Prem Narayan struggled in that psychological no man's land . . . somewhere between sleep and wakefulness . . . his subconscious mind disturbed by sounds barely audible. Years of tracking the most desperate of criminals had developed in him a sixth sense of subtle awareness, even while asleep, and this unusual perceptiveness more than once had saved his life. Over and above the steady, almost hypnotizing, sound of water gently lapping against the side of the houseboat, there were dissonant notes which he recognized as those of wood softly scraping against wood.

For: Pam Anderson
with best wishes

Melvin A. Casberg

Dr. Casberg is also the author of
DEATH STALKS THE PUNJAB and of FIVE RIVERS TO DEATH,
the first two of the Prem Narayan stories.

Strawberry Hill Press

DOWRY OF DEATH

Melvin A. Casberg

illustrations by Matt A. Gouig

Strawberry Hill Press
2594 15th Avenue
San Francisco, California 94127

Manufactured in the United States of America

Wordprocessed by No. One Press, San Francisco, California
Typeset by Cragmont/ExPress, Oakland, California
Printed by Edwards Brothers Incorporated, Ann Arbor, Michigan

Library of Congress Cataloging in Publication Data

Casberg, Melvin A., 1909-
    Dowry of death.

    I. Title.
PS3553.A78975D6   1984   813'.54   84-8655
ISBN 0-89407-062-2

To Bobbie and Glen Liddiard
whose encouragement watered the tender
roots of my early creative writing.

CAST OF PRINCIPAL CHARACTERS
(In Order of Their Appearance)

Captain Prem Narayan—*Crack sleuth of the Indian Criminal Investigation Department (C.I.D.); assigned the task of solving the çobra murders in Kashmir. Wife: Bubli.*

Pritham Singh—*Deputy Inspector General of the C.I.D. to whom Captain Narayan is directly responsible.*

Doreen Duncan—*Stewardess for Indian Airlines and sister of Doctor Bruce Duncan, herpetologist.*

Douglas Gordon—*American Consul in Bombay; born in India. High school classmate and long-time friend of Captain Narayan.*

Montague Brown—*American geologist on sabbatical leave from the University of California; studying Himalayan rock formations.*

James Appleton—*American discharged from the Diplomatic Service under questionable circumstances; gathering information for a book on the Indian/Pakistani border conflicts in Kashmir.*

Lieutenant Ali Aurangzeb—*C.I.D. representative at Srinagar, Kashmir.*

Major Ram Sunderam—*Retired from the Indian Army following combat-incurred disabilities; manager of the Military Officer's Club in Delhi; Military Academy classmate and close friend of Captain Narayan.*

Allabaksh—*Kazak Muslim from Xinjiang Province, Peoples Republic of China; first victim of the cobra murders.*

Doctor Pran Sahgal—*Civil Surgeon at the Srinagar Government Hospital, with a particular interest in herpetology.*

Ahmed Feroze—*Srinagar merchant trading with Pakistan, China and Afghanistan; second victim of the cobra murders.*

Rustum Sharif—*Driver and cook for Captain Narayan and his C.I.D. party in Srinagar. Wife: Fatima.*

Lieutenant Ian McVey—*Chief of the Chandigarh, Punjab, branch of the C.I.D. Associate of Captain Narayan in the investigation of the cobra murders. An Anglo-Indian greatly respected by his fellow officers. Wife: Joyce.*

Sergeant Major Sardar Khan—*Retired from the Indian Army; currently employed by the C.I.D.*

Maya Reznikoff—*White Russian married to a wealthy Frenchman and a resident of Delhi.*

John Parkozian—*Armenian citizen of Lebanon; temporarily a resident of Srinagar dealing in international intrigue.*

Colonel Wilhelm Vandermeer—*Commander of the United Nations Observer Team patrolling the Indian/Pakistani Cease Fire Line.*

Kafir Jacub—*Renegade resident of Srinagar.*

Mohammed Mohidin—*Proprietor of the Suffering Moses merchandise houseboat on the Jhelum River in Srinagar and close friend of Captain Narayan.*

Mos (Osmosis)—*Orphan waif from the Srinagar streets adopted by Montague Brown.*

Doctor Bruce Duncan—*Herpetologist researcher at the Kasauli Institute in the Punjab developing cobra and viper antivenin. Wife: Maureen. Sister: Doreen.*

Abdul Ashok—*Srinagar confidant and friend of Sergeant Major Sardar Khan.*

Lieutenant Baldev Raj—*Superintendent of Police, Srinagar.*

Sayad Khan—*Expatriate Afghani residing in Srinagar and trading in dowries.*

Lakshmi and **Ram**—*Mother and son supplying milk to the houseboats on Dal Lake.*

Aisha—*Female leader of a band of expatriated Pakistani dacoits.*

Captain Ashok—*Ranking military officer serving under Aisha of the Pakistani dacoits.*

Achmed—*Member of the communist puppet Afghani band working undercover in Kashmir.*

Ameena—*Elderly housekeeper for the communist puppet Afghani band.*

Ram Singh—*Indian Police Intelligence Division liaison with Interpol.*

Ivan Dostovitch—*Officer in the U.S.S.R. Embassy, Delhi.*

Note to the reader: In the text of this novel, Indian words are spelled according to the Standard System of Roman Transliteration approved by the Government of India!

Chapter One

Shortly after midday, early in November, Indian Airlines flight one eight five rose steeply from the main runway of what the old-timers still called the Santa Cruz airport on the northern outskirts of Bombay, climbed over the escarpments of the Western Ghats and headed inland toward Delhi. As the No Smoking and Fasten Seat Belt signs turned off, Captain Prem Narayan of the Indian Criminal Investigation Department stood and removed his trench coat, folding it neatly on the empty seat beside him. Then ... still standing ... he reached into the ample side pocket of his bush jacket and retrieved a cloisonne cigarette case of exceptional beauty. Selecting his favorite brand ... a Camel ... he rolled it gently between his fingers before raising the smoke to his lips and torching it with a flourish from an attached and equally beautiful cloisonne lighter. Inhaling deeply and then exhaling with a languid sigh, the Captain sat down, tipped his seat to a reclining position and stretched both legs forward under the passenger ahead. With eyelids narrowed against the acrid tobacco fumes, he commenced blowing a series of smoke rings only to have the jet of cold wind from overhead destroy the symmetry of his cigarette artistry. Grunting his annoyance, he reached above and turned off the forced-air nozzle.

The day's activities had been initiated rather abruptly by an early morning telephone call from Pritham Singh, Deputy Inspector General of the Department, asking the Captain to fly to Delhi immediately for an assignment which probably would extend over a period of at least a fortnight and would require warm clothing. Such meagerness of instructions came as no particular surprise to him, dictated as it must have been by the demands of security. Fortunately, except for a few minor details which could be left in the hands of subordinates, he had just completed the investigation of a sensitive espionage case involving a freighter docked at Ballard Pier of the Bombay Harbour District. The details of his coming mission would be discussed over breakfast at the Military Officers Club in New Delhi on the morrow.

Anticipating a long and full day for her husband, the Captain's wife, affectionately nicknamed Bubli, prepared an early luncheon of more than usual proportions. Each of them having lost their lifelong mates quite recently, and having married in Canada during the past summer, now were enjoying the excitement of a newly found love.

"Any idea, Prem, how long you'll be away?" Bubli's eyes scanned her husband's face expectantly.

He did not reply immediately but for a fleeting moment affectionately studied his wife over the top of his steaming cup of coffee.
"Dashed if I know, my dear, except that Pritham Singh spoke of a
fortnight. Perhaps I might cut that short by a few days."

Drawing a deep sighing breath, Bubli rose from the table and walked
around to the other side. Encircling Prem's neck with her arms, she
whispered, "It's going to be lonesome around here without you." A
deep sincerity flooded her words.

"These separations aren't exactly my cup of tea," he said with a
frown, rising to gather her into his arms. On tiptoes, she stretched until
their lips met.

Captain Narayan gave the appearance of a college professor rather
than one whose career had been devoted in large part to the hunting
down of criminals. His closely cropped black hair showed beginning
streaks of gray matching the shade of his eyes. Of average stature, his
body was lean of build but muscular. He walked and stood with an
erect bearing, showing the ingrained habits of past military training.
His movements were carried out with a measured deliberation, belying
an ability to act physically with a lightning swiftness should the
circumstances demand. The Captain conversed unhurriedly . . . at times
almost in a hesitant manner . . . as though analyzing each word before
using it. He was wont to quip that whereas Hindustani was his mother
tongue, English was his father tongue, the latter of which he spoke
precisely and with a clipped British enunciation.

"A drink sir?" The airline stewardess, smartly dressed in a colorful
sari, leaned forward balancing a tray with a variety of cold soft drinks
and a pot each of hot coffee and tea.

"Ah . . . my dear . . . sounds like a splendid thing . . . yes indeed!
Let's make that hot coffee . . . a cup of hot coffee," the Captain
repeated as if the the words themselves were warming.

"Very good sir," she responded, deftly filling a paper cup.

"And a spoon of sugar as well as a spot of cream, if you will," he
added, looking up just in time to catch a fleeting grimace disrupt the
young lady's smile.

"Sugar and cream," she murmured, quickly looking away from his
disfigured face and giving her whole attention to stirring the drink.

"Thanks," he responded, almost as an aside to himself, accepting
the cup and noisily sipping the hot liquid as the flustered stewardess
moved on up the aisle offering drinks to passengers in the forward
seats.

An ugly scar slashing across the left side of his face, from temple to
the angle of his mouth, cruelly branded the Captain. Tissue contrac-
tures and muscle injuries had distorted the eye and the upper lip
creating an appearance of a permanent snarl. The result of this

unfortunate state of affairs was that it created two profoundly different facial expressions depending on which profile happened to be exposed. Seen from the left he gave the impression of a savage ferocity, whereas simply by turning his head he reflected a benign serenity. Meeting the Captain, a stranger might have the distinct conviction that he or she was facing a Dr. Jekyll and a Mr. Hyde at the same time and all in one person.

Having finished his coffee, Prem Narayan rested his head against the back of the seat with eyes closed, placing himself in a state of total relaxation. Through the years it had become an established custom on his part, particularly during the more recent stressful periods of his professional life, to practice a form of autogenic mind and body control, using for that purpose any available scraps of time such as the present. His reasoning on this matter had been quite basic, namely, if the mind can create and pass on negative and destructive emotions precipitating mental and physical distress, then why not deliberately generate and disseminate positive thoughts with their creative potential for the better?

A light touch on his arm aroused the Captain from his reverie. He turned to find the stewardess seated beside him holding his trench coat on her lap and smiling contritely.

"Feel a bit of a cad ... " she hesitated, dropping her eyes self-consciously before going on ... "please accept my apologies."

"No need ... no need my dear," he repeated softly, patting her hand. "Jolly well used to it, don't you know."

"Lost my Daddy in Kashmir ... the border fighting with Pakistan. I was just a child but shan't ever forget Mummy saying he was hit in the face by a mortar fragment. Your wound ... well it made me think ... " her words came to a halt as she pursed her trembling lips.

"Sorry ... Miss ... Miss ... " he broke off and waited for her reply.

"Doreen ... Doreen Duncan. Mummy is Indian."

"Prem Narayan here ... Captain Narayan of the C.I.D." He threw her a reassuring smile. "I too lost a dear friend in the same fighting."

Tears began to well up in her eyes.

"Now ... now my lass, cheer up, eh what?" He reached over to pat her hand again. "What say we change the subject?"

She threw him a wan smile and nodded her head in agreement, batting her eyelashes to shed the accumulated teardrops.

"And where's your home, Doreen?"

"Mummy lives with my brother and his family. He's a doctor on the staff of the Kasauli Institute. Do you know where ... "

"Yes," he cut in with a wave of his hand, "been there several times. Antivenin for snake bites and antiserum for rabies."

"Just below Simla."

Prem Narayan nodded knowingly. "Kasauli ... nestled in the Himalayan foothills above Chandigarh."

"My brother, Bruce, is quite an authority on poisonous snakes. Last year he laid on an invitational lecture at the London School of Tropical Medicine." Her voice projected overtones of pride.

Charming lass, the Captain thought to himself as he basked in the warmth and enthusiasm of Doreen Duncan's vivacious personality. She had inherited a beauty so often found in those who carried a mixture of genes from the Orient and Occident. It would seem that Nature in her creative generosity often deliberately selected the more positive genetic attributes as gifts to racial hybrids. Flashing dark blue eyes dominated a face whose rich olive complexion contrasted pleasantly with even rows of white teeth. Her sculptured features broke into smiles frequently and with ease. In typical Indian fashion, her dark hair was knotted into a tight bun at the nape of her neck. She moved with a lissome fluidity accentuating the charms of her comely feminine contours, all fetchingly wrapped in an attractive sari.

"You're a ruddy liar, Rudyard Kipling," Prem muttered in an aside to himself, "this business about East is East and West is West and never the twain shall meet."

"Sorry ... Captain ... you said something?" Doreen asked, leaning closer.

He shook his head and repeated quietly, "Nothing ... nothing really."

A passenger's call light flashed nervously overhead and Doreen Duncan slipped down the aisle to respond. Prem Narayan soberly stared after her, a touch of sadness in his eyes. One of the tragic inequities of British Colonialism, he reflected, was the social ostracism of the Anglo-Indian by both the rulers and those ruled. Strange to say, this racial prejudice was much less evident in the British Isles, the home of these very same colonials.

Her duties to the passengers having been discharged, Doreen returned to exchange a few more pleasantries with the Captain.

"Shan't let you see my ferocious side, only the more photogenic right profile," Prem confided with a chuckle. She joined easily in his laughter before excusing herself for other tasks.

Captain Narayan rarely alluded to the circumstances under which he had acquired the deforming facial injury, but through the years since those turbulent days of partition, the story had become a living legend in the military and police academies across the land. The event took place early one morning during the first week of September, 1947. With her independence not yet quite a month old, the government of India trembled under the pressures of terrorism and uncontrolled chaos. The stench of rotting bodies rose from sections of Delhi where communal gangs stalked and wantonly murdered those not of their faith. It was within this environment of anarchy that young Lieutenant Narayan, recently out of Dehra Dun Military Academy, in a single-handed foray had stemmed the tide of a rampaging wave of Hindu fanatics led by a slogan-shouting member of the Rashtriya Swayam Sewak Sangh, an extremist organization which later planned and carried out the assassination of Mahatma Gandhi. Completely outnumbered and desolately alone in a seething caldron of hatred, he drew his automatic and shielded with his own body the quarry of the crazed mob, a terrified Muslim lad not yet in his teens. Raising his voice above the noise about him, the Lieutenant shouted, "To kill this Muslim child, you first must kill me a Hindu!"

The hoodlums hesitated but for a moment then surged forward again, enraged by this attempted denial of their blood lust. Suddenly a sword flashed, glinting wickedly in the morning sunlight, and simultaneously the sharp report of a gun reverberated within the narrow confines of the compound. The sword-wielder crumpled to his knees as if paying homage, then with a sighing groan toppled forward to lie prone before the officer. But the sword had taken its toll as well. Blood covered the left side of the Lieutenant's face, momentarily blinding him, and flowed down over his shoulder and onto his chest. The sight of this symbol of law and order, bloodied but resolute, was too much for the now leaderless rabble. They broke ranks and fell back, leaving the dead hostage at the feet of the victor still clutching the sword in his lifeless fingers.

Captain Narayan's thoughts were brought abruptly out of the past as the plane banked sharply downward into the landing pattern. First in Hindustani and then in English, a feminine voice announced over the speaker that flight one eight five was making its approach to Palam Airport, Delhi.

Prem Narayan moved with the other disembarking passengers to the baggage claim section where he procured the services of a coolie to carry his trunk and bedding roll. The man selected was lean and rawboned, wearing a soiled and nondescript brown sweater over a frayed khaki shirt whose tails fell freely over a pair of oversized pants. In sharp contrast to the drabness of his clothes was the very red and ample turban, snugly spiraled over his scalp from just above the eyebrows to the nape of his neck, with a loose tail end dangling down his back. From a distance the coolie gave the appearance of a crimson flower whose stem split somewhere below into two walking limbs. The colorful headdress cushioned the weight of the baggage which he skillfully hoisted one above the other to tower over him, affording an easy landmark for Prem to follow through the airport crowds.

At the taxi stand a Sikh driver welcomed the Captain, who barely had time to pay the coolie and seat himself beside his tin trunk and bedding roll, before the vehicle took off through the congested Delhi streets as if all the devils in hell were in hot pursuit. This mad dash was carried out to the accompaniment of a constant and deafening cacophony of horn blowing. The maneuvering between and around pedestrians, cyclists, motorized rickshaws, wandering cows, horse tongas, bullock carts and other taxis, was carried out with an aggression which dared others to contest the driver's right to any spot on the thoroughfare. As was his custom, Captain Narayan sat quietly in the back seat, arms folded across his chest, resigned to any eventuality.

The resplendently vested and turbaned doorman at the Ashoka Hotel, whose stance and colorful attire reminded Prem of a Bengal Lancer in formal uniform, swung open the lobby door and haughtily waved the Captain inside. Reservations having been made by Pritham Singh's office under a previously agreed upon pseudonym, the registration formalities were perfunctory and swift. Showering and stretching out on the comfortable bed, he exploited the opportunity to erase ... at least in part ... a sleep deficit incurred over the past fortnight by the demands of the espionage investigations in Bombay.

Captain Narayan awoke with a start. It was dark. Turning on a light he opened the tin trunk and retrieved an egg sandwich Bubli had packed for him that morning. Sitting on the edge of a chair he moodily munched the food, washing it down with drinks of tap water from a paper cup. If only Bubli could've come with me, he mused, sensing the loneliness of the coldly impersonal hotel quarters.

Prem showered, dressed and took the lift down to the hotel bar. Finding a small table at the periphery of the room, he sat down alone and ordered a drink. As was his wish, he became an ill-defined shadow barely discernible in the subdued light. A background murmur of conversation, indistinct and low, was supplemented by the soothing music of a softly plucked sitar, courtesy of All-India Radio. His half-closed eyes stared abstractedly at the glass of gin and tonic which he rotated slowly on the table between the fingers of both hands. One fraction of his senses, that part on sentry duty as Prem would describe it, constantly screened the movement of people about the room, diaphanous shadows flowing through the varying shades of subdued illumination still further darkened by floating layers of tobacco smoke.

Alerted by the actions of a patron very deliberately moving toward his table from the bar counter, the Captain quickly stubbed out his cigarette and slipped his hand over the holster under his coat.

"I thought it might be you when I first stepped into the bar but had to wait until my eyes adjusted to the dim lights." The words were spoken with a distinctly American accent.

Grasping the extended hand, Prem Narayan waved the newcomer to an empty chair across the table. "Doug! I must say this is a bit of alright. Do sit down, old chap. What a ruddy coincidence meeting you here."

"Not so much of a coincidence, Prem. Caught a fleeting glimpse of your back in the lobby this afternoon just as the doors of the lift swallowed you. Knowing your habit of signing in under an assumed name, I didn't try locating you through the registration desk."

"*Accha*—Alright." The Captain frequently prefaced his remarks with this Hindustani word. "And who's tending shop at the American Consulate in Bombay?"

Consul Douglas Gordon chose not to respond to the question but leaned forward, elbows on the table and chin cupped in both hands, quietly studying his companion's face. After a moment he glanced around cautiously and dropped his voice to confide, "The Ambassador called us in for a two-day conference. Things are getting a bit sticky in the Northwest Frontier."

"You're bloody well right they're sticky," Prem muttered, "and all hell could break loose up there at any moment."

Doug shrugged his shoulders as a preface to his observation, "Sort of a catch 22 situation, I'd say."

Shaking a finger solemnly at his friend, Prem resumed his dire predictions, "We'd better play a damned straight bat or our wickets'll be knocked all over the field."

"I'll hazard a guess as to where you're headed," Doug broke in without looking up at Prem.

"*Accha*. And just where in hell am I headed?"

Doug drew in a quick breath and announced in a matter-of-fact voice, "Kashmir."

The Captain chuckled out loud. "Could be. My orders do call for warm clothing ... " he began and then stopped to dissipate the collected cloud of cigarette smoke by vigorously fanning with his hands before going on to say ... "and if you're right, Bubli and I'll take Sharon and you out to dinner at Fernando's when I get back to Bombay."

Doug grinned his agreement. "Incidentally, how's the charming bride?"

A shy and soft smile stole across the Captain's face as he replied, "Bubli's just great. She's just great," he repeated as if he liked the words.

Prem Narayan and Douglas Gordon, both of them born in India, had been close friends since their days at Breeks Memorial School in the Nilgiri Hills of South India. Over the four years at Breeks, they had been classmates, rooming in the same dormitories and playing together on the school soccer, hockey and cricket teams. After their Senior Cambridge examinations and graduation, Doug had gone to the United States where, on completion of college, he had entered the Foreign Service of the State Department. Prem, on the other hand, had been admitted to the Military Academy in Dehra Dun and shortly after graduation had been recruited by the Criminal Investigation Department. On Doug's return to India, the two classmates renewed their long-standing friendship and, as both currently were stationed in Bombay, frequently shared social and official contacts. When Anandi, Prem's first wife, died a few years back, the Captain suffered a period of despondency which Doug and Sharon did their best to alleviate. They had invited Prem as a guest to their bungalow in the Himalayan resort village of Landour, where the companionship and outdoor life had contributed to a rapid convalescence. This experience had deepened even more the ties of friendship between the two men.

"Say ... Prem ... " Doug paused to scratch his head thoughtfully before going on ... "wish you'd do me a favor and check on a fellow who's currently headquartered in Srinagar."

"You're really convinced I'm headed for Kashmir, aren't you?"

Doug nodded and pushed his glasses up higher on the bridge of his nose.

"*Accha*. If I land in Kashmir, I'll do the necessary. But who is this chap?"

"Montague Brown ... Monty for short. A young professor on leave. He's into academic geology."

"Academic geology? What the hell is that?" Prem's eyebrows rose questioningly.

"Well ... let's see ... he's an associate professor at the University of California, Los Angeles. His investigation is purely theoretical ... I mean he's not exploring for oil or minerals. First met him and his parents a few years back when his father was an exchange professor with the Maulana Azad Medical College in Delhi."

"Doug ... precisely what is the blighter doing?" Prem persisted.

"Actually the fellow's researching the rock formations of the Himalayas and Siwaliks ... the age of the mountain upheavals and all that geological stuff. Works out of Srinagar and wanders all over Kashmir."

"Hell of a place to be wandering over just now ... wouldn't you agree?"

Little shadows of worry pulled at the corners of Doug's eyes as he nodded in agreement. "Prem, he's involved in areas outside geology."

"The chap's an American?"

Again Doug nodded.

"Are we ... this Monty and I ... supposed to have common interests of some sort?"

Doug frowned and pursed his lips in thought for a moment before replying, "Could be. Actually Monty just might be of help to you."

"Help to me? Doug ... there you go talking in riddles again."

The American grinned enigmatically at his companion and urged, "Look ... Prem ... just contact the guy."

"*Accha*. Where's he staying?"

"Nedou's." Doug sounded relieved.

"Anything else ... I mean what else can I do for you up in Kashmir?"

"Actually I was just about to ask your help on another situation," Doug chuckled and added as the Captain waved him on with his hand, "we're a bit worried about another American ... in a different way altogether. This fellow's been spending time up around Srinagar. He used to be in our diplomatic service during the so-called 'Cold War' period. Was attached to the American Embassy in Warsaw, Poland. Helped in the very discrete negotiations between us and the Peking ambassador, Wang Ping-nan, when we were feeling out the Chinese about renewing diplomatic relations. After that he was moved to Moscow where the bugger got into some sort of trouble resulting in his being asked to leave the service. Chap was alleged to have passed classified documents to the Russians. All kinds of messy investigations."

"Just what's the bloke supposed to be doing here?"

"Writing a book on the India-Pakistan border conflicts ... particularly the Kashmir."

"Is he official in any sense?"

"No sir!" Doug shook his head emphatically. "No official governmental connections whatsoever. He's a private citizen in every sense of the word. We're damned worried that the man might become an embarrassment to our government. After all he's dealing with a damned emotional and sensitive matter ... sensitive to both India and Pakistan."

"What's the blighter's name and what does he look like?"

"James Appleton. Sixty-seven years old. Five feet eleven inches tall and of slender build. Balding gray hair and closely trimmed beard. Swarthy skin. Left eye artificial and immobile ... World War II injury. Wears an eye patch a good part of the time."

"*Accha*. I'll check him out for you. Anything particular ... I mean anything particular you want to know about him?"

"If he's not playing cricket, pass me the word, eh?"

The two men rose and left the bar separately, the American leading off and heading directly for the lift and his room. Prem casually sought out the hotel gift shop and replenished his supply of cigarettes. While waiting for the lift, he removed the Camels individually from the pack and meticulously arranged them in his cloisonne case, placing the last one between his lips.

"May I?" A man stepped around from behind the Captain and raised a flared lighter to the unlit cigarette.

"Thanks, old chap," Prem responded, bending forward to accommodate his benefactor.

"Don't mention, please," the stranger admonished, snapping the lighter cap closed. For a fleeting moment his eyes intently studied the Captain, particularly the scarred left side of his face.

Any further conversation was interrupted by the single clang of a bell announcing the lift's arrival. As the operator opened the door to admit the few waiting passengers, Prem lingered and unobtrusively studied the man with the lighter. A caracul astrakhan cap rested jauntily on a head of closely cropped black hair. The man's face was framed by a neatly trimmed beard, while a bristling mustache clung fiercely to the ramparts of his upper lip. Coatless, he wore a smartly tailored open vest over an expensive collarless shirt whose tails, in front and behind, draped over ballooned heavy cotton pants snugged at the ankles. An Afghani . . . probably a Pathan . . . Prem thought to himself, disturbed by the stranger's apparent recognition of his identity.

Reaching his quarters, the Captain quickly undressed and slipped on his pajamas before pulling out the tin box from under the bed. This small metal trunk, showing the marks of hard usage, belied its strength, looking just like the many thousands of similar pieces of baggage traveling the thoroughfares of India. Closer inspection however, revealed it to be a veritable safe with steel reinforcement strips welded into its sides. The securing device was a small but sophisticated combination lock. Kneeling on the floor before the box, he opened it and removed a folder containing documents pertaining to Kashmir. Fingering through the material he selected a letter of recent date from Lieutenant Ali Aurangzeb, the Criminal Investigation Department representative stationed in Srinagar. It was a personal chit covering the final disposition of a case both men had investigated the year before. Prem carefully read a postscript to this correspondence before replacing it in the tin box.

"I am more than a little concerned," Ali wrote, "by the travels of an American, name of Brown. The blighter wanders all through Kashmir and God only knows where else. I fear for his safety. He states that he is studying the geology of the Himalayan ranges. The chap laughs off my warnings with a shrug of his shoulders. At least he is aware of my apprehension on his behalf."

Prem sat in bed smoking, his forehead wrinkled in thought. If I'm actually headed for Kashmir, he mused, I'd better bloody well contact this Monty bloke early in the game. Taking a final draw on his cigarette, he ground out the stub in the ash tray and after turning out the reading lamp, slipped down between the sheets.

Chapter Two

Prem Narayan's taxi cautiously wove its way into Connaught Circus, the commercial heart of New Delhi, ringed by a conglomerate of shops, restaurants, banks and other assorted business ventures. Virtually stalled by the pedestrian and vehicular rush of patrons exploring these numerous facilities, the Captain ordered his driver to pull over to the curb and stop. Jumping out of the vehicle, he paid his fare and spryly ran up four steps onto a porticoed walk which offered a common thoroughfare to all customers. A few brisk paces brought him to a large wooden door with shiny embossed letters spelling out: Military Officers Club. The uniformed Gurkha seated on a stool beside the entrance sprang to attention, saluted smartly and swung open the door.

"Well I'll be buggered!" Major Ram Sunderam exploded, reaching across the registration desk to grasp the Captain's extended hand.

"Ram, you're still laying on weight," Prem teased, "and those jacket buttons are about to pop off."

"Not much to do but sit on my ass around here," the Major grumbled with a self-conscious grin, "and down chota pegs."

"Pritham Singh here yet?" Prem asked, glancing around the room cautiously.

Ram shook his head and leaned forward to whisper, "Due any time now. Made reservations yesterday for a small table in a quiet corner . . . " he frowned and drew in a deep breath before going on . . . "so you're the chap he's meeting. I wondered who the bloke would be."

Major Sunderam moved out from behind the desk and, placing his arm around the Captain's shoulders, led him down the hall toward the officers' mess. Classmates during their military academy days in Dehra Dun, the two men had remained close friends during the ensuing years. Wounded in a border clash with Pakistan and now retired, the Major managed the Club.

"Here's what I've laid on for the two of you." Ram stopped beside a table in a corner of the mess room. An attractive bouquet of bright orange marigolds decorated the breakfast setting.

"*Accha.*"

"New assignment, eh?" Ram studied Prem's face inquisitively before continuing, "Bet I know where you're going."

"The hell you say! You know you're the second bloke since I landed here in Delhi yesterday who knows more about my destination than I do."

The Major shrugged his shoulders noncommittally and broke out laughing. Pulling out a chair, he waved Prem to be seated. "Make yourself comfortable, my good chap, and I'll have the bearer fetch you a cup of coffee." With that, Ram disappeared into the kitchen.

The walls of the mess displayed the familiar tiger and leopard skins of varying sizes and beauty alternating with stag horns of substantial spreads. A large and somewhat worn sharply-tusked wild boar's head snarled down upon the room from its vantage point above a window. Around the periphery of the floor, resting on brightly varnished wooden pedestals, stood numerous traditional trophies vaunting regimental prowess in pigsticking, hockey, cricket, soccer, polo and tennis. One whole side of the mess wall was devoted to portraits of various dignitaries, military and otherwise, their underwritten autographs in some instances faded beyond the point of legibility. From a central prestigious position, Lord Louis Mountbatten's sharp-chiseled and handsome face surveyed his surroundings in rather a detached manner. With special defference to the aphorism that rank has its privileges, the importance of the pictured personages appeared to decrease with their distance from Lord Louis.

Prem's study of the familiar wall photographs was interrupted by a bearer who set a cup of coffee before him. As he lifted the warming brew to his lips, a tall turbaned Sikh with a commanding bearing stepped into the mess hall and threw the Captain an informal hand salute. Pritham Singh, Deputy Inspector General of the C.I.D. with particular jurisdiction over the Punjab and Kashmir, approached the table smiling broadly. He wore a winter khaki uniform ... bush jacket and long trousers ... with a military trench coat draped casually over his shoulders. His graying hair was covered by a snugly applied turban and his beard held tightly against his chin and cheeks by a fine-meshed hair net.

"I say, it's jolly good to see you again, Prem!" The Sikh's greeting was warm and vigorous. After shaking hands he sat down at the table, briskly rubbing his palms together and blowing on them.

"The same goes for you, Pritham."

"Your trip from Bombay ... " he scanned the Captain's face closely before continuing ... "it was pleasant?"

Prem nodded and said, "Caught up on my sleep on the plane. That ruddy espionage case at Ballard Pier left little time to rest over the past fortnight."

"Damned glad you're here ... " Pritham dropped his voice and looked about the room ... "big assignment for you, my dear chap. A really important assignment." The Sikh's words projected worry.

"You don't say?"

"The chief himself asked me to lay the case on for you."

"The Inspector General ... P.K. Datta?"

Pritham nodded impressively. "Precisely! the *barra sahib* himself."

"We who are about to die salute you," Prem said with a mirthless chuckle.

"Dash it all, man, it's not that bad."

"Just ragging you a bit." The Captain broke out laughing and was joined by his companion.

The bearer interrupted their conversation, bringing in a pot of coffee and handing each of them a menu. While the patrons studied the breakfast list, he stood obsequiously to one side poised with pencil in hand. His dress was standard for the more posh clubs of India. As an embattled fortress rises sheer on the summit of a hill, a turban crested his head, plumed at the top like a cockscomb by one protruding end of the wrapped cloth, the other end dangling free down his back. A knee-length white coat was gathered at the waist with a broad belt fastened in front by an impressively large brass buckle, monogrammed with the intertwining letters M and C. White loose-flowing pantaloons and leather sandals completed the uniform.

'Bowl of sliced bananas with cream, two soft boiled eggs, toast and marmalade,' the Sikh checked off each item on the bill of fare with his finger.

"Papaya, bowl of oatmeal, toast and guava jelly," Prem followed in rapid suit.

Having taken the orders, the waiter turned and headed for the kitchen.

After covertly surveying the room, Pritham dropped his voice to confide, "We've problems ... really serious problems ... in Kashmir. It's a damned sticky wicket if you ask me."

"That bad, eh?"

The Sikh frowned and pursed his lips a moment before going on "International implications."

"Such as?"

"Secretary for External Affairs has been pressuring us and the whole blooming C.I.D. is in a ruddy funk."

"Pritham, for God's sake, you'll have me climbing the walls. Tell me what's going on ... let's on with it, eh?"

"Talking about walls ... before we go any further ... wish the Club would take that damn stuffed boar's head and throw it out. I'm sick to death of looking at that frozen sardonic grin on its snout."

Prem exploded in unrestrained laughter. Finally, gaining control of himself, he muttered, "My dear chap, you say the damndest things at the damndest times."

"Such as?" He raised his eyebrows in piqued surprise.

"Jumping at random from the subject of serious international implications to that of a stuffed boar's head." Prem resumed his laughter and ... after a brief hesitation ... his companion joined in.

"Anyway ... that sickly tusker bothers me." The Sikh frowned his displeasure.

'*Accha*. I'll use my influence with Major Sunderam to take care of same," Prem countered tolerantly.

Pritham shifted uneasily in his chair then leaned forward, elbows on table, to whisper, "A Chinese citizen ... Peoples Republic Chinese ... murdered in Srinagar this past week. For a couple of days the police couldn't identify the bloke. Thought he might be a Kashmiri or Pakistani."

Prem, who was in the process of lighting a cigarette, stopped abruptly, holding the flaming cloisonne lighter in mid-air. "Peoples Republic Chinese?" His eyebrows were raised in surprise. "A Chinese mistaken for a Kashmiri or Pakistani?"

"The victim was a Kazak from the western part of China, Xinjiang Province."

"*Accha*. I'm with you. A Muslim from over the Himalayas to the north of Kashmir." Prem completed lighting his cigarette.

"Name of Allabaksh."

For a moment the conversation came to a halt as the bearer approached with the ordered dishes.

"How was the chap finally identified?" Prem broke the silence.

"An inquiry from the Peoples Republic Embassy here in Delhi."

"Leads as to how, by whom or why?"

Pritham fastidiously touched his napkin to his lips and quietly belched before replying, "Positive on the first and negative on the second and third."

"So ... how was he killed?"

"Cobras."

"The hell you say ... " Prem raised his eyebrows incredulously before going on ... "but couldn't it have been accidental? I mean after all the poor blighter could've ... "

"Murder," Pritham cut in with a wave of his hand, "cold blooded assassination, if you will. The victim's body was found in a lily pond in the Shalimar Gardens just off Dal Lake."

"You used the plural ... cobras."

"Two sets of fang marks. Both on the right forearm. The Civil Surgeon at Srinagar interpreted his findings as indicating that two snakes were involved. Fortunately for us, Doctor Pran Sahgal's an avid herpetologist."

Prem stared thoughtfully at the Sikh a moment before asking, "Just how did the man come to this conclusion ... the two snakes conclusion?"

"To begin with the bites were on opposite sides of the forearm. But even more convincing were his descriptions and explanations of the reactions about the wounds. Each site showed equally violent tissue deterioration and . . . ''

"*Accha*," the Captain broke in , "I follow Sahgal's reasoning. It appears that equal and substantial amounts of venom were injected into each of the two areas. A snake usually empties the greater portion of its poison sacs at the initial strike, leaving much less venom for a second or third."

"Precisely," Pritham agreed, nodding vigorously, "the two equally destructive reactions on opposite sides of the forearm convinced Sahgal that more than one cobra was involved in the attack."

Major Sunderam approached the table to ask if all was in order. Prem grabbed his arm to share with him the matter of the boar's head.

"Quite . . . quite . . . a splendid idea really," the Major expressed his approval of the change with unusual enthusiasm. Turning to stare at the mounted specimen on the wall, he commiserated, "Poor chap who donated it to the Club passed away just a couple of months ago."

"Be a good fellow and throw the thing out, eh?" Pritham suggested.

"No botheration at all. I shall do the necessary," Ram promised as he left the room.

"The reason for the Department calling you in on this . . . " the Sikh paused to stroke his beard and finger his mustache . . . "is that the I.G. is convinced there's more to this than just some routine homicide investigation. He insists that the whole thing could blow up into a bloody international nightmare. Whether Datta is right or wrong, we've little choice but to follow through."

Selecting a Camel from his cloisonne case, Prem rolled it gently between thumb and forefinger, feeling the resilience of its fresh tobacco, tapped it vigorously against the surface of the case and lifting it to his mouth flamed the tip with the lighter. Inhaling deeply and then exhaling with a sigh, he squinted against the acrid smoke. Pritham watched the entire procedure in a tolerant silence, aware that the Captain was giving deep thought to the matter under consideration.

"And what about the Peoples Republic?" Prem broke the silence.

"Meaning?"

"How did Peking react to the assassination?"

"Official and quite formal but courteous. Called our Foreign Secretary and asked for the body. Just how they found out about the murder, we really don't know."

"Our police didn't pass them the word?"

The Sikh shook his head.

"If we knew who the informant was it just might give us . . . " the Captain broke off and drew on his cigarette.

Pritham nodded soberly. "Actually, we discretely broached the subject . . . as to how they found out . . . but met a wall of silence. With Government's permission, flew a plane into Srinagar and air lifted the body out to China. One of our military aircraft escorted them to the border near the Karakoram Pass.''

"Doctor Sahgal's still in Kashmir?''

"Uh-huh,'' the Sikh grunted his affirmation, "we've contacted the chap and he'll give every assistance. Then you'll ... '' he paused and studied Prem's face before continuing ... "you'll take on the assignment?''

"Do I have a choice?'' The Captain's eyes danced mischievously.

"There you go ... ragging me again. Of course you've a choice!''

"*Accha* ... I'll ...''

"Splendid old chap!'' Pritham cut in, disallowing him a chance to complete his sentence. "The I.G. will be frightfully happy, don't you know.''

Prem shrugged his shoulders self-consciously and announced, "I've a couple of requests.''

"Yours for the asking, old chap ... as long as they're within reason.''

"Two people to work with me on this assignment ... Lieutenant Ian McVey and Sergeant Major Sardar Khan.''

The Sikh chuckled happily and confided, "My office already has contacted both men.''

"Splendid!''

Obviously delighted by the Captain's decision, Pritham Singh pushed his chair back and stood, extending his hand across the table. "Agreed then, eh? It's a *pakka* ... a solid agreement?''

'*Pakka*,'' Prem repeated, nodding soberly.

"Absolutely smashing!'' The Sikh was ebullient, but then turned serious to add, "Not a cushy job this. But then I've never seen you walk away from a difficult challenge.''

The Captain gave a self-deprecating wave of his hand and chose to remain silent.

"Righto then, Prem, drop over to my office around three this afternoon and pick up the dossier on the victim Allabaksh as well as your ticket for the morning flight to Srinagar.''

Captain Narayan walked his chief to the door where he paused to watch the tall Sikh disappear into the Connaught Circus flow of pedestrians. The constantly changing and ceaseless stream of humanity provided a panoramic fashion show, a colorful physical action, an incarnation of Mother India. The varieties of dress seemed unlimited, a beautiful blend of colors woven into a living tapestry by the shuttles of an animate loom.

Turning to reenter the Club, Prem sensed a warm pride welling up within himself, a pride encompassing all the people who had been parading before him. These were his kinfolk, he mused, a melding of races and religions which had been evolving for thousands of years in this vast subcontinent of India. Flowing in their veins was the blood of the Dravidian aborigines to the south as well as the blood of the people who over the centuries had swept down through the Himalayan passes to the north, including the Indo-Aryans, the Greeks under Alexander the Great and the Monguls from the vast plains of Central Asia.

"Prem, my dear fellow, how about a cup of coffee for old times' sake?" Major Sunderam grabbed the Captain's elbow and led him back toward the mess hall. As the two stepped through the door, Ram called out to the bearer in Hindustani, *"Aur kuc kafe jaldi lao*—Bring some more coffee quickly."

While the hot drinks were being poured, the Major studied his companion's face soberly. Then waving the bearer away, he leaned forward and dropped his voice to comment, "Kashmir's becoming a hotbed of intrigue. Yesterday a chap came through from there and said the place now was the Switzerland of the Far East . . . full of espionage agents."

Prem listened quietly as he sipped his coffee, noting that all the humor had drained from his companion's face.

"A lot of talk flows through the rooms of the Club . . . some of it is bloody serious and some a bit daft . . . but adding it all up one must come to the conclusion that Kashmir no longer is a quiet holiday hill station."

"You're damned right, Ram, what with the ruddy invasion of Afghanistan by the Russians, and that no man's land of constantly shifting international boundaries between India, Pakistan and China, it's a blooming mess to say the least."

"Be a good chap and take care." A deep sincerity flooded Ram's words.

Half smiling, Prem shrugged his shoulders and countered, "Plan to do the same. You know me . . . cautious Narayan."

"Cautious Narayan . . . hell!" Ram snorted. "You're a damned fearless fool when it comes to tracking down criminals. I heard Pritham Singh say in this very room that under stress your blood automatically turns to ice water."

Prem grinned sheepishly and dismissed the subject with a wave of his hand.

"Changing the subject, how does it look?" Ram nodded toward the wall where the boar's head had been replaced by a mongoose engaged in a death struggle with a hooded cobra whose coils encircled the ferret-like creature.

'I'll be!" Prem broke out with a loud guffaw. "And may I know where they came from?"

"Shot the cobra in my yard a couple of years ago."

"And the mongoose?"

"Always wanted a cobra and mongoose in combat like that . . . " Ram waved his hand toward the specimens . . . 'so I sent the snake skin down to Van Ingen and Van Ingen, taxidermists in Bangalore, and asked them to mount the combination for me.''

"Good job . . . I mean the taxidermy . . . and I know Pritham will be happy." Prem felt an inner revulsion as he studied the head and lifelike eyes of the reptile.

As the two men walked toward the Club entrance, Ram stopped and grasped his companion's arm to say, "One last thing before you leave, Prem, a chap just down from Srinagar came through here a couple of days ago and related a rather bizarre tale concerning a band of dacoits roaming the Vale of Kashmir."

"*Accha.*"

"They're a gang of expatriate Pakistanis who fled Karachi right after the execution of the late Prime Minister Bhutto."

Prem nodded the Major on.

"They've taken on a Robin Hood air . . . robbing the rich and giving to the poor. The villagers like them and hide the blighters from the authorities. They all are Muslims and find support from a fairly good number of Kashmiris. But there's one thing about these dacoits you'll find hard to believe."

"Try me."

"The leader is a woman . . . a fetching young woman at that."

"The hell you say!"

"That's right . . . a woman."

Chapter Three

The midafternoon Delhi traffic unobtrusively absorbed a taxi pulling out from the Ashoka Hotel enroute to the Criminal Investigation Department headquarters. In the back seat, withdrawn into his own thoughts, Prem Narayan reflected on his new assignment. Cobra murder, he mused, frowning and pursing his lips, a reptile which took thousands of innocent lives every year. How he despised the venomous creatures, in spite of the fact that Hindu folklore attributed to them a mystical potency to engender fertility. Then too, a new dimension had been added to the case. Only that morning Pritham Singh had inferred that the assassination of Allabaksh, the Chinese, might well precipitate international complications. Prem shook his head unhappily at the thought of the Vale of Kashmir ... beautiful jewel of the Himalayas ... experiencing the blight of malicious intrigue and the foul play of hostile espionage, for the Jhelum valley was his favorite vacation spot.

Deftly guiding his taxi through the vehicular traffic, impeded by capricious pedestrians, including children just released from school, the driver finally braked sharply in front of the C.I.D. headquarters entrance. Having paid his fare, Captain Narayan jumped out of the vehicle, climbed the steps and showed his identification card to the sentry just inside the door. The uniformed employee saluted and waved him on to an office servant, known as a *peon* or *chaprasi*, who escorted him into the building. Prem and his guide moved along the halls in a continuous flowing motion, unhampered by such obstructions as doors or bamboo screens, all of which were quickly and silently opened by fellow *peons*. These ubiquitous servants were scattered throughout the building, seated on benches, stools and chairs, even on the floors along verandahs and hallways. Some stood statuesquely outside office doors at the beck and call of clerks inside, enthroned behind their desks.

Far in the interior of the headquarters complex, isolated from the distractions of the lower ranking offices, was a room served by two chaprasis, one on either side of the door. A neatly painted wooden sign jutted out at right angles from the lintel above, identifying this particular domain as that of Pritham Singh, Deputy Inspector General, C.I.D. One of the chaprasis, recognizing the Captain, quickly swung open the door and asked him to enter. Stepping over the threshold, Prem paused in silence surveying his surroundings. Pritham, at the moment unaware of his visitor, continued to pore over papers spread

out before him. Small steel rimmed glasses, perched low on the bridge
of his nose, softened the austerity of his bearded and mustached
features. The desk displayed the organized untidiness of a busy man. A
stack of documents occupied the right side of its top and appeared to
flow over the edge into an equally substantial collection on the floor.
The other side of the table boasted a ponderous lamp and shade
supported on the head and trunk of a kneeling elephant artistically
carved out of rosewood. Directly across from the seated Sikh, on the
very front border of the desk, a tall and slender bronze vase fought to
hold aloft a drooping and wilted rose.

Moving forward, Prem announced his presence with a discreet
cough, which he repeated several times until it was noticed.

"Ah! So here you are, my good chap. Come in . . . do come in,"
Pritham repeated with enthusiasm, rising to reach across the desk and
grasp Prem's outstretched hand. "A spot of tea . . . yes?" He waved his
guest toward a chair.

"Don't mind if I do."

Clapping loudly for attention, the Sikh called out in Hindustani,
"Chaprasi, do chay lao- Chaprasi, bring two teas."

Prem, dressed in a khaki woolen bush jacket with matching long
trousers, placed his military cap and swagger stick on a side table and
sat down. Reaching into a drawer, Pritham pulled out a large brown
envelope which he pushed toward his guest.

"Dossier on Allabaksh, including Sahgal's post-mortem findings.
We've alerted the Doctor as to your arrival. Addresses and telephone
numbers . . . all in there." The Sikh pointed at the envelope.

Steaming cups of tea were poured by the chaprasi for each of the
men who paused to sip noisily of the brew.

"And Ali Aurangzeb?" Prem asked about the C.I.D. man in
Srinagar.

"He's expecting you," Pritham cut in with a wave of his hand, "and
is familiar with the case. Better consider this as a classified paper . . . "
he paused to tap the document with his finger before continuing . . .
"and here's your plane ticket."

"Thanks." Prem reached across to pick up the dossier and the
smaller envelope stamped "Indian Airlines."

"The flight makes two intermediate stops . . . Amritsar and Jammu.
Lieutenant Aurangzeb will meet your plane at Srinagar and place a jeep
at your disposal. The Kashmir Princess, a houseboat on Dal Lake has
been reserved for your party. Much better security than hotel rooms.
The driver, Rustum Sharif, has a wife who'll cook for you. Rustum's a
young chap . . . a local lad . . . been mucking about the Jhelum valley all
his life and knows it like the palm of his hand. Works for the C.I.D.
out of Ali's office." The Sikh took a vigorous sip of tea while he
surveyed his companion's face.

Prem sat quietly making mental note of his chief's comments and intermittently drawing on his cigarette.

"Damned important to the Department . . . the solution of this case. In fact it's extremely important to Central Government," Pritham broke into the silence.

Prem soberly nodded in agreement and asked, "Ian McVey and Sardar Khan . . . Where'll they be joining me?"

"Amritsar."

"And as in the past I'll be directly responsible to you?"

"Directly to me. And we've notified the Srinagar Superintendent of Police and the Provincial chaps as well."

"*Accha*. That about ties things up . . . " Prem began and then continued in Hindustani . . . "*Ab mai jata hu* - I'm going now."

Pritham rose and walked around the desk to place his arm around Prem's shoulders and confide, "If anyone can resolve this ruddy mess . . . it's you, old chap."

"Hope you're right," the Captain responded self-consciously.

"Haven't been wrong about you yet."

"Changing the subject, that boar's head no longer looks down on the Club mess hall."

"The hell you say!" Pritham squinted in surprise over his glasses.

"Major Sunderam chucked the moth-eaten tusker out and replaced it with a mongoose in the clutches of a cobra."

"Ah . . . an omen . . . that's it . . . an omen," the Sikh broke in excitedly, "portending to the success of your assignment."

"I don't exactly follow you?"

"My dear chap, in such a duel the mongoose is invariably the victor."

"So?"

"Damn it Prem, the instrument of death in Kashmir has been a ruddy cobra and you're a helluva lot brighter than a mongoose!"

"*Accha* . . . I'll accept it as a good omen," the Captain admitted with a broad grin.

"I say, Prem, one final thing before you leave. Our office here's been worried about leaks in security up in Kashmir. Just haven't been able to put a finger on the source but it could be someone in Ali's office. We've alerted Ali and I want you to be cautious. Might be careful about classified information anywhere off the Kashmir Princess."

"Well, cheerio, Pritham." Prem Narayan saluted with his swagger stick and walked out of the office.

Rising early the next morning, Prem prepared for the flight to Kashmir, packing and locking the tin box and then snugly compressing a reluctant and corpulent bedding roll with two encircling leather straps attached to each other by a looped handle. He had compared this

procedure with that of saddling a horse, intimating ... with profanity
... that there were times when the inanimate baggage could be far more
stubborn than its equine counterpart.

Notifying room service of his intended departure, Prem stood at the
window surveying an awakening Delhi. A hesitant dawn, detained by its
winter schedule, squinted through the haze of countless fires warming
chilled bodies and cooking the first meals of the day. The combination
of smoke and a subdued dawn softened the sharpness of Delhi's
serrated skyline, wrapping the ancient city in an aura of mystery.

Indian Airlines morning flight to Srinagar impatiently lifted off the
Palam Airport runway, retracting its wheels into their separate pods
with vibrating thuds. Climbing rapidly to a cruising level, the aircraft
nosed into a northeasterly direction toward Amritsar. The brisk winter
air was exceptionally clear, affording Prem an unlimited visibility. He
watched the flat farmlands of Haryana and the Punjab slip by below, a
vast mosaic of verdant fields, irregular in size and shape, pasted over
the face of the earth like hundreds of colorful postage stamps across a
gigantic brown envelope. Scattered as punctuation marks over this
agricultural panorama were the villages hiding their mud and brick
houses in the lush camouflage of green trees.

Punjab ... Punjab, Prem reflected as he scanned the seeming
endless stretches of land passing under him. Comes from the Sanskrit,
he continued in his reverie, meaning five rivers, 'panch' denoting five
and 'jeb' river. These plains flow northward into the stunning grandeur
of the Himalayas, whose melting glaciers and snows perpetually
replenish the five tributaries of the Indus nourishing the fertile fields
below. The Captain appeared half asleep, lost in his musings.

"I say, you're headed for Kashmir, eh?" A voice from behind
roused Prem from his daydreaming, and he turned to look back down
the aisle into the face of the man who had lighted his cigarette while
waiting for the lift at the Ashoka Hotel, the night before.

"Right you are." The Captain's reply was noncommittal.

"Business or holiday?" the man persisted.

"Business," he replied good humoredly, wondering what the
stranger's inquisitiveness could mean.

The stewardess broke into the conversation to announce over the
loudspeaker that the plane was commencing its approach to Amritsar,
the holy city of the Sikhs. After the partition of India, this ancient and
revered site would have been the logical capital of the Punjab, except
for one fact, it lay only a few miles from the border of Pakistan. Thus
an entirely new city, Chandigarh, rose in the open fields against the
foothills of the Himalayas, some one hundred and fifty miles southeast,
to become the home of the provincial government. As he had done
many times before, Prem loosened his seat belt and leaned his head
against the window to catch a better view of the Sikh Golden Temple.

Although not large by comparison with some of the world's religious sanctuaries, this sacred shrine made up in dignity and simple beauty for what it might have lacked in size. Like a golden lotus it appeared to float in the center of a small lake. A short causeway, commencing in an ornate arch on the shore side, led across the water to the temple crowned with a central dome and surrounded by four minarets, one at each corner. Bordering the esplanade about the shrine were several smaller canopied minarets raised on supporting pedestals. The unruffled surface of the lake reflected the golden dome with a mystical perfection. Drawing in a quick breath of admiration for what he had just seen, the Captain settled back in his seat and awaited the plane's landing.

Amritsar was a brief stop. Through passengers were denied debarking privileges. Lieutenant Ian McVey and Sergeant Major Sardar Khan boarded the plane together. Seeing Prem in the rear, they came down the aisle all smiles, the Lieutenant heading for the seat beside the Captain and the Sergeant Major taking the one just behind. Winter being a slacker period for the Kashmir tourist trade, passengers were fewer and the three men were able to converse quietly without fear of compromising security.

Prem briefed the two on the facts Pritham Singh had disclosed and concluded, "We'll study the dossier on Allabaksh in the privacy of the Kashmir Princess."

"Well . . . a bloody cobra, eh? Not exactly my cup of tea," Ian muttered, shaking his head and scowling. "Despise the blasted reptiles. They scare the hell out of me," he admitted, his voice projecting a deep disgust.

"Two of them according to the civil surgeon," Prem countered grimly.

"Can you believe it, a friend of mine raises the damned things at the Kasauli Institute," the Lieutenant confided in a barely audible voice.

"Bruce Duncan?" the Captain asked.

"How'd you know?" Ian raised his eyebrows in surprise.

"On the flight from Bombay . . . "

"Ah . . . Doreen," Ian cut in and added, "Bruce's baby sister."

"What do you mean . . . baby? She's a lovely young lady."

The Lieutenant broke out laughing. "Aye, that she is, a bonnie lass, but Bruce still refers to her as his baby sister. Mrs. Duncan and my Joyce are cousins. All four of us, Bruce, Maureen, Joyce and I attended school together at Woodstock in the Himalayas."

"I think we'll be needing Doctor Duncan's help in Kashmir," Prem observed quietly, a pull of worry about his eyes. Having said this, he tipped his seat back for a cat nap.

Lieutenant McVey headed up the C.I.D. office in Chandigarh, capital of the Punjab, and Sergeant Major Khan was his second in

command. On receiving particularly difficult assignments, Captain
Narayan was wont to petition Delhi headquarters for the services of
these men and the petitions were rarely denied. The trio made up an
effectual team ... rational, cool, fearless and usually successful in their
mission. Because of this efficiency, and somewhat to their embarrassment, they were becoming a legend in the matter of criminal
investigations, both among those enforcing the law and those breaking
it.

A smile of satisfaction touched Prem Narayan's face as he mentally
reviewed the character of the young man seated beside him. Over the
several years of their professional association, the two had become fast
friends. Ian McVey displayed his dual ethnic background, the blue eyes
and the sandy hair of the Scotsman combined with the swarthy
complexion of his Indo-Aryan heritage. He stood just under six feet in
height and demonstrated the proportioned contours of well-exercised
muscles without evidence of excess fat. His facial expression bordered
on the dour, projecting the firmly-etched lines of solemnity. Bushy
eyebrows jutted out like eaves. He smiled infrequently when not around
close friends but on those occasions when he did, his entire face
participated in the action. Although outwardly the Lieutenant usually
displayed a reserved sobriety, underlying this show of austerity there
existed a defensive ... almost shy ... mien. Prem attributed these latter
characteristics in great part to be expressions of a social insecurity
associated with his being an Anglo-Indian.

Sergeant Major Sardar Khan, a Muslim, was a man whose dress and
bearing exhibited the epitome of military spit and polish. His trim and
amply beribboned uniform, flamboyant khaki turban, neatly trimmed
beard, bristling mustache ... waxed and pointed like the curving horns
of a buffalo, and ramrod posture, all attested to years in the Indian
Army. After his recent retirement from the military, the C.I.D.
recruited his services. The Sergeant Major's untiring persistence in
following through on the exasperating minutiae of investigation had
won Prem Narayan's admiration. Steeped in military discipline, Sardar
Khan maintained a rank-conscious reserve in his relationship to the
Captain and Lieutenant, a situation which neither officer was able to
break down completely in spite of their close associations during these
investigative forays.

North of Amritsar the plane banked eastward to circle a finger of
Pakistan stabbing into India from the west, then turned back to touch
down at Jammu, the winter capital of Kashmir. The stop was brief ...
just long enough to unload and load. Rising with a vibrating full thrust
of its turboprop engines, the aircraft climbed rapidly to clear the crests
of the Siwaliks, a range of foothills almost lost against the towering
mass of the Himalayas. Like a colored picture suddenly flashing on a
screen, the Vale of Kashmir broke into view, with the city of Srinagar

hugging the banks of the serpentine Jhelum River. Meandering in wide coils through a patchwork of green fields, this watercourse ... one of the five tributaries of the Indus ... with its numerous interlacing canals was transformed by the reflecting sunlight into dazzling channels of quicksilver. Between Srinagar and the wooded Shalimar Gardens lay the smooth waters of Dal Lake mirroring the abruptly rising mountains beyond. Prem pressed against the window, absorbing the breathtaking view of the valley below, eighty-five miles long and twenty-five across at an average elevation of over five thousand feet, surrounded on three sides by the glittering tiara of snow-capped Karakoram and Himalayan peaks thrusting skyward from the borders of the Vale.

Chapter Four

Lieutenant Ali Aurangzeb, the Kashmir representative of the C.I.D., a slender young man in uniform whose bearded aquiline face sported an awesome handlebar mustache, stepped out of the crowd at the Srinagar airport and grasped Captain Narayan's hand. Taking the three men aside from the debarking passengers, he greeted them soberly, "Glad to see you chaps ... " he began and then paused to look around cautiously before continuing ... "there's been another murder." His voice was barely more than a whisper.

Prem caught his breath sharply and asked, "Cobra?"

Ali frowned and nodded his head in agreement.

"When?" The Captain pressed his questioning.

"Last night. Body was found this morning. A repitition of the Allabaksh case except ... " Ali paused, a perplexed look in his eyes, then went on ... "except this time the blooming bites all were in the left forearm."

"Bites, you say. How many?" Ian asked.

"Three separate wound sites and ... according to Doctor Sahgal ... made by three different snakes."

"And we can examine the victim?" Prem asked.

Ali nodded. "Sahgal's expecting you at the hospital morgue."

"See that chap," Prem whispered to Ali as they approached the baggage claims counter to retrieve their gear, "the bloke in the astrakhan cap just climbing into the horse tonga. Anybody you happen to know?"

"From this distance, with his beard and all ... " Ali squinted and stared for a moment and then shook his head before continuing ... "it's hard to say, but I'm willing to bet you a dozen rupees the bugger's an Afghani."

"Your rupees are safe," Prem countered with a chuckle, "I'd come to the same conclusion."

"Why ... I mean what's the bloke done?" Ali asked.

"Oh ... nothing much really ... at least he's done nothing but been inquisitive. I've an uncomfortable feeling he knows who I am. Ran into him at the Ashoka night before last and then again on the plane this morning. The chap's a bit patronizing. Then too, funny thing, he has a falcon tatooed on the backs of his hands."

"Lots of Afghanis running around Srinagar these days," Ali observed in a matter-of-fact voice.

Picking up their baggage, the four men compressed themselves into a jeep and headed for the Srinagar Government Hospital. Conversation was limited to generalities as their thoughts concentrated on the bizarre circumstances of the two murders.

Doctor Pran Sahgal rose from his desk to greet the visitors as they stepped into his office. His glistening pate was wreathed with a narrow fringe of closely cropped white hair, while steel-rimmed eye glasses perched precariously near the tip of a thin and curved nose. Larger than average sized ears jutted out from the sides of his head. His likeness to the late Mahatma Gandhi was quite startling.

After introductions, the Doctor beckoned his guests to follow and led the way into the morgue, waving them to gather around the table on which lay a sheet-covered body. Removing the shroud with a dramatic flourish, he lectured his captive audience with an over-abundance of medical terms, lisping slightly because of ill-fitting dentures. Having completed explanations of the post-mortem findings which were interrupted frequently for clarification, he imperiously marched the entourage back into his office where a peon was pouring out four cups of steaming tea.

"Victim's been identified from papers on his person as Ahmed Feroze, a local tradesman," Ali confided between sips of the hot drink.

"An Indian citizen?" Ian asked.

Ali nodded in affirmation.

"Sir, I take it you're certain that each of the three wounds came from a different cobra?" Prem framed his words slowly and distinctly, all the while studying Doctor Sahgal's watery eyes for any evidence of hesitation.

"Yes! Yes!" he repeated emphatically.

"Please, sir, would you summarize your reasons again?" Prem posed the question deferentially.

Before replying, the doctor shot a quick condescending glance at the Captain, betraying an obvious pleasure in his superior role as a teacher. "Each of the sites showed an equal reaction to the venom. Stated differently, each showed almost identical necrosis or destruction of the adjacent flesh." He paused to adjust his glasses and survey his audience, as if waiting for his words to sink in.

"And the type of snake . . . a cobra?" Ian asked.

The doctor nodded so emphatically he almost lost his glasses, pushing them up on the ridge of his nose with both hands before responding, "We definitely are dealing with the cobra rather than with the viper or krait. The former carries a neurotoxic and the latter a hemolytic venom . . . "

"Meaning?" Prem broke in quickly.

Pran Sahgal continued his dissertation as if he had not heard the question, "Cobra poison paralyzes the nervous system ... the spinal cord and brain in particular, frequently involving the respiratory center. On the other hand, the viper venom harms the blood, interfering with the clotting mechanism and destroying red cells. The victim actually may bleed to death within his own body. Viper fang marks usually are more evident than those of the cobra. The surrounding flesh deteriorates into guava jelly-like rotten tissues. As the viper toxin spreads, large black and blue areas develop ... hemorrhage into and under the skin." The Doctor stopped, grimaced and shrugged his shoulders as if apologizing for the gruesome details he had recounted.

"*Accha.*" Prem nodded his head and swallowed forcefully at the unsavory thought of the venom-poisoned tissues being likened to guava jelly, his favorite breakfast spread. Why does the medical profession liken disease processes to food, he mused. Coffee ground vomitus ... thick pea soup pus ... " he stopped and swallowed hard again.

"As in the case of Allabaksh, the victim's body was thrown into a pond ... the same pond ... in the Shalimar Gardens," Ali explained.

"Were they alive when thrown into the pool?" Ian asked.

The Doctor shook his head. "Neither one drowned ... no water in the lungs."

Reaching into an inner coat pocket, Prem Narayan retrieved his cloisonne case and opened it to offer Pran Sahgal a cigarette, which he crustily refused. The Captain smiled tolerantly and proceeded to select and light his Camel with an air of detached indifference. After blowing several smoke rings up at the ceiling, he turned abruptly in his chair and asked, "Doctor, by any chance was Ahmed Feroze left-handed?"

The slightest glint of admiration flashed in Doctor Sahgal's eyes as he nodded in assent.

"And was Allabaksh right-handed?" Prem pressed his questioning.

The Doctor hesitated and nervously adjusted his glasses before responding, "Yes ... yes he probably was."

"Then you're not certain?" The Captain enjoyed a touch of personal pleasure at Pran Sahgal's discomfiture.

The Civil Surgeon stared at his clasped hands on the desk before him and shook his head. "Not certain. I really gave the matter no thought until this morning and by then the first victim's remains had been flown out of the country. No doubt in this case. Chap's left-handed. Muscular variation between right and left sides leaves no doubt."

"The Chinese probably was right-handed," Prem agreed good humoredly.

"Another finding, a bit strange I must say," the doctor was explaining, "were ... were ... " he paused and groped for the proper wording ... 'were the remains of a crushed chicken's egg in the hand of each victim. In the first case I thought this might just have been a coincidence, but when again today there were the remnants of a crushed egg, well . . . ' his voice trailed off into silence.

"On the same side as the cobra bites?" Ian asked.

Pran Sahgal nodded and added in an aside to himself, "Allabaksh in the right hand and Feroze in the left."

Touched by the slanting rays of an afternoon sun and shining white in its recent coat of paint, the Kashmir Princess floated proudly on the pellucid waters of Dal Lake. The picturesque flat-bottomed houseboat was secured by thick hemp ropes fastened to two posts embedded in the bank alongside. A narrow gangplank, bordered by slackened rope banisters, bridged the short watery gap between shore and an open stern deck. There were two stories to the floating residence. In the center of the upper deck was a large breezy room, roofed and with walls insect-proofed by finely meshed wire netting, all surrounded by a broad uncovered promenade with regular ship's side rails. This section, while delightful for summer months, was infrequently inhabited during the cold winter. The lower and main deck embraced three small but comfortable bedrooms and an ample mess hall which also served as a living or front room . . . all heated by individual charcoal open braziers. There being no electricity aboard, kerosene not only fueled the various conveniently located lamps but also a large antiquated refrigerator standing in one corner of the dining room. A hastily rigged telephone connection had been installed just that morning on Lieutenant Aurangzeb's order. On the houseboat's exterior, slanted white canvas awnings, six to either side, sloped down from their attachments along the upper borders of the windows to be held out from the ship's sidings below by carved wooden props.

Tied up to what might be considered the stern of the floating living quarters, with a connecting catwalk, was a less pretentious ark-like craft which incorporated kitchen facilities as well as housing for those servicing the Kashmir Princess. In addition to a very much occupied and noisy chicken coop and a nondescript dog, the deck was cluttered with a variety of articles ranging from towels drying on a clothesline to an assortment of pots and pans. Two braziers, fueled by charcoal, were the sole sources of heat for cooking and baking. On the lake side of this service boat was moored a much smaller and narrow hand-propelled craft known locally as a *shikara*. This floating taxi afforded passenger and marketing transportation not only to the far shores of Dal Lake but also, over numerous connecting canals, to many parts of Srinagar. Hanging from the gunnels of the service vessel was a pilot's rope ladder permitting access to the *shikara*.

As Ali Aurangzeb swung the jeep around to an abrupt and gravel-scattering stop on the bank beside the Kashmir Princess, Rustum Sharif and his wife ran to the ship's end of the boarding gangplank to welcome the new guests. A sheer scarf modestly covered the lower portion of Fatima's face, accentuating the animation of her dark eyes. She was dressed in the Punjabi *kamiz* and *salwar*, a practical costume consisting of a knee-length tunic or sheath, split on the lower sides, and full pantaloons close-fitting about the ankles. A knitted woolen sweater worn over the upper portion of the *kamiz* added necessary warmth. Rustum was clad in a woolen military outfit including a long overcoat. After introductions, Prem unobtrusively studied the man and his wife, surprised at their apparent youth. Rustum must be in his early twenties, he thought to himself, and Fatima not yet out of her teens. Could either or both of them be the security leak out of the local C.I.D. office?

Under Ali's directions, the baggage was sorted and distributed to the designated billets, each member of the trio having a private cabin which opened into a short enclosed hall running along the shore side of the houseboat as an extension from the dining-living room combination. Because of the telephone connection, Prem Narayan was assigned the first room, while Ian McVey bedded down in the adjoining and central quarters, with Sardar Khan occupying a bedroom at the far and blind end of the corridor. A water closet . . . with washbowl, bath-shower and toilet facilities . . . was crowded into this complex between the billets of the Lieutenant and Sergeant Major.

"My transportation is arriving," Ali announced, hearing a vehicle pull up on the shore driveway. "The jeep we drove in from the airport is yours for the duration."

"*Accha* . . . and you'll be joining us in the morning . . . say around nine?" Prem suggested.

Ali nodded his agreement and confided, "Rustum's a bally good driver. Knows every nook and cranny around these parts. Born and raised here."

"Thanks for everything and cheerio." Prem raised his hand in an informal salute as the young Lieutenant headed ashore across the gangplank.

Darkness and a biting chill permeated the Kashmir Princess as Prem and Ian pulled their chairs up around a charcoal brazier by the dining room table. Ian took his shoes off and alternately warmed his left then right foot over the glowing coals. Rustum Sharif and Fatima were scurrying about lighting the kerosene lamps and preparing to serve dinner. The two officers were enjoying their usual preprandial drinks, the Captain his gin and tonic and the Lieutenant his scotch and soda. Sardar Khan, being an orthodox Sunnite Muslim who shunned all alcoholic beverages, was pacing briskly about the upper deck promenade, his quick measured steps easily heard by those below.

"Allabaksh and Feroze, both done in by cobras," Ian mused aloud as he filled his pipe from an ornately tooled leather tobacco pouch. "Awful way to die, eh?"

Prem chose not to reply immediately other than to nod his head in agreement. With eyelids almost closed, he continued to bob the ice in his drink with a section of lime peel. Suddenly he straightened in the chair to comment, "Both Muslims and from the evidence so far it appears both were murdered by the same party. Now what in God's name is the linkage between the deaths of a Chinese Muslim and an Indian Muslim? Get the answer to that question and we'll be well on our way to the solution of our problem." The Captain followed his words with a stiff drink which initiated a bout of coughing.

"Think there'll be more?" Ian asked after Prem settled down and cleared his throat.

"God only knows. I've an uneasy feeling . . . a gut sensation . . . that there will be more."

"Good to have a chap like Sahgal about . . . I mean a specialist on snakes. Reminded me of Sherlock Holmes . . . that magnifying glass."

"Comes on a bit strange at first but the bloke's sharp. In fact I'd say he's damned sharp."

"Reminds me of Gandhi. If they make a movie of Mahatma Gandhi there's your man to play the part."

Prem laughed out loud and nodded his agreement.

Ian was in the midst of his pipe ritual, a meticulous transaction which the Captain watched in amused silence. First came the filling of the bowl, then the precise tamping of the tobacco with a specific instrument released from his many-bladed pocket knife, followed by a dramatic lighting with the flourish of a wooden match. As a benediction to this ceremony, the Lieutenant concluded with a series of short quick draws on the pipestem creating billows of exhaled smoke.

"A right-handed person usually defends with his left arm, using his right for attack," Prem mused, breaking the silence.

"So why should a right-handed man be bitten on the right forearm?"

"Precisely," the Captain cut in, stabbing the air with his cigarette.

"Unless the victims weren't permitted an opportunity to defend themselves and were forced to carry out some procedure exposing an arm to the cobras."

Prem nodded soberly, continuing to bob the ice cubes in his drink. "The crushed eggs," he muttered, "just where in hell do the crushed eggs fit into the picture?"

"A gruesome way to commit murder," Ian grumbled, reaching over to stir the brazier with charcoal tongs.

"Psychological warfare. The bastards want to terrorize as well as murder," Prem elaborated grimly.

The unique aroma of Punjabi cooking pervaded the room as Rustum and Fatima brought in covered dishes of food. Ian sniffed the air and smiled his pleasure.

"We can always order European food," Prem teased.

"Though I'm half a Scotsman, the Indian half caters to my appetite," Ian countered. "Cookng here is an art and spices are the foundation of this cuisine, a careful blending of ingredients so that the variety, amounts of each and even the order of their addition must be correct. One good Indian cook is worth a dozen European chefs."

"Can't believe that you prefer this Indian *khana* to clear soup, boiled potatoes and fish cutlets," Prem continued his ragging.

Rustum rang a small brass bell announcing dinner. The three men needed no second invitation. In the center of the table was a large bowl containing the main dish, mutton curry. Encircling this were many supporting servings: A platter of fluffy yellow saffron rice; *muttar pannir*, peas and cubes of homemade cheese; *kheera-ka rayta*, yogurt with sliced cucumbers; *pakoras* and *samosas*, deep-fried lentil pastries filled with meats and vegetables; *naan*, a thick leaf-shaped bread; and *gajar halva*, a sweet dessert made of cooked wheat and finely grated carrots.

"*Jo khana apne pakaya, vah bahut accha tha*—The food which you cooked, was very good," Prem complimented the couple in Hindustani.

"*Dhanyavad*—Thank you," Rustum replied with an appreciative grin while Fatima giggled self-consciously and slipped out of the room.

After dinner Prem invited Ian and Sardar to his quarters for a discussion of procedures to follow in the investigation. Closing the door into the hallway, he lowered his voice to announce, "Ali will join us here after breakfast in the morning. He'll have to be kept informed of all our plans. This is a helluva dangerous assignment, no worse than some in the past, but certainly no cushy job ... " he studied his companions' grim faces before going on ... "and I needn't remind you that death from the fangs of a cobra is a ghastly death."

"As we usually do, let's settle on a password," Ian proposed.

Prem nodded. "I've already selected one," he dropped his voice before continuing, "the written, drawn or spoken swastika, from Sanskrit, meaning 'benediction.' "

"Jolly good," Ian agreed, "a word as ancient as the Hindu Vedas."

"And in contrast to the Nazi party emblem, this 'swastika' has the arms bent counterclockwise," Prem reminded, picking up a pen and drawing the design on a scratch pad under the light.

"I understand, sir," Sardar Khan conceded, after studying the sketch.

The Captain continued his discussion of plans, "After our session with Ali in the morning, I want Ian to get in touch with Montague Brown, Monty for short, who's staying at Nedou's Hotel. He's an American and a geology professor on leave studying rock formations in the mountains around here. Doug Gordon, my friend the American Consul in Bombay, asked me to check on this chap."

"How old ... I mean this Monty?" Ian asked.

"I'd guess just a bit younger than you."

"You'd rather meet him here in private?"

"Precisely, that is if you can persuade him."

"Challenge accepted," Ian responded with a grin, reaching out to warm his hands over the charcoals.

"And Sardar," Prem turned to face the Sergeant Major, "I want you to comb this area and find out all you can about cobras. Who's selling them and who's buying them. The Jhelum valley ... at this altitude ... isn't exactly the most natural habitat of those damned snakes but some blighter's supplying the murderers with cobras. Of course you'll check out the local snake charmers."

'*Accha, ji*—Alright, sir," Sardar Khan chose to reply in Hindustani, his eyes bright in anticipation of the assignment.

"Why don't I put a call through to my friend Bruce Duncan at the Kasauli Institute. They keep those bloody cobras and vipers to collect their venom for the preparation of anitvenin," Ian proposed.

"Smashing idea!" Prem approved enthusiastically.

"How much should Bruce know about ... " Ian began.

"He's certainly read about the murders," Prem cut in, "and at the moment we don't know a lot more, do we? Just keep quiet about possible international complications, eh? I would like to meet the chap and discuss some of my ideas with him."

A discrete knocking on the bedroom door interrupted their conference. Sardar Khan admitted Rustum Sharif who asked, "At what time breakfast, gentlemens?"

"How about seven?" Prem suggested, surveying his companions who nodded their agreement.

Rustum accepted the time and announced, "Cooking for breakfast, hot dhalia porridge, eggs, toast and coffee." He surveyed the three questioningly, all of whom gestured their approval.

"What about these during the night?" Ian asked, pointing at the glowing bed of charcoals in the brazier on the floor.

"Please, leaving them in hall outside when sleeping. I am moving them to deck till morning time when they move at six o'clock to outside door again. Also, please gentlemens, tonight doors are closing and windows are opening."

"Or get a terrible headache," Ian interjected with a wry smile.

Prem rose and stretched, wishing his companions a good night's rest. The water closet, without any heating device, discouraged loitering, so he hurried through the routine of showering in tepid water and brushing his teeth, then retreated quickly to the somewhat greater warmth of his bedroom. Slipping the brazier out into the hall, he locked the door and raised the window, folding back the awning to permit a full view of the lake. Finally, turning the lamp wick low, he blew out the kerosene lamp. Shivering, in spite of the pajamas and wrap-around blanket, he stood before the open window. The night was quietly beautiful, delicately illuminated by a half-moon floating weightlessly in a star-decked winter sky, its subdued light intensified as it caressed the gossamer of fog flowing like the sheerest of white chiffon over the lake. Rising wraith-like from their foundations in the shadowed valleys below, pinnacle after incandescent pinnacle of the Himalayan ranges thrust upward into the pale moonglow, as if reaching out to finger the sky.

A lone shikara silently floated past the Kashmir Princess, poled through the water by its navigator standing in the stern. The boat portrayed an otherworldliness as it slipped silently . . . almost illusively . . . in and out of the hovering mists. A kerosene lantern on the prow intermittently reflected from the water a long undulating shaft of light like a writhing phosphorescent reptile. Squatting in the center of the craft was a blanketed and barely discernible form. Prem watched as the shikara slowly turned in a wide arc to retrace its course, this time coming closer to the houseboat. He quickly stubbed out his cigarette and stepped back from the window to be absorbed by the darkness of the room. The inadequate light outdoors, abetted by the enshrouding fog as well as the fact that both men were bearded, made identification impossible. It was evident that both of the shikara's occupants were interested in the Kashmir Princess, for the poling of the boat stopped and the two men conferred for several minutes, one of them repeatedly pointing in the direction of the houseboat. The conference completed, the navigator stood and walked back to the craft's stern to pick up his pole and push off into the night's fog.

For some time Prem stood scanning the mist-shrouded lake hoping the boat might return, but finally relinquished his vigil to enjoy the warmth of a thickly-blanketed bed. Lying in the hush mantling of the night, he savored with pleasure his isolation from the rest of the world. As was sometimes his custom under such circumstances, he began a game of environmental exploration, an exercise in sharpening his sensory acuity. Under the rules of this pastime, he must recognize at least one almost subliminal sensation before permitting himself to fall asleep. To his distinct pleasure, he identified the subtle whispered sound of the lake lapping against the houseboat's hull.

Before courting sleep, Prem Narayan turned his attention to the salient facts just observed through the window. Two somewhat surreptitious persons in a shikara had shown an unusual interest in the Kashmir Princess. Both men displayed beards trimmed after the fashion of Muslims. Of significance for the purpose of identification, was the observation that the navigator of the prying craft was missing his left hand.

Chapter Five

As Fatima was gathering up the dirty breakfast dishes and stacking them into a large brass tray on the floor, Lieutenant Aurangzeb's vehicle pulled up alongside the Kashmir Princess.

"I say old chap, how about a cup of hot java?" Prem asked, stepping out onto a frost-covered gangplank to welcome Ali aboard.

"Frightfully decent of you," he responded, blowing on his cold hands.

Once inside, the men pulled their chairs up close to the two charcoal braziers in the dining room while Rustum poured steaming coffee.

"So . . . anything new?" Prem put the question to his guest.

Ali set his cup on the table beside him and fingered his mustache thoughtfully before replying, "An informant of mine who works at Nedou's Hotel, called me last night and said he's noted some unusual activity in room seven over the past few weeks, particularly the past fortnight . . . " he took several noisy sips of his drink.

"*Accha*." Prem urged him on with a wave of his hand.

"This blighter's been a reliable source," Ali confided.

"Yes . . . yes," The Captain broke in impatiently.

"Well, he's noted people slipping in and out of the room during late hours of the night . . . very mysteriously."

"What sort of people?" Prem pressed his questioning.

"Hard to tell. They move quietly and in the shadows. One consistent visitor is a woman . . . not an Oriental."

"A Western woman!" Prem sounded incredulous.

Ali nodded impressively "Russian. She flies up from Delhi for a couple of days at a time. Makes her reservations at the hotel under the name of Maya Reznikoff."

"And the regular occupants of room seven?" Ian broke into the conversation.

"Just one chap . . . wears European clothes. Registered under the name of Parkozian. Speaks good English but his Hindustani is quite mediocre."

"Probably Armenian," Prem interjected.

"Any chance of having the room bearers pick up information?" Ian asked.

Ali shook his head. "We've tried, but the chap treats his room like a fort . . . brooks no strangers. Permits the bearers entrance only under his surveillance."

"He'll bear investigating," Prem muttered as an aside to himself, then added out loud, "If your man could give us some idea of the people dropping in on Parkozian."

"I only learned about this last night. We'll try and do the needful." Ali appeared irritated at the barrage of questions.

The four men sat quietly a moment drinking their coffee and warming themselves over the two braziers which Rustum kept replenishing with charcoal.

"I say, Ali," Prem broke the silence, "a friend of mine in Delhi told me you have dacoits running about this place led by a woman."

"Right. The blighters are Pakistani expatriates who fled their country for political reasons after the new regime took over."

"And the woman leader?" Ian interjected.

Ali nodded. "That's what the police say. They've been buggering up the countryside. Thank God it's their problem ... problem of the police. They've been having a hard time getting their act together."

"Meaning?" Prem raised his eyebrows.

"Devilish hard to nail the dacoits down. They move quite freely through the territory and often with the help and protection of the local citizenry. It seems their major attention is directed toward the incumbent Pakistani government rather than India."

"Changing the subject ... " Prem selected and lit another Camel before continuing ... "Sardar Khan's going to muck about today exploring the cobra market."

"Been checking on this but haven't come up with anything significant," Ali grumbled.

"And I've asked Ian here to contact Monty Brown," Prem reported, "Have any suggestions?"

"Haven't seen Brown for several days. He's headquartered at Nedou's, you know."

"By the way, Ali, while we're on the subject of Americans, have you run into a chap by the name of James Appleton? He's supposed to be writing a book on the border problems between Kashmir and Pakistan. It's to be sort of historical, if you know what I mean."

"I've met the bloke," Ali nodded and frowned, closely studying Prem's face, "he travels back and forth between here and Delhi. Carries an American passport. I've seen him in Nedou's dining room eating with Vandermeer, commander of the U.N. patrol on the Cease Fire Line."

"That would be natural in the light of Appleton's interest in border problems." Prem conceded, staring over the brim of his coffee cup.

"Uh-huh," Ali grunted.

"Ian, you and Sardar take the jeep on your errands. I'll ask Ali here to drop me off at Mohidin's Suffering Moses shop on the Jhelum. Might have Rustum pick me up there around noon."

Prem and Ali rode in silence for several minutes, trench coats buttoned high against the cutting wind. Intermittent wisps of congealed breath played about their faces.

"As I was about to retire last night a lone shikara with two occupants poled past the Kashmir Princess," Prem said, breaking the quiet. "Actually, they came by twice, much closer on the second approach."

"Checking things out, eh?"

"Must've been."

"Come close enough for identification?"

"Couldn't see the blighters all that well. Fog, don't you know. Both were bearded with shawls over their heads ... Muslim trim to their beards."

"Too bad. Too bad," Ali repeated.

"The bugger with the pole had only one hand ... the left was missing below the wrist."

Ali turned quickly to say, "They were that close."

"You know the chap?" Prem's voice projected surprise.

"Probably Jacub, Kafir Jacub ... " he broke off and stared down the road ahead biting his lower lip.

"And?" Prem prodded him on impatiently.

"Just a local renegade," Ali countered with a shrug of his shoulders.

"In what way?"

"He peddles information to any interested party for a price. An Indian citizen who holds no allegiance except to the rupee."

"Could he be connected in any way with the cobra murders?"

"Could be," Ali replied with a mirthless chuckle.

'*Accha*. But how could they know that we're ... "

"That you're here?" he cut in with a wave of his hand. "Chap was at the airport yesterday when you landed."

The ample houseboat store was moored securely to the bank of the swiftly flowing Jhelum River. Large letters in English emblazoned over the side of the craft identified the floating merchandise shop as that of "Suffering Moses." A wide gangplank, carpeted and with substantial side rails, welcomed the shoppers. Mohammed Mohidin, the proprietor, warmly greeted Prem as he stepped through the entrance. Grasping his arm, he led his visitor toward the stern of the houseboat, passing through a seemingly endless array of salable Kashmiri items. These included carpets, table cloths, woolen shawls with beautiful needlework designs, soft silk saris, bed linens, artistically embroidered blouses and dresses, tooled leather goods, carved wooden tables of all sizes and hundreds of other articles for sale. An aroma, distinct and singular, pervaded the shop. It was a blending of odors from many sources, not always individually identifiable, an essence originating from an amalgam of linens, cottons, freshly sculptured wood and tanned leather. Prem Narayan and Mohammed Mohidin had been friends for many years, each visiting the other on their trips to and from Bombay and Srinagar. A respected Muslim businessman with an intense interest in and an understanding of the Kashmir Valley, Mohidin's customers came from all parts of India as well as many points abroad. According to his explanation of the houseboat's name ... possibly apocryphal ... a visiting British dignitary at the turn of the century, on seeing the intricate wood carvings of his great-grandfather had exclaimed in wonderment, "Suffering Moses." The name had been appropriated by the family and carried on through following Mohidin generations.

In the stern of the boat was a small office, separated from the shop proper by heavy hanging drapes. Entering and pulling the partition closed after them, Mohammed waved Prem to a bench built into the hull of the craft and then sat down beside him. Occupying the floor directly before them was an intricately carved walnut coffee table on which rested two porcelain pots, each jacketed with a colorfully knitted woolen cozy. Removing the covers from these vessels, Mohammed ambidextrously and simultaneously poured hot milk and black coffee to concoct an aromatic and steaming blend in each of their cups. After tasting the delightful brew, Prem, with the suave grace of an accomplished magician, retrieved his cloisonne case from an inner pocket and offered his host a Camel which he accepted. Selecting one for himself, the Captain flamed both cigarettes and then leaned back to blow a perfect smoke ring above their heads.

"You're going to have to give me lessons on how to do that," Mohammed said, pointing at the spiraling circle rising toward the ceiling.

"It's simple ... quite simple," Prem said with a self-conscious grin.

"So ... back in Srinagar, eh?" The Muslim shot an inquisitive glance at his guest.

"Back in Srinagar," Prem repeated, carefully picking an adherent tobacco shred off his lower lip and flicking it into the ashtray.

"Big problems?" Mohammed persisted.

"Tell me something about Ahmed Feroze," Prem asked without answering his question.

The Muslim's eyes narrowed and his jaws clenched producing muscular bulges on the sides of his face. Then taking in a quick breath, he muttered, "So ... you're investigating the cobra murders?"

Prem quietly nodded in assent.

"Just what I thought when you called last night." Mohammed shifted in his seat nervously before cautioning, "Then it's a damned dangerous game you're in, my dear fellow. This bloody assassination probably reaches beyond Kashmir ... for that matter probably beyond the borders of India."

For a moment both men smoked and sipped their coffee in silence.

A rapping on the outside of the boat's hull interrupted their thoughts. Mohammed opened a sliding window on the river side and, after the Muslim greeting, "*Salaam Aleikom,*" accepted a bundle of letters from the postman seated in a shikara. In return the proprietor transferred a stack of parcels for mailing back into the small craft. With the transactions completed, the postal boat continued its deliveries along the Jhelum River.

"Ahmed Feroze?" Prem persisted in his questioning.

Mohammed stared at the cup of coffee in his hand as if he had not heard the question and his guest exercised the wisdom of keeping silent. After a moment the Muslim set his drink down on the table and took a deep breath. "A fine man he was. We both grew up here in the Jhelum Valley. We've worked together on various civic projects over the years. His main business was trade with adjacent countries. Shipped out condiments, spices of all kinds, nuts such as cashews and peanuts. Used hill ponies to distribute his wares through the mountain passes into China, Afghanistan, Pakistan and even Tibet."

"Was Feroze smuggling?" Prem asked.

The Muslim shook his head vigorously. "No ... the chap wasn't a smuggler in the ordinary sense of the word."

"Any ideas why he was murdered?"

"I've been asking myself the same question."

"His business in international trade, could that be linked to the killing? You know the first victim was Chinese."

Mohammed shrugged his shoulders. "Might have some link. A portion of his trade was with China. Goods sent from here over treacherous mountain roads to Western China ... Xinjiang Province."

Prem stared at his companion incredulously. "What a trade route ... bloody hard to believe."

"Not exactly a cushy enterprise."

"Precisely. Last year I had reason to study that route for the C.I.D. From here it goes to Kargil and then northwesterly down the Indus River and up its tributary, the Gilgit. From there north up into Hunza and after that through the Mintaka Pass at well over fifteen thousand feet elevation down into Western China. And that all adds up to some four hundred miles!"

"The goods are light weight and compact. Took a bit over a fortnight one way."

"For a considerable distance that route goes through territory now controlled by Pakistan."

"In far away places like this, a little money under the table takes care of that. Also being a Muslim oils a transaction with the Pakistanis."

Mohammed stood and refilled their cups with an equal mixture of coffee and hot milk, all sweetened with raw honey.

"Does the name Kafir Jacub mean anything to you?" Prem asked, watching his host's face closely.

"Kafir Jacub!" he spat the words out as if they burned his mouth.

"Yes ... Kafir Jacub."

"Swine!" the Muslim exploded, his eyes narrowing to fine slits. "May a camel spit in his face!"

"Why?"

"That dog is a scoundrel ... a disgrace to our Muslim community," Mohammed muttered angrily.

"I think the bloke could be ... " Prem searched for a proper word ... "implicated in some way with the murders."

"You've seen the bloody fool?" He threw a questioning look at the Captain. "Left hand missing."

Prem recounted the sighting of the two men in a shikara the previous night.

"Black sheep of a respectable family. Ran off to Baluchistan for several years. Supposed to have joined a gang of bandits raiding travelers. Came back with a missing left hand. Those Baluchis are strict Muslims. Probably lost his hand for breaking one of their laws."

A small boy parted the drapes and looked in to announce, '*Apka motar jane-ko taiyar hai, ji*—You car is ready to go, sir."

"*Driver-ko andar ane do*—Let the driver come in," Mohammed instructed the lad.

Rustum Sharif stepped though the curtain and greeted his fellow Muslim, "Salaam Aleikom."

Placing his hand on the driver's shoulder, Mohammed confided, "This young chap's my cousin's son and used to work for me until Ali stole him away."

"Really?" Prem expressed surprise.

Pointing at his guest, Mohammed counseled Rustum in Hindustani, "*Yah Capitan mera dost hai*—This Captain is my buddy."

Out on the gangplank of the merchandise houseboat, the proprietor pulled Prem aside and reported, "The chief of the United Nations Mission ... Cease Fire Line border patrol ... a Dutchman by the name of Colonel Vandermeer, frequently buys things from me to ship to Holland. A few days ago he asked me an unusual question."

"*Accha?*"

"Asked if I traded in merchandise with Afghanistan."

"And what did you say?"

"Just laughed and said that I didn't."

Captain Prem Narayan, seated behind the driver and partially hidden by side curtains raised to protect against a raw wind, reflected on the activity in the Srinagar bazaars. The narrow streets and congestion ... vehicular, human and animal ... slowed the jeep's progress to a crawl, but on this particular occasion the dawdling pace served the Captain's purpose. Through his years of criminal investigative efforts, he had nourished what some psychologists would describe as a sixth or visceral sense, an ability to reach beyond the customary avenues of awareness. Entering a community such as this which harbored malicious action, it was his habit to sample ... by physical proximity ... the rising and falling of human tides, best sensed in environments such as the busy market places. Steeped in the oriental mysticism of Hinduism, Prem reasoned that he must be absorbed into the total human community, one drop in the ocean of mankind, in order to grasp the local ethos and thus better to discharge his assigned task.

The wares of the bazaar were displayed in a variety of ways, some on the bare ground or stacked on carpets and sheets of cloth, others on boxes or crudely constructed wooden stands. In the background ... crowded wall to wall ... stood small and narrow shops. Along the sides of the streets, arranged for all to see, smell, feel or taste were fresh vegetables, dried lentils, brown lumps of raw cane sugar, varieties of flour, spices, meats, Dal Lake or Jhelum River fish and numerous other foods of interest to the housewife or houseboat cook. In addition to the edible items, ardent entrepreneurs noisily called attention to the excellence of their particular brands of astrakhan caps, leather slippers, shirts, carved wooden hiking canes, carpets, bolts of cloth for immediate tailoring, silver jewelry and a variety of esoteric goods.

Behind the more or less temporary facilities outdoors, stood the rows of shops, almost crushed together, huddling close as if seeking each other's warmth. There were few doors at the entrances, these being replaced by metal barricades folded on either side of the store front, which could be pulled across to secure the premises at night. Corrugated iron eaves or slats of wood jutted out above the entrances a couple of feet as protection against rain or sunshine. Two or three wooden steps admitted the customers from the street level directly into a small room with shelves on either side displaying commodities for sale. The shop section was separated from the living quarters in the rear by hanging curtains. The proprietor usually sat cross-legged in the center of the store within easy reach of all his wares and with the ubiquitous hookah close at hand.

The varieties of clothes worn by the bazaar patrons were not so obvious due to overcoats, wrap-around shawls and blankets thrown over shoulders and heads as protection against the cold. With the large Mohammedan population of Srinagar, the burqa, worn by many conservative Muslim women, was much in evidence. This one-piece garment ... resembling a ghostly shroud ... covered the body from head to toes, except for a narrow transverse window to accommodate the eyes, usually screened by a mesh see-through cloth.

"Righto ... let's go," Prem addressed Rustum, who turned the vehicle about and headed out of the bazaar for Nedou's to pick up the two other members of the party. Stepping inside the hotel, the Captain found Ian standing at the registration desk reading a chit from Sardar Khan.

"Shan't be back until later. Do not wait for me," Ian read the Sergeant Major's message out loud.

With the two men crowded into the back seat, Rustum steered the jeep out the hotel compound gate and headed for Dal Lake.

"Not used to this ruddy cold," Prem muttered through chattering teeth, drawing his coat tightly about him.

"Same here," Ian agreed, rubbing his hands together briskly.

"Did you make your contact?"

"Montague Brown's in Pahalgam, a bit over an hour's drive from here. Talked to him on the phone. Invited him to have breakfast with us in the morning on the Kashmir Princess."

"*Accha.*" Prem threw his companion an approving glance, before asking, "What about Bruce Duncan?"

"Bruce, his wife and sister, all three are coming up for a fortnight in Kashmir. They'll be arriving tomorrow."

"The sister Doreen, whom I met on the flight from Bombay?"

Ian nodded. "They'll be going on in a couple of days to Nedou's in Gulmarg. Be staying with friends here in Srinagar before moving on. There's snow up there and they all three are ardent skiers."

"Ah ... Gulmarg. My favorite spot in Kashmir. From behind Nedou's main building and dining room below, the hotel cottages climb the hill behind in single file like giant steps rising into a forest of pines aproning a backdrop of snowy mountains."

"At this rate you'll become the poet laureate of Kashmir," Ian complimented with a broad grin.

"Must see this Duncan chap when he comes through. I've some questions to ask him. He just might be of critical assistance in our investigation," Prem mused out loud.

"Took the liberty to invite all three for dinner with us on the houseboat tomorrow night."

"Splendid!" Prem exclaimed, obviously pleased.

Fatima was setting the dining room for tea when the two men stepped aboard the Kashmir Princess. After washing up, they met beside the table. Ian no sooner had seated himself than he rose again to fetch an extra brazier from his room which he placed between their chairs. "Bloody cold," he commented tersely, picking up his steaming cup of tea and cradling it in both hands for warmth.

"What say after this we take a dekko at the pond where the two victims were dumped," Prem suggested.

"Righto. Rustum knows the spot."

Centuries past, Mogul Emperors of India fashioned the Shalimar

Gardens for their own personal enjoyment as an escape from the searing heat of the plains. Fronted by the cool waters of Dal Lake and nestled back against the sheer wall of towering Himalayas capped by everlasting snows, the royal retinues luxuriated while their less fortunate subjects sweltered through the scorching hot season five thousand feet below. Ever-flowing mountain springs, fed by melting snow and glaciers, replenished brooks and ponds which, under the supervision of an army of gardeners, watered flower beds so carefully rotated that their beauties were on constant display. Lofty Persian chinar trees, a landmark of the Shalimar Gardens, brought into the Vale of Kashmir by the Moguls, rose high above all other growing things pointing to the grandeur of mountains beyond. November frosts had turned their large maple-like leaves into varying shades of copper. These leaves had become the trademark of Kashmiri weavers, seamstresses, tailors and woodcarvers. Delicately embroidered fabrics and finely sculptured walnut carried the decorative festoon of chinar leaves far beyond the Jhelum Valley and drew travelers from all parts of the world to admire and purchase these works of art.

"A couple of feet deep ... maybe three," Prem concluded, staring down into a small pond whose surface was covered with floating lotus leaves.

"A bit shallower than I'd expected," Ian commented.

Prem stooped over and with the aid of his swagger stick pushed aside some of the lotus leaves for an inspection of the pond's floor. Suddenly he pointed at a small white object resting on the bottom. Rustum quickly removed his shoes and socks, rolled up his pants legs and waded in to retrieve a half-rupee size of broken eggshell.

"Ali didn't quite do the needful here," Prem muttered testily, then went on to say, "I can't make out any connection between this damned shell and the two murders." He repeatedly turned the newly-found object over in his palm, inspecting its every detail.

Ian shook his head in exasperation. "Chicken eggshells ... chicken eggshells," he repeated slowly as if the repetition of the words might reveal their hidden meaning.

Rustum Sharif accelerated the jeep over a narrow road hugging the shore of Dal Lake. Evening shadows paced languidly eastward as the sun lowered over the serrated and white-crested Karakoram ranges to the west. High in the east, a lopsided moon struggled upward toward the sky's zenith in pursuit of the molten solar sphere gently resting on the western horizon. Winter twilight was short-lived in the shadowed Jhelum Valley, lying sequestered at the feet of the lofty Himalayas. Light from kerosene lamps, feeble but hospitable, reached out through the windows of the Kashmir Princess as the vehicle pulled up alongside the gangplank. From a distant minaret, wafting through the evening's hush, came the muezzin's shrill and alliterative call to prayer, '*Laa*

ilaaha illa llaah—There is no god but God!" Summoning the faithful to worship, it was chanted in Arabic, the language of the Prophet Mohammed and the Koran, holy book of the Muslims. Having discharged his passengers, Rustum quickly pulled out a prayer rug from under his seat, unrolled it on the ground beside the jeep and prostrated himself facing Mecca. It was time for evening prayers.

Prem Narayan and Ian McVey drew chairs away from the dining table and arranged them around two braziers. Each had mixed his own drink.

"Cheers," Prem proposed, raising his glass. "Here's to the solution of the cobra murders."

"To the cobra murders," Ian returned the toast.

Taking a heavy drink of his gin and tonic, Prem made a wry face after he swallowed. Then clearing his throat, he observed impatiently, "That chicken shell business could drive us both daft, and I'll be damned if I know just what the connection is ... " his voice drifted into silence.

Ian looked up from tamping down the tobacco in his pipe to propose, "It's ruddy confusing but let's not make the mistake of bogging down on this one clue to the neglect of others."

"Here, here. Well said," Prem agreed quickly, "don't want to come a cropper over cracked eggs, eh?" He directed a rueful smile at his companion.

Fumes billowed about Ian's head as he repeatedly drew on his pipestem, making the tobacco glow like a bowl of small golden nuggets.

Sardar Khan stepped inside and walked directly over to the brazier, warming his open hands over the charcoal embers. Throwing the Captain a self-conscious look, he apologized, "A bit late, sir. Sorry."

"Join us," Prem invited, pointing at a chair, "a hot drink and you'll jolly well feel better."

"Thank you, sir. Be right back." He turned and left for his quarters.

Just as the Sergeant Major reentered the dining room, Fatima rang the brass bell calling the three men to the table. In the cold air the large bowl of lentil soup steamed like a miniature volcano. Silence fell on the men as they warmed themselves internally with the tasty and highly seasoned dish. In spite of the curious glances of his two companions, Sardar Khan quietly continued spooning his soup.

"A long day, eh?" Prem directed a searching look across the table at the latecomer. "Anything new on cobras?"

Enjoying the prestige of his current role, the Sergeant Major studied both men quietly without slackening his attack on the hot soup. Finally, putting his spoon down and wiping his mustache with the tip of a napkin, he began, "My friend from military days, Abdul Ashok, he is retired here in Srinagar. This person owns basket shop in the bazaar ...

'' he broke off to take a long and noisy sip of tea.

"And?" Ian urged him on.

"First thing today, I visit Abdul and ask many questions . . . '' again he paused to drink tea.

"*Accha*." There was a note of exasperation in Prem's voice.

"Then all day Abdul and I visited many snake charmers. My friend knows snake charmers because he sells them baskets for snakes."

"Good show, Sardar, and what came of this?" Ian asked expectantly.

"This evening we found a person in the bazaar who sold five cobras," the Sergeant Major reported triumphantly.

"Sold them to whom?" Prem questioned.

"To someone not a snake charmer."

"Splendid!" Prem's eyes flashed excitement.

Sardar Khan paused dramatically to stroke his beard before going on, "Fortnight ago he sells three and then yesterday he sells two more."

"All to the same man?" Ian asked incredulously.

The Sergeant Major nodded. "To the same man."

"The hell he did! Sold two more cobras just yesterday," Prem exploded, leaning forward over the table to stare at Sardar Khan. "Dash it all, man, do you know what that means? It means the bloody bastards are planning to murder again!" The Captain punctuated his remarks by pounding the table with his fist, jangling the dishes and silverware, and startling Fatima.

"Did he . . . the snake charmer . . . describe the man who bought the snakes?" Ian pursued his questioning.

"A Muslim . . . a Muslim beard," Sardar Khan replied soberly, "and his left hand was missing."

"Kafir Jacub!" Prem and Ian exclaimed in unison.

Chapter Six

Montague Brown, wearing a one-piece ski suit with an attached hood, moved across the gangplank onto the Kashmir Princess with the quick flowing rhythm of a panther, body rolling slightly at each step and the chill morning air condensing his breath into short intermittent puffs of misty white. Ian McVey met him on the rear deck and led the way into the dining room. Stooping to clear the door lintel, the American reached forward to grasp Prem Narayan's hand.

"Nice to meet you, Captain," his basso profundo voice boomed.

"Good of you to take the time . . . " Prem began.

"No problem," he broke in with a wave of one hand, using the other to push the hood back off his head.

Prem led his guest to a seat at the breakfast table and Fatima began serving the three, Sardar Khan having left earlier on his continued investigation of the cobra sales.

"So . . . I understand you're into geology," Ian opened the conversation.

Monty gave the Lieutenant a quick but penetrating look before replying, "That's right. Currently on leave from my teaching at U.C.L.A. or University of California, Los Angeles."

"Our mutual friend, Doug Gordon was quite insistent that I meet you, but the chap gave no particulars as to why," Prem said.

Setting his knife and fork down on his plate, Monty leaned back from the table to say, "Doug's known my family for quite some time . . . sort of a Dutch uncle as we say . . . and the guy worries about me. My parents probably are behind some of this worrying. They see me as a young man all by himself in a corner of the world where intrigue and revolutions seem to be the order of the day."

"Perhaps there's just cause for this worry," Prem countered, "I understand you're not just the run-of-the-mill tourist. You wander off the beaten paths a bit, eh?"

The American shrugged his shoulders and scanned his interrogators somberly, before replying, "My particular interests do take me out into the boondocks."

"Boondocks?" Prem raised his eyebrows questioningly.

"Just another slang word for 'off the beaten paths,' " Monty retorted with a chuckle.

"And just how off are some of these trips?" Ian asked.

"Well ... my last trip of any distance was to Leh."

"Really, that far. That's almost two hundred miles." Prem's voice projected surprise.

"Uh-huh," Monty agreed, between sips of coffee, "Hired two Kashmiris and a hill pony to lug our baggage. We were back in Srinagar in about three weeks."

"*Accha*," Prem commented, a worried look crossing his face.

"You ... you learned something from your trip to Leh ... I mean there were matters of geological interest?" Ian asked with hesitation.

Monty nodded. "Been studying the relative ages of rock formations in the Himalayas as well as the Siwalik foothills. I'm sure you're aware of the fact that the diminutive Siwaliks are much older than the Himalayan peaks towering above them."

"In this trip to Leh on the Indus River, did you note anything out of the ordinary?" Prem asked.

"Geological or otherwise?" Monty's eyes danced mischievously.

"Otherwise," Prem came back with a laugh.

The American cleared his throat and took in a deep breath before replying, "Besides the usual traffic I did note several pony trains of boxes ... wooden boxes ... not the routine trade in those parts."

"Any identification on the boxes?" Ian queried.

"Lettering there was, but it was in Urdu or Arabic, neither of which I read."

"Please bear with another question, Mr. Brown ... " Prem began, only to be cut off by his guest.

"Captain Narayan, may I ask that you call me Monty. And that goes for you also, Lieutenant McVey."

"*Accha*, Monty if you will," Prem agreed with a wave of his hand, "but how do you handle the language problem?"

"*Mujhe torda Hindustani ata hai*—I understand a little Hindustani," the American replied with a self-conscious grin.

"Splendid!" Ian countered with enthusiasm. "A pakka accent if I may say so."

"My dad, a professor of surgery at Howard University in Washington, D.C., was involved several years ago in a faculty exchange with Maulana Azad Medical College in Delhi. Being a young and adventuresome lad of nineteen at the time, and with the approval of my folks, I opted to take a year out of college and join them here in India. A good pundit and plenty of language confrontations with the local citizenry gave me my foundation in Hindustani. As to Kashmir, even among the Muslim population, I find little difficulty in communication. As far as Urdu, the written Muslim language, I can't read it. But this hasn't proven to be a problem because the two spoken languages are practically the same."

Prem quietly studied the American through wisps of smoke rising shore end of the gangplank was parked a fairly recent vintage red Chevrolet station wagon. "That's my Red Chariot," Monty announced, pointing at the vehicle. "Bought it from a staff member of the Canadian High Commission in Delhi. The old buggy rolls along quite well in spite of its mud camouflage."

"Be expecting you around seven-thirty, eh?" Prem reminded his guest as they shook hands.

"Cheerio," Ian joined in the farewell.

"*Phir jaldi milege*—We'll meet again soon," Monty paraded his Hindustani with a friendly grin. Then pulling the hood over his head, he loped across the gangplank and climbed into the car to drive off toward Srinagar.

Returning to the dining room, Ian removed the cozy from the coffee pot and filled their cups again. Fatima replenished the braziers, blowing gently and transforming the black charcoal into glowing ingots of warmth.

"Did you notice someone in the front seat of the Red Chariot?" Prem asked, warming his hands over the hot coals.

Ian nodded. "Looked like a child wrapped up in a blanket."

"That's what I thought . . . a child," Prem mused.

"Seems like a jolly good chap, the American," Ian volunteered.

"Need to find out more about him. That's why the invitation to dinner tonight. He's studying more than Himalayan rocks . . . " Prem's voice drifted away as he turned to stare abstractedly out the window.

Rustum interrupted to announce that their vehicle was ready.

"*Accha*," the Captain acknowledged, rising and stretching both arms toward the ceiling. "We're going to try and find a friend of mine, if he's still living. Had a home on the eastern outskirts of Srinagar, a devout and quite elderly Mohammedan. He's been a practitioner of traditional medicine . . . *unani* medicine, as the Muslims call it."

"Or *ayurvedic* medicine according to the Hindus," Ian added.

"Doesn't have much of a practice now. Too old, really. As a young man he taught English in a Srinagar middle school for many years. Currently he keeps abreast of activities in the Jhelum Valley . . . political and otherwise. Then besides all of these interests, the old chap dabbles in soothsaying . . . a teller of future events."

Leaving Srinigar, the country road meandered cautiously through farmland, for the most part already harvested for winter. Poplars in stately single file flanked the route, their golden leaves enticed into graceful pirouetting dances by each gust of morning breeze. The village, less than five miles out of the city, boasted a handful of humble houses, for the most part humble single-roomed homes with walls of field stone mortared by mud and with roofs of shale or corrugated iron. Open fires indoors vented their smoke to the outside through any available cracks in the roofs, the walls or around poorly fitted windows and doors. A from the cigarette in his hand. He wondered why Doug had wanted the two of them to meet. The Captain found himself impressed by his guest's straightforwardness and the way he looked directly into one's eyes during conversation. Monty maintained a confident and easy informality without giving the appearance of a lack of respect or a discourteous indifference. He displayed a disciplined self-control. There had not been the slightest evidence of surprise at the Captain's disfigured face ... not the quick second look most strangers were wont to take. The man exuded a sense of physical strength ... a controlled muscular power. Although of African heritage, somewhere in his lineage there had been an infusion of white blood, blunting the negroid characteristics to a point where his physiognomy and the shade of his skin were not all that different from the Kashmiris around him. One genetic feature had persisted in spite of miscegenation, a thickly curled crop of black hair which he kept cut close to his scalp.

"Now that you've heard my story, may I ask a couple of questions?" Monty threw an enquiring look at each of the men.

Prem nodded. "Certainly ... do go ahead."

"You're here to investigate the cobra murders?"

"Precisely. But may I ask how you knew this?"

"Well ... in the first place the murders are common knowledge in the bazaars of Srinagar. In the second place a fellow I know saw Lieutenant Aurangzeb of the C.I.D. meet you at the airport two days ago. Putting these bits of information together adds up to ... " he broke off and scanned the faces of his hosts.

"You've met Ali Aurangzeb?" Ian asked.

Monty nodded "The guy checks up on me from time to time and warns me of my exposure to dangers. Doesn't bother me ... I mean his keeping an eye in my direction. He sure gets about the country ... out into the boondocks."

As Rustum and Fatima began removing the dishes, the three men got up from the table and stood in conversation around the braziers, each holding a cup of coffee.

"Thanks for the delicious breakfast and the pleasure of your company," Monty expressed his appreciation, backing up his words with a warm smile. "And Captain, would you help me keep Doug from worrying?"

"If you'll keep me from worrying," Prem retorted with a lusty laugh in which the others joined.

"Touche," the American countered, still laughing, "I'll do my darndest."

"*Accha*. And Monty, could you join us for dinner here, say around seven-thirty tonight?"

"You bet your life, I'd be delighted to."

The three moved out onto the rear deck of the houseboat. At the few pariah dogs and a scattering of well-bundled children scouted the narrow passages between the huts.

The closed door was solid wood ... heavy vertical slats with supporting bolted crosspieces ... and from near the center of the margin on the opening side dangled a crudely forged iron chain of large oval links. A ponderous but simple lock was hooked into a metal loop on the doorjamb.

"*Hakim, Hakim*—Doctor, Doctor," Prem repeated, knocking against the door with the free end of the hanging chain.

"*Kaun hai*—Who is it?" a fragile voice responded from within.

"Captain Prem Narayan."

"*Andar aiye*—Please come in.' The words were stronger.

Prem pushed the heavy creaking door inwards and ... followed closely by Ian ... stepped over the threshold. For a moment they stood waiting until their eyes adjusted to the dimness of light inside. Slowly the outline of a man seated in a large chair by a brazier began to take shape.

"*Baithiye, Capitan ji*—Please sit down, Captain sir," the Hakim invited, waving toward an Indian wooden bed.

"This is Lieutenant McVey, my assistant," Prem introduced his companion.

"A real pleasure to meet you Lieutenant." The Hakim shifted from Hindustani to English so smoothly that the change almost went unnoticed. "And what an unexpected pleasure to meet you again, Captain Narayan."

The charcoal in the brazier suddenly crackled and flamed, momentarily lighting the room. Reclining in a rattan chair, the Hakim firmly grasped the enlarged forward end of the arm rest with his right hand and with his left held the mouthpiece of a long tubed smoking connection with a hookah pipe sitting on the floor beside him. Perched on his head was a gray astrakhan caracul cap, jauntily tipped to one side. An ample woolen shawl draped around both shoulders, enwrapped his frail body down to thickly stockinged and slippered feet. From his bearded face, eyes ... deeply sunk into their orbital sockets ... burned brightly.

"We've come for some words of advice," Prem stated in a deferential tone of voice.

The Hakim chose not to reply immediately, but paused to draw on his hookah, sending the smoke bubbling through the water bowl. After a siege of coughing, he cleared his throat and addressed his guests, "If I can be of assistance, I shall be happy to do the needful."

"What are the unani antidotes for poisonous snake bites?" Prem asked.

"So, my dear Captain, you're here to solve the cobra murders and may Allah grant you protection and success."

"Thank you. We shall need all the help we can get."

Again there was silence, except for the soft bubbling sound of the hookah and the occasional crackling of charcoal in the brazier. After another bout of coughing, the Hakim continued, "Of course, my dear fellow, the most effective remedy is antivenin, but very few rural folk have such specifics available ... " he broke off and shook his head disconsolately.

"I've heard of a black stone used by villagers," Prem said.

The Hakim nodded. "Yes a black stone used to draw out the poison of a snake bite."

"How does it work?" Ian sounded incredulous.

"Incise the area across the fang marks until the blood flows freely, then apply the stone to the wound. Hold it with slight pressure for about a minute and the stone will become attached firmly ... almost as if glued ... until the venom's drawn out or the stone saturated, when it will fall off. To prepare the stone for use again, it must be placed in boiling water for thirty minutes. Bubbles and tiny congealed particles ... the venom ... will be observed escaping from the stone. Finally, it is soaked in milk for a couple of hours then dried thoroughly in the sun. After this it is ready for use again."

"You feel that it ... the stone ... is effective?" Ian asked.

The Hakim nodded, his tongue moving across his dry lips.

"Lives have been saved by the black stone. Repeated applications may be necessary over a couple of days. May I loan you one of mine?"

"Oh no ... no ... but thank you just the same." Prem raised both hands in a gesture of appreciation.

"I understand," the Hakim responded, stroking his beard, "you must have antivenin available, yes?"

Prem nodded. "Might you have comments or words of advice about the cobra murders?"

The hookah bubbled as the Hakim drew on it, turning the coal in its clay bowl into glowing embers. Meticulously his eyes studied the faces of both his guests. "Friends have kept me informed of the devilish killings. Two Muslim brothers, one of whom I knew. May satan and his evil angels throw the souls of these murderers into the abyss for eternity." A bitterness flooded his words.

Sensing his host's rising anger, Prem had the wisdom to keep quiet. The three men sat in silence for a moment.

"There are doubts in the minds of my people that the dogs who perpetrated these crimes are Kashmiris. It is more likely that they are outsiders ... foreigners," he spat the words out.

"Outsiders?" Prem asked cautiously.

"Infidels ... infidels of a godless nation ... " the Hakim's voice, trembling with anger, faded into silence.

A knocking on the door was followed by the entry of the

housekeeper, who immediately busied herself in the business of replenishing the charcoal in the brazier.

"And what of this method . . . this method of assassinations with cobras?" Prem pressed his questioning.

"Not just the game of a twisted insane mind but a cunning and sadistic scheme. It combines the elements of physical and psychological torture. An attempt . . . a desperate attempt . . . to dissuade someone." The Hakim shrugged his shoulders despondently.

"Might you have particulars as to the killers?" Prem persisted.

Drawing heavily on his hookah, the Muslim withdrew into himself for a moment staring at the burning coals in the brazier. Then he raised his hand for attention and spoke as if in a trance, "Three riddles I share with you. Beware of the hooded bird with slashing beak and tearing talon. Trust not the unseeing eye that hides a festering hatred. Fear the official who barters justice for wealth and prestige."

"Thank you for the words of wisdom," the Captain rose and shook the Hakim's hand. Ian in turn grasped the host's extended fingers in farewell, noting how frail and cold they felt.

As they pulled the door open to leave, both men turned and offered the Muslim salutation in unison, "*Salaam Aleikom*. The Hakim waved and replied in the same words.

Rustum Sharif painstakingly guided the jeep through the crowded bazaar streets while the two officers conversed in the back seat.

"Damn it! Three ruddy riddles," Ian burst out. "Why in hell didn't the Hakim just out with it?"

"No doubt about his feelings toward the cobra assassins . . . infidels . . . sadists . . . foreigners," Prem mused.

"Only two godless nations about here are Russia and China."

"The hooded bird with slashing beak and tearing talon must be the falcon. The Afghani with the tattooed falcons on the backs of his hands certainly fits the case."

"Right you are," Ian agreed, "and as the plot unravels we'll probably find the unseeing eye and the . . . the . . . " he threw the Captain a questioning look.

"The official who trades justice for wealth and prestige."

"So we look out for three blokes," Ian grunted with distaste.

Suddenly Prem ordered the driver to pull over on the side of the road beside a gathering of people observing the performance of an itinerant snake charmer, turbaned and squatting on the ground surrounded by his flat woven baskets of reptiles. Both officers remained inside the vehicle and watched a hooded cobra, tongue flicking the air, uncoil slowly from its container and rise to face the to-and-fro movements of a wailing flute made from the combination of two perforated bamboo rods inserted into the end of an elongated hollow gourd. The climax of the performance came as the artisan, while still playing the instrument with one hand, reached forward with the other in a series of hypnotic gestures to stroke the back of the cobra's hooded neck.

"Awful way to make a living," Prem said with disgust and ordered Rustum to drive on.

On board the Kashmir Princess, Fatima had set up for tea. After washing, the two men gathered around the table. Barely had they settled, when Sardar Khan entered.

"Join us, " Ian invited with a wave.

"Shan't be long." The Sergeant Major disappeared into his quarters and returned shortly to sink into his chair at the table with a loud sigh.

"That bad, eh?" Prem asked solicitously.

"Thought I had laid it on good but ... " he sighed again and reached over for his teacup to take a long hissing sip.

"So what?" Ian asked.

"Most of the day I visited my retired army friend, Abdul Ashok, in his basket shop. We watched people passing in the bazaar. About noon my friend catches my arm and points to man with red shawl. Man has left hand missing. I follow the bugger to Dal Lake where another man waits for him in shikara and they quickly leave for across the lake."

"Did the chap recognize you?" Prem asked. "Remember he saw us at the airport when we arrived."

Sardar Khan shook his head. "Shawl over his head ... not look around."

"Good work Sergeant, bloody good work," the Captain repeated, throwing a complimentary smile. "That bastard just might play an important role in the solution of our problem."

Fatima kept replenishing their cups of tea as Prem and Ian discussed with Sardar Khan the meeting with the Hakim. He sat and listened intently to the narration without asking any questions.

"So ... what do you think?" Ian directed his question to the Sergeant Major.

"About the Hakim's words?"

"Uh-huh. His words and particularly the riddles," the Lieutenant said.

Sardar Khan twirled his mustache reflectively before replying, "The old Muslim is a wise man and respected here in Srinagar. He is listening to words from many people. He is knowing much."

"What about the riddles?" Ian persisted.

"Soothsayers are using riddles very much. The falcon we are now recognizing and the other two we shall recognize along the investigation," Sardar Khan nodded knowingly.

Chapter Seven

Intermittent flurries of a chill late evening breeze prankishly played tag with trees along the banks of Dal Lake, sending their colorful fall leaves into nervous fluttering dances, while at the same time rustling the drier foliage into tapping accompaniments not unlike the sound of muffled Spanish castanets. Having tired of teasing the landed flora, these same zephyrs moved on and mischievously touched down at random on the glazed surface of the lake, tickling the water and sending it into uncontrolled giggles of fast spreading ripples. The immature moon, having climbed to its zenith, delicately caressed the Vale of Kashmir, transforming the harsher light of day into a velvety nocturnal luminescence. On the far side of the valley, beyond the lake, rising straight from their obscure understructures, the Himalayas pushed their snowpacked peaks and massive glaciers skyward into the cold tranquillity of a pale moonglow.

On board the Kashmir Princess, Rustum Sharif and his wife Fatima were embellishing the dining room for the special dinner. She had spent the greater part of her day preparing food. The menu was to be of the Northwest Frontier ... or Mohammedan ... with a main dish of Moghlai Kabob, broiled skewered ground lamb. In deference to the Hindu and Muslim members of the party, neither beef nor pork would be served. A delicate and savory awareness of spices, an artful blending of aroma and taste, pervaded the houseboat. Four guests were expected: Bruce Duncan and his wife Maureen; Doreen Duncan, Bruce's sister, and Montague Brown.

The first to arrive was the American, who parked his Red Chariot on the lake shore and then trotted across the gangplank onto the rear deck of the Kashmir Princess, almost colliding with Rustum carrying two folding chairs. After apologizing, he unceremoniously relieved the driver of one of the chairs and followed him into the dining room.

"*Ap kaise hai*—How are you?" Ian inquired as he stepped forward to shake Monty's hand.

"*Mai bahut accha hu, dhanyavad*—I am very well, thank you," he replied in a straight face.

Hearing the exchanges in Hindustani, Prem joined the two and added his greeting, '*Apse phir milkar mai bahut khus hu*—I am very glad to meet you again."

After this game of linguistics carried out at Monty's expense, the three men broke out into boisterous laughter, causing Rustum and Fatima to pause in their work and stare at them in wonderment.

Still chuckling, Prem admitted, "Shan't question your ability to communicate with the local folk ... " he drew on his cigarette before going on ... "Dash it all man, you speak Hindustani with a better accent than many foreigners who've lived in this country for years."

Choosing not to reply to the compliment, the American grinned self-consciously and nodded in appreciation.

Sardar Khan, hearing the loud laughter, entered the dining room and greeted Monty in English. The Sergeant Major was dressed impeccably in army uniform, including a flamboyant military turban.

"I say, my good fellow, what'll you have for a drink?" Ian asked their guest.

"We're drinking?" Monty shot back quickly.

"Jolly well right we are. Prem enjoys his preprandial gin and tonic ... the quinine in the tonic keeps his malaria under control," Ian stage whispered with a supporting wink.

"Well ... how about a scotch and soda?"

"Splendid ... splendid," Ian repeated approvingly, "You'll be joining me in the finest of drinks ... straight from the heathered hills of Scotland." He set about mixing the liquors, singing sketches from "Ye Banks and Braes O' Bonnie Doon."

Each of the two officers was dressed in winter uniform, less ostentatious than that of the Sergeant Major. The American wore a dark woolen suit with a white turtle neck sweater, the latter contrasting pleasantly both with his charcoal gray coat and his tawny complexion.

"Cheers!" Prem raised his glass. "To the solution of our problems."

"Here, here," Ian followed suit in the proposal.

Joining the others in the toast, Monty raised his glass then lowered it to take a sip. His eyes thoughtfully studied the faces of his hosts as he repeated, "To the solution of our problems." Further discussions were interrupted by the arrival of the Duncans in a dark green Land Rover.

After welcoming Bruce enthusiastically, Ian gathered Maureen and Doreen into his arms for a warm and exuberant greeting. Doctor Duncan, although not portly, was approaching such proportions. His complexion and features were surprisingly similar to those of Ian McVey. Both men were of Scottish-Indian heritage with evident carry-throughs from each of the ethnic sources. Ian's dourness was not apparent in Bruce, who tended to be outgoing and animated. Maureen Duncan, also Anglo-Indian, was statuesque and of an athletic build, but not blessed with the natural beauty bestowed on her sister-in-law Doreen. The symmetry of her face was blemished by a fiercely aquiline nose. However, she compensated for this unfortunate feature with a personality which made one soon forget the physical imperfection.

"Ah ... here's my charming airline hostess," Prem said, reaching out to shake Doreen's hand.

"Captain Narayan," she sang out happily, "hardly expected to meet you again so soon."

"Doreen, I'd like to present our American guest, Montague Brown," Ian announced, guiding Monty over to her side.

"A pleasure, Miss Duncan," he boomed, his voice reflecting the sincerity of his words.

Doreen was dressed in a pair of dark blue slacks with a matching blazer bordered in a gold cord. Covering the left breast pocket of her jacket was an embroidered patch showing two crossed racquets, denoting athletic achievement in tennis. Around her throat was a loosely knotted lighter blue scarf with its free ends dipping inside the front of a white blouse. A large bun gathered her black hair on top of her head, exposing the sensuously sculptured curves of her face and neck.

"So you're an American," Doreen responded, extending her hand.

Monty nodded and scanned her face intently for a moment, then broke out apologetically, "I was staring ... Please excuse my boorish manners. But at least accept my attention as a genuine compliment." He smiled good humoredly.

"That I'll do," she countered, a flicker of amusement crossing her eyes.

"Which ... my staring or my compliment?"

"Why both, of course," Doreen replied with a laugh.

Rustum rang the brass handbell for dinner and the seven moved toward the table where Prem directed the seating. Fatima in her freedom of imagination had created a flower and leaf festoonery of unusual attractiveness. Small lotus leaves and tiny wildflowers followed each other in close single file, crisscrossing the table with a bucolic abandonment. From a central brass vase rose a dozen or more cattails, their brown cylindrical stalks huddled together like arrows in a quiver. Besides the usual settings of china, silverware, glasses and serviettes, there were individual brass finger bowls, each with floating wildflowers and a thin slice of lime.

Much to his delight, Monty found himself seated next to Doreen and evinced his pleasure by throwing her a warm smile.

"So you're an American?" she repeated for the second time, more as a statement of fact than a question.

Again Monty acquiesced with a nod, 'Right ... an American."

"We're Anglo-Indian," she volunteered, glancing across the table to include her brother. "Daddy was a Scotsman and mummy's Indian."

And I'm Afro-American," Monty countered, "a mixture of black and white." Doreen sensed a touch of pride in his voice.

Rustum entered the room from the adjacent kitchen houseboat, resplendent in his bearer's uniform including the ornate cockscomb turban, carrying a large oval platter heavy with the main dish of Moglai Kabob. Fatima followed demurely in his wake, dressed in a colorful Punjabi kamiz and salwar, serving the thick wheat bread known as naan.

"Doctor Duncan, the three of us . . . " Prem waved toward Ian McVey and Sardar Khan . . . "have been assigned a sticky task, that of running down the killers of two men. What makes this a bit unusual is that the instruments of murder were cobras."

Bruce Duncan brought his spoonful of food to a halt in mid-air and admitted, "Yes. I've heard of the killings. You're sure the bites were from cobras?"

Prem nodded. "Cobras according to Doctor Pran Sahgal."

"A damned good herpetologist," Bruce acknowledged.

The Captain related the murders of Allabaksh and Ahmed Feroze without going into the possible motivations or potential international implications. He dwelt on the matter of multiple fang marks in each case and the nature of the wounds.

"Sahgal's a bright chap really. A bit dogmatic and opinionated at times but jolly good on snakes."

"Bruce, if I may call you that . . . " Prem waited for his approval.

"By all means . . . by all means," he repeated amiably.

"Bruce, would it make sense to immunize a person before the bite of a snake? Protection before the fact?" Prem asked.

"A smashing idea, if I may say so," the Doctor exclaimed enthusiastically. "You three may be exposed to the venom, so why not be prepared, eh?"

"Exactly!" Prem interjected.

"What we call passive immunization. Effective almost immediately and gives coverage for several weeks. Could make the difference between life and death."

"You said passive immunization?" Prem raised his eyebrows questioningly.

"That's the immunization by introducing into one's body an antivenin produced actively by another body, such as a horse, sheep or rabbit. Immediate but relatively short term immunity. On the other hand, active immunization is the process by which one's own body develops the antivenin as a result of direct exposure to the poison, in this case the cobra venom. Repeated injections of the toxic material are needed to accomplish this. In other words, while the process of active immunization takes time, the immunity is long term. Because of the time element in your situation, the passive method would be necessary."

"Wouldn't this be the same antivenin ordinarily used for a snake bite?" Monty asked.

"Quite right. Immediate results are needed, the immediate neutralization of the snake venom."

"*Accha,*" Prem interrupted, toying thoughtfully with the floating flowers in his finger bowl, "I've been thinking that we give serious thought to immunizing ourselves ... the three of us. After all we're going to be, or already are, targets of the killers."

"Sounds like a ruddy good idea to me," Ian said, nodding his approval.

"And you Sardar?" Prem looked across the table at the Sergeant Major.

"Yes, sir, I too shall receive the medicine."

"Splendid!" Bruce set his glass down on the table with a thud, spilling the water. "Always carry an ample supply of antivenin with me. I'll fetch some here for you first thing in the morning, eh what?"

"Precisely! The sooner the better." Prem sounded pleased.

"How long does the protection last?" Ian asked.

"A bit unusual ... I mean giving the shot before the snake bite." Bruce pinched his nose between thumb and forefinger and surveyed his three patients thoughtfully a moment. "Should cover you for at least a fortnight, but I'd want to repeat the procedure in about ten days."

"Need another patient, Doctor Duncan?" Monty broke in.

"You?" Prem threw the American a surprised look.

"Why not?" Monty shrugged his shoulders. "I'm climbing about these mountains. Never can tell when I might cross paths with a cobra."

"You're quite right," Bruce chimed in, "mucking about these places can be frightfully dangerous. Our cobras don't give a warning like the American rattler. Be happy to lay on a shot for you."

"Good. Then I'll be here in the morning to get in line."

Prem raised his hand for attention, leaned forward over the table and dropped his voice to say, "This antivenin project must be kept an absolute secret. No one ... let me repeat ... no one outside this circle should know that we are being immunized against cobra venom."

"Not even Ali?" Ian asked.

"I said no one beyond the seven of us around this table." The Captain's voice left no doubt as to what he meant.

Ian nodded in acquiescence.

As Rustum and Fatima served the after-dinner coffee, Monty leaned over to Doreen and suggested quietly, "Let's take our drinks to the upper deck and enjoy the moonlight?"

"Sounds romantic," she whispered back.

"An old American custom," he confided with a grin.

Excusing themselves they put on warm outer garments, Doreen a woolen cape and Monty his trench coat, and with their cups of coffee climbed the stairs topside. Out on the deck a wintry night breeze nipped at their faces. Sipping the hot drinks intermittently, they stood in silence sensing the beauty of the moonlit night.

"Breathtaking ... isn't it?" Doreen spoke in a subdued voice, and went on, "like a vast cathedral, beautiful and sacred." She leaned closer to Monty and he felt her shiver.

"Cold?" he asked solicitously.

"My shivering?"

"Uh-huh."

"A bit so, perhaps, but also just being thrilled at the night around us," she responded in a pensive voice.

"In the interest of warmth, may I?" He slipped his arm around her waist and gently drew her close. Doreen said nothing and did not resist.

"Monty, tell me something about yourself?" She looked up into his face curiously.

"Name, rank and serial number?" His eyes teased.

"You were in the military?"

"Marines for three years. A year in Nam ... Viet-Nam that is."

"Daddy was in the Indian Army, Major Sean Duncan," she said with a note of pride. "He was killed in Kashmir ... not far from here. It was the war against Pakistan ... " she broke off with a catch in her voice. Monty's arm tightened about her as she continued, "Sorry, beastly sorry to burden you this way ... "

"Not at all," he cut in, "My mother used to say that those who refuse to share each other's sorrows have no right to share each other's joys."

A warm smile transformed her face as she repeated, almost to herself, "How sweet ... how very sweet."

"Not to continue with my curriculum vitae," Monty chuckled, "After college I did graduate work in geology. In fact I'm on the faculty of the University of California in Los Angeles."

"Really?" She looked up at him in surprise. "You're a professor?"

"Uh-huh. An associate professor," he replied self-consciously, and went on to say, "and now you're wondering what I'm doing here in Kashmir?"

"Should I be?"

They both broke out laughing and Monty enjoyed the rich music of her laughter.

"To answer my own question, I'm on leave from U.C.L.A. studying the geological formations of these mountains." He swept his arm across the skyline.

"Family?"

"Dad's a professor of surgery at Howard University and Mother teaches art in a private school."

"You're married?"

"No. Just haven't found the time or the right girl."

"So you're a bachelor," Doreen countered, and Monty thought . . . or possibly hoped . . . he detected a note of relief in her voice.

"Now it's your turn to confess," he suggested, looking down into her upturned face.

"Not much really. High school at Woodstock in the Himalayas, four years of college in Lucknow, a couple of years with relatives in Scotland, airline hostess school in Bombay and with Indian Airlines for the past four years."

"You look younger than that."

"Younger than what?"

"Oh, I just did a bit of mental arithmetic and came up with your age."

"And what is it?"

"Let's say around twenty-seven."

Doreen broke out laughing. "You're quite a mathematician. The answer is twenty-seven and a half to be exact. And how about you?"

"Well . . . five years in college, one of them here in India, three years in the Marine Corps, three more in graduate school and four years teaching."

"I come up with the number thirty-one . . . thirty-one years old."

"I'll be jiggered. You've hit it right on the head, short just a couple of months. Now I'd say that's good figuring."

"Monty, changing the subject, I'm glad my brother's giving you the antivenin shot in the morning." Her words projected a sense of uneasiness. "Are you in some kind of danger?"

"Don't let your pretty little head worry about that." Her concern triggered a warm happiness within him.

In a silent mood, they leaned against the deck rail overlooking the lake and watched the fidgety reflection of the low-hovering moon squirm across the water. A frosted moonglow highlighted the snow on the Karakoram peaks pinnacling the western skyline. The Vale of Kashmir had fallen a willing prey to the night's quietness, a hush broken only by the distant beating of a lone drum and the more proximate music of waves lapping softly against the houseboat.

"How long are you up here in Kashmir?" Monty broke the silence.

"I'm here a fortnight, and then back to Indian Airlines . . . " Doreen took in a long deep breath and went on to ask . . . "and you?"

"About another month, maybe less. I'm due to head for home shortly. My sabbatical leave from the university's about up."

From below came the sounds of the party breaking up. The two moved slowly toward the steps, Monty's arm still about her waist.

"Doreen, would you have dinner with me tomorrow night?" he asked expectantly. "I'm staying at Nedou's here in Srinagar and I'll make reservations at their dining room."

"So sudden?" she came back with an infectious laugh. "Seriously,

I'd be happy to accept.''

"Great!'' he boomed enthusiastically. "Where can I pick you up?''

"We're with friends here a couple of days before going on up to Gulmarg ... Nedou's in Gulmarg. But in answer to your question, let me meet you at the hotel tomorrow night. I'll ask you to drive me back after dinner, if you will?''

"Very good. In the hotel lounge at seven-thirty, eh?''

"Righto. Shan't be late.'' She gave a happy little laugh and, pulling away from his encircling arm, ran down the steps to join the party.

After the Duncan's Land Rover drove away from the lake shore fronting the Kashmir Princess, Prem invited Monty and Ian to his quarters. Sardar Khan, an early riser by habit, had retired for the night.

"Ruddy charcoal fumes,'' the Captain grumbled, blinking his smarting eyes, "what say we open up a bit.'' He waved his guests to the two chairs and, after pushing open the window casements, returned to sit on the bed's edge.

"Hope you didn't mind my butting in about the antivenin,'' Monty apologized, reaching over to warm his hands over the brazier.

Prem shook his head. "Not in the least, my dear fellow, not in the least.'' Retrieving his cigarette case from the bedside table, he selected a Camel and lit it with slow deliberation. After several deep draws and exhalations he focused his attention on the American. "I'm of the opinion that your interests in Kashmir extend beyond the field of geology.''

A flicker of amusement played around Monty's eyes. "Captain Narayan, I'd be sorely disappointed in your professional competence were you to think otherwise.''

Prem waved his hand deprecatingly. "It's neither my right nor my intention to delve uninvited into your activities, but I do have a concern as to your safety. Doug Gordon's a close friend of mine and in our last conversation I sensed an uneasiness on his part as to your welfare. At Doug's urging I promised to look you up. Please assess my questions in the light of the same.''

"Okay ... my words are in the strictest of confidence.''

Prem and Ian nodded their agreement.

"While I do admit to certain interests other than geology, for the time being these must remain my secrets.''

"*Accha.*'' Prem squinted his eyes against the acrid smoke of his cigarette. "You might give thought to the possibility that we have a mutual need ... we need you and you need us.''

For a moment Monty held his lower lip tight between his teeth and scanned the faces of his hosts. Then with a shrug of his shoulders he admitted, "I've had thoughts along these lines. You're probably right and when the proper time comes along I'll be consulting with you. Anyway, I do appreciate your interest.''

"You're in a position to protect yourself?" Ian asked solicitously.

Monty nodded with a self-conscious smile. "For three years I was a Marine and one of those years was spent in Nam with the Special Forces behind enemy lines ... "

Prem interrupted with a wave of his hand, Nam?"

"Viet-Nam ... we all referred to the place as Nam."

"Please continue," the Captain urged.

"Well ... Surviving in the jungles behind enemy lines wasn't exactly a tea party, and I should add that I've confronted cobras before now."

Prem nodded soberly. "Glad to see you're carrying a gun."

Monty reached under his coat on the left side and removed an automatic from its holster. "I'm a fairly good shot with this if I do say so," he confessed, patting its steel blue barrel. "Part of my survival kit."

"*Accha*," Prem grunted in satisfaction, throwing his Camel stub into the charcoals where it flared momentarily like a flashing meteor.

Standing and stretching, Monty excused himself, thanking his hosts for a delightful and interesting evening. "I'll be around first thing in the morning for my antivenin."

Both officers accompanied the American to the gangplank from whose vantage point the Red Chariot stood out clearly.

"Looks like you've a passenger," Ian observed, pointing toward the vehicle.

Monty chuckled, nodding in agreement. "My shadow," he admitted, "the kid adopted me and I finally just gave in and reciprocated. Nothing legal mind you ... just an adoption of convenience. At first I thought all the convenience was his but now he's carrying a share of the load."

"A waif ... an orphan perhaps?" Prem suggested.

"Must be. At least that's what he says. His parents moved to Pakistan and left the kid with an aunt who later died. Must be around ten years old. A dirty little ragamuffin when he first took to following me around. I tried to lose him but just couldn't. Finally, with a bit of help from a bearer at Nedou's, I cleaned him up and found some clothes which fit him after some of my custom tailoring. Some good food ... and ... and a bit of love ... " Monty swallowed hard a couple of times before going on ... 'Anyway the kid's become my number one handy man. He runs errands, polishes shoes and tries to keep the car clean ... in fact he sleeps in the back of the Red Chariot. I'm warned that the rascal will steal me blind, but I'm not sure that he does ... no proof."

"And what's the lad's name?" Ian asked.

"He told me it was 'Abdul' but I call him 'Osmosis' or 'Mos' for short. The kid permeates any barrier ... nothing seems to stop him."

Prem broke out laughing after repeating the physiological name given the waif by the American. "Actually, the abbreviation 'Mos' is quite acceptable as a Muslim name," the Captain observed, "although most will interpret it as 'Moshe' for 'Moses'."

After a round of handshaking, Monty sprinted across the gangplank and up the bank to his waiting Red Chariot. As the rumbling starter ignited the motor into a steady purr, Prem and Ian watched a diminutive figure climb from the rear of the vehicle into the front seat and disappear behind the American's substantial shadow.

Chapter Eight

Prem Narayan struggled in that psychological no man's land ... somewhere between sleep and wakefulness ... his subconscious mind disturbed by sounds barely audible. Years of tracking the most desperate of criminals had developed in him a sixth sense of subtle awareness, even while asleep, and this unusual perceptiveness more than once had saved his life. Over and above the steady, almost hypnotizing, sound of water gently lapping against the side of the houseboat, there were dissonant notes which he recognized as those of wood softly scraping against wood.

Quietly Prem retrieved the automatic from under his pillow and raised himself up on his elbows. Partially open window casements faintly framed the starlit night. The sound, he thought, could be driftwood or a shikara riding against the hull of the Kashmir Princess. He slowly changed his position, sitting upright in bed, knees drawn under his chin. He waited in a hushed suspense as time moved at an exasperatingly slow crawl. Prem felt that surely his pulse pounding in both temples could be heard by anyone else in the room.

An amorphous shadow began to rise slowly above the lower border of the window, in part blocking out the faint glow of outside light. Probably a turbaned head, he reasoned, watching the intruder silently work his way indoors. Having stepped inside the cabin, the entrant warily straightened and paused, glancing about trying to penetrate the room's darkness. Prem's thumb pushed forward to release the safety latch of his automatic. It would not move. Using both hands he tried to unlock the mechanism but to no avail. Realizing that he must change his tactics, he quietly slipped his bare feet out onto the floor and positioned his body in a manner that would permit him to spring forward. Cautiously he removed the uppers to his pajamas, thus denying his antagonist a handle by which to grab him. Prem clung to the inoperative automatic hoping to use it as a bludgeon.

Hesitantly placing one foot before the other, the prowler began moving forward. Then for a fleeting second the man turned sideways, silhouetting his right fist against the open window. There was a dagger in his hand. Good, Prem thought, the odds have improved a bit in my favor. Actually, he had expected this ... a dagger instead of a gun ... for the assassin would want to escape unnoticed after the deed and the firing of a shot, even with a silencer, would decrease by a considerable margin his chances of successful flight.

The outside source of starlight, faint as it was, favored Prem, being insufficient to expose him in the back of the cabin and yet giving a bare outline of the trespasser. The Captain studied the man's approach in terms of determining the ideal position for a surprise attack. To stop him at the desired point, he used a simple ruse known to ventriloquists. Holding an open palm before his mouth to disguise the exact source of his voice, he barked tersely in Hindustani, '*Kaun hai*—Who is it?''

The startled intruder froze into inaction and in that same instant Prem leaped forward to bring his automatic down hard on the knife-wielding wrist. There was a gasp of mixed pain and rage as the dagger clattered across the floor and out of reach. With the loss of the weapon, the terms of combat had equalized and the Captain ... a master in the art of jujitsu ... pressed his attack, soon becoming the aggressor in the engagement. Appreciating this turn in the tide, the would-be assassin began a deliberate retreat toward the open window. In an attempt to thwart the escape, Prem seized his opponent's left wrist in a maneuver to throw him, but to his dismay his fingers slipped off ... the hand was missing. The violent unchecked momentum of this action unbalanced the Captain, hurling him to the floor and permitting his assailant to scramble precipitously through the window and into a waiting shikara.

"Kafir Jacub," Prem muttered bitterly as he watched the boat and its lone occupant quickly disappear into the misty dark. For a moment he stood leaning against the window, out of breath, listening to the soft splashing sounds of the craft hastily being poled across the lake.

Responding to the pounding on his cabin door, Prem released the bolt and admitted Ian and Sardar, each carrying an automatic and a torch, the lights from the latter nervously tunneling holes through the darkness. Beckoning his two associates inside, the Captain lit the kerosene lamp and retrieved his gun which had been discarded after the initial blow of the skirmish. Sardar Khan picked up the dagger with a kerchief, studying it closely.

"So the bloody fool funked and ran," Ian observed at the conclusion of Prem's terse account of the confrontation.

"What about the knife?" Prem looked at the Sergeant Major.

"Blooming good steel, home forged. It is coming from Afghanistan, near Pakistan. Probably Jalalabad."

"*Accha*," the Captain acknowledged the assessment, knowing Sardar Khan's expertise in weaponry. "The damned bugger got away for two reasons ... " he drew forcefully on his cigarette before continuing ... "and for the first of them, the jammed safety latch, *mea culpa*. Let me add, not by way of an excuse, this has never happened to me before and I'll bet it'll never happen again. As for the second mishap, the missing left hand, in view of the poor lighting there was little chance of recognizing the deformity."

Suddenly Ian walked over toward the window to pick up a metal object from the floor. "I'll be ... if it isn't a key ... a door key," he exclaimed, scrutinizing its outline under the beam of his torch. "No markings," he added, passing the object to Prem.

The Captain in turn studied the metal piece, his forehead wrinkled in thought. "Ian, check this out in the morning, old chap. I think you're right. It does look like a door key. Might lay it on at Nedou's Hotel, eh?"

The Lieutenant nodded and took the object back. "Righto, I'll do the needful. Dropped by Kafir Jacub?"

"Must have been. Wasn't there before the encounter," Prem replied.

"The automatic, sir?" Sardar asked, holding up the Captain's hand gun.

"Still jammed?"

The Sergeant Major nodded.

"You're the specialist, and dash it all, let me know what's gone wrong with it. I've another in my tin box."

"*Accha, ji*—Alright, sir." He nodded again.

"What say we all turn in for the night," Prem suggested. "I'll give Ali a ring first thing in the morning ... ask him over to breakfast."

Both men rose and wished their chief a goodnight before heading for their quarters.

Procuring an alternate weapon from the strongbox, the Captain carefully checked the gun and slipped it under his pillow. Then securing the window and door he crawled under the covers and heaved a deep sigh. Very shortly the cabin fell quiet except for the steady breathing of sleep.

Prem awoke to the tread of Sardar Khan's footsteps on the deck overhead ... his usual constitutional ... and the sound of dishes rattling in the dining room. Slipping out of bed, he moved over to open the window and look out into a somber dawn. Glowering clouds swollen with moisture recklessly chased each other across the Jhelum Valley and on up into the forbidding Himalayas. The usually blue water of Dal Lake had turned gray overnight with a surface wind-blown into the fine irregularity of ground glass no longer capable of reflecting the surrounding beauty. Taking deep breaths of the chill air, he sat down on his bed and telephoned Lieutenant Aurangzeb.

"I say, Ali, deuced sorry to ring you at this early hour."

"Don't mention, quite alright, quite alright," Ali's sleepy voice repeated.

Prem briefly related the night's encounter in his room and invited the Lieutenant over for breakfast. "I think we've a couple of things to talk about, don't you know."

"Jolly good. Be over shortly. You may have another visitor before long ... Baldev Raj, Deputy Superintendent of the Srinagar Police Department."

"*Accha.*" Prem hung up the receiver and hastened to finish his routine in the W.C. Following this, he dressed, putting on heavier clothing in anticipation of a colder winter's day. My dearest Bubli, he thought, unpacking a muffler she had knitted for him. The wool felt warm and for an instant he fantasized the softness of his wife's arms around his neck.

"By Jove, Ian, you're up early," Prem greeted his associate who was seated in the dining room, pipe in one hand and a cup of hot coffee in the other.

Ian grinned sheepishly. "Couldn't get back to sleep after the affair last night. What with the wind banging the window shutters and a thousand and one thoughts swirling through my restless mind ... " he shrugged his shoulders and made a wry face.

Seating himself, Prem accepted a cup of coffee from Fatima and, after carefully balancing the drink on the edge of the brazier, selected a Camel which Ian lit with a flaring wooden match.

"So. Kept awake by a thousand blithering thoughts, eh?"

Ian soberly chewed on his pipestem for a moment before responding. "Just trying to make sense out of all this mess. What's going on in room seven at Nedou's? Of what significance, if any, are the broken eggshells? Where does the goonda Kafir Jacub fit into the picture? Is Monty involved in this bizarre series of events? During my fitful sleeping last night I dreamed of long rows of hands and every damned one of them was tatooed with black falcons." He shook his head in exasperation.

Angry bursts of wind-slanted rain began to thrash the sides of the Kashmir Princess, rattling windows and whistling eerily through the houseboat's superstructures. Fatima moved quickly from room to room tightening the casements and then, throwing a shawl over her head, ran up the stairs to secure those articles topside that might be exposed to the storm's capricious fingers. Meanwhile Rustum replenished the charcoal in the braziers.

Ali Aurangzeb and Lieutenant Baldev Raj arrived at the same time in separate vehicles. They sprinted down the bank and across the gangplank to get out of the rain, Ali slipping on the wet boards but regaining his compromised balance by grasping the thick rope siding.

"Jolly good of you to drop by," Prem welcomed the police officer, shaking his hand.

"Beastly weather this," Ali muttered, removing his heavy topcoat, shaking off the excess water and throwing a look of disgust at the rain-pelted lake.

Prem waved everyone inside off the rear deck, closing the door behind against the damp cold. Baldev Raj, in spite of his first polite protests, was persuaded to join the group for breakfast. Rustum rounded up three more braziers and, after fanning each into a glowing warmth, placed them about the room. Fatima busied herself setting the table. Soon hot cups of coffee warmed hosts and guests alike, dulling the sharp edge of the cutting outdoor chill.

"*Accha*, let me brief you on last night's encounter," Prem announced, interrupting the light chitchat of conversation. An immediate silence prevailed; all eyes focused on the Captain as he related the details of the skirmish, all the details except the finding of the crude metal key. Having finished the account, he took a last draw on the short stub of his cigarette and then flicked it into the brazier near his seat. The room fell quiet except for the sound of a restless wind and driving rain. For the moment, each of the five men about the table appeared engrossed in his own thoughts.

Coughing to break the silence, Baldev Raj, the police officer, observed, "The bloody fools have exposed their hand by the attack last night. I'm a bit surprised that the perpetrators of the murders would let the chump, Kafir Jacub, be the first to lay it on. The bloke's not frightfully bright, you know."

Prem nodded in agreement. "Quite right, quite right," he repeated thoughtfully. "The cobra murders can't be resolved merely by capturing some henchman or accomplice. We've got to collect sound evidence, evidence that'll hold up in court."

"Precisely!" Baldev Raj interjected. "Furthermore, a clumsy pursuit could frighten the quarry into flight."

"The situation's compounded by its international implications," Ian reminded.

The police officer rose and excused himself, "Just wanted to drop by and pay my respects." After shaking hands around the table, he stepped out onto the deck and walked briskly through the rain to his chauffeured vehicle.

"We've several things to discuss," Prem suggested, waving the party back around the breakfast table.

"Chap acted quite decently," Ali said with a wry smile.

"Meaning?" the Captain asked.

"The blighter really resents the C.I.D. moving into his territory and usurping the rights of local authority."

"Quite understandable don't you think, Ali? I'm afraid I'd feel very much the same were I in his shoes."

"Agreed. But I'll repeat that he acted quite decently. He's been showing an extraordinary interest in the cobra murders. Constantly calls me to ask how far along the C.I.D. is in the solution of the crimes. Might add that the chap seems to have developed an intense hatred for me."

"Hatred for you?" Prem raised his eyebrows in surprise.

Ali nodded soberly. "We used to be good friends but . . . " his voice drifted off into silence.

"He has an unfortunate lisp . . . almost whistles as he talks," Ian noted.

"Hard to forget. Hear his tiresome voice over the phone almost every day," Ali admitted with a scowl, then went on to add, "Anyway he knows of your past records in criminal investigations and respects you, my good fellow."

"*Accha* . . . " Prem coughed self-consciously before going on . . . "I didn't tell all about last night's affair. After the bugger escaped we found this on the floor."

Ali studied the key, holding it forward under the kerosene lamp. "Door key, I'd say."

"That's what we thought. I've asked Ian here to check the blooming thing out. Possibly fits something at Nedou's." Prem studied Ali's face intently a moment before adding, "We dropped in yesterday on a friend, the old Hakim on the eastern edge of the city. You must know the chap."

Ali nodded. "He's sort of a grandfather to the Muslim community here in the Jhelum Valley."

"He gave us three riddles: Beware of the hooded bird with slashing beak and tearing talon; the unseeing eye that hides a festering hatred; and the official who barters justice for wealth and prestige."

"Chap's a bit off his chump . . . getting a bit senile. He's always telling riddles. Probably slips a pinch of hashish into that hookah of his. Wouldn't give much thought to his babblings." Ali sounded irritated with the attention given the Hakim.

"You won't forget to keep us informed on foreigners coming into Srinagar," Prem reminded.

"Our office keeps close watch on the airport and hotel registrations. It's damned difficult to cover other facilities such as private transportation. With Kashmir's rugged boundaries, people come and go pretty much as they please. The Mohammedans throughout this part of the world . . . Pakistan, Afghanistan, the Soviet Socialistic Republics and China . . . can mingle with the Kashmiri Muslims without much difficulty."

"From the opening encounter last night we must assume that the bastards are playing a no-holds-barred type of game," Prem spoke in a subdued voice, sounding cold and hard like a mixture of ice and steel, "and we'll be totally daft if we don't function from here on under a tight security." A background noise of wind and rain heightened the sense of sobriety.

"Murder by cobra fangs, a gruesome form of physical and psychological warfare," Ian broke in, scowling with distaste. "The killers have introduced elements of suspense and mystery, all tied into man's inbred fear of snakes. It's not just bizarre, it's bloody awful if you ask me."

A heavy knocking on the door admitted Montague Brown, raincoat still buttoned high up his neck and water dripping on the floor.

"Monty did you have breakfast?" Ian called out as the American closed the door behind him.

"Thanks, yes . . . " he paused to struggle with the removal of his wet coat before continuing . . . "but at this point I'd sell my birthright for a cup of hot coffee." His contagious laugh rolled through the houseboat as he stepped forward and stooped over a brazier to warm his hands. Pulling a chair up to the table he accepted the steaming drink from Fatima and savored its warmth, odor and taste with a grateful sigh.

Studying his face intently, Prem briefed Monty on the night's confrontation with Kafir Jacub. As he listened, the American's eyes narrowed and gradually all humor drained from his features.

Rustum admitted Bruce Duncan who joined the party to enjoy the external comfort of the braziers and the internal warmth of hot coffee. After downing his second cup, Bruce stood and suggested that he get on with the typhus injections, this spurious naming of his medical administrations having been agreed upon the night before. Prem led the Doctor to his cabin and became the first recipient of the needle, followed in turn by Ian, Sardar and Monty. Having completed the immunizations, Bruce packed his medical valise and scurried through the rain to his Land Rover, heading back to Srinagar.

"Thanks for the hospitality," Monty addressed everyone in general as he again wrestled with his wet coat. Slipping out of the door he dipped his head against the driving rain and ran to the Red Chariot.

"Ali . . . a bit of a botheration . . . but could you drop me off at Mohidin's, old chap?" Prem asked.

"No botheration."

The Captain nodded and smiled his appreciation.

"I'll be laying on the door key investigation," Ian proposed.

"*Mai bazar jaa rahaa huu*—I'm going to the bazaar," Sardar Khan announced in Hindustani.

"Jolly good," Prem approved, "and besides checking out more on the cobra situation, see if you can find out something about the bloke who tried to do me in last night."

The Sergeant Major nodded his acceptance of the further responsibility.

"I'd like to suggest that Rustum remain aboard the Kashmir Princess whenever possible," Ian proposed.

"Any particular reason?" Prem asked.

"Let's just call it a gut feeling."

"Good enough reason for me, and Ian, I shan't be using the car so the two of you take it. Might brief Rustum and Fatima on the seriousness of our mission before you take off. Better tell them about the attack last night as well."

"Righto."

"Let's on with it lads," the Captain admonished as he and Ali stepped through the door on their way out.

Mohammed Mohidin met Prem as he walked onto the Suffering Moses merchandise houseboat and led him directly to the rear through heavy hanging curtains into his office. The two men were alone.

"Rustum gave me your message this morning," Prem reported, and went on to ask, "Anything new on the murders?"

The proprietor nodded, waving his guest to a seat and pouring a coffee mixture into two cups.

"Last night I had a visit with my friend, Sayad Khan, who is visiting here from Afghanistan, northeastern part, town of Faizabad in Hindu Kush mountains. For many years he has traded here in Srinagar arranging marriage dowries for wealthy Muslim families in Afghanistan, Pakistan and Western China . . . Xinjiang Province. After Russia invaded his homeland, Sayad fled the country and now helps the freedom fighters . . . mujahidin . . . supplying them with arms, warm clothing and medical goods."

"And these supplies are sent all the way from here in Kashmir?" Prem sounded incredulous.

"Precisely! Pakka organization. Goods are taken in through back door of Afghanistan. Mountain paths and along stream beds which Russian vehicles can't patrol."

"The hell you say!"

"The two cobra victims, Allabaksh the Chinese and Ahmed Feroze the Kashmiri, were a part of this operation. Allabaksh appeared to have the unofficial blessings of Peking."

"And of course this all adds up to a pakka motive," Prem muttered in low voice, closely studying his companion's eyes.

The Muslim nodded, his face distorted by a scowl.

"Dash it all man, this chap's marked for death. The bloody assassins will be after him twenty-four hours of the day. Can't we protect the chap in some way?" The Captain's voice was urgent.

"Sayad's a very proud man."

"Would he talk to me . . . confidentially of course?"

Mohammed Mohidin paused to sip on his coffee, while his eyes carefully scanned Prem Narayan's face. Setting his cup down on the table he fingered his mustache a moment before confiding, "Sayad is most suspicious of any official. He does not trust anyone in uniform."

"But Mohammed, surely you can convince the chap that we're allies against a common enemy."

"I shall see. Perhaps he'll meet you here in my office."
"Splendid! Let me know, eh?"
The Muslim nodded soberly.

Chapter Nine

Prem Narayan arrived back at the Kashmir Princess late in the afternoon. A wet winter already was drawing the curtains of dusk about the Jhelum Valley, diminishing even further the pale light filtering through the angry scurrying clouds. Stepping out of the taxi, he pulled up his pant legs above the ankles and cautiously maneuvered his way down the soggy bank onto the gangplank. Rustum Sharif, waiting on the rear deck, helped Prem remove his dripping coat, then pointed at a stranger squatting to the side of the entrance door and announced, "This hill woman is wanting with you to speak."

The wisp of an elderly woman sat under an awning on the deck, her back against the wall and knees drawn up under her chin. She smiled shyly at the Captain. A gunny sack, one corner folded inside the other to make a peaked hood, covered her head and shoulders like a monk's cowl. Her basic garment was a once-white thick cotton caftan enveloping her miniature body and draping down to the ankles, exposing leather-sandaled feet. White hair, jeweled by entrapped raindrops, framed her pixyish face, bronzed and deeply furrowed by years of exposure to the elements, giving the appearance of a wrinkled and shrunken apple that had fallen from its tree and lain on the ground through several frosts. Three large but plain gold rings hung from the pierced lobe of each ear and a beaded steal ring penetrated the left nostril to dangle across the corner of her mouth. Around the neck, as if supporting her dewlaps, circled a snug choker of turquoise beads.

With a wave of his hand, Prem invited the visitor into the dining room and directed her to be seated near a brazier. Wordlessly, she accepted the bidding, leaving her gunny sack cowl on the deck just outside the door. Rustum was invited by the Captain to remain for possible assistance in understanding the hill dialect.

"Mother, you have a message for me?" Prem asked with a kindly smile.

She hesitated briefly but finally, with Rustum's urging, nodded and said in a voice barely above a whisper, "Someone plots evil against you, Sarkar."

"And just who is this someone?"

She shrugged her shoulders and shook her head.

"Then what is the evil?" Prem pressed his questioning.

"They wish to do away with you." She warned solemnly.

"Do away with me?" His voice projected surprise.

The little woman nodded a vigorous affirmation and then blurted out her story in a torrent of words. She, Lakshmi, and her son, Ram, routinely supplied the Kashmir Princess with milk. They had been doing this for years, delivering their produce every morning by shikara from across the lake. Today two strangers in another shikara accosted them enroute and offered a substantial bribe if they would put a medicine in the milk. Under the duress of threats, Lakshmi and Ram accepted both the bottle of liquid and the money.

"Tell me more about the strange men," Prem urged.

She dropped her eyes in thought for a moment before replying, "Both men were bearded . . . one a Kashmiri and one not."

"Did you recognize the Kashmiri?"

She shook her head. "It was dark and I could not see well," the woman replied apologetically, "but he spoke like a Kashmiri."

Rustum handed over a small bottle which the Captain inspected fastidiously, then removed the cork and sniffed its contents. He drew his head back quickly and muttered, "Burnt almonds. Cyanide." Replacing the stopper with an expression of disgust, he set it on the table beside him.

Lakshmi, who had been searching nervously in the folds of her skirt, pulled out a wad of paper money. "Here!" she exclaimed, impulsively thrusting her full fist toward the Captain as if the currency burned her hand. There were ten damp ten rupee notes.

Throwing the hill woman a kindly smile, Prem said, "For your protection this money and bottle must be left with me. You are a brave and honest woman and I shall see that a proper reward comes your way. Be certain to report any future incidents like this to me."

She dropped her head self-consciously and murmured, "Thank you, Sarkar, for your kindness. I shall report to you."

Rustum beckoned Lakshmi to follow him out of the room. As she rose to leave, her eyes fleetingly scanned Prem's face and he caught a hint of fear in their depths.

The Captain showered and changed into more comfortable clothes before putting a call through to Delhi. Pritham Singh at C.I.D. headquarters, listened intently to a recounting of recent developments, expressing a particular interest in the cobra antivenin immunizations.

"Absolutely smashing idea!" the Sikh's voice boomed over the telephone. "Hope none of you have to prove the protective powers of the injections, but I'll rest easier knowing you've done the needful."

"We've pretty good motivations for the assassinations. Both victims were engaged in smuggling supplies to the Afghani rebels, the mujahidin. So far, although there are some leads, there are no pakka suspects."

"Righto, old chap, good step in the right direction. You know we must have solid evidence against the killers. Facts which will stand up in court, especially seeing there are international implications. Facts so accurate that no one can point a finger at the same.''

"Quite right, Pritham, and I'll be summarizing all this in my report."

Appreciating the precarious nature of criminal investigations, the C.I.D. required a daily log of case progress as insurance that, in the event of a detective's untimely demise, there would be available sufficient evidence to facilitate a continuing effort on someone else's part.

Ian McVey and Sardar Khan stamped onto the rear deck, removing their coats and shaking off the residual water before stepping inside. Prem invited them to confer with him when they had changed into dry clothes and washed up for dinner.

"Cyanide!" Ian spat out the word with a grimace after hearing Prem recount his interview with the hill woman. "Damned easy to slip the bloody stuff into food. Takes only a few drops."

The Captain nodded and stared abstractedly at the glowing tip of his cigarette. For several minutes the three men sat in silence, alternately warming their feet and hands over the crackling embers. Rustum and Fatima hustled about the dining room, replenishing charcoal in the braziers, lighting kerosene lamps and setting the table for dinner.

"Sir, I am making a suggestion ... '' Sardar Khan paused deferentially.

"*Accha,*" Prem waved him on.

"A good thing for me to ride in the shikara tomorrow morning with the milkwoman and her son."

Both officers nodded and Prem admitted, "Could pay off, don't you know."

"I shall sit in the bottom of the boat and cover with a shawl. This is a most good camouflage."

"A bit of alright, Sardar," Ian interjected enthusiastically, and went on to add, "not only a protection for the milkwoman but you might pick up some information. Those bloody cads won't be all that friendly toward them once it's found out they turned the evidence over to us."

"Uh-huh," Prem grunted his assent as he warmed both hands over the brazier. "We're beginning to worry the bastards and that's when the game becomes dangerous ... '' his words drifted off into silence.

Ian called Rustum over and, after briefing him on the Sergeant Major's proposed plans, asked if he would contact the milkwoman or her son tonight. He promised to cross over in the shikara later and arrange for the subterfuge.

With the ringing of the dinner bell, the men gathered about the table to continue their discussions. Prem suggested that Sardar lead off to report on his day's findings.

"No cobras sold by that snake charmer. I visit and ask him. But my army friend . . . "

"Abdul Ashok," Ian broke in.

"Yes," he assented with a tolerant smile, "my good friend Abdul Ashok of the basket shop, he is thinking he knows where the cobras are going."

"The devil you say," Prem exclaimed, and added, "where?"

Sardar Khan took several noisy sips of hot tea and enigmatically scanned his companions over the rim of his cup. Then setting the drink down, he fastidiously patted his lips and mustache with a napkin. Appreciating the Sergeant Major's proclivity toward the dramatic, Prem and Ian waited patiently for his reply.

"A small village about ten miles west of Srinagar. It is called Narangwal. A few huts for fishermen along south bank of Jhelum."

"And how did Ashok . . . Abdul Ashok . . . find this out?" Prem asked.

"He is learning this from Forest Officer friend."

"Just that . . . I mean nothing else about the matter?" Ian questioned with raised eyebrows.

Sardar Khan shrugged his shoulders and conceded, "That is all. Abdul is telling me no more."

"*Accha*," Prem broke in, staring at the Sergeant Major across the table through narrowed eyelids, "Tomorrow you will get into that village and explore. Find out what in the devil's going on there. But be careful . . . damned careful, eh?"

"Jolly good, sir." Sardar Khan's face broke into a broad smile of anticipation. "Abdul Ashok already is talking with me plans to do the needful."

"Don't forget the early morning shikara ride with the milkwoman," Ian reminded.

He nodded his assent.

A particularly heavy downpour of rain, abetted by squally gusts of wind, thrashed the Kashmir Princess, making further conversation difficult. For the moment the three men gave their undivided attention to enjoying dishes of savory chicken curry and rice. To Fatima's particular delight, second helpings became the order of the evening. As the storm ameliorated, there was a resumption of dialogue. Prem nodded at Ian and suggested that he make his report.

"A proper bloke, that chap at Nedou's, the assistant manager. Gave me all the assistance I needed . . . " Ian pulled out a wooden match and relit his pipe before continuing . . . "and I learned some interesting things."

"Such as?" Prem urged him on.

"The key dropped by Kafir Jacub last night in your cabin, has the same serrations as the one that fits the door to room seven."

"So ... the bloody thing fits room seven," Prem muttered in a barely audible voice.

"The assistant manager bloke was quite surprised. Agreed that it had been forged."

"So ... we now know that Kafir Jacub had in his possession the means to enter room seven," Prem observed reflectively, "and either the goonda is an accomplice of the room's occupant or was planning to break in. Probably the latter, because if he was an accomplice, why should he have to make a key?"

"In room five, two doors down, the occupant is the commander of the United Nations Observer Team which keeps watch on the Cease Fire Line between Pakistan and Kashmir. He's a Dutchman name of Colonel Wilhelm Vandermeer."

"The Colonel been here long?" Prem asked.

"Fourteen months according to the assistant manager."

"Which is Monty's room?"

"Blighter moves around a bit. When he's gone for a time, he'll sign out and then sign in again on return. Right now he's settled in room six."

"Going back to the Dutchman ... anything unusual about the chap?" Prem asked.

"Has little to say. Close-mouthed bugger with rare visitations from anyone. Spends most of his time riding about Kashmir in the blue and white vehicle with the United Nations insignia and flag."

"*Accha*, go ahead," Prem nodded Ian on.

"Monty Brown makes occasional trips down into Himachal Pradesh to the Bhakra-Nangal dam and hydroelectric plant just below us here on the Sutlej River."

"Now what in the devil interests Monty down there?" Prem's forehead puckered into deep furrows.

"Also India's largest fertilizer factory," Sardar Khan interjected.

"Dash it all, that's a bit off geology," Ian muttered, chewing on his pipe stem.

As Rustum and Fatima began clearing off the dinner dishes, the men moved away from the table and converged around two braziers.

"And how's Mohidin?" Ian asked.

"Spent a bit of time with him. He wanted to clue me in on conversations with his friend from Afghanistan, a chap named Sayad Khan." Prem took the time to light a fresh Camel and then shared the details of his visit aboard the Suffering Moses.

"So now we have the motive for the cobra murders!" Ian exclaimed at the close of Prem's recital. "The assassins are trying to break up the flow of supplies to the Afghani mujahidin."

"Agreed," the Captain chuckled with a twinkle in his eyes, "but a major part of the puzzle's still missing ... who dunit?"

Ian broke into a self-conscious laugh. "But damn it, that is a big step in the right direction."

Prem nodded good humoredly. "You're right, old fellow. It is a major step forward."

"Going to see the Afghani?" Ian asked.

"Mohidin's arranging for me to meet him at his office in the morning."

"On the Suffering Moses?"

Prem nodded. "I'm scared as hell for Sayad Khan's security. He's a marked man. I'll try and do something about this when we get together in the morning."

Sardar Khan rose and excused himself to retire, adding, "Early in the morning Rustum and I shall cross the lake to join Lakshmi the milkwoman. Then after that I shall leave by bicycle to investigate Narangwal."

The two officers sat in a reflective silence for a moment, each privy to his own thoughts. Bursts of wind-swept rain intermittently drummed against the sides of the houseboat, agitating the window shutters and making them clatter like nervous castanets.

"*Bhakra-Nangal*," Prem mused out loud, resuming the conversation, "wish I knew what Monty's business is down there."

"Let me check that out," Ian countered, "I've an engineer friend on the staff and I'll contact the chap."

"*Accha*, I'll leave you to do the necessary on that, eh?"

"Righto. Guess I'll turn in for the night," Ian announced.

Prem rose from his chair with a sigh and stretched. "Going to do the same as soon as I get a letter off to Bubli. Dear woman, she worries about me too much. Then a few notes into the C.I.D. log for our good friend Pritham Singh ... " his further words were lost in a loud and prolonged yawn.

Chapter Ten

Montague Brown leaned effortlessly against a post supporting the verandah entrance to Nedou's Hotel watching rivulets of water trickle from corrugated eaves above and splash into their individual miniature pools on the ground near his feet. The night was black and two electric lights, one on each side of the courtyard gate, struggled to brighten the dismal damp darkness. He listened abstractedly to the lonely hoofbeats of a trotting horse pulling a two-wheeled passenger tonga down the road just outside the compound wall. As the sound of the vehicle faded into the distance, it was replaced by the splashing of a mud-soiled blue and white car moving through the rain puddles just within the lighted entrance. Still visible on its sides, in spite of the smeared dirt, was the United Nations global insignia. Braking to a squeaky stop, it disgorged a rotund and uniformed European well-bundled against the inclement elements.

"Managing to keep dry, Colonel Vandermeer?" Monty asked the Dutch officer with a good humored grin.

"Ya. But it is vet and cold and miserable," he grumbled in his thick accent. Climbing up onto the dry verandah, he vigorously shook the excess water off his trench coat.

"Come on, Wilhelm, it's not that bad. Dry clothes followed by a couple of Holland beers and you'll forget all about the weather."

"Ya, ya," the Colonel conceded with a mirthless laugh as he turned and marched toward his quarters.

A taxi, whose blinding lights swept callously across the hotel's front, came to a sudden and ungracious halt some distance from the protective roof of the portico. Doreen Duncan, struggling to open an obstinate umbrella which she had pushed out through the car door, suddenly felt someone gently remove the reluctant article from her grasp and unfurl it with a flourish. Next she found herself propelled out of the rain and onto the verandah, barely having set shoes on the sodden ground between.

"There you are," Monty chuckled, releasing her elbow and turning to look down into her face, "didn't want you to sit through dinner with wet feet."

"You're very thoughtful," Doreen responded gratefully. "It's beastly . . . I mean the weather." She shivered involuntarily.

Monty frowned and nodded in agreement. "Let's get inside out of this cold." Again taking her elbow they moved into the foyer and toward the dining room. The white-turbaned bearer led them to a reserved table for two. Before seating Doreen, Monty helped remove her rain cape and hang it on an adjacent clothes rack. This being an off-season for tourists, only a few scattered patrons were present, lending a pleasant sense of privacy. Soft electric lights were positioned strategically about the room. In the center of each table stood a single lighted candle.

"You do know how to lay on a pleasant dinner date," Doreen complimented with a shy smile.

"Only do this for very special occasions," Monty responded, and added in a stage whisper, "for very special guests."

"A bit of a contrast. " She nodded toward the window, "That out there and the coziness inside."

"You're warm now?" he asked solicitously.

"All but my hands . . . see." She reached across the table and Monty felt her icy fingers.

"We'll take care of that," he said, rubbing her hands briskly between his palms.

"Do you provide this service for all your dates?" she teased.

He shook his head and countered, "Only for the beautiful ones."

"Must admit it's a bit of alright." Her eyes danced mischievously.

Bruce had warned his sister to be very proper with Monty and not let him become forward. She wasn't quite sure what he had meant by that but decided her brother had been watching too many American flicks. Even though she had met him only once before, Doreen felt quite at ease with her escort. She rather enjoyed the gentle and protective aura which flowed from this physically large and powerful man. Monty's frequent smiles appeared to be straining at a leash, ready to break out into the open at the least enticement. His eyes were the windows to his thoughts, portraying on the one hand a sensitivity bordering on shyness and at the other extreme a brittle, almost frightening, hardness. Doreen reasoned that Professor Montague Brown, the academic geologist, must be engaged in something more portentous than the study of Himalayan rock formations. As these thoughts crossed her mind, a cloud of worry darkened her face.

Monty took pleasure in what he saw across the table. Seated before him was a beautiful young woman dressed in a stylish blue form-fitting suit, matching the color of her eyes. A delicately embroidered white blouse contrasted attractively with the coat and a narrow black velvet choker. Her dark hair, parted in the middle, was gathered in a single large bun at the back of her head, while a few maverick wisps strayed teasingly about the nape of her neck. The faint titillating aroma of gardenia perfume crowned her presence with a sense of excitement.

"Like what you see?" Doreen asked, leaning forward with a puckish grin.

"Oh yes . . . you bet I do," Monty came back with a start, laughing self-consciously. "There I go again, being rude. Shouldn't be staring at you like that, should I?"

Doreen reached across the table and placed her hand over his. "You know, I've been staring a bit myself." She began to laugh and he joined in, the music of her alto and his bass harmonizing most pleasantly.

"I've done something tonight I can't remember ever having done before," Monty confessed with an apologetic look, "and that's ordering the menu beforehand."

"I shan't have a choice?" she asked in mock surprise.

"That's right, no choice."

"I was only ragging you . . . " she threw him an impish smile before going on . . . "and what may I ask is this surprising dish?"

"Lamb."

"Lamb curry?"

Monty shook his head. "*Shahjahani biryani* . . . Moglai cuisine."

Doreen looked puzzled. "*Shahjahani biryani*," she repeated, her forehead wrinkled, "That's new to me."

Named after Shah Jahan, the fellow who . . . "

"Yes. The Mogul Emperor," she cut in, "The chap who built the Taj Mahal."

"Right. The dish is named after him. A mixture of spiced saffron rice and lamb with shredded coconut and bananas as well as a dish of yogurt on the side. First tasted this at a small Muslim eating place in Chandi Chowk bazaar . . . Old Delhi. I've talked the cook here into preparing it for us tonight."

"Oh Monty, how nice of you." She paused at a loss for words and threw him an appreciative look.

"Sure hope you like it," he said expectantly.

The candle at the table's center obstructed their view of each other, so Doreen moved it to one side and as she did so, Monty observed a shadow of worry about her eyes.

"Problems?" he asked, dropping his voice.

"Possibly . . . " she lifted the glass of water to hide the movement of her lips . . . "A couple of tables directly behind you there's a man watching us intently."

"Do you have a small mirror? A make-up mirror?"

Doreen nodded and began exploring the contents of her purse, retrieving a small compact which she pushed across to Monty. Unsnapping the cover, he manipulated it on the table until he could see the reflection of the man to his rear.

"Can you see him?" she asked in a whisper.

"The fellow with the Muslim cut of beard wearing the caracul astrakhan hat?''

"That's the bloke.''

"Seen him about the hotel here for several weeks now.''

"Blighter's been staring at me over his cup of coffee. Can you see that tattoo on the back of his hand?''

"Uh-huh,'' Monty grunted, "looks like a hawk. Hard to make out the detail at this distance.''

For a moment Doreen bit her lower lip nervously. "That look on his face scares me. You will be careful, won't you?''

A warm smile fleetingly touched Monty's features as he reached across the table to pat her hand. "You're worried about me, Doreen?'' It was more a statement of fact than a question.

She dropped her eyes and a pink blush . . . starting low at her throat . . . spread upward to envelop her face.

Their further conversation was interrupted as the bearer brought on the lamb dish exuding an appetite-triggering aroma.

"You know,'' Monty began, savoring his first spoonful of the biryani, "I find it difficult, quite difficult really, when eating Indian food, to determine the relative roles of taste and fragrance, where one begins and the other ends. The pleasure of eating in this country is the extraordinary simultaneous titillation of the taste buds and olfactory nerve endings.''

Doreen broke out laughing. "You sound just like my brother Bruce. Loves his Indian khana, as he calls it. On trips to England he about goes daft putting up with their bland diet of boiled potatoes, kidney pies, beef or fish cutlets and Brussels sprouts, all washed down with tea.''

"The fellow's leaving,'' Monty whispered as he monitored the mirror before him.

"His baggy trousers and open vest . . . '' she raised her glass of water to hide her face . . . "could be from one of the Soviet Socialistic Republics such as Uzbek or Tadzhik or Kirgiz, all having substantial Muslim populations. But I think this fellow is Afghani.''

"Doreen, I've decided to share something with you . . . '' he began and broke off to study her face thoughtfully.

"Yes?'' She threw him a puzzled look.

"Besides being a geologist studying the Himalayas, I'm also involved in other activities.''

"I've wondered if you weren't.''

"These other activities expose me to a certain amount of danger.''

Doreen nodded, her face fixed in a worried frown.

"I'm not bringing this up because of my own exposure to danger. What worries me is that our association could place your safety in some jeopardy, danger from the same source. You should know this.''

She shrugged her shoulders and gave out a short mirthless laugh.

"I've already told you that Daddy gave his life for India. And as for danger, I don't funk easily." Her dark blue eyes flashed defiance.

"I must say you're quite a gal, Doreen, quite a gal," he repeated with a shake of his head. Monty felt a glow of admiration for the mere slip of a young woman seated across the table from him.

"Sorry. Didn't mean to lay it on that heavy ... but ... " she broke off with a sigh and flashed a winsome smile.

"How do you like it?" He pointed at her dish.

"Delicious! A bit of alright. Takes a foreigner like you to introduce us to our own gourmet foods."

"And I've ordered something sweet for dessert. *Gaj . . . Gaj . . .* " he *groped for the right word.*

"Gajar halva," Doreen interrupted, "shredded carrots, milk, cream and gur or unrefined brown sugar ... all cooked together and then sprinkled over with nuts."

"That's it ... *gajar halva* ... carrot dessert."

"It's actually one of my favorite dishes."

Monty brought his cup of coffee to an abrupt stop, suspended halfway between its saucer and his lips. "Take a look," he said, nodding toward the entrance door.

Doreen turned to stare at two men conversing in the foyer just outside the dining room. One of them was the Afghani who had left the table near them a few minutes earlier. The other was a man in European dress. Both appeared to be engaged in a heated argument.

"I've seen the guy in the suit a couple of times about the hotel here," Monty admitted, "We've chatted. Name's Appleton, he's an American. Stands out like a sore thumb with that eye patch."

"International intrigue, eh?" she quipped with a frown.

'Not quite what I'd planned for our evening together, I mean all this cloak-and-dagger stuff," he apologized.

"No matter. To be quite honest, I'm enjoying myself, all this excitement," she confessed with a laugh. Then turning sober she asked in a subdued voice, "This, this thing you're doing, not exactly a cushy job, eh?"

Monty nodded. "A bit ticklish," he admitted, "but let's not bother your pretty head with that, what?"

The rain had abated somewhat by the time they left the dining room. As they walked along the verandah toward the parking lot in the rear of the compound, a small boy came running and stopped breathlessly in front of them, bringing their progress to an abrupt halt. Tossing his head back, he flashed an infectious grin up at the both of them. Stooping forward, Monty picked him up and, holding the giggling child out at arms length, playfully shook him before setting the lad down again. Doreen noted how the boy continued to cling to the American's hand.

"This is Mos, short for osmosis," Monty announced.

"Mos . . . osmosis?" Doreen repeated with a perplexed look.

"The kid'll permeate anything. He'll manage to get through any obstacle."

She broke out laughing. "Clever name. I just recollected my college physiology lectures . . . uh-huh . . . osmosis."

"You know this moppet adopted me. He's an orphan, a Srinagar waif. I tried to stop him from following me around but finally just gave up. Calls me 'Monty Cha-Cha'."

"Uncle Monty," Doreen interpreted, patting the boy's head.

"Sleeps in the back of the Red Chariot, my Chevrolet car. With the help of a few rupees the cook feeds him regularly. Then just to be sure his ravenous appetite is satisfied, I usually put some of my extra food in a doggie bag for him . . . "

"Doggie bag?" Doreen cut in with a bewildered look.

Monty chuckled out loud. "An American custom of taking home restaurant leftovers for the dog or . . . more frequently . . . later snacks for the humans. Anyway, we call them doggie bags."

He couldn't be more than ten years old, Doreen thought as she studied the child standing beside her. His face was pinched, looking much more mature and wise than his probable age. Pulled down over his forehead and ears, a knitted khaki stocking cap accentuated dark penetrating eyes fluctuating between flashes of humor and sobriety. A woolen coat falling down to his knees, obviously originally intended for an adult, revealed an attempted re-tailoring of size to accommodate a small body. The sleeve of his right arm was turned up freeing the hand, but on the left even the fingers were totally hidden by an extended cuff. An excess girth of the coat resulted in a double-breasted effect, which was maintained in position by a cloth sash firmly encircling the boy's midriff. The ample trousers had been cut off at the ankle level from which protruded stockingless feet strapped into leather sandals.

"Mos loves that coat . . . his most prized possession," Monty confided, "Functions as his security blanket, I guess."

"You made that outfit, didn't you?"

"It's that bad?" He chuckled self-consciously.

"No, no. I think it's great." There was a catch in her voice and she swallowed hard to control her emotions.

"I'm trying to teach him English. He's catching on at a surprising rate, really."

"You don't say?" Doreen raised her eyebrows in surprise.

Monty looked down at Mos and spoke slowly, enunciating each word, "What have you been doing?"

The boy's face brightened as he replied, "The shoes and room I am cleaning."

"Good. Now you go back to my room and wait for me. I shall

return in one hour, okay?"

"Okay, Monty Cha-cha. I to the room am going," Mos replied with a happy laugh, turning to run down the verandah.

"Hard to break that Hindustani syntax ... verb last," Doreen observed.

"Hi there," the man with an eye patch approached with his hand extended to Monty, "Miserable night out."

"Mr. Appleton, I'd like you to meet a friend. Miss Duncan this is Mr. Appleton."

"What a pleasure! Just what I needed on a dismal night like this, an opportunity to meet a charming and beautiful lady. May I say that after this the day won't be a total loss." His exposed right eye stared coldly into hers, negating the pseudo-warmth of his words.

As Monty and Doreen walked on arm in arm, he felt her shudder. "Cold?" he asked, his voice showing concern.

She shook her head. "That fishy look in his eye as it bored into mine was repulsive." Doreen shuddered again. Monty squeezed her arm reassuringly.

In the deserted back compound of the hotel, the Red Chariot sat surrounded by large puddles of water. Raindrops splattered on the vehicle's top, sending a continuous spray of moisture in every direction. A dim ceiling light automatically turned on as Monty opened up the car and hustled Doreen inside. Quickly stepping back preparatory to closing the door after her, he froze in horror at what he saw. A large cobra, hood spread widely, was rising slowly from its coils on the driver's seat directly adjacent to her.

"Don't move! Don't speak!" His clipped whispered words sounded strange, almost mechanical. "And for God's sake don't panic," Monty continued in the same tone of voice. "There's a cobra within striking distance of you on the left. Doreen ... now listen carefully ... " he swallowed hard before continuing ... "I'll be going around to the other side to distract the snake. When I give the word, start turning your whole body away from the cobra and face out the door. Move slowly ... almost imperceptibly if you can ... and get your feet on the ground. Then bend forward and using your legs as purchase slide off the seat. No jerky actions. When you're clear of the car ... out of reach ... with one fast shove, slam the door shut. That's it."

With a brave smile, she nodded her head ever so slightly, just enough to signal a comprehension of his message. My God, what a gal, Monty thought as he quietly circled the Red Chariot. Reaching the closed window on the driver's side, he commenced a slow to-and-fro movement with his open palm just outside the glass. The snake turned quickly, attracted by the pendulum-like action, and began swaying to the metronomic rhythm. After a few slow passes, he changed his tactics and became more aggressive, cupping his hand to resemble a cobra's head and hood, hitting the window with his finger tips. Responding to the hostile challenge, the reptile began striking back angrily, hissing and slobbering its frothy venom against the glass until the poison ran down in spittle-like rivulets.

"Start moving and steady does it," Monty urged quietly, carefully maintaining his distracting hand action. He watched anxiously as Doreen turned in her seat and eased toward the outside. The cobra, hissing noisily, continued its frenzied battle, senses dulled by rage and seemingly oblivious to what was happening just beside it. Then the car door slammed shut, like the final curtain on a horrendous drama.

"Glory be!" Monty shouted as Doreen ran around the vehicle and buried herself in his arms. Her body trembled as he held her close and felt the intermittent shudders of her suppressed sobs. They stood in silence for a moment, unmindful of the rain, until she lifted her face and broke out into a struggling smile. Suddenly their lips met . . . hungry lips . . . wet from the blending of salty tears and raindrops.

"Oh Monty," she sighed, pulling away from his arms and wiping her eyes with the backs of her hands, "the sickening feeling as I turned away from that . . . that loathsome thing. Its hissing rang in my ears like the music of death. Each second I expected to feel its fangs sink into my back."

"You're brave, extraordinarily brave," he repeated quietly.

"And what's next?" she asked, looking up expectantly.

"To get you out of this wet and onto the verandah."

"I'll stay." Her voice carried a sense of determination which Monty decided not to contradict. Reaching into her cape pocket she retrieved a small torch and handed it to the American.

"The creature's still coiled up on the seat," he muttered, shining the flashlight through the venom-streaked car window, "head raised a few inches but the hood's collapsed."

"Yes . . . yes I see it . . . and what's that on the floor?"

"A wicker basket. What they brought the snake in."

"The cads must've chucked it in there, slipped the lid off and closed the car door. Oh, Monty, what if you had gotten in first!"

"Pays to be a gentleman and seat the lady first," he countered with a grim laugh.

Monty walked over and picked up a gardener's hoe lying in a water-soaked flower bed against the compound wall.

"Why don't you leave the blooming thing in there till daylight?" Doreen suggested.

"Not on you life," he retorted, "that blasted reptile's not going to deprive me the pleasure of driving you home tonight. In fact I can hardly wait to do the damned thing in. I've a score to settle with all cobras. A buddy of mine got bitten by one of them in the Vietnam jungles.

"Righto then, let's carry on, give me the torch and I'll assist in your vendetta."

Warily opening the car door, Monty quickly stepped back out of striking range, holding the hoe between him and the snake. It began to raise up, tongue darting in and out and its hood again spreading. For a moment the light appeared to blind the creature and it made no attempt to advance. Using the hoe as a rake, he started to pull the reptile off the seat down onto the ground. It struck out vehemently and repeatedly at the weapon, all the time hissing loudly. As the forward coils slid down into a pool of water, Monty brought the sharp metal edge of the hoe down on the neck with a force that broke the cobra's back, reducing its actions to purposeless thrashings. Further well-placed blows ended all major movement.

"My gosh, it's over five feet long!" Monty exclaimed after straightening the reptile out and pacing its length. Taking the flashlight he explored the interior of the car. Throwing the wicker basket out, he carefully coiled the dead cobra inside it and replaced the lid. Then procuring a rag from the glove compartment, he dampened it by sopping up pools of water collected on the hood of the vehicle and washed off the inside of the window.

"Be sure you don't have any cuts or bruises ... open sores ... on your hands," Doreen cautioned, "Bruce once got some viper venom into a finger wound and was terribly sick for a couple of days."

"No wounds," Monty replied, "and besides, I had antivenin this morning, remember?"

"Just the same, don't take any chances," she urged anxiously.

"I won't," he shot back, warmed by her interest in his personal welfare.

"And the snake ... you're going to leave it there?"

"Yup ... right there in that basket. Can't hurt anyone now. I'd give a month's pay just to see the faces of the guys who take that lid off, especially if they're the same ones who left it."

"Monty do you have any idea who put that thing in your car?"

He scowled and shook his head. "Not sure ... suspicious perhaps ... but not sure."

"It's a bit sickening, don't you know. Blighters must be off their chumps to do a thing like this."

"Doreen, let's take off that cape. It's sopping wet. I'll pull out one of my old surplus army blankets." He stooped over and rinsed his hands in a clear puddle of rain water, before opening the rear of the station wagon and rummaging in a footlocker.

"And look at you. That coat of yours is soaked through."

"Okay. I'll take it off if you'll share the blanket," he countered with a teasing chuckle.

Although the streets for the most part were deserted because of the lateness of the hour as well as the inclement weather, progress was slow. Large pools of water obscured the chuckholes along the way. Many little fingers of rain drummed incessantly across the top of the vehicle. Nervous windshield wipers jerkily thrust their rubber blades back and forth over the glass, erasing in wide swaths the myriads of scattering wind-blown droplets, permitting quick intermittent glimpses of the road ahead. Clods of mud flung off the tires splattered noisily against the undersurface of the car. For some moments Monty and Doreen rode in silence, their emotions drained by the harrowing encounter with the cobra.

"Cold?" Monty broke the quiet, his voice projecting concern.

"Not really," Doreen responded, drawing close to his warmth.

"Good. Being wet in this kind of weather can be miserable."

"Monty?"

"Uh-huh."

"What was that you shouted right after I slammed the car door shut on the snake?"

"Did I shout something?" He threw her a puzzled look.

"Something about glory."

"Oh that." Monty broke out laughing. "Glory be! My grandmother's favorite exclamation."

Doreen lay her head on his shoulder, the dampness of her hair wetting the side of his neck. He put an arm around her under the blanket, bringing them closer together.

"Here we are," she announced, directing him into the driveway. Braking to a stop, he switched off the lights and ignition. For a while the two sat in an awkward silence. Then Monty turned and, gently cupping her face in his hands, kissed her on the lips. She drew to him, slipping her arms around his neck and prolonging the embrace.

"Better not discuss tonight's ordeal with anyone," Monty suggested as he walked her to the front door. "I'll clue Prem Narayan in on our confrontation. And, Doreen, could you get your brother to give you cobra antivenin?"

Smiling up into his face she said, "He'll do just about anything for his little sister."

"You'll do it soon?"

She nodded her assent.

"Leaving for Gulmarg tomorrow?" he asked.

"Yes. We'll be staying at the Gulmarg Nedou's. This cold may fetch us some snow up there . . . skiing snow."

"I'll ring you up, if that's okay with you?" he proposed expectantly.

"By all means." There was excitement in her voice and then in a sober vein she urged, "Monty, please take care."

"That I'll do, Doreen," he promised quietly. In the subdued light of the verandah he studied her face and recognized a hint of worry.

Chapter Eleven

The pointed prow of the shikara moved out into a darkness as yet barely penetrated by the first pink glow of dawn. Pulling away from the Kashmir Princess, the boat headed across the lake, silent except for the intermittent muted splash of the propelling wooden pole breaking the water's surface. Rustum Sharif, standing in the stern and softly chanting a rhythmic ditty, pushed the craft forward in surging thrusts. Wrapped in a blanket, his face shrouded in bearded shadows, Sardar Khan sat motionless in the prow scanning the waterway ahead. During the night the wind and rain had abated, enhancing the creature comforts of the two shikara occupants.

Well informed in the navigation of this particular area of Dal Lake, Rustum moved the boat rapidly through the water. As they neared the opposite shore he poled the craft into narrow channels between floating vegetable gardens looming up as shadowy islands in the cloud-filtered light of a murky daybreak. Buoyant logs lashed together and covered with shredded bark, straw, moss and soil, provided fertile vegetable beds with natural irrigation of lake water seeping upward between the timbers and moistening roots embedded in the overlay. To the discomfort of ignorant or careless navigators, heavy growths of lotus water lilies and reeds often camouflaged these floating gardens, erasing boundaries between penetrable and impenetrable vegetation.

Lakshmi, the milkwoman, and her son Ram were seated in their shikara moored to a post supporting a narrow planked pier jutting out from the shore. As had been arranged, Sardar Khan joined them, sitting on the bottom of the craft between a variety of tin milk containers and concealing himself under a shawl. With his diminutive mother perched motionless on the bow like a carved ship's figurehead, Ram poled the boat out into the lake, skillfully evading the log-supported floating gardens and on occasion forsaking open channels to short cut through growths of reeds and lotus. Rustum followed at a distance, moving cautiously over more orthodox waterways. Although breaks in the clouds gave sporadic glimpses of Himalayan peaks silhouetted in the light of an advancing dawn, visibility on the lake remained limited, due in part to shifting fingers of mist exploring the water's surface.

"*Dekko*—Look!" Lakshmi gave out in a hoarse whisper, pointing forward into the haze.

A shikara, barely visible and directly ahead, floated motionless, its outline appearing and disappearing eerily in the restive fog. Ram reacted quickly, carrying out a strategy born of the fact that he was familiar with the varying and intricate waters of this particular shore line. First he must determine whether or not this was the enemy. Changing course slightly to pass the other craft's stern, he continued his rhythmic thrusts. Lakshmi slid down off her perch and picked up an extra pole, taking her position near the prow ready to give auxiliary power if needed.

As they drew closer to the other shikara carrying a boatman and two passengers, it turned in pursuit. Instead of returning to the shore, Ram continued his course, heading out into the lake and drawing his adversaries after him. Suddenly he turned sharply and began retracing his route back to land, slowing down deliberately for a moment in order to narrow the distance between the two boats. Then as they drew near to shore he called for his mother's assistance and increased the craft's speed to the limit of their combined effort. Struggling to overtake his quarry, the boatman in the other shikara grunted and cursed with each thrust of his pole.

Leaving the open lake, Ram headed directly into a growth of lotus lilies and reeds, showering his passengers and himself with water droplets accumulated from the night's rain. Then, swerving abruptly with a force that threw his mother to her knees on the boat's bottom, he narrowly evaded the corner log of a floating vegetable garden and skillfully maneuvered into an open channel. Howls of dismay and rage broke out from the occupants of the pursuing shikara as its momentum forced the craft high onto logs where it balanced precariously for a moment and then capsized, throwing all three men into the water. Disregarding Sardar Khan's plea to return and identify the pursuers, Ram invoked his prerogative as captain of the ship and poled his way back into the lake to continue his milk deliveries. Behind them, as they moved away from the catastrophe, the furor of shouts and curses soon attracted the interest of a few early risers, a couple of whom attempted to give halfhearted assistance to the shipwrecked passengers.

Rustum returned to shore and after securing his shikara to a pier post, joined the few curious onlookers surveying the accident. Amid continued profanity, the three men hurriedly righted their craft and sped off, obviously shunning identification. In the short period of exposure at the scene of disturbance, Rustum noted several significant findings: All three men appeared to be Muslims; the boatman's left hand was missing; and the two passengers conversed in a dialect, of Arabic derivation, foreign to Kashmir or Pakistan.

Around the breakfast table Sardar Khan reported on the early morning encounter, including the observations of Rustum Sharif, and concluded by announcing, "Lakshmi and Ram will have always as

passenger her brother who is retired from the police here.''

"Good show, old chap," Ian commended with a wave of his cereal spoon.''

"Quite," Prem chimed in enthusiastically.

Rustum admitted an excited Lieutenant Ali Aurangzeb, who announced as he approached the table, "We've another cobra victim, Sayad Khan!''

"Good God!" Prem exploded, rising to his feet. "I was just leaving to meet the fellow at Mohidin's.''

"Found the body an hour ago in the same pond . . . Shalimar Gardens," Ali went on to add.

"How tragic!" Prem made a wry face. "The poor chap would have given us some crucial evidence, but now . . . " he threw his hands up in dismay.

"And what happens to the project the three victims were carrying on?" Ian asked.

"It'll go on," Prem interjected with an emphatic nod. "The undertaking's well organized. There are other leaders involved in the action.''

"So this will mean the cobra murders haven't ended," Ian muttered.

"I definitely want to see the post-mortem," Prem retorted, leaving for his cabin to dress for the outdoors.

"I shall be doing the needful in Narangwal," Sardar Khan announced when the Captain returned to the dining room. "Rustum is borrowing a cycle for me.''

"Ian, old chap, carry on at Nedou's, will you? I'm convinced there're some clues lying about that hotel.''

Doctor Pran Sahgal was waiting for the two officers and invited them into the morgue where he began the examination of the body of Sayad Khan. There were two sets of fang marks, one set on either side of the left forearm just below the elbow. After stooping to inspect the sites of injury with a magnifying glass and meticulous palpation with his rubber gloved hands, he straightened and nodded knowingly.

"Cobra?" Prem asked quietly.

"Yes.''

"Chap's left handed?" the Captain persisted in his questioning.

"Uh-huh," Doctor Sahgal grunted, and went on to add, "The left shoulder and arm . . . " he pointed at the parts before going on . . . "definitely better developed than on the right.''

"And the hand?" Prem asked.

Prying open the victim's tightly clenched left fist, the Doctor exposed the remains of a crushed egg, fragments of shell mixed with the usual yellow and white contents. He felt and smelled the mixture then stepped over to wash his gloved fingers under the faucet at the head of the morgue table.

"Time of death?" Ali asked.

"Man's been dead twelve to sixteen hours; let's say he died last evening."

"Other injuries than the snake bites?" Prem questioned.

The Doctor shook his head, peering in succession at his two guests over steel-rimmed glasses. "Only a couple of post-mortem abrasions ... skin bruises made after death ... probably when the body was thrown into the lotus pool."

Shortly after leaving the hospital, Ali dropped Prem off at the Suffering Moses houseboat. Mohammed Mohidin whisked him back to his office.

"The third victim ... Sayad Khan ... " Prem studied his host's face before continuing ... "Did he tell you anything night before last that I should know?"

Mohammed shifted uncomfortably in his chair as if hesitant to join in an unpleasant discussion, then leaned forward toward his guest and muttered, "Sons of Satan ... these cobra killers!"

Prem nodded in solemn agreement and waved him on.

"Of course you know I am not a part of the smuggling program. It just happens that the last two victims were friends of mine. Although Sayad Khan realized the possibility of his assassination, he refused assistance from me or from anyone else for that matter. The Afghani was a brave man, stubborn perhaps but brave."

"Coming back to my question, did he pass on to you any information that might help us apprehend the criminals who killed him? We know that he worked with the other two victims?" Prem pressed his questioning.

"The Afghani planned to meet you here this morning and I'm certain he had information for you."

Prem shook his head sadly. "Should've insisted on meeting the poor blighter yesterday but that's all water under the bridge now." He forcefully stubbed out his cigarette in the ashtray.

"There is one thing ... " Mohammed's eyes probed those of his guest for a moment before he went on ... "Sayad did give me the secret ... the secret ... " he groped for the proper word.

"Password?" Prem broke in.

"Password, that's right, the secret password."

"*Accha*," Prem urged him on.

"Dowry of Death."

"In English?" Prem sounded surprised.

Mohammed nodded. "In English because it was the only language commonly known to the leading participants."

Both men sat in silence for a moment. Prem tapped his Camel hard against the cloisonne cigarette case several times before lighting it and drawing deeply. Breaking out in a coughing bout, he expelled the smoke through his mouth and nostrils at the same time in explosive puffs. Clearing his throat, he conceded in a subdued voice, "Makes sense. After all the Afghani was an arranger of dowries ... so Dowry of Death."

Mohammed Mohidin nodded soberly.

By midmorning the skies had cleared and a warm sun moderated the winter's chill pervading the Vale of Kashmir, extracting from its wet soil wisps of ephemeral mist. Sardar Khan pedaled his rented three-gear B.S.A. bicycle westward out of Srinagar on the road to Baramula between lines of stately poplars standing at parade attention. In the interest of anonymity he had discarded his uniform and dressed more in conformity with the local citizenry. The muddy status of the footpaths along the side of the gravel roadway encouraged all ancillary traffic, including cyclists, pedestrians and beasts of burden, to flow hesitantly along the center of the crushed rock thoroughfare, giving way on demand to the occasional automobile and more frequent animal-drawn vehicle. Just beyond the bridge over a rain-swollen tributary of the Jhelum, a rutted dirt path branched away from the road, heading through drenched woods and fields toward the village of Narangwal, not more than a few furlongs distant. Surveying the mucky route ahead, Sardar Khan removed his shoes and stockings, placing them in a knapsack around his neck, then rolling up his trousers and hanging the bicycle over his shoulder, he moved forward through ankle-deep mud toward his destination.

In the days of the British Raj, before Indian independence, Narangwal had been a private gun club of sorts with a rifle range and facilities for skeet shooting. All that remained of this once posh association was the central bungalow, a stone edifice in need of repair. The grounds long since had reverted to wild shrubbery and trees, and scattered about ... like planets orbiting a central sun ... were a dozen or more dilapidated huts with walls built of stones cemented together with mud. A few small boats of varied sizes and shapes had been pulled up on the land alongside some of the shanties. Fishing nets hung from posts, either drying or in the process of being mended. Less than a furlong distant to the north ran the Jhelum River, the source of livelihood for the Narangwal residents.

"Salaam Aleikom," Sardar Khan greeted an elderly fellow Muslim squatting on the threshold of his hut smoking a hookah.

The fisherman responded in kind and, pointing at a nearby reed stool known as a morah, bid his guest to be seated. Propping his bicycle against the side of the house, the Sergeant Major accepted the offer and seated himself with a grateful sigh.

"You come from Srinagar?" The question was asked in Hindustani.

Sardar Khan nodded. "Survey ... survey of occupations ... what villagers are doing." He removed a small notebook and a pencil from his pocket as a gesture of authenticity.

"Ah yes. Surveys. The government always is making surveys."

Sardar Khan threw his host a wry smile as if in apology and then went on to inquire, "You all are fishermen here?" He waved his hand to include the circle of huts.

The white-bearded resident nodded, while continuing to suck on the mouthpiece of the long flexible tube of his hookah, drawing the tobacco smoke bubbling through the water bowl at its base. Then rising and pointing at his visitor's muddy and cold feet, he proposed, "Let me fetch a cup of hot tea and some water to wash."

A few minutes later, with his hands and insides warmed by the steaming drink and feet again encased in stockings and shoes, Sardar Khan continued his questioning. "The bungalow ... " he turned and nodded toward the building ... "Who lives there?"

"Until some two months ago it was empty except for an occasional transient squatter. At the time of partition a family of Hindus was murdered in there and since then there has been a superstition about the place. Then, as I said, about two months ago the inside was cleaned and some people moved in. They come and go, only adults; we see no children."

"How do they come and go?"

"Horse tonga. Usually the tonga is closed in with purdah curtains so we can see no passengers."

"What do they look like ... I mean the men?"

"What do they look like ... " the fisherman stroked his beard thoughtfully before going on ... "well most are dressed and look like Mohammedans. They could be Kashmiris, Pakistanis or Afghanis. Never talk to us. If our children stray near their quarters, they drive them away ... even throw stones at them."

"That bad, eh?" Sardar Khan commented solicitously. "Any foreigners ... Europeans?"

"Only Allah can say. We have seen none for certain, but they could come and go in the curtained tongas unknown to us."

"Do the bungalow folk ever travel by the Jhelum River?" Sardar Khan nodded toward the path leading northward through the underbrush.

"Never." He shook his head vigorously. "The waters are swift and constantly changing. Very dangerous to those unfamiliar with the currents."

"May I walk down to the river's edge?"

"And why not?" The old fisherman waved toward the narrow gravel trail. "I shall go with you."

A small tributary flowing into the Jhelum had created a sand bar affording a haven for the half dozen fishing craft tied up to a crude but functional pier at the end of the pathway leading from the huts of

Narangwal. Two fishermen were gathering their morning's catch into reed baskets preparatory to marketing. The Sergeant Major carefully studied the layout, memorizing all salient landmarks, not only of the boat moorings and pier but of the village and bungalow as well.

An ox cart was preparing to leave for Srinagar as the two men returned from the river, and with his host's assistance, Sardar Khan procured transportation as far as the hard road, thus sparing himself the unwelcome task of trudging back in his bare feet over almost a mile of treacly mud.

"Salaam Aleikom," Sardar Khan bade the old fisherman farewell, while making room for himself and his bicycle between baskets of freshly caught fish.

The small lounge at Nedou's Hotel had two occupants when Ian McVey entered and seated himself across from a window giving a view of the registration desk in the hallway directly adjacent. He busied himself filling his pipe from the artistically tooled leather pouch, fastidiously tamping down the tobacco and lighting it with a flaring wooden match. Then procuring portions of a day-old issue of the *Hindustan Times* from a vacant chair beside him, he pretended to be absorbed in its contents, taking cover behind the open paper. A fireplace in the back corner sputtered with less than ordinary enthusiasm, but in spite of its meager flame, managed to throw out a modicum of warmth.

Apparently the mail had just been distributed, for the other occupants of the lounge were engrossed in checking out an assortment of letters and papers. Ian, who was waiting for an appointment with the hotel's Assistant Manager, covertly studied the two, a man and a woman. The man, a stocky European in his middle fifties and dressed in a dark green jump suit, was leafing though a magazine whose words, although printed in an alphabet similar to English, were foreign to the Lieutenant. The woman, blonde and quite attractive, was of indeterminate age but certainly younger than the European male. She kept her face buried in a letter. Neither evidenced any recognition of the other, though the man did throw an occasional curious glance in the woman's direction.

"Car is ready, Colonel," a bearer announced, sticking his head in through the door.

The stocky European jumped to his feet, slipped on a trench coat over the jumpsuit, stuffed his mail into a pocket and strode out of the lounge. Ian rose and crossed the room to the window, ostensibly to empty out his pipe into an ashtray on the coffee table. He kept a surreptitious eye on the Colonel, watching him walk down the verandah, climb into the blue and white United Nations vehicle and drive out through the compound gates. So that's Wilhelm Vandermeer, Ian thought as he returned to his seat and resumed a pretense of scanning the newspaper.

Having completed the reading of her letter, the blonde reached down to tuck it into her purse resting on the floor and at the same time retrieved her make-up cosmetics. In the transaction she inadvertently dislodged a room key so that the metal identification disc dangled out of the zippered opening. Number seven was stamped clearly on the tag.

"She's got to be Maya," Ian muttered in an aside to himself as she left the room, "Maya Reznikoff." Again he walked to the window and tapped his pipe free of tobacco ashes, all the while closely observing the woman as she engaged the desk clerk in a conversation inaudible to him in the lounge. During this action Monty Brown came up, followed close at his heels by Mos the Srinagar waif. Having procured a room key, the American paused briefly to exchange a few words with the lady, then strode down the verandah. Ian quickly stepped out into the hallway and, catching up with Monty, invited him to share a couple of cups of coffee.

"Don't mind if I do," he replied, turning and instructing Mos to wait for him on the verandah.

A bearer seated them at a small table and then left to return shortly with a pot of coffee, several toasted and buttered crumpets and a jar of marmalade.

"Was that woman you talked to just now Maya Reznikoff?" Ian asked as he poured their hot drinks.

Monty looked up in surprise. "You know her?"

Ian shook his head. "Not really. Her name's come up in the process of our investigation."

"Now that's interesting," he commented, continuing to look surprised.

"Who is she?"

"A Russian who lives in Delhi and visits Srinagar rather frequently. Stays here at Nedou's."

What does she do?"

The American shrugged his shoulders and shot an enigmatic look at his questioner. Ian decided not to pursue the matter.

"Something I wanted to share with you and ask that it be passed on to Captain Narayan," Monty confided as he spooned marmalade onto his crumpet.

Ian nodded and waved him on.

"Might keep this classified as the military say . . . just the three of you."

"Righto. Carry on."

Monty proceeded to describe Doreen's and his encounter with the cobra the night before.

"How bloody awful!" Ian exclaimed at the conclusion of the recital. "Those bastards really are trying to put us into a funk. But why you?"

Monty's eyes narrowed into slits and the expression on his face hardened. Again he chose not to answer Ian.

"I'll brief Prem on the matter this evening ... " Ian stared out the dining room window a moment and added bitterly ... "such damned cheek!"

"Hate to think of Doreen being exposed to this danger." A wave of unhappiness flooded his eyes.

Ian rose and extended the American his hand. "Must be off to an appointment. Get in touch if you need help."

"Thanks." Monty's face melted into a warm smile.

A few minutes later, the Assistant Manager of Nedou's Hotel beckoned Ian into his office and waved him into a seat. "Anything new has happened?" he asked solicitously.

Choosing not to reply, Ian countered, "Room seven ... have things changed in any way?"

He nodded hesitantly, his tongue moving nervously across dry lips. Then after swallowing hard, the Assistant Manager confided in a low voice, "Someone tried to break into the room last night."

'Really!"

"About two this morning the occupant heard a key being used in the door and when he checked, the intruder fled into the night."

"They didn't see the person ... no identification?"

The Assistant Manager shook his head, giving Ian a suspicious look. "You were not involved ... I mean the C.I.D.?"

"Involved in the attempted intrusion?"

He nodded.

Ian broke out into a mirthless laugh before replying, "No we had nothing to do with this ... this attempted break in."

He looked relieved.

"Maya Reznikoff ... she's here?" Ian asked.

Again he nodded and went on to say, "She's staying in room eleven."

"And carries a key to room seven," Ian countered.

He made an attempt to smile but ended up frowning and pursing his lips. "She confers with the occupant of room seven."

"Any one else ... I mean does anyone else confer with the occupant?"

"The American geologist."

"Montague Brown?" Ian asked incredulously.

"Yes, Montague Brown." The reply was precise.

After dinner that evening, while Rustum and Fatima cleared the table, Prem Narayan and his two cohorts drew their chairs about a couple of braziers and shared the details of their day's investigations. The Captain described the post-mortem findings on Sayad Khan.

"What a hellish way to die!" Ian muttered, his face distorted with a scowl. "Another left handed victim and a crushed egg, eh?"

"Right ... " Prem leaned forward and warmed his hands over the glowing charcoal before continuing ... "Damn it, we've bloody well got to find a way to stop the bastards."

"Thank god for Bruce's antivenin," Ian murmured, almost to himself.

"Mohidin shared with me the code name for the smuggling being carried out by the three victims. He called it, Dowry of Death'."

Ian nodded knowingly. "Makes sense. The Afghani was a merchant dealing in dowries."

The dishes having been cleared, Rustum and Fatima excused themselves for the night and in the interest of greater warmth the three men retired to Prem's quarters for further discussions.

Sardar Khan gave the details of his trip to Narangwal, outlining the precise layout of the village huts and the old gun club bungalow as well as the sand bar inlet harboring the fishing boats in the Jhelum River.

"*Accha*" the Captain interjected as the Sergeant Major completed his report, "I want you to make Narangwal a priority project. Find out what the devil's going on in that old gun club, eh?"

"Jolly good, sir, I shall do the needful." Sardar Khan's eyes flashed in anticipation of the assignment.

Ian McVey recounted his spotting of Colonel Vandermeer and Maya Reznikoff in the hotel lounge, with particular emphasis on the key to room seven which he had surreptitiously observed in the latter's purse. He relayed the statement by the Assistant Manager that Monty Brown had been a visitor to room seven. Finally, Ian shared the story told him by the American of the harrowing cobra encounter in the Red Chariot.

"Dash it all, " Prem exclaimed, stabbing the air with his cigarette, "wish I knew where Monty fits into this picture. We've got to find out sooner or later ... wish it could be sooner ... might just save some lives. Chap's bloody close-mouthed about the whole thing."

Sardar Khan rose to leave the room, pleading a need for sleep after a day which had commenced very early with the shikara ride across the lake. Throwing an informal salute to the two officers, he stepped out into the corridor quietly closing the door behind.

"Ian ... " Prem stared seriously at his companion before going on ... "How about getting together with Monty tomorrow ... the two of you alone ... and convincing the blighter that it's to our mutual advantage for him to share at least some of his information with us. The bloke's in danger ... danger of his life ... and the stakes of the game he's playing are bloody high."

"Righto. I'll take a dekko around Nedou's in the morning and catch up with him. See if I can fetch back some information."

"Pritham Singh called me from Delhi this afternoon. His office had a session yesterday with the top intelligence officer of the Chinese

Embassy . . . Peoples Republic Embassy. Seems that Allabaksh was one
of their better undercover agents. A Kazak and a Muslim, he'd been
headquartered in Kashgar, or Kashi as it's now called, an important
town in Western Xinjiang Province along the ancient Silk Road. Until a
couple of weeks ago the chap had been supervising the shipment of
arms from China to the Afghani mujahidin. They were transporting
these supplies along the narrow finger of Afghanistan extending
eastward to the Chinese border . . . through the Pamir plateau.''

Ian chewed on his pipestem and nodded thoughtfully. "Bloody
awful terrain through the Hindu Kush,'' he observed quietly.

Prem grunted in agreement. "According to Pritham, Allabaksh met
the two other victims while engaged in these clandestine operations and
agreed to join up for a fortnight or so to integrate their operations.''

"A bit of a difference between the two operations,'' Ian broke in,
"Allabaksh must have been operating under the aegis of the Chinese
government, while Ahmed Feroze the Indian and Sayad Khan the
Afghani were functioning privately . . . pretty much on their own.''

"Precisely. Pritham admitted that the Chinese agent was in Kashmir
without the knowledge or permission of the Indian government.''

"Must have caused some embarrassment to both countries.''

"Quite. This probably was a bargaining point in favor of our
government.''

"Meaning?''

"Getting information concerning the Chinese trade with the Afghani
mujahidin.''

Ian nodded his understanding. "So now the Dowry of Death goes
under other leadership.''

Prem shrugged his shoulders. "Regardless of the future of the
smuggling activities, we still have a binding mission . . . a mission to
find the assassins.''

"We jolly well do,'' Ian sighed, standing and knocking out the ashes
from his pipe bowl into the brazier, creating a series of miniature
fireworks as the shreds of residual unburned tobacco touched the
glowing coals. Then straightening and stretching his arms toward the
ceiling, he yawned loudly and headed for the cabin door. With his hand
on the knob, he turned and mumbled sleepily, "Cheerio. See you at
breakfast, Prem.''

The Captain remained seated on the edge of his bunk and went
through the routine of retrieving his cigarette case, selecting a Camel,
tapping it against the cloisonne container, slowly raising it to his lips
and finally flaming the end with his colorful lighter. Then he reached
again into an inner pocket and brought out a letter which he handled
with an unusual tenderness. A gentleness settled over his face as he
opened the envelope and read for a second time the intimate message.

Prem Narayan was very much in love with his wife Bubli, and this was the first letter he had received from her since their parting in Bombay just a few days ago, an airmail letter in reply to one which he had posted immediately on his arrival in Srinagar. After reading the message he replaced it in his pocket and heaved a contented sigh.

With Rustum's warning in mind, Prem moved the brazier out of his cabin into the hallway, then secured the door and outside window before undressing and quickly sliding into bed to escape the cold. For a couple of minutes he shivered involuntarily until his body heat had warmed the chill of the sheets. The night was still except for the occasional creak of the houseboat's wooden hull as it gently rose and fell on the waters of Dal Lake. After taking a last draw on his cigarette, he reached over and stubbed it out in the ash tray on the night table, then drew the covers up around his neck. In the distance a night bird repeated its eerie cries.

Chapter Twelve

Startled from his sleep, Prem Narayan stiffened a moment and then reflexly reached for the ringing telephone. While doing this, he swallowed hard to moisten his throat and repeatedly licked his dry lips. Putting the receiver to his ear, he listened in silence for a few seconds, a customary precaution developed toward calls at unusual hours from those who might be interested solely in his absence or presence. A nervous cough at the other end of the line broke the quiet.

"Captain Narayan here," he barked into the phone, as if perturbed by the disturbance.

"Beastly sorry, Captain. Bruce here . . . Bruce Duncan."

"Carry on, Doctor," Prem continued in a more solicitous tone of voice.

"Sorry for the botheration but I . . . we need your advice." His words projected an urgency.

"*Accha*, Bruce how can I help?"

"Doreen. A short while ago we thought we heard a noise in her quarters next to ours and by the time we got over to look in she was gone. The far window had been pried open and the room was empty."

"You're at Nedou's in Gulmarg?"

"The top cottage . . . last in line above the administrative offices and dining room."

"No note or clue of any kind?"

"Maureen and I immediately took a torch and searched inside and outside. Couldn't find a thing except that the snow on the ground without her window was trampled."

"You've notified no one?"

"Not a soul."

"Good. Leave things as they are and I'll have Ian up there *bahut jaldi*—very fast."

"Righto." The word was followed by a sigh of relief.

Prem returned the telephone to the bedside table and slipped on his bathrobe and slippers with a synchronized swiftness that would have made a choreographer envious. Then moving down the corridor he awoke Ian and shared with him the few details the Doctor had supplied.

"I'll take the jeep and be on my way," Ian responded as he hurriedly dressed.

"Let me give the American a call . . . just a hunch," Prem muttered, moving off toward his quarters.

"Bruce'll take this bloody hard," Ian groaned to himself.

"Nedou's?" The Captain was on the telephone.

"*Ha ji*—Yes sir," a sleepy male voice responded.

"Give me Mr. Brown . . . room six."

"Sorry. At this time of night we do not disturb."

"This is Captain Narayan of the C.I.D. and you'll bloody well disturb. Get Brown on the phone *ek dum*—at once!" The words were as cutting as honed steel.

"Hello?" The American's response was part enunciation and part yawn.

"Monty . . . Prem Narayan here."

"Oh," he punctuated his yawn, "something wrong?"

"Bruce Duncan just called from Gulmarg. Doreen's disappeared. He thinks she's been abducted."

"Great Scott!" Monty was wide awake. "Abducted you say!"

Prem quickly gave the meager details of the telephone message at the conclusion of which there was silence except for the sound of heavy breathing at the other end of the line. Then Monty broke in to announce, "I'll be leaving for Gulmarg pronto," adding as an afterthought, "anything I can do for you, Captain?"

'Ian McVey'll be on his way up there in a couple of seconds."

"Why don't the two of us join forces?"

"Splendid idea!"

"If he'll meet me here we'll drive up in the Red Chariot."

"*Accha*. He should be there in fifteen minutes."

When Prem returned to notify Ian of Monty's offer, he was in the W.C. washing up. Speaking through the partially open door, the Captain shared the American's suggestion.

"And you think this'll be alright . . . the two of us joining forces?"

"Quite!" The Captain sounded convinced. "The chap's a damned bright lad and, as the saying goes, two heads are better than one. We must consider the possibility that he may have contacts not available to us. After all he's been roaming over these parts for the past several months. And finally, you were to meet him today and try to find out what the blighter's up to besides his geological interests."

"Righto. Let's have Rustum drop me off at Nedou's here and bring the jeep back for you."

As the C.I.D. vehicle entered the compound, the electric lamps atop the pillars on either side of the gate appeared to be welcoming the first fragile light of dawn as an ally in a common campaign against the last bastions of the night's darkness. Quietly depositing Ian at the hotel entrance, Rustum turned the jeep about and headed back to the Kashmir Princess.

Monty was dressed in heavy winter clothing, including a thick woolen turtle neck sweater and hiking boots. After a sober and terse greeting, the American led the Lieutenant to the rear compound parking lot.

"Good-a-morning, Monty cha-cha," a muffled and sleepy child's voice rose from under a tangle of blankets in the rear of the Red Chariot.

"Mos always greets me as his uncle," Monty explained and reached under the assorted covers to tickle his adopted waif, who responded with giggles of delight.

The vehicle's engine broke into a satisfactory purring after a couple of remonstrative backfirings. In short order the trio were headed out of Srinagar toward Gulmarg. A murky darkness still partially obscured the landscape and the car's headlights tunneled into the ebbing night, lighting up a meandering rural road bordered by trees marching past in single file. Sitting tense and silent behind the wheel, Monty pushed the Red Chariot's throttle hard, weaving around the sparse traffic of occasional bullock carts and pony trains. Mos stood behind the two adults, staring ahead through a narrow slot between their shoulders.

"Why Doreen?" Monty broke the silence in a voice both anxious and puzzled. "I'm afraid it's because of her association with me."

"Damned if I know," Ian muttered angrily. "Possibly it could be the stigma of the Duncans' meeting with the C.I.D. on the Kashmir Princess the other night."

"God help the son of a bitch who dares lay a hand on her." The cold fury in Monty's voice startled his companion.

"She's something special to you," Ian volunteered softly, more as a statement of fact than a question.

Choosing not to reply in words, the American nodded as he reflected agonizingly on the morning's turn of events. It's my fault, he thought, blaming himself for the dinner at Nedou's and the cobra episode which followed. Dear God, he ventured a silent prayer, grant that she's had the antivenin.

A small village with a handful of huts marked the point where the Red Chariot would be exchanged for sturdy hill ponies and a steep zigzag trail climbing up into the Gulmarg vale. Monty admonished Mos to remain in the car until they returned, an order to which the waif reluctantly consented. Daylight had dissipated the night's darkness as the two men mounted their steeds and headed up the twisting path. Each horse was followed by a *syce*—groom hanging tenaciously onto his charge's tail and thus easing his ascent. Were it not for the seriousness of the occasion, the sight of Monty's tall and ample frame draped over the back of the pony with his boots almost dragging along on the ground would have been cause for hilarious repartee. Within a few minutes both horses were perspiring profusely as they struggled up the mountain side. At times the riders found the going uncertain and even dangerous, for there were sections of the trail covered with loose rocks denying their mounts a sure footing. From time to time both men dismounted and walked to ease the plight of their animals. With a sense of relief the entourage crested the final range and looked down on the houses of Gulmarg huddled protectively in the embrace of a ring of white-topped mountains. A light snowfall covered the ground, beautifying the panoramic view and hiding any areas of village drabness. Riding beyond the few huts and shops, Ian and Monty approached their destination.

Nedou's Hotel was clustered over the side of a hill with the administrative unit, which also included the dining room, centered at the base. From behind this larger building a long covered stairway climbed to reach a line of cottages rising step-like toward a forest of pine trees.

Dismissing the two syces with a commitment that they remain available for the return trip, Ian and Monty climbed the stairway to the highest quarters where Bruce and Maureen were waiting. Although the Duncans were unable to conceal their surprise at the American's unexpected presence, they welcomed him warmly.

"The noise that alerted you during the night, what did it sound like?" Ian asked as they searched the vacated half of the duplex cottage.

"Scraping on the floor, like shoes or something being dragged. It wasn't loud really . . . sort of soft," Bruce reflected.

"What about voices?" Ian pursued his questioning.

"No voices that we could hear. Not surprising considering the thickness of the wall planks. We never could hear Doreen unless she shouted."

"What did you do immediately after awaking?"

"I woke up first," Maureen picked up the conversation, "and lay in bed listening for several minutes, thinking that Doreen was moving her bed toward the window. She's a fresh air addict. Then the sound stopped. I couldn't get back to sleep and became worried enough to rouse Bruce."

"What happened then?" Ian urged her on.

"Putting on dressing gowns and slippers, we grabbed a torch and came in here to find Doreen gone." There was a catch in her voice.

"The door and window were open," Bruce continued the recitation, "but things were pretty much in place. She must have been able to put on her ski suit and boots . . . they're missing."

"Did you hear any noises outside?" Monty broke in to ask.

Bruce scratched his head thoughtfully before responding, "I thought I heard horses . . . hoofs on the footpath circling the hill just above us here. Maureen couldn't hear them."

At this point Monty took the Doctor by the arm to ask, "Did you give Doreen antivenin?"

"Yes, last night."

'Thank God," the American said under his breath.

"We've reserved a table for breakfast," Maureen offered with an apologetic smile, "I know you've not had time to eat."

"Give us thirty minutes or so to look things over before we join you," Ian proposed.

A rough-hewn finish to all the interior woodwork ... walls, doors and solid paneless window ... as well as the fact that there were no dishes or glasses lying about, left little chance of finding fingerprints. The orderliness of the room belied any serious struggle. On the ground just outside the window the snow had been trampled down in a fashion precluding the clear outline of footprints. The abductors had descended directly across a grassy hillside from a footpath about a hundred feet above the cottage. On this narrow trail there was evidence that the intruders had come on horses ... hoof marks and fresh manure.

Monty slowly retraced his way down the slope toward the cabins, leaving Ian to explore the pathway above. Enroute he studied the grass with its speckling of snow and made note of the bootmarks. As best he could surmise there were two kidnappers. Suddenly he paused and knelt on the ground to retrieve a shiny brass button about the size of a half rupee piece.

"I'll bet it came off a military jacket," the American speculated as Ian turned the object over in the palm of his hand.

"Splendid, old chap," Ian bubbled with excitement, "and it's from a military uniform alright. Insignia's from a Muslim country ... crescent and star."

Bruce Duncan rose and welcomed the two men to a table in the dining room at which he and Maureen had been waiting their arrival. The bearer took the orders after serving a round of coffee. Intermittently sipping his drink, Ian gave a resume of the inspection and a reconstruction of what probably happened during the night.

The intruders ... probably two ... must have found the window to Doreen's room open or unlocked and crawled through without waking her. Then using a knife or a gun they intimidated her into going along with them without creating a disturbance. Either the abductors suggested that she put on the ski suit and boots, or Doreen persuaded them to permit her to dress warmly. Opening the door from within, the captors and captive made their way up to the waiting horses.

"What're we going to do?" Maureen asked plaintively.

"I just don't believe her life's in immediate danger," Ian announced attempting to project a sense of optimism. "If they'd wanted to kill Doreen, she'd be dead now."

"Oh my God, don't say that! I mean ... " Maureen's grief choked her into silence.

"Sorry my dear," Ian's voice was apologetic.

"What's just been said is true," Monty interjected. "Doreen's a hostage for bargaining. She's much more valuable to them alive. I'm certain we'll be hearing from the kidnappers. Thank God this gives us time."

"And you two . . . what're you going to do now?" Bruce asked, anxiously scanning the two men's faces.

"Back to Srinagar. That's where we'll probably hear from the cads," Ian replied.

"What do we do?" Maureen's lips trembled and there were tears in her eyes.

"Stay right here for the time being in case the buggers try to contact you. Report the matter to the hotel authorities and I'll see that the police in Srinagar are informed. We'll keep in touch with you." Ian tried to sound comforting.

A bearer brought something wrapped in a paper napkin and set it on the table beside Monty, who confided with a self-conscious smile, "Toasted egg sandwich for Mos."

Ian excused himself and put a call through over the telephone to Prem Narayan. Then, following a few minutes of desultory conversation, the two men rose and expressed their appreciation of the breakfast. The syces and hill ponies awaited them outdoors.

The downhill trek, while probably easier on the horses, required of the riders fatiguing acts of balance just to maintain their positions. This complication was abetted not only by the frequent stumbling of their mounts, but also by the absence of pommels on the front of their saddles. Finally, in frustration, both men dismounted and trotted down the trail ahead of the ponies.

The Red Chariot . . . ominously quiet . . . stood abandoned where it had been parked some two and a half hours earlier. Mos was not to be found. After searching the vicinity, Monty asked a grain merchant seated cross-legged on the floor of his shop and within easy sight of the vehicle, if he had seen the lad. At first hesitant and nervous but eventually encouraged by the authoritative insignia of Ian's uniform, the man described in detail the kidnapping. Two men had pulled up in a small black car and tried to coax the reluctant waif outside. Frustrated by their failure, one of the abductors finally crawled into the Red Chariot and physically extracted the kicking, biting and screaming captive, who was then quickly and forcibly transferred into the other vehicle which sped off toward Srinagar. The kidnapping had taken place about an hour earlier. From his dress, one of the men appeared to be an Afghani . . . possibly a Pathan . . . and the other a Kashmiri Muslim. Both were quite heavily bearded. A final comment by the grain merchant was that the Kashmiri had no left hand.

A somber and taciturn Montague Brown guided his vehicle back toward the city. In deep thought, he drove slowly and deliberately. His face was furrowed by the deep lines of a scowl and his eyes almost closed by narrowed lids. At first Ian thought the American was grunting intermittently, but then ... above the rough purr of the motor ... he heard fragments of a doleful tune, the sad melody of a grieving heart. After a moment, words replaced his humming and the Lieutenant picked up a barely audible line, "Nobody knows the trouble I've seen." A furlong or two down the road Monty pulled the Red Chariot to the side, shut off the ignition and turned to face his companion.

"Ian, the abduction of Mos changes the picture of this whole thing. I'm strongly of the opinion that these two kidnappings are directed against me rather than the C.I.D. There may be some overlapping of their intent, but I've become the fall guy. What they're planning God only knows, but I'll be getting a ransom note ... want to bet?"

"You may be right, Monty. It is a bit difficult to tie your lad Mos into the C.I.D. investigation." Ian stared at his companion a moment before breaking into a mirthless laugh and conceding, "We've the same bloody bastards working against both of us, and that's why it's vital to share our information."

Monty nodded but made no immediate reply. Both men sat engrossed in their thoughts for a period of time until the American broke the silence to confide, "I've a feeling that what I'm about to share with you will be to our mutual benefit, that of the C.I.D. as well as mine."

"Go ahead." There was a sense of excitement and urgency in Ian's words.

"About four months ago ... at night ... driving on the road to Pahalgam, I was stopped by a barricade ... a bullock cart turned sideways. A gang of men overwhelmed me. After the free-for-all brawl, and a sworn assurance that I would not be harmed, they led me through the dark about a mile away from the road to a small building on the outskirts of a village. Inside a dimly lit room, there was a cot on which lay an obviously sick man. According to my informants, the fellow had fallen with his horse and sustained a severe abrasion of the right leg. I examined the extremity after removing a pus-soaked dressing and found serious infection with marked swelling. I didn't need a thermometer to tell he was running a high fever. After advising frequent changes of hot wet packs ... towels that had been boiled for sterilization ... I informed them that in the Red Chariot were medications which the sick man must have. Stepping back from the cot, I almost knocked over an attractive young woman who apologized in precise English for the manner of my capture. It appears that they had anticipated my return on that particular road and were waiting for me. Traveling about the villages, I had made it a habit to dispense medications ... a sick call of sorts . . . basic medications like antibiotics. In fact in some parts I had acquired the name of the American Hakim. When I asked the woman why they didn't get a Srinagar physician, she smiled enigmatically and replied that dacoits were denied such privileges."

"My God!" Ian exploded. "Pakistani dacoits!"

Monty nodded and continued, "She's the leader and her name is Aisha. After a conference, they escorted me back to the Red Chariot. But before I left, she handed me a slip of paper with a phone number and told me to call if she could ever be of assistance. I sent back antibiotics and antipyretics for the patient and found out later that he had recovered completely."

"You've contacted this Aisha since then?"

Monty nodded. "Several times. Actually they've been of real assistance in some of my efforts."

"I'll be damned!" Ian exclaimed incredulously. "What an alliance . . . how extraordinary!"

"I'm going to bring Aisha and her dacoits in on Doreen's and Mos' abductions. They've an excellent communication system . . . mostly by word of mouth . . . covering the entire Jhelum Valley."

"You are!" Ian's voice projected alarm.

"Of course you and Prem won't have an official connection of any sort with such illegal trafficking. This will be my show . . . entirely my show."

"Dash it all, Monty, the whole thing's bloody dangerous . . . dacoits . . . Pakistan . . . " Ian's words trailed off into silence.

The American nodded solemnly. "Illegal as all hell and the odds probably will be high, but look at the alternatives. I'll be meeting Aisha tonight. I'm going for broke."

"Going for broke?" Ian raised his eyebrows questioningly.

"A Japanese-American slogan meaning going all the way."

"For God's sake be careful, Monty." A shadow of worry darkened the Lieutenant's face as the Red Chariot again headed for Srinagar.

Chapter Thirteen

A sudden draft of icy air played over Doreen's face, rudely awakening her from a warm and deep sleep. Without moving, she swiftly scanned the bedroom faintly outlined by the delicate glow of a setting moon. An uneasy silence prevailed for the next few seconds broken abruptly by the noise of a shoe shifting on the wooden floor. She tensed the muscles of her jaw and felt a rising pulse pound in her temples. With a repetition of the noise, she cautiously drew in a deep breath and prepared to throw off her covers and dash for the door, only to be thwarted by the feel of cold steel pressed tightly against her throat. An involuntary chill coursed through her body. Hot breathing against her cheek preceded whispered words in English warning of instant death in the event of an outcry. On command, Doreen sat on the edge of the bed and then at the further order of the intruder, donned her ski suit which had been tossed across the davenport the night before. Without requesting permission, she put on woolen socks and hiking boots lying on the floor.

There were two trespassers, bearded men with shawls draped around their heads and shoulders. Each carried a small torch and one of them hovered close to Doreen flourishing an unsheathed dagger. Unlocking the cabin door and turning out their lights, the abductors, one in front of the captive and the other behind, stealthily moved out of the building and started up the hillside powdered by a light fall of snow.

A tumultuous array of thoughts assaulted Doreen's mind, each intent on gaining immediate recognition. Appreciating the destructive potential of uncontrolled mental turmoil, she selected an immediate objective and, to the neglect of all else, focused on its fulfillment. She must escape. In the realization of this goal, every potential opportunity to gain freedom had to be assessed swiftly. Time was precious, to be measured in seconds rather than minutes. Strangely enough, with a definitive purpose in mind, her spirits rose. Doreen checked off the immediate advantages. There was darkness to conceal her flight and a pine forest near at hand offering refuge. The grassy slopes were slick and with her instinctive aptitudes as a skier, she should be able to maintain her balance and outdistance any pursuers. Preparing for action, she unobtrusively slackened her pace to permit the forward man to increase his lead. Directly behind her, the knife-wielder panted nervously as he urged her on. Glancing up the hill, she could barely see

the outlines of two . . . or maybe three . . . horses and the vague shadow
of someone standing watch. The action could not be postponed.

Suddenly Doreen swung around to leap out from between her
guards, but slipped and lost control of her momentum, falling heavily
on the ground. In her bitter disappointment she scarcely heard the
curses of her captors as they ran to her side. Hot tears of frustration
and anger melted small holes in the snow pillowing her cheek.
Determined to hide any semblance of fear, she turned and stared
defiantly into the two faces looking down on her. Roughly pulling their
captive to her feet, the abductors shoved her ahead. As she stumbled
forward, she felt the sharp sting of a dagger pricking her buttock.

"Bloody Anglo-Indian slut," one of the men muttered through
clenched teeth.

Stopping in her tracks, Doreen demanded, "Which of you blithering
cads said that?"

Taken aback by the fury of their captive, both guards stood
speechless for a couple of seconds, then with a sneering laugh the
knife-wielder admitted authorship, his words cut short by a cry of rage
as Doreen struck him hard across the mouth with her hand. For a
second time she found herself lying in the snow, knocked down by the
blow of a fist to her chest. While on her face, one of the men kicked her
hard in the head and groin. Dazed and nauseated by this last assault,
she painfully struggled to her feet and climbed the few remaining steps
to the narrow trail where three horses awaited them. For a moment as
she tried to mount a designated pony, Doreen paused with a hand on
the saddle and one foot in the stirrup, then slowly slumped to the
ground unconscious.

Mos was shoved into the dark room with such force that he fell to
his knees. Behind him the door was slammed shut and bolted with an
ominous finality. His head throbbed with pain and both sides of his
face were sore where the men had struck him for resisting capture. But
in spite of physical discomfort and the mental anxiety of an uncertain
future, the waif's heart was troubled by something else, the gnawing
worry that Monty Cha-cha would think he had abandoned his charge,
the Red Chariot. His clenched fists dug at his wet eyes as he cried
softly, still kneeling on the cold stone floor. As the weeping gradually
wore itself out, Mos dried his tears and running nose on the sleeves of
his coat. Changing to a sitting position, he encircled both legs with his
arms and drew up his knees as a chin rest. Low sobs were replaced by
an aftermath of hiccoughing sniffs.

As his eyes gradually accommodated to the dimness of the room,
Mos soberly surveyed his surroundings. Directly across from the closed
door behind him was a window with secured shutters admitting a
minimum of light from outside. In one corner stood a round table on
which rested a metal washbasin and a matching water pitcher. One of

the other corners was closed off with a hanging cloth curtain. Then he noticed for the first time in the shadows directly under the window, an Indian bedstead or charpai, with someone lying on it. Mos held his breath between involuntary hiccoughs and listened. There were sounds of rhythmic breathing punctuated by an occasional moan. At first the waif was frightened by this discovery but in the end curiosity overcame his fears and he tiptoed over to investigate.

"The Lady . . . Monty Cha-cha's Lady!" he blurted out in surprise, kneeling down to study her face closely.

Mos had seen Doreen but once, that night on the verandah at Nedou's in Srinagar as Monty and she strolled out from dinner heading toward the Red Chariot and the cobra. But there was no doubt in his mind as to who lay there in front of him. She gave no response to the sound of his voice and this disturbed the little orphan who, in the light of his discovery, had forgotten his own physical aches and mental fears. This person was special . . . Monty Cha-cha's very own friend . . . and as such warranted his loyalty and protection. Although a mere slip of a lad, the orphan's exposure to the give and take of Srinagar slums had aged him far beyond his years. His struggle for survival had denied him the carefree pleasures of childhood and catapulted him into premature adulthood. There were advantages to this rapid maturation, not the least being that adults grossly underestimated the child's capabilities.

Leaning closer he inspected his charge's face more intently, gently touching a wisp of hair spread in disarray about her head. Then straightening, he whispered, "Not you worry, Lady, Mos now here." Having made this solemn pronouncement, he moved a morah, or cane stool, over beside the charpai and sat down to commence his quiet vigil over Monty Cha-cha's Lady.

Floating in and out of a painful consciousness, Doreen struggled to recollect the events of the day which presented themselves in a piecemeal fashion and not always in their chronological sequence. After some effort, she finally succeeded in mentally retrieving and setting in order all of her activities from the time of the abductors' intrusion into her quarters until her falling unconscious while trying to mount the horse. Having salvaged the happenings of the past, she now cautiously explored the present. The pleasant smell of a wood fire offered a tangible grasp on the reality of her immediate environment. The sound of an occasional sniffle quite nearby caught her attention. I must have a guard, she thought, and opened her eyes a bare slit to investigate her surroundings. At first she found it difficult to focus on the person seated beside her cot but with effort the image began to clear. The face that appeared was small, probably that of a woman, she thought at first. Then as her vision cleared further, she recognized the features of Monty's adopted waif.

"Mos," she whispered, reaching out toward him, "What . . . what are you doing here?'' her voice broke and drifted into silence.

The waif grasped her hand tightly and struggled to smile, holding his lower lip between his teeth as the tears overflowed. "Lady . . . you not worry . . . please . . . " he wiped his eyes with a coat sleeve before going on . . . "Mos here, Monty Cha-cha's boy.''

Doreen never could remember whether she laughed or cried as she drew the brave lad down into her arms and mothered his sobs against her breast. Soothed by her tender stroking of his wet cheeks and whispered words of comfort, his weeping subsided.

"Mos,'' she leaned forward to speak in a subdued voice.

"Yes, Lady?'' His reply was wedged in between sniffs.

"Where is Monty Cha-cha?''

A frown of worry crept across his lifted face. "I not know. Monty Cha-cha in the Red Chariot is leaving me and riding horse to Gulmarg. Then two badmans take me.''

There were sounds of voices in the adjacent room and Doreen placed a finger across the waif's lips.

"You struck and kicked her?'' There was a strong guttural European accent to the question asked in English.

"But she tried to escape . . . and . . . and besides she struck me in the face first,'' a man replied in an obsequious whine.

Doreen immediately recognized the voice as that of the knife-wielder who had knocked her down and kicked her.

"Achmed, you bloody fool!'' The European cursed loudly and then dropped his voice to add, "You're daft . . . hopelessly daft.''

"But . . . but sir . . . " Achmed began hesitantly only to be cut short.

"You ver told to bring her here unharmed,'' the words were spoken in icy anger. "Vat in the devil's the matter vith you . . . can't you follow orders?''

"Sorry, sir . . . " again he was interrupted by the European.

"Disobey vonce more and ve'll bloody vell give you the cobra treatment!''

"We did her little harm,'' Achmed countered in a final attempt to solicit his superior's understanding.

"Did her little harm you say! Vy you bloody fool, you yourself told me she vas brought here unconscious. You know damned vell she's to be used as a hostage and ve can't afford to have her hurt at this stage.''

So I'm a hostage, Doreen thought, and not to be hurt for the time being at least. And the knife-wielder . . . the cad who savaged me . . . is Achmed. They're coming in to look us over and I'll be damned if they're going to intimidate me. Still in her ski suit, she threw off her covers and sat upright on the edge of the cot, holding Mos tightly to her side within an encircling arm. With her head throbbing painfully and dizzily, she struggled successfully to remain seated. The bolt unlocked with a metallic rattling and then the door slowly swung inward with protesting squeaks from the hinges.

A heavy figure of medium height moved cautiously across the threshold into the room, followed by a man of equal stature but lesser girth. As the intruders' eyes grew accustomed to the darkness within, both moved closer toward the cot, but not close enough to make identification easy. The stocky European, wearing a thick fur cap and a long sheepskin coat with a knitted woolen scarf about his neck and lower face, stood arms akimbo staring in the direction of the two captives. Doreen could not recognize the foreigner as anyone she had seen before, but immediately identified Achmed who still wore the baggy Pathan pants and the shawl wrapped around his shoulders and head. Suddenly she recognized that this was the same person who had stared at them the night that she and Monty had dined out at Nedou's. At that time he was wearing an astrakhan caracul cap.

"There they are," Achmed announced smugly, waving an arm in the direction of the cot.

Doreen felt Mos tremble under her arm and drew him closer.

"You are conscious now?" the European asked solicitously.

"Conscious but a bit bruised, thanks to the ministrations of your loutish henchman." Her words dripped with sarcasm.

Achmed cleared his throat as if to speak but the European interjected, "He tells me you struck him first."

"That I did, but has he told you why?" she asked defiantly.

"Vy don't you tell me."

"The oaf called me a bloody Anglo-Indian slut."

"Is that vat you said?" The European turned to face Achmed who chose to remain silent.

"I don't know who you are or your relationship to this game of abduction, but you should be damned proud of your cutthroat goondas who beat up this defenseless child," Doreen spat the words out in a scathing denunciation.

Caught by surprise at the prisoner's fearless attitude, the European coughed self-consciously and, at a loss for further words, moved to leave the room with Achmed close at his heels. Grasping the doorknob, he turned and called back gruffly, "There vill be hot meals for both of you tonight."

Mos was showing signs of becoming sleepy, so Doreen wrapped him up in a blanket and lay him across the foot of the charpai. The room was cold and she was grateful for the warmth of her ski suit. Washing her hands and face in the chill water poured into the basin from the pitcher, she carefully combed her tousled hair and wove it into a single braid to hang down her back. In order to loosen up her stiff muscles and improve her circulation, she did a dozen quick push ups. The soreness in her groin, chest and head where Achmed had kicked and struck her, appeared to be no worse. With pulse racing and short of breath, she pulled the reed morah up beside the cot and sat down, resting her head on a pillow.

Who could the European be, Doreen wondered. His accent most certainly wasn't British. Was the chap German or perhaps Russian? She changed her train of thought to their hostage status. Why should Mos have been kidnapped? The waif hardly could be involved with Prem Narayan's investigation. And of course her own association with the Captain was tenuous to say the least, except for the fact that her brother had administered the antivenin to the C.I.D. team members. After a few moments of analysis, Doreen came to the conclusion that their abduction must be directed against Monty. In a short time ... possibly already accomplished ... demands would be made on the American in exchange for the two hostages. She gave out a deep sigh. That's what he was worried about, she mused sadly, worried lest harm befall her because of association with him.

A rattling of the lock bolt interrupted Doreen's thoughts. She quickly straightened and turned just in time to watch the door slowly swing open and admit an elderly woman carrying a charcoal brazier. She appeared to be a Muslim and was wearing a kamiz and salwar. Stepping to the center of the room, she glanced around hesitantly as if waiting for an order.

"*Yaha per rakko*—Place it here," Doreen directed in Hindustani, pointing to the floor beside her morah.

Maintaining an expressionless composure, the servant followed her instructions and on their completion turned to leave without saying a word.

"*Dhanyavad*—Thank you," Doreen called after her with a friendly wave.

The woman stopped and stared back with curiosity for a moment before breaking out in a smile. Then she stepped out into the hall and bolted the door behind her.

Mos was sleeping soundly, undisturbed by the goings on about him. Doreen barely had finished checking to see if the lad was warm when the door opened again to admit the same woman carrying a kerosene lamp. After adjusting the wick, she set it on the table beside the washbasin. Mos whimpered in his sleep and tossed restlessly under the cover. The servant woman quickly moved over to the bedside.

"*Yah apka chokra hai*—Is this your boy?" she whispered, peering down into the sleeping child's face.

"*Mera nahi hai*—He's not mine," Doreen replied, a touch of tenderness in her voice.

The woman pursed her lips and frowned. Then staring at the door she muttered in a barely audible voice, "*Sur-ka baccha*—Son of a pig." Her hatred had flared against someone not in the room. Turning to leave, she paused to study Doreen's face and as she did so, her grimace of abhorrence dissolved into a warm smile.

Small as it was, the kerosene lamp added a psychological warmth to the room. Doreen stirred and fanned the charcoal in the brazier until the embers sent out salvos of tiny crackling sparks like miniature meteorite showers. Exploring behind the corner curtain, she discovered a mobile toilet which she gratefully used. The room showed the ravages of age and lack of maintenance. Mud plastering had crumbled in spots baring the underlying field stone wall. As far as she could determine, the building was not just a village hut but rather a substantial single story structure, quite possibly the home of an agricultural landowner. Sounds filtering in from outdoors were typical of rural India, the lowing of cattle and buffalo, bleating of sheep and goats, clucking and crowing of poultry and the raucous calls of crows noisily settling in the trees for the night. Moving over close to the window, she tried to peek out but the slanted louver boards limited her range of vision to a distant field surrounded by woods and rolling hills. The sun had set and a winter's dusk was lowering rapidly. Returning to the cot, Doreen lay down with a discouraged sigh. Very shortly she fell into an uneasy sleep, her taut muscles trembling nervously from time to time.

A rattling of the metal bolt was a prelude to the swinging open of the door and a return of the servant woman bearing a tray of hot food. The noise had startled Doreen and Mos out of their sleep. Rolled up in his blanket, the waif gave the appearance of a caterpillar larva in its cocoon. Standing just within the door, Achmed sullenly surveyed the room. Removing the washbasin and pitcher, the woman set the steaming dishes of curry and brass tumblers of hot tea on the table and then stepped back into the shadows.

"Damned cheeky on your part," the knife-wielder sneered condescendingly as he walked toward the cot.

"Telling the European of your foulmouthed comment this morning in Gulmarg?" Doreen stood and took a step toward Achmed.

"You know bloody well what I mean."

"I'd slap your filthy mouth again if you repeated it," Her words rang with contempt.

Achmed growled angrily under his breath and turned to urge the servant woman out of the room ahead of him, slamming the door shut with such force that the building shook.

Doreen shuddered at the thought of the man and decided not to goad him as she just had done. The look on his face when she threatened him was evil and vindictive. She wondered why she hadn't noticed the marks on her captor earlier, then realized that he had worn gloves during the abduction that morning. A falcon was tattooed on the back of each of Achmed's hands.

Even with the glowing charcoal embers, the room remained cold, but the hot food and drink helped blunt the sharp edge of the chill. After eating, Doreen washed Mos' face and hands before wrapping him in a blanket again and laying the waif across the foot of the charpai. Then she moved the brazier to the far side of the room in order to dissipate the noxious effects of its fumes, and, after washing up, curled up across the remainder of the cot.

"Are you warm?" Doreen asked as she patted the bundled lad at her feet.

"Yes, Lady."

"Have a good sleep."

"Lady, I ask you something?" His voice trembled.

"Yes, Mos."

"Allah know I am here?"

"I'm sure Allah does."

"Allah know you are here?"

"Yes Allah must know."

The waif took a deep sighing breath. "I now have good sleep, Lady."

Doreen struggled mentally in an effort to rescue herself from a nightmare, only to realize that she had wakened to a reality. A hand covered her mouth firmly ... scarcely permitting breathing ... and for a second time in the past twenty-four hours the cold sharpness of a steel blade pressed firmly against her throat. Again she heard the hoarse whisper, "Make a sound and I'll slit you from ear to ear." She shivered involuntarily, twisting her head to the side so she could breathe more freely. The threats continued, "If the little bastard gives trouble he'll get the same." She shivered again as her toes felt Mos stirring under the blankets.

"What do you want?" Doreen asked quietly, concealing her inner fear with a casual tone of voice. She had recognized the words as those of Achmed. Except for a slight glow from the brazier it was dark.

"What do I want?" I want you, you little bitch," he sneered.

"We're going to my quarters and don't forget this knife." He increased the pressure of the blade against her neck.

"And what will the European have to say about this?" she asked defiantly.

"Not a damned thing because I'm not telling the bastard. What's more you had better bloody well keep your mouth shut or somewhere along the way I'll be using this knife on you for the last time."

Having delivered his warning, Achmed waved his hand signaling her to get up.

"Both my feet are numb," Doreen whispered, sitting up on the edge of the charpai and massaging her calves. "The cold and the cramped space in bed ... " her words ran out as she stretched her legs one after the other. She deliberately prolonged these exercises as her mind explored potential avenues of escape. Achmed grunted angrily at the delay, rubbing his hands together to warm them.

Mos had been roused by the sudden stiffening of Doreen's feet against him when she had felt the cold knife and suffocating hand. Out of the corners of his eyes he quickly assessed the urgency of their predicament and ... still feigning sleep ... began to free himself from the blankets. His instincts for survival came to the fore as he moved imperceptibly off the charpai onto the shadowy floor. Then with a feline quietness he crawled to a position behind the abductor. Doreen, seeing the waif on the move, prepared herself for any eventuality, in the meantime making an important contribution to the boy's continued concealment by an increased action in leg massaging.

With a hideous shriek of raw terror, unbelievably coming from a human of such modest proportions, Mos threw himself against the backs of Achmed's knees.The vehement assault knocked the surprised intruder off balance and sent him tumbling to the floor, bellowing with rage. Without slowing in the momentum of his attack, the waif appeared to bounce off the knife-wielder's legs and dash unerringly across the floor to pick up the brazier of burning charcoals which he adroitly hurled at the kneeling victim's head.

Screams of pain now substituted for the howls of rage as Achmed danced his way about the room trying to free himself of the searing embers. A sickening smell of burning clothes, singed hair and scorched skin accentuated the uproar of shouts and curses. After a halfhearted attempt to catch his nimble tormentor, the intruder rushed to open the door and let himself out of the room.

Doreen lit the kerosene lamp and helped Mos pour water from the waste bucket beside the table to quench the few active coals on the floor, creating a thick irritating smoke. After a bout of coughing, Doreen sat on the edge of the cot and began to laugh. Not quite certain as to whether the recent encounter called for laughter, the waif frowned soberly a moment before joining in with a chuckle.

"Did you see that lout break into a fast jitterbugging?"

Doreen asked of no one in particular, fully aware that her words would be totally foreign to Mos.

In his haste to leave, Achmed left the door unbolted and the servant woman entered noiselessly. She surveyed the room and must have recreated in her mind something of the action which had taken place. Doreen explained in Hindustani the events of the past few minutes. The woman scowled angrily and spat out the words she had used earlier, "*Sur-ka baccha* - Son of a pig." Then her face softened as she invited Mos, "*Ao beta* - Come son." Patting him on the head, she complimented the waif, "*Shabash* - Well done!"

Doreen asked the servant woman her name. It was Ameena. In a few minutes she had refurbished the brazier with glowing coals. Then she took a broom and swept the floor, placing the trash in a waste bucket.

Pausing at the door, Ameena turned to smile and wave.

Again Doreen bundled Mos in blankets after removing his prize coat. Then she lay down for the night and noted it was just ten o'clock. A variety of thoughts troubled her and precluded sleep. For the time being Achmed had been held at bay, but for how long? Certainly the humiliating torment he had been subjected to would intensify his hatred of them. Ameena was friendly but what authority, if any, did she carry? Their major immediate protection appeared to be the European. At least he castigated Achmed for the rough treatment of his captive. But again, how long would this apparent benevolence last? Doreen was convinced by now that she and Mos had been abducted to place some kind of pressure ... blackmail ... on Monty. The very thought of this probability depressed her. How terribly unfair to the American, she thought, particularly in the light of the consequences should he not bend to their demands. At this stage Monty must be strongly suspicious that these abductors were linked with the cobra murderers. She began to weep quietly, releasing her tensions in the hot tears of emotional exhaustion. After a few moments the accumulated fatigue of the day's activities gently nudged her toward the frontiers of sleep, but just before crossing this threshold, she felt small exploring fingers touching her arm. Tenderly grasping Mos' hand in hers, she whispered, "Dear God have mercy on the both of us."

Chapter Fourteen

Prem Narayan had been unable to sleep after dispatching Ian McVey and Montague Brown to Gulmarg. Tired of tossing in bed, he quickly performed his morning ablutions in the cold W.C. and returned to his cabin to dress. Buttoning his trench coat high, he climbed to the upper deck of the houseboat and restlessly paced back and forth. Dawn's many luminous fingers were creeping over mountain silhouettes in the east, reaching resolutely to pry loose the night's shadowy grasp on the Vale of Kashmir. There was no wind and the surface of Dal Lake was slate-gray with the smoothness of glass. The Captain's forehead was furrowed with numerous worry wrinkles as he walked, body bent forward, apparently oblivious to the natural beauty surrounding him.

"Why Doreen Bruce?" Prem asked in an aside to himself. The very thought of her being held hostage disturbed him deeply. She had no connection whatsoever with the C.I.D. investigation, except for the fact that her brother had administered antivenin, a matter which was supposed to be classified. Rubbing out his cigarette stub on the deck, he rested his elbows on the rail and shredded its tobacco content overboard onto the water. Then retrieving and lighting another Camel, he continued to stare out over the lake.

"Could Doreen's kidnapping, if such it were, be a red herring to throw us off the assassins' scent?" Prem continued his musings. "Another possibility could well be that Monty was the target of Doreen's abduction." The Captain moved to the rail and spat into the lake. "Damn it!" he exploded with a vehemence that startled even him, "We've got to find out more about the American's activities."

Fatima, noting Prem's preoccupation, solicitously served a breakfast with which he toyed absent-mindedly. Sardar Khan had left quite early for his further investigation of Narangwal as well as an arranged interview with the Forest Officer concerning the supposed transportation of cobras to the village. The anticipated jangling of the telephone broke into the Captain's breakfast and he quickly moved to his cabin.

"Captain Narayan here," he tersely announced into the receiver.

"Ian here, calling from Nedou's in Gulmarg."

"*Accha.*" Prem's voice was tense.

"Kidnappers, probably two of them, broke into Doreen's quarters around three this morning and absconded with her. No evidence of a struggle. Came into her room ... the last in the string of cottages ...

through a window. Short distance above the cottage ... say about a hundred feet at the most ... horses were waiting and took them in from there. Bruce and Maureen heard indistinct noises but by the time they got there Doreen and her captors were gone.''

"No clues?''

"On the hillside above the cottage, Monty picked up a brass button about the size of a half rupee.''

"Military?''

"Uh-huh. Muslim insignia ... crescent and star ... I'd say it was off a Pakistani uniform.''

"Ian ... '' Prem cleared his throat before continuing ... "did Bruce give his sister antivenin?''

"Aye ... that he did.''

"Thank God for that,'' Prem muttered in a barely audible voice, and went on "When'll you be back here?''

"Monty and I'll be leaving for Srinagar very shortly.''

"Better report your findings to Ali Aurangzeb here. Try to find out what the American's doing, eh?''

"This abduction's hit him harder than I'd anticipated and he just may open up a bit.''

"It's in Monty's interest as well as ours to synchronize our acts. Dash it all man, we probably have the same enemies!''

"Righto, Prem, I'll be working on him. Be seeing you on the Kashmir Princess in a jiffy.''

"Not until around noon.''

"And where'll you be in case of an emergency?''

"Nedou's here in Srinagar. I've got to find out what the hell's going on in room seven.''

"Not alone, for God's sake man, wait until I get there!'' Ian sounded exasperated.

"It'll be alright, my good fellow, I'll have Rustum with me.''

"Well ... '' he began hesitantly and broke off.

"*Accha*. I'll see you for tiffin here on the Princess.''

Following the Captain's instructions, Rustum parked the jeep in the hotel compound directly adjacent to room seven. The driver was apprised of the potential hazard in the morning's venture and prepared to give support as needed. Prem paced the length of the front verandah in a quick surveillance before returning to the door in question. Loosening his automatic in its holster, he knocked firmly.

"I can't be disturbed. I'm too busy.'' The words from within projected annoyance.

Prem continued his knocking even more firmly.

"Oh hell, who is it?'' the occupant called out petulantly.

"Captain Narayan ... the C.I.D.''

There were shuffling footsteps inside before the door was unbolted and opened a slight crack, revealing a single dark eye ogling him. Prem produced an identification card and held it at a proper reading distance from the solitary staring orb. This action resulted in the door opening quickly and his being invited within by a curt nod. Carefully replacing the bolt, the occupant waved the Captain to a wickerwork chair.

"Parkozian here, John Parkozian." He extended his hand in greeting, all the while scrutinizing his guest.

"And of course I've already introduced myself," Prem countered, as he in turn took stock of the occupant of room seven.

John Parkozian displayed a Near Eastern aura, as was borne out by his mannerisms, swarthy skin, aquiline features and the Armenian name. His build was portly and his breathing labored even with minor exertion. He spoke English with a nondescript accent, neither British nor American, but with the easy flair of an educated person. A striking characteristic of the man was the probing nature of his dark eyes. They presented an uncanny sense of being able to penetrate surface boundaries and explore deep within. Prem watched him scan the scarred left side of his face without evincing the least flicker of surprise.

"I've a pot of tea on the hot plate. Will you join me?" the Armenian asked as he still studied his guest's features.

"Don't mind if I do," Prem responded with a disarming smile.

There was silence in the room while the steaming tea was poured into two cups. Having creamed and sugared the drinks, the host settled his ample frame into another wicker chair facing the Captain.

"Old ticker's been acting up a bit," Parkozian confessed, dramatically tapping the front of his chest with a long forefinger.

"Sorry old chap. Must be a bit of a botheration getting about at this elevation."

"Really don't get about much ... " he stooped over to remove his slippers before adding ... "and it's not just because of this." He again tapped his chest knowingly. "But let's not get bogged down in the trivia of my infirmities." Winking good humoredly, he raised his cup of tea in a toast. "Cheers."

"Cheers," the Captain responded in kind.

For a moment both men noisily sipped their hot drinks, while eyes and minds alertly parried for the appropriate time and words to attack or defend.

"The C.I.D. is involved in the investigation of three recent murders in this area," Prem broke the silence, appreciating that, as the intruder, the rules of the game called for him to make the first move.

Parkozian, a chain smoker in spite of his supposed heart trouble, drew on his cigarette and then simultaneously exhaled through mouth and nostrils, all the while nodding vigorously and repeating, "Yes ... yes ... yes I know of the cobra murders."

"Very simply stated, the purpose of my visit is to find out just where you fit into this witches' brew." Prem stared quizzically at the Armenian.

Parkozian broke into a mirthless laugh as he stubbed out his smoke in an ash tray on the arm of his chair. "You're convinced I'm involved with the murders?" he wheezed, still chuckling.

"No." The Captain waved his hand in absolution. "I'm not charging you with complicity in the assassinations, Mr. Parkozian," he added dispassionately.

"Now that is a relief." There was a hint of sarcasm in his voice.

"My purpose isn't to bandy words," Prem countered acidly, "Three men have been murdered in a most brutal fashion and the C.I.D. is determined to find the killers."

"Sorry, my dear chap, really didn't mean to nettle you. In a way I am involved but on the receiving end."

"Meaning?"

"Actually I consider myself a potential victim."

"A potential victim?" Prem raised his eyebrows in surprise.

"My heart deficiency isn't the major reason I don't run about in Srinagar." The tip of his tongue moved nervously across his lips.

The Captain studied Parkozian over the rim of his tea cup and caught a flicker of alarm in the depths of his dark eyes. "Might be to our mutual advantage for you to share your problem with me," he suggested to the Armenian.

Parkozian chose not to reply immediately but sat staring at the floor, cracking his knuckles one by one. Prem coughed and stirred in his creaking chair. Stimulated by this distraction, the host leaned forward, elbows on his knees, and spoke in slowly measured words, "You must be aware of the Dowry of Death?"

"Uh-huh," Prem grunted his assent.

"A private organization supplying arms, clothing and medicine to the Afghani mujahidin, the freedom fighters."

Prem nodded knowingly.

"Well ... " Parkozian interrupted his words to light another cigarette before continuing ... "I'm the executive director of the Dowry of Death."

"The hell you say!" Prem exclaimed in surprise and went on to ask quietly, "You're a Muslim?"

"An Armenian Christian. I work for a Lebanese arms exporter headquartered in Beirut. My relationship to this Afghan project is quite mercenary really. The leaders here asked my company to loan them an organizer to expedite the smuggling and that's why I'm here. Quite simple, you see."

"Then the three victims, Chinese, Afghani and Kashmiri, were a part of your organization?"

"The Afghani and Kashmiri were. The Chinese was consulting."

"Just how extensive is the Dowry of Death?"

"Modest but effective. Mostly people from Kashmir and Afghanistan, Muslims who despise the Russians and their Afghani lackeys."

"Just how do you function in this . . . this . . . " Prem groped for the right word . . . "this international consortium?"

"It's quite clandestine . . . sort of an underground action . . . all steeped in intrigue."

"What about the various officials, the governments of India and China?"

"Officialdom for the most part considers the Russian invasion of Afghanistan an international obscenity. They just look the other way and, so far, haven't disturbed our activities."

"What about loss, pilfering let's say, of goods enroute to Afghanistan?"

Parkozian frowned and pursed his lips in thought before replying, "Losses? Yes we've had losses through raids on our pony trains."

"By whom?"

"By those sons of bitches . . . " he broke off into a bout of coughing and after clearing his throat went on . . . "those sons of bitches the cobra murderers."

Prem stood and asked his host if he could peek outside just long enough to assure his driver that all was well. Rustum, who was leaning against a verandah post, recognized the Captain's signal and nodded his reply.

"But in Srinagar of all places, how in hell do you get supplies here? At a port city . . . Bombay or Calcutta . . . I could understand . . . " Prem's voice drifted off as he continued to stare incredulously at Parkozian.

With an enigmatic smile, the Armenian responded, "I'm certain you're aware of the Bhakra-Nangal hydroelectric plant just at the foot of the mountains below us?"

The Captain nodded. "Probably the largest in Asia. Uses power from the Sutlej River."

"There's a large fertilizer plant connected. Well, in their maintenance program, portions of machinery are being replaced constantly."

"*Accha*," Prem interrupted with a wave of his hand, "The light begins to dawn."

"Boxes of arms, specially marked, are interspersed with the machinery shipped in for the power and fertilizer plants. These are surreptitiously smuggled here by trucks and repacked in smaller boxes for transshipment across the mountains to Afghanistan."

"You must have accomplices at Bhakra-Nangal . . . accomplices at a pretty high level."

Parkozian nodded. "Precisely . . . from plant management to the Punjab State Electricity Board and on to Delhi. Word has been passed down to let the arms go through.''

"I'll be damned!" Prem muttered. "Permits the sending of arms to Afghanistan unofficially without raising diplomatic outcries from Russia or their puppet Afghani regime."

"Of course there has been a response, unofficial perhaps but deadly serious, in the form of the cobra murders," Parkozian countered, nervously moistening dry lips with his tongue.

"And then I'm certain the Indian Government takes care that these arms actually go on to Afghanistan and aren't cached somewhere in Kashmir for possible future trouble."

"You're correct on that. I've an unofficial official who shadows me in this regard."

"Where do these murdering bastards hide out?"

"Wish to hell I knew," Parkozian retorted angrily. "The top man or woman probably functions out of here, somewhere in Srinagar. But those who do the dirty work move about this area and along the road west into Pakistan running along the Jhelum. Best I can get from my informants is that one of their centers has been in the vicinity of Baramula about thirty miles west. But they move from place to place."

"Any leads as to who the top person is?"

"Just intelligent guesses ... " the Armenian took a big gulp of tea before going on ... "but we think that he or she might be a Pakistani or Indian, more likely the latter."

"An Indian ... " Prem broke off with a scowl.

"That's right, an Indian. Let me add that a Russian from their embassy in Delhi comes up here fairly regularly and, we're certain, consults with the cobra goondas. The bugger's not their top one ... probably just a liaison of some kind."

"*Accha.*"

"Shows the Russians have an interest in the murders."

"This wouldn't be Maya Reznikoff?" Prem pressed his questioning.

Choosing not to reply, Parkozian grunted a noncommittal evasion. The Captain offered him a cigarette, took one himself and torched both with a flourish of his cloisonne lighter. For a moment the two sat in silence broken only by the Armenian's wheezing and the metallic throbbing of an alarm clock on a bedside table.

"Pardon the botheration of my pursuit, but all of this information is ... is ... " Prem probed for the proper word ... "is inextricably tied into our investigation of the cobra murders."

Parkozian nodded soberly, dislodging a shower of cigarette ashes onto his lap. "Agreed," he responded, vigorously brushing his pants.

"Where do you transfer and repack these supplies before sending them on to the mujahidin?"

"Various facilities. Mostly warehouses of Muslim merchants here in Srinagar. For obvious reasons we change the location from time to time."

Prem studied Parkozian's face closely as he asked, "Do you know the American, Montague Brown?"

Without hesitation the Armenian replied, "Yes, I'm acquainted with the fellow, but I'll be damned if I know just exactly what he's doing here."

"He's been seen entering this room, number seven."

Parkozian shuffled his feet on the floor a moment then leaned forward in a confidential posture to concede, "Our organization has dealings with him."

"Dealings?" Prem raised his eyebrows in surprise.

"I've been instructed to supply the American with single samples of all military ware, and ammunition to match, which the Dowry of Death has been moving to Afghanistan."

"Whose instructions?"

"Can't say," Parkozian said succinctly.

"What's the chap doing with the stuff?"

"You may not believe this but it's God's truth, I just don't know."

"I must agree that what you've just admitted is damned hard to believe."

"You know, I've wondered if he's recruiting some sort of a raiding party."

Prem disagreed with a shake of his head. "If he's getting just a single sample of each type of firearm, the distribution's not right for the equipment of a small fighting unit."

A knocking on the door interrupted their conversation. It was Rustum checking on the Captain's safety. After exchanging prearranged signs . . . signals that would thwart any forced validation . . . the driver withdrew.

As Prem sat down again and sipped tea, he studied his host over the rim of his cup and noted that the Armenian's previously benign features had hardened. His dark eyes probed those of the Captain, projecting a touch of belligerence. Leaning forward in his chair, Parkozian spoke in a formal tone of voice, "Sir, I have shared secret information with you for one purpose and that is to assist the C.I.D. in bringing the cobra murderers to justice. May I urge that you not use these data in any way that might jeopardize the Dowry of Death. Not as a threat but as a statement of fact, should the Indian Government interfere in this undertaking, it most certainly would estrange Kashmir's prominent Muslim leaders. I hardly need remind you that such a reaction would be most detrimental to the continued harmony of this province."

Captain Narayan listened soberly, aware of the significance of the Armenian's words. Nodding placatingly, he responded to the appeal, "As long as my Government's security is not compromised, your confidence will remain inviolate."

Parkozian's harshness melted into a broad smile and he volunteered, "Thank you, Captain. We have a common enemy and be assured I shall share with you any pertinent evidence."

It was just past noon as Rustum guided the car out through the gates of Nedou's compound, heading for the Kashmir Princess. The session in room seven had been revealing, Prem thought, riding with eyes narrowed to slits. What in the devil is Monty doing with the military equipment, he asked himself. In some way the American must be connected with the Afghani mujahidin. No wonder he wanted cobra antivenin. Then, what about Parkozian, could he be trusted? I'd be a blithering idiot, the Captain continued his musings, not to check the bloke out carefully. A first step in that direction might be to confront Monty with what I've just learned. His attention turned to Doreen's abduction early that morning. "The swine, the bloody swine!" Prem swore out loud. Hearing the words, Rustum quickly turned to investigate and the cold fury he saw in the Captain's narrowed eyes sent a shudder through his body.

Chapter Fifteen

Tiffin on the Kashmir Princess that day was light: fresh fruits, toasted crumpets and jams, bolstered by hot drinks, either tea or coffee. All four of the C.I.D. contingency sat around the table, the three men from without Kashmir as well as Ali Aurangzeb, the local representative.

"Let's have a dekko at that button you found," Prem interrupted Ian's reporting on the trip to Gulmarg. After inspecting the embossed crescent and star, he passed it over to Sardar Khan for his comments.

"Obviously from a military uniform of a Muslim country," the Sergeant Major mused out loud as he fingered the object. "Pakistan flag has this crescent and star, Afghanistan flag does not." He handed the brass button to Ali.

"*Accha*. Do I gather then from what you've just told us, Ian, that Monty knows the leader of the Pakistani dacoits and plans to contact her for assistance in locating Doreen?" Prem asked.

"Precisely." Ian McVey nodded soberly. "The American's an angry young man."

"Ali, you're the local authority," Prem conceded, turning to face the Lieutenant, "what about this business with the outlaws?"

"We're fools, quite daft really, if we have anything to do with the dacoits," he retorted angrily.

"As long as it remains unofficial and without direct contacts, what then?" Ian countered.

Choosing not to reply, Ali merely shook his head in disgust.

"This damned well is Monty's doing and we're in no position to stop the bloke. But in the future we may become involved, who in hell can say? After all, it would appear that we have common enemies, the cobra assassins. Beggars can't always be choosers. There will be no official documentation of collaborations and let me emphasize, that's an order." Prem's voice was firm.

"What a buggered up situation," Ian broke in, "The American now becomes our unofficial liaison with the dacoits."

"The blighter will be done in," Ali muttered in scarcely audible words, going on to add, "and that'll bring an international hornet's nest about our ears."

After a moment's silence, Prem initiated the conversation to say, "This abduction of Miss Duncan and the waif points the finger of danger at Monty. He's become the target of an organization apparently dedicated to the disruption of his efforts here in Kashmir, whatever those may be.''

"As one corollary to your statement, let me add that the abductors hounding Monty and the cobra murderers are one and the same gang of goondas," Ian offered soberly.

Ali shook his head vigorously. "Too many missing links in your chain of evidence. I doubt there's any connection."

Fatima entered the dining room to replenish the hot drinks and add more charcoal to the braziers. The four men sat quietly for a moment creaming and sugaring their fresh tea and coffee.

"Ian," Prem broke the silence, "how about ringing up the Duncans in Gulmarg and sort of encouraging them ... you know ... bringing them up to date on things, eh?"

"Should I tell them about Monty and the dacoits?"

The Captain stared thoughtfully at the thin line of smoke curling up from the tip of his cigarette without responding to the question.

"What say?" Ian verbally nudged his chief.

"Sorry, my thoughts were elsewhere," Prem apologized.

Ian repeated the question.

"Better not, later perhaps but not just now. Telephone lines have listening ears, you know."

Lieutenant McVey excused himself and placed the call to Gulmarg, returning shortly, his mission accomplished.

"How did they take it?" Prem asked.

"Quite well, deeply worried but in control. Talked to Bruce," Ian reported.

"*Accha.*" The Captain nodded approvingly and then turning to Sardar Khan asked him to make his report on Narangwal.

Clearing his throat several times, the Sergeant Major began his account, "A bit of a surprise ... " he stroked his beard and mustache before continuing ... "It is a ... a ... a brothel."

"That bungalow is a whorehouse?" Ian raised his voice in surprise.

Sardar Khan nodded solemnly.

"Go ahead. Give us the details." The Captain waved him on.

"The horse tongas in purdah ... with curtains ... they bring ... are bringing customers from Srinagar and as well take ladies to private homes. Very much secret."

"Damn it!" Prem swore under his breath, then raised his voice to ask, "What about the cobras in baskets?"

"Fish baskets. To take fish to markets. The Forest Officer is mistaken. He is just thinking cobras are carried in baskets."

"A worthy effort, Sardar, even though the results were disappointing,"Prem commiserated with an obviously embarrassed and disheartened Sergeant Major.

"Your turn," Ian said, pointing his pipestem at the Captain.

Prem discarded his cigarette stub in the brazier and lit another before repeating almost verbatim his dialogue with Parkozian: The activities of the Dowry of Death; the procurement of arms by way of Bhakra-Nangal Hydroelectric; Monty's receiving single duplicates of arms and ammunition being shipped to the mujahidin by the Dowry of Death; and the Armenian's fear for his life.

"His story . . . I mean Parkozian's . . . it's reliable?" Ian asked with eyebrows raised.

"I think the bloke's pakka, but needs checking out," Prem admitted.

The telephone began ringing. The message was for Prem.

"Captain Narayan here," he barked into the receiver.

"This is Monty. I want to read you a note I've just received. It didn't come through the mail but was left at the hotel desk for me. The clerk didn't see anybody leave it."

"*Accha*, Monty, I'm listening."

Prem could hear a rustling of paper at the other end of the line before the American read the brief message, "If you leave Kashmir immediately, Miss Duncan and the Srinagar waif will be released unharmed. Otherwise neither will be seen again."

There followed a brief silence while each could hear the other breathing into the phone. Prem broke the quiet, clearing his throat before asking, "That's all, not even a signature?"

"Not even a signature."

"Typewritten?"

"The message was typed and on good bond paper, twenty-five per cent cotton paper."

"Be sure and let me have the letter."

"Yo."

"Yo?"

"American navy and marine slang. Means yes."

"Monty, Ian has passed on to me your conversation with him this morning. Have you contacted the dacoits?"

"Yes, as soon as we got back from Gulmarg."

"And?"

"I'm meeting with them at midnight."

Prem drew in a deep breath and exhaled with a sigh. "You know we can't officially participate in a thing like this. These people are outlaws."

"I understand."

"Monty, for God's sake be careful." A deep sincerity flooded the Captain's words.

"Thanks. I appreciate your interest."

"What're you going to do about the letter?"

"Perhaps after tonight I won't have to do a damn thing."

"I'll be expecting you to contact me immediately after your action, eh?"

"We'll take care of ourselves and I'll be reporting later."

"Cheerio, old chap." Deep in thought, Prem held the receiver in his hand a moment before replacing it on the phone. "Wish I could join the American tonight," he muttered, as he walked back to the dining table.

Lieutenant Aurangzeb excused himself and drove off toward Srinagar. The Captain invited his two companions to the cabin.

"That was Monty on the phone," Prem announced soberly, then went on to describe the blackmail letter and the American's plan to meet with the Pakistani dacoits that night.

"A raid of some sort," Ian conjectured.

Prem nodded. "He didn't say outright but intimated that it was to be a raid. Chap actually sounded confident and cheerful."

"Damn," Ian swore angrily, "What a chance to round up the whole bloody lot of the bastards."

"*Hasti, hasti*—Slowly, slowly," the Captain cautioned in Hindustani, "We've got to have evidence ... pakka evidence. No use having the culprits in hand unless we can convict them in our courts. Don't forget, these murders have international implications."

"Wish I could join them," Ian confessed, banging a fist in the palm of his hand.

"The American and the Pakistanis just may get us some evidence tonight. If not, I've a plan for direct action," Prem announced grimly.

"Such as?" Ian asked.

"Let's wait until we learn what happens on tonight's raid."

"Sir, a question?" the Sergeant Major broke in, directing his words to the Captain.

"*Accha*," Prem nodded him on.

"I am having a good friend of the Srinagar police. He is a policeman now for many years. The Lieutenant Aruangzeb is saying of his botherations with Baldev Raj, Deputy Superintendent. If you are wishing it, I may find out reasons and very much in confidence."

"Why not, and of course confidentially," Prem agreed.

"I'd like to have a go at something this afternoon," Ian interjected.

"*Accha*, let's hear it."

"Check out this bloke, James Appleton."

"Good project." Prem nodded his approval.

"Appleton hangs around Nedou's, so that's where I'll be if you should need me."

"Jolly good. I've got my report to get off to our Delhi office," the Captain concluded, standing to stretch and yawn.

Chapter Sixteen

Dropping Ian McVey off at the Kashmir Princess, Monty Brown drove to the hotel and parked the Red Chariot in the rear compound. Entering his quarters, he bolted the door and went directly to the telephone. Giving the desk clerk a number he listened for the telltale faint buzzing which might indicate an eavesdropper. Hearing none, he leaned forward in his chair and waited impatiently for the call to be completed.

"*Kaun hai*—Who is it?" a male voice answered cautiously in Hindustani.

"*American Hakim hai*—It's the American Doctor," Monty enunciated the words slowly and precisely, for the phone connection was not the best.

"*Accha ji*—Alright sir," the man responded, this time with enthusiasm.

After a brief pause, a feminine voice greeted, "Hello American."

"Aisha?"

"Yes, Aisha here. You're in trouble?"

"Need your help . . . must meet with you tonight." Monty went on to explain the story of Doreen's and Mos' abduction.

"You're in love with this Doreen." It was more a statement of fact than a question. "I am a woman and your voice tells me this. Alright, we shall meet tonight."

"Great! When and where?"

There was a moment of background conversation at the other end of the line before Aisha replied, "Go east on the road from Srinagar toward Baramula. Between the third and fourth furlong markers beyond the twenty-fourth milestone there's a small bridge. Pull off past this into the trees on the left side. Turn the car lights out and wait inside quietly. About five minutes after your arrival my men, who'll have been watching for any possible pursuers, will contact you and do the needful."

"And the time, Aisha, the time?"

"Midnight. At the stroke, if you understand what I mean, and exactly what's your watch say now?"

"Ten sixteen, a.m. of course," Monty reported after a pause and heard her chuckle over the phone.

"I know it's morning, American." Again she laughed contagiously and he joined in with her.

"Okay. I'll be seeing you, Aisha." There was a note of relief in his voice.

"Cheerio American and don't forget the directions and exact timing ... " she breathed a deep sigh before going on teasingly ... "So I'm losing you to an Anglo-Indian."

A cold wind from the southwest sprang up late that evening and chased billowing moist clouds up into the fastness of the Himalayas. As night advanced the darkening skies glowered sullenly on the Vale of Kashmir. With infrequent success a partial moon sought breaches in the overcast through which to direct its fragile beams into the blackness below.

Monty ate a late dinner in the hotel dining room and then retired to his quarters to slip on a water repellent ski suit and marine hiking boots. He checked out his automatic, carefully oiling its intricate mechanism, and then changed the batteries in his small but powerful flashlight. Slipping along the verandah shadows to the rear compound, he started the Red Chariot and headed out of Srinagar eastward toward Baramula. As he urged the vehicle along, Monty missed the incessant chatter of Mos, his adopted waif. Poor helpless little kid, he thought sadly, and all this because of me.

A fine drizzle began to fleck the windshield, moistening a layer of dust into a thin brown syrup which the double wipers spread across the glass in two large dirty arcs. Monty slowed down until the visibility improved, due in large part to the increased tempo of the rainfall. The impending storm and the lateness of the hour had curtailed traffic, so the Red Chariot was able to pick up speed, guided by its lights probing the darkness ahead. A few minutes before midnight, the American passed the twenty-fourth milestone and slowed down to count off three furlong stone markers to a bridge before turning into a grove of thickets and trees on the left. Switching out the lights and cutting the ignition, he waited in silence as instructed by Aisha. Rain drops tapped over the parked car in a rapid drum roll of muted beats.

Suddenly nature's tranquil sounds were ravished by the harsh noises of a motorized vehicle approaching from the direction of Baramula. The car stopped at the bridge, then slowly turned into the thickets, finally coming to a halt not far from the Red Chariot. Monty drew his automatic, cradling it in his lap, and watched the scintillating rain droplets pass as meteor showers through the vivid beams of the headlights. Then the illumination and engine of the second vehicle were turned off and the darkness with its background sounds of rain again held sway.

Hope these are Aisha's men, Monty mused, but if not, someone tapped our phone conversation and I'm in one helluva spot. He slouched down in the seat to offer a smaller target for any would-be assassin. The doors of the other car opened and closed. Suddenly there was the sickening thud of a heavy object striking flesh, followed by the bedlam of physical combat. Quietly but quickly the American slid out of the Red Chariot to engage in the fight, but hesitated and then just as quickly scrambled back into his car. What a damned fool, he muttered, I don't know the good guys from the bad, and what's more, in the dark, they wouldn't know me from Adam.

The battle continued, and from the sounds there appeared to be two separate skirmishes in progress. As time advanced, so did the heavy breathing and grunting, until it became evident that the encounter was over. But which side had won, Monty wondered. At this stage, he decided to get out of the car into the trees where, if necessary, he could defend himself better. Leaning against a tree trunk he waited, water dripping on him from the leaves overhead. He could hear low muttered conversation, punctuated by swearing, all in Hindustani or its Pakistani equivalent, but only an occasional word filtered through clearly enough to be understood. However, even from such meager comprehension, Monty felt assured that Aisha's men were the victors, and with this certitude he climbed into the Red Chariot out of the chilling rain. Lowering the windows, he strained to understand the continued conversation at the conflict site.

"No ... no ... no!" a man screamed in English, followed after a few seconds of silence by a wild shriek which carried over into a flow of uncontrolled sobbing. Shortly after this nerve-wracking episode, it was repeated except that the remonstrance was in Hindustani, "Nahi ... nahi ... nahi!" trailed by hysterical wails.

There had been no shooting, Monty noted, so the Pakistani dacoits must have surprised the occupants of the other car and brought them down by physical force. But what in God's name had they done to their captives, he wondered. Then he heard someone start the motor and drive the vehicle further off into the underbrush. From the continued howling in that direction, Monty surmised that the two victims were passengers.

"Salaam Aleikom," a voice greeted from the shadows.

"Salaam Aleikom," the American repeated, reaching out through the window to shake an extended hand. The man standing beside the car was clean-shaven except for a bushy mustache. Two other men of similar bearing materialized out of the night, each reiterating the Muslim salutation. Unnoticed in the darkness, Monty grimaced as he recognized the trophies carried by one of the dacoits, two hands, each amputated at the wrist.

"See ... good punishment," the man announced, holding up both severed members by their fingers.

"A bit barbaric, isn't it?" Monty questioned, staring with

repugnance at the bloody specimens.

"Barbaric," the first man, whom the American recognized as the leader, repeated with a harsh laugh, "those bastards are fortunate to be alive. Not only are both of them murderers, but my dear fellow, they came here tonight to execute you. Perhaps this seems a severe penalty to the eyes of a Westerner, but it is proper justice according to our Koran."

"Please get into the car," Monty invited and the three men quickly climbed in out of the rain. The Pakistanis were dressed in olive drab military jump suits, with thick pull-over khaki sweaters and knitted woolen stocking caps.

"Bloody awful weather this, eh what?" the leader volunteered, rubbing his hands briskly. At the American's invitation he was occupying the front seat, while the other two sat in the rear.

"You know them?" Monty asked, pointing toward the source of cries still issuing from the other vehicle.

The leader nodded. "One is an Afghani ... a shame to the Muslim brotherhood ... a damned puppet of the godless Russian invaders."

"And the other?"

"A renegade Kashmiri despised by his own community in Srinagar."

"And they'll die ... bleed to death?"

"I doubt it, although they should die; they sure as hell deserve it. We bound up their amputated stumps very tightly with strips of cloth."

"American Hakim," the man in the back seat carrying the specimens spoke out, "there is a mark here."

Monty turned to inspect the gruesome trophies under the beam of his flashlight. On the back of one hand was tattooed a black falcon. He also noted that the other dismembered part was from the left side. He brought this difference to the attention of the leader seated beside him.

"But the left hand already was missing from the Kashmiri," he explained dispassionately.

"You mean to say that this fellow now has neither hand?" Monty asked incredulously.

"Neither hand," the Pakistani repeated.

"I'll be damned," the American muttered under his breath.

"We'd better leave," the leader suggested, pointing westward in the direction of Baramula.

Rain was falling steadily, creating shallow splashy pools in the ruts of the road. Shortly they reached Baramula and found the main street deserted by man and beast alike, all seeking an escape from the inclement weather. Just beyond the town, the leader directed Monty onto a narrow gravel driveway cutting off toward a house nestled against the side of a hill, and soon the Red Chariot disappeared inside its walled compound. A sleepy chowkidar closed the gates behind them.

"We walk about four furlongs," the Pakistani whispered, pointing up into the hills to the south.

The blowing rain slowed their progress, not only because of the treacly mud on the steep and winding path, but also due to the sheer discomfort of the moist cold. By now water was beginning to penetrate their outer garments and with each step wet socks squished within waterlogged shoes. The trail was well camouflaged, in some parts barely discernible. Growths of pine huddled together, shivering in the wind as if seeking each other's warmth. As the four climbed higher, they were engulfed by waves of moisture-laden clouds which deposited beads of water on their eyebrows and mustaches.

"Righto ... we're there ... almost," the leader panted as he struggled to catch his breath. "Wait here, please, just one moment." Stepping a few feet off the path, he used what Monty recognized as a military field telephone cleverly hidden in the hollow of a tree. After a brief conversation, inaudible to the rest of the party, he again led the way up the trail.

"Halt!" The startling command came out of an adjacent wooded knoll, terse and very military. Coming to a standstill, all four faced the source of the order as their leader gave out a password which Monty could not understand. A torch inquisitively played over them until the sentry, apparently satisfied, called out, "Carry on."

From the outside, the dilapidated stone building enfolded in the hollow of a hill, appeared to be in the process of capitulating to an encroaching jungle. As they drew closer, Monty surveyed the crumbling bungalow and concluded that in the days of the British Raj it probably served as a hunting lodge. The calculated neglect of the grounds and house exterior had created an effective camouflage. A partially dismantled chimney emitted wisps of smoke which were sheared off intermittently by gusts of wind.

In response to the leader's knocking, a massive weather-beaten wooden door slowly swung inwards with resentful squeakings from its hinges. Following the Pakistani, Monty paused just inside the threshold, accommodating his eyes to the brighter light within. A kerosene table lamp with frosted glass shade rested on the mantle of the fireplace as the main source of illumination. A wood fire burned on the grate, discharging occasional puffs of smoke into the room whenever gusts of wind outdoors created down-drafts in the chimney. Crouched on the floor before the hearth, with head resting on its forepaws, lay a young white snow leopard, collared and leashed to the leg of an overstuffed couch. The four men moved over toward the fire while the maid closed and bolted the entrance door and then slipped out of the room through a curtained exit.

"Ah, American, welcome," Aisha called out as she crossed the floor to shake Monty's hand. "Kindly oblige and take that chair by the fireplace. You must be chilled through. I shall have a word with these chaps before I join you." She beckoned the three Pakistanis to follow her into an adjoining room.

The shapely Muslim woman, probably in her early forties, Monty surmised, was comely in a mature way, moving about with an authoritative yet graceful bearing. Even a prosaic military jump suit failed to hide her attractive feminine form. In the depths of her animated eyes, he recognized an emotional warmth as well as the potential for ruthlessness should the occasion demand.

Slowly the snow leopard rose, stretched and yawned, exposing four large and sharp canines, before padding over just within the permissive radius of its leash, to sniff suspiciously at Monty's wet boots. Pretending not to notice the big cat's presence, he leaned forward to warm his hands over the wood flames. Having satisfied itself as to the harmlessness of the stranger, the animal sauntered back and dropped to the floor, announcing its lack of concern with a deep rumbling purr.

"You are wet, yes?" Aisha asked, as she re-entered the room and pulled up a chair beside the American.

"Not too wet, really," he responded, shifting his position to face her, "My socks are soaked but this ski suit is surprisingly dry inside."

"Jolly good! Kick the boots off and put them by the fire. I'll have some thick woolen socks for you." She clapped loudly for the maid and ordered the dry apparel.

"That leopard," Monty nodded toward the purring cat, "how'd you come by it?"

"Found it half starved near here. Someone must have shot the mother." Aisha turned and placed her hand on the American's arm. "Thank Allah you're safe. Sorry about the botheration of that fight with those two goondas, but we planned it that way."

"Planned it?" His voice projected surprise.

She nodded. "We deliberately leaked the fact of your being at that spot at midnight, then dropped our three men off a couple hours earlier. They were hiding under the bridge when you drove up."

"But why?"

"To incapacitate two people who planned to do away with you."

"How'd you leak the facts?"

"That's my business," she countered with a teasing grin.

"Sorry ... didn't mean ... " he began apologetically.

"Don't mention," Aisha broke in, "You'll have to accept some of our activities without understanding just how they're accomplished. But enough of this ... " she waved her hand and went on ... "I've good news for you."

"Doreen?" Monty asked quickly.

Aisha nodded with a good humored smile. "Not only Doreen but your little Muslim waif as well."

"So they're together ... " he drew in a breath and asked ...

"where?"

"Easy American, not so fast ... " she patted his arm before going on ... "They're still captives but we're about to do the needful to free them."

"Count me in on it!"

Aisha laughed out loud. "I expected as much. But you will go with my men, the same ones who brought you here, on one condition."

"And that is?"

"You will be under the command of Ashok, the leader and do nothing against his orders."

"I've not much choice, have I?" he countered with a resigned grin.

"Precisely!" Her voice was unyielding. "The three are just now changing clothes and getting something to eat. You will be leaving in thirty minutes. The timing must be just right."

The maid parted the curtains and brought in a tray of hot food and drinks which she placed on a morah between them. Aisha removed a cozy from the tea pot and poured out two cups of the steaming drink, sugaring and creaming Monty's according to his specifications. Then she dished out generous helpings of rice and curried lamb for him. The American needed no urging to eat.

"Quite a hide-out you have here," he conceded between bites, waving his spoon in an inclusive sweep.

"The most pretentious of our hide-outs. Actually, for reasons quite obvious, we move about quite frequently."

"How come you didn't blindfold me this time?"

"How come we didn't blindfold you? Well American, we've learned more about you since then and like what you're doing at the risk of your life. And as you must have observed, our security at this place is pretty damned good."

"Quite military."

Aisha nodded. "Most of us are from military backgrounds. My husband was a colonel in the Pakistan army ... tanks."

"Was?" Monty paused in his eating to study the face of his hostess.

"Killed in the clashes when Prime Minister Bhutto was overthrown."

"I'm very sorry."

"So you might call us military exiles waiting until the political climate permits our return."

"But why this dacoit status?"

"Little choice really. India doesn't want us and yet we have to be near to settle old scores."

"Scores with India?"

She laughed mirthlessly before responding, "With Pakistan. The border's just a few miles from here and we can watch from the side lines."

"And who supports you?"

"You know, American, you're an inquisitive and cheeky bounder," Aisha countered, feigning irritation at the question, "but for your information, we support ourselves. Our methods may at times be a bit unorthodox but they're successful."

"Touche," Monty responded with a self-conscious grin. "If you'll pardon my cheek, I'll quit badgering. But may I hand out a compliment?"

"What female doesn't appreciate a compliment?"

"Besides your beauty and personal charm, you speak such a fluent English ... your accent and all ... " he paused, at a loss for words.

"There now, you've made me blush ... " she laughed and refilled Monty's empty tea cup before going on ... "I attended college in Lahore, an American institution."

"Aisha, I meant what I just said."

She dropped her eyes and whispered in a barely audible voice, "Thanks, American." The two sat quietly for a moment watching the flames in the fireplace.

"We'll be coming back here after the raid?" Monty broke the silence.

She nodded. "You'll come back here and then to your car. From there you're on your own."

"Is it far, the place we're raiding?"

Aisha shook her head. "About thirty minutes of fast hiking. You'll be approaching the building in the dark and from the wooded side. We've learned they're planning to move in the morning so there's a time limit."

"Again, the leader's name is Ashok?"

"Uh-huh. Ashok's an ex-captain in the air force, electronics and communications. Rigs up all our telephone connections. He's a tough and reliable chap. You can depend on him, American."

"These people who abducted Doreen, who are they and why did they do it?"

"Why did they kidnap your Anglo-Indian and the orphan child? They did it to hurt and frighten you, American. They don't like what you're doing here. And as to who they are, they're traitorous swine ... puppets of the damned Russians in Afghanistan." Her words projected hatred and bitterness.

"The cobra murders?" Monty asked quietly.

Aisha stared at the fire as if she hadn't heard the words.

"The cobra murderers?" He changed the question slightly.

She turned slowly and stared into his eyes, but instead of speaking, merely nodded in assent.

Parting the door curtains, the maid stepped into the room and announced, "*Ashok jane-ko taiyar hai*—Ashok is ready to go."

"*Us-ko andar ane do* — Let him come in," Aisha ordered.

The three men entered as Monty was giving the final touches to lacing up his boots. Rising, he joined them.

Aisha addressed the men in English, "Ameena will be waiting at the window of her room, next to the kitchen, at three o'clock sharp. She will make no moves related to the captives until you actually contact her. After the alert, she will bring the two and deliver them to you just outside the back entrance of the compound. One of you will then return to the building with Ameena and handcuff her to a verandah post, leaving the key on the ground where she could reach it if necessary. Should it not be possible to do this, handcuff her, pretend to strike her on the head so she can fall to the ground as if unconscious. Under all circumstances it must be made to appear that Ameena was overcome and forced to release the captives against her will."

"There are dogs?" one of the men asked.

"We supplied Ameena with drugs which she will add to the dogs' food. They'll sleep soundly through the night."

Outside, the weather had deteriorated. The four men fell into single file with Ashok in the lead. The party climbed the hill sheltering the bungalow and then moved along its crest over a poorly discernible trail. At one point they came to an abrupt halt as a frightened hill deer barked and crashed off through the brush.

"You have a gun?" Ashok turned and asked Monty without slowing their pace.

"Yes," he responded, patting the bulge of his holster.

"Keep it ready, old chap ... " the leader mopped his rain wet face with a large khaki kerchief tied around his neck, before continuing ... "and don't hesitate to use it if the bloody goondas misbehave."

"It' a good gun and I've used it before."

"I happen to know that you're jolly well familiar with automatic arms."

A mountain leopard on the prowl coughed its warning from the hillside below, sending an antlered sambar stampeding across their path.

"Ashok, one thing worries me a bit," Monty confided.

"And what's that?"

"Those two men you tackled tonight, couldn't they have made it to their place and warned of a possible attack by us?"

"Believe me, American, those bastards won't bugger off anywhere tonight. We told them that one of our men would be mucking about in the bushes to shoot the first person to step out of the car before daylight. No, those two blokes were in a bloody funk when we left them stuck in the mud."

Ashok called a brief halt under a large pine tree, checking out last minute instructions on the assault plans. "It's ten minutes to three and we're almost there. From here on we talk in low whispers and let's step quietly. Free up your guns and knives and let's be damned sure that in the dark we don't get excited and start shooting the wrong blokes. If you have the choice, use a knife, it's a lot quieter. I'm the lead man to contact Ameena. The three of you will watch from without the compound gate and get into the fracas only if you're needed. As soon as the two hostages are outside with us, I'll return with Ameena and handcuff her to the verandah post. Any questions?"

"What about this?" One of the men held up a rainsoaked and bloodstained bundle wrapped in newspaper. "You know, the hands."

"Give the blasted things to me when we get there. I'll drop them onto the verandah as a warning."

"I'm not carrying a knife," Monty interjected.

"I take it you want one?" Ashok asked.

"Yes."

"Extra knife anyone?" The leader looked at the two other men.

Shifting the package of dismembered hands, the Pakistani passed over a stiletto to the American.

"Righto lads, let's on with it," Ashok announced in a whisper and stepped ahead on the trail.

As a dike holding back a flooding sea, the meandering brick compound wall stemmed a jungle encroaching from the west side. In a mute warning to would-be trespassers, a line of glass shards impaled in concrete ran along the top of the barrier, like the bony plates cresting the vertebral column of a dinosaur. Although successful in withstanding the onslaught of the forest, the elements over the years had compromised the wall to a point where it no longer posed an obstacle to human penetration. The decaying wooden gate stood fixed in an open position, its lower border locked in mud.

Ashok stationed the three men outside the compound wall beside the gate. From their vantage point, the west side of the building and most of the grounds were in full, if shaded, view. Except for the sound of rain on the roof and the steady dripping of water, the place was eerily quiet.

"Righto, carry on. I'm on my way," Ashok announced in a barely audible whisper. Then crouching low, he stole toward the verandah, a knife in his right hand and an automatic in the other. In a matter of seconds he had faded into the shadow of the building and in an equally short time was recrossing the compound to join his companions. Ameena had been alerted and the amputated hands deposited beside the rear doorsteps.

Doreen awoke to a gentle nudging of her shoulder which, at first, she thought was Mos, but seeing a blanketed form bending over her she jumped out of bed.

"*Hasti, hasti*—Slowly, slowly," a woman's voice spoke softly, as she reached over to awaken Mos and wrap him in a shawl. With both captives fully aroused, Ameena signaled silence with a finger pressed across her lips, and beckoned them to follow. As they passed one of the rooms, someone grunted and mumbled in his sleep, bringing the three to a breathless halt. With quietness again prevailing, they moved forward through a door out onto the verandah. Ameena paused and listened for any indication of trouble, but the house was silent, so she grasped the hands of the two captives ... one on either side ... and started across the compound. Ashok met the escape party halfway.

"Quickly, to the gate," he whispered, shoving Doreen and Mos in that direction. Then propelling Ameena by the arm, he headed for the verandah where he seated her against a pillar and handcuffed both wrists around it, placing the key on the ground near her feet.

"*Bis minut me bhot awaj karo*—In twenty minutes make a lot of noise," Ashok whispered in Ameena's ear before turning to join his group.

Just outside the compound gate, Doreen nestled silently within Monty's encircling arms, trembling from excitement and the wet cold.

"What the hell!" Ashok muttered, as Mos threw aside his shawl and broke from the party to run back across the grounds.

"Coat ... Monty Cha-cha," they heard him cry out as he disappeared into the shadow of the building.

"Oh my dear God!" the American groaned, "he left his coat behind."

"Let's move," Ashok urged, "The lad'll alert the blokes and they'll be on us like a pack of wolves."

Monty, oblivious to the leader's words, gently released Doreen and sprinted after the waif. Before he reached the verandah there was the sound of a shot fired indoors. The raiding party waited, transfixed by the drama. A door slammed loudly, breaking the quiet, and then shouts punctuated by the report of another gun. On Ashok's command the three Pakistanis fanned out over the compound and closed in on the building. Suddenly the large shape of Monty broke out of the shadows, running toward them carrying Mos under his left arm and a gun in the right hand.

"Look out!" Doreen screamed, as someone rushed from the verandah to cut off Monty's escape.

Hearing the warning, the American in one continuous movement laid Mos on the ground and pivoted to face his knife-wielding adversary. With the three Pakistanis rapidly drawing in, Monty feared to use the automatic lest he injure them, so slipped it into his pocket and crouched as a boxer parrying for a breach in his opponent's defense. At precisely the right second, he leaped forward with a shout, knocked the attacker's knife out of his hand and, encircling his neck with one arm, threw him to the ground mortally injured. The snapping

MATT GOLIC 83'

of the man's cervical vertebra resounded through the compound like a pistol shot.

"Let's get out of here pronto," Monty called out, stooping to pick up Mos and running toward the gate where the party joined forces in preparation for the trek back through the jungles.

"How's the lad?" Ashok asked, unable to see details in the darkness under the trees.

"He's dead ... shot through the head." The American's words were mechanical, as if they were trying to disassociate themselves from his inner emotions.

"Oh dear God," Doreen sobbed, clinging to Monty's free arm, "and he was so alive just a minute ago."

"Murdered in cold blood ... an innocent little kid ... " Monty choked up and then cleared his throat to go on ... "the killer received payment in kind ... a bullet through his skull."

"Bloody cads!" Ashok swore bitterly, then turned abruptly to lead at a fast pace over the ridge trail. One of the men followed about fifty yards behind, covering as a rear guard. Biting cold rain, fast turning into sleet, was driving into their faces as the wind increased in tempo. At Monty's suggestion, Doreen followed close in his steps, both as a partial shield against the stinging droplets, as well as to keep her near at hand for assistance over rough terrain. At a section where the path leveled and straightened, she moved ahead beside the American and held onto his hand. Smiling up into his face she watched its icy hardness melt into tenderness.

"Did he get ... " the rest of her words were drowned out by the storm.

Monty understood and nodded, turning so she could see the coat draped over Mos' body, its lapel held firmly in the death grip of the child's pale fingers. Doreen swallowed again and again as her throat tightened painfully and tears flowed mixing with the rain coursing down her cheeks.

Drawing her close, almost lifting her off the ground, Monty leaned down to kiss her lips and whisper, "My sweet, you're either crying or it's raining salt water, but in either case, I love you." She nodded up into his face, holding her lower lip tight between her teeth, afraid to trust her voice in a reply.

The party was about twenty minutes into the return march when Ashok called a halt. Because of the worsening force of the elements and in deference to the female member, he had tempered their pace. Permitting the rear guard to catch up, he assured himself of the fitness of his party, giving particular attention to Doreen's welfare. Satisfied with the results of his investigation, he announced, "Although the rain and wind will pretty thoroughly erase our trail, I'm choosing to be extra cautious as we get nearer to our headquarters and we'll be crossing over to follow another ridge for the rest of the way.''

The new route offered less of a recognizable path, in fact Ashok in the lead had to open up routes through heavy brush over long sections of the way. The party's progress slowed and the five members pushed to maintain the pace. Leaning forward against the soaking wind, stooping under branches, stepping high over fallen logs and fighting to preserve her balance on slippery terrain, began to take its toll of Doreen's endurance. Her legs, numb with fatigue, began to move mechanically as if they were separate entities and no longer under the control of her brain. Monty, sensing the cumulative effects of her emotional and physical exhaustion, halted for a moment, freed a leather strap from his gun holster, buckled it over his belt in the back and placed the loop in her hand.

"Doreen," he said, raising his voice against the wind, "we've not much farther to go. Hang onto the strap and let me pull you along. Please do this, will you?"

She nodded and smiled up at him through the slanting rain and sleet pelting her face. The noise of the storm drowned out a happy smothered sob birthed by the realization that now she could draw on Monty's strength.

Chapter Seventeen

Aisha was seated by the fireplace reading a book when the party entered, their shoes squashing noisily with each step and water dripping from soaked clothes into pools about their feet. Faces were taut with fatigue brought on by the psychological tensions, sheer physical exertion and penetrating wet cold. For a moment the room fell silent except for the sound of the driving wind and rain outside. The Himalayan snow leopard, lying on the hearth, rose on its front paws and surveyed the intruders suspiciously.

"Splendid!" Aisha exclaimed, throwing the book aside and rising from her chair to advance toward the bedraggled raiders. Halfway across the room she paused, hands on hips, to survey the group more closely, giving particular attention to Doreen. Then seeing the bundle in Monty's arm, she pointed and asked, "The lad's asleep?"

The American stared at her sadly and shook his head. "He's dead . . . shot during the escape."

"Oh Allah," she groaned with a deep sigh. Reaching forward, she took the body wrapped in its sopping wet coat and gently laid it on the floor before the fire.

"Aisha, this is Miss Bruce," Monty said quietly, taking Doreen's wet and cold hand in his.

The Muslim woman stared wordlessly at the Anglo-Indian for a brief moment, then broke out into a friendly smile and admitted, "She is beautiful, American. Even the merciless elements haven't been able to erase her beauty."

"You're most kind," Doreen replied.

"But there you are shivering and miserable," Aisha observed, taking Doreen's other hand in hers and calling for the maid, who responded immediately. "Quickly now, get out of those wet clothes and return for some hot drinks. Sorry, not enough toothbrushes to go around but there are neem twigs . . . just as good . . . in the washrooms. Nahid here will direct you to quarters for the changes." She pointed at the servant girl who led the entourage out through the curtained door.

A few minutes later, straying back and sitting on the white sheepskin rugs scattered about the fireplace, the party members were served hot chocolate drinks, replenishing and warming tired bodies. Ashok recounted the details of the raid, stopping from time to time to sip noisily at the nourishing liquid. A row of shoes were propped up against the bricks around the hearth, wisps of steamy moisture rising from the wet leather. At Aisha's command, Nahid had taken down Doreen's braids and was drying her hair briskly with warmed towels.

"So you disobeyed my orders, eh?" The question was directed to the American.

Monty nodded in admission of the fact.

"Why did you take such a risk?" Aisha persisted.

"Why did I do it? Because I'd come to love Mos." He stared disconsolately at the waif's body wrapped in the coat.

"American, you have a warm heart ... a tender heart ... " her voice drifted off into silence.

Monty remained quiet, his attention still absorbed by the lifeless form before the fire.

"But according to Ashok you're frightfully good at committing mayhem," Aisha remarked, throwing Monty an admiring look.

"Only to protect the lives of our party." he responded defensively.

"No offense, American, no offense," she repeated, and added as an aside, "Might just be asking you to train my men in hand-to-hand combat."

"Your men are plenty good," Monty conceded with a wave.

The Muslim woman turned to Doreen and murmured in barely audible words, "I find it hard to believe. The American's not only courageous and tender of heart but humble as well."

Nodding in acquiescence, the Anglo-Indian returned a shy smile.

"Aisha ... I've a favor to ask." Monty's eyes pled compliance.

"Another favor?" She observed the deep sincerity of his request.

"Would you see that Mos has a proper Muslim burial? The kid's real name's Abdul. Never did know his family name."

Aisha paused to cough self-consciously. Monty watched as her eyes brimmed with tears. Gaining control of her emotions, she replied in a subdued voice, "The lad will be buried as you have asked with Islamic rites recited by an imam."

"And I'll stand good for any expenses involved."

"American, you've just insulted me," she retorted, half crying and half laughing.

"One last thing."

She nodded him on.

"Please bury him in that coat. He was so proud of it."

The room stood silent as Nahid the maid replenished the fire with wood and turned the shoes for different exposures to the drying heat. Moving from one stockinged foot to another, the Himalayan leopard made the circle warily sniffing each individual.

Aisha rose with a sigh and suggested that Ashok take the American and his freed hostage friend back to the Red Chariot while it was yet dark. She insisted that the two guests wear the dry jump suits just put on, ordering Nahid to bundle the wet discarded outfits to make them more portable.

Holding Doreen by the hand, Monty stepped toward Aisha. "We're deeply indebted. I'll never be able to settle with you for this."

"Poppycock, American, you've already repaid me many times over. And dash it all, someday I may be calling on you for help."

"It's yours for the asking," Monty responded gratefully, walking over and stooping to brush the tousled damp hair off the dead boy's forehead. Then reaching over and borrowing Ashok's dagger, he cut a button off the wet coat. "Just something to remember my side-kick . . . " his grief choked him into silence.

Impulsively, Aisha took Doreen into her arms and whispered, "Take good care of the American. We're both in love with him but you've won out. You will keep my secret . . . at least until after you're married?"

"Don't worry, it'll be safe . . . your secret. Thanks for saving my life. May Allah preserve you for a long future of happiness," Doreen whispered, placing a kiss on her cheek.

Ashok and one other Pakistani accompanied the two of them over the tortuous path down the hill. Maintaining a balance on the wet slippery trail was the major physical effort of the descent. With surprising verve, Doreen had recuperated from her earlier state of physical exhaustion. The rain continued unabated, although the wind appeared to be ameliorating. It was still dark as the party reached the hard road just outside Baramula. Inside the compound, the Red Chariot waited in the splattering downpour. After brief but warm farewells, Monty and Doreen climbed into the welcome shelter of the vehicle. Throwing the wet bundle of their ski suits into the back seat, they started down the road toward Srinagar. The car heater functioned superbly, blunting the cutting cold. Doreen slipped off a plastic rain hood Hahid had fitted over her head and shook out her hair to cascade over both shoulders. With painstaking detail, each of them recounted the events of the past twenty-four hours, pausing at intervals for requested clarifications. As they drove over the bridge where Monty had been picked up by the Pakistanis, he wondered about the status of the two amputees. A barely perceptible light of dawn seeped through the clouds as the Red Chariot approached the outskirts of Srinagar.

"My sweet . . . " Monty turned to kiss the top of Doreen's head resting against his shoulder, before going on . . . "You're a mighty brave one. I'm so proud of you . . . the way you've held up under this terrible stress. And, darling, you're probably aware of this, but let me go on record again. I'm hopelessly in love with you."

She looked up into his face and smiled through tears, unable to trust her voice. Finally, after swallowing hard she responded through trembling lips, "I'm in the same . . . the same fix . . . hopelessly in love with you. And to think ... we almost lost each other last night.''

Drawing her close with one arm, he looked down into her tear-brimmed eyes and observed with a broad grin, ''Heart's water.''

''Heart's water?'' she repeated perplexedly.

''Your tears. Grandmother always called tears 'heart's water'.''

''Your 'glory be' grandmother?''

''Yup. My 'glory be' grandmother.'' Doreen joined in Monty's laughter.

For several minutes they drove in silence, their attention absorbed by the early morning Srinagar traffic.

''You'll miss him, I know,'' Doreen broke in quietly.

''Mos?''

She looked up and nodded.

''Funny how you can become attached to an abandoned and homeless ragamuffin. Actually I'd been worrying about what to do with the little tyke when I left for the States. Even gave serious thought to taking him with me. Well, that problem had a tragic resolution. No longer have to worry about ... '' Monty broke off, unable to complete what he was saying.

Splashing along the wet streets, the Red Chariot rolled through the town on toward Dal Lake and the Kashmir Princess. A fine drizzle had replaced the night's heavy rain.

''Must get this information to Captain Narayan pronto,'' Monty confided. ''We'll call Bruce and Maureen from the houseboat. God, are they ever going to be relieved! Prem sounded tight as a drum over the phone yesterday when I told him of my plans to meet with Aisha.''

''And you weren't tight as a drum?'' Doreen countered with a teasing chuckle.

Monty laughed. ''You can bet your bottom dollar I was scared as all get out ... '' he turned and stared at her seriously before continuing ... ''scared mostly that I might lose you.''

''I've never been as frightened as I have over the past twenty-four hours.'' Doreen's words were barely audible.

''I received a threatening note yesterday,'' Monty confided and proceeded to quote the message.

''What hellish blackmail!'' Doreen broke in, then added quietly, ''I'm glad you didn't have to make that decision.''

''So am I,'' he groaned. ''There just wasn't an alternative. I had to get you away from those kidnappers.''

The mongrel houseboat dog barked everyone awake seconds after the Red Chariot came to a halt beside the Kashmir Princess. Fatima wept happily as she led Doreen by hand across the gangplank. Rustum collected the bundle of wet ski suits in the back seat and carried them aboard to dry. After a warm and emotion-filled welcome, Prem and Ian turned over their cabins as dressing rooms where cold and clammy clothes were exchanged for ill-fitting but dry ones.

With its long extension cord, the telephone was carried out to the dining table where a call was placed for the Duncans in Gulmarg. After several irritating delays, a sleepy operator finally made the proper connection.

"Doctor Bruce Duncan here." The words were clipped and taut.

"Captain Narayan . . . good news."

"Yes?"

"Doreen's safe and unharmed."

Prem heard the Doctor shout the message to Maureen, who sobbed, "Oh, thank God!"

"Where is she?" Bruce asked expectantly.

"She's here with us on the Kashmir Princess, and we'd better keep her here for her safety, at least for the time being. And Bruce . . . are you still on the line?"

"Sorry old chap. Just lost my voice for the moment."

"*Accha* . . . You've Monty to thank for Doreen's rescue."

"The American, eh?"

"Uh-huh."

"We'll be down to see all of you today and bring Doreen's things."

"Why don't both of you join us here for tiffin around noon. And, Doctor, bring a vial of antivenin with you please."

"Righto. Be seeing you shortly. Cheerio." Bruce Duncan's voice carried a sense of profound relief.

Rustum and Fatima began their clattering activities in a prelude to breakfast or *chota hazri*, as they preferred to call this first meal of the day. Just who assumed which particular responsibility in this team effort was never quite clear to an observer and probably never was repeated in exactly the same way for any two consecutive meals. With the arrival of a large steaming kettle, the tantalizing aroma of coffee pervaded the dining room, blending shortly thereafter with that of bread toasting on a wire mesh overlying charcoals in a brazier. Fanning the glowing ingots and turning the browning slices, was one duty which usually fell to Fatima's lot.

Monty was the first to join the C.I.D. trio, followed shortly by Doreen. The American's borrowed clothes gave the appearance of an outfit distorted by substantial shrinkage with hands and feet protruding in an ungainly fashion far beyond the cuffs. On the other hand, exactly the opposite was Doreen's situation, with a petite form almost lost within the ample folds of her appropriated clothes. After an instant of amused staring, both broke out into uncontrolled laughter joined by the others, including Rustum and Fatima.

At Captain Narayan's suggestion, they all moved up to the table where they were served coffee; hot cracked wheat porridge flooded with the white cream of buffalo milk and generously sprinkled with raw brown sugar; toast in all stages of fruition, from slight singeing to charring, spread with butter and layered with bitter marmalade; and fresh apples.

Slowly, between spoonfuls of porridge, bites of toast and sips of coffee, Monty and Doreen recited their stories. First came the details of the kidnapping from Nedou's in Gulmarg and the sequential incarceration with Mos. Following Monty's modest narration of the raid, Doreen insisted on embellishing the action, describing the American's heroism in entering the building to retrieve the Muslim orphan's body and the destruction of the would-be interceptor in the compound. A barrage of questions and answers filled in the gaps until the chronicle was complete.

"The Hakim's riddle about the hooded bird," Ian observed with a knowing look, "a tattooed falcon."

"This Aisha ... I take it she's an intelligent leader?" Prem asked.

"I'll say," Monty replied without hesitation, "that gal's mighty bright. Right, Doreen?" He looked at her for confirmation.

"Rather!" She nodded vigorously in agreement.

"We may need the help of those Pakistanis," Ian ventured, adding quickly, "unofficially of course."

"Precisely," Prem interjected, "and I'm not too proud to ask for help ... unofficially of course." He broke out in a self-conscious laugh which was joined by the others.

"That European who came into your room with the Achmed bugger, could you guess as to where he was from?" Ian asked.

Doreen shook her head. "He wasn't American or French and could have been German, Scandinavian or even Russian. His voice was husky, sounded like he might have had a bit of a cold."

"Ian, would you move in with Sardar so we can let Doreen have your quarters?" the Captain proposed.

Both men nodded.

"I'll have to be gone overnight," Monty said apologetically, "be back early in the morning."

Prem shook a coffee spoon in the American's direction and cautioned, "You're more than a bit daft if you don't button up your security until it hurts. Last night you killed two of their men and those bloody bastards neither forget nor forgive. Dash it all man, why the hell don't you lie low for a couple of days?"

Monty scowled and shook his head. "Thanks for the advice, Captain, but I have an obligation ... must go."

Doreen's hand reached over to cover his and her eyes pled with him. He leaned across and touched the top of her head with his lips.

"Be back tomorrow ... and ... and thanks for everything," Monty said as he rose from the table, "especially for watching her." Doreen stood to be encircled by his arms and kissed. Picking up his bundle of wet clothes, the American headed for the Red Chariot. She accompanied him out onto the rear deck and waved him off toward Srinagar.

"Your brother and Maureen will be having tiffin with us," Prem announced as Doreen stepped back inside. "I've an appointment with a chap at Nedou's this morning, but I shan't be gone all that long."

"I'll ride over to the hotel with you," Ian proposed, "and muck around there checking out this bloke, James Appleton."

"*Accha*. And Sardar I want you to hold things down here on the Kashmir Princess. Don't forget things are getting a bit tight. Cover the telephone and in an emergency you can get me at Nedou's."

"Jolly good, sir."

Prem walked over to Doreen, who was standing warming herself over a brazier, and took her by the hand, triggering a sighing sob. "I'm sorry ... a bit childish ... " her words drifted off as she blinked hard to stem the flow of tears.

The Captain took her into his arms and patted her heaving shoulders. "My dear child, you've been through hell ... enough to break down a seasoned campaigner. Please lie down and make up for lost sleep. Fatima will have your room ready shortly."

A half hour later, Prem and Ian, with Rustum at the wheel, drove off toward the city. There was a lull in the rain and drizzle, although the clouds continued to scramble nervously toward the mountains in the northeast.

"So you got an appointment with Vandermeer?" Ian said, more as a statement of fact than a question.

"The bounder didn't seem all that happy but I used a bit of legitimate pressure and he finally capitulated. Admitted that the roads were too muddy to patrol."

Rustum pulled into the hotel compound. The two officers jumped out and climbed up onto the verandah.

"*Accha*. Cheerio Ian. Carry on old chap."

"I'll keep Rustum informed as to my whereabouts." Ian threw an informal salute and walked off toward the hotel registration desk. As he walked past the dining room door, he caught a glimpse of Montague Brown and Maya Reznikoff seated at a table, engaged in conversation over cups of coffee.

Chapter Eighteen

"Come in, do come in out of the damned cold," Colonel Wilhelm Vandermeer's words boomed out as he stood almost filling the width of the doorway to Nedou's room five. He was dressed in mufti with slacks and a knitted woolen sweater. Accepting the invitation, Captain Prem Narayan stepped inside on the heels of the Dutchman.

"Hope this isn't an inconvenience, my coming here," the Indian apologized.

"Not really." The words were spoken without particular enthusiasm, as the Colonel waved his guest to a chair beside an electric heater resting on the floor. "A terrible mess . . . roads . . . they're impassable."

"Rather," the Captain concurred, "damned unusual weather for this time of the year. The monsoon should be over, don't you know."

"Try one of these?" The Dutchman held out an open box of select Cuban cigars.

"No thanks." He waved a hand in negating the offer. "Never been a weakness of mine . . . cigars." While speaking, he reached for his cloisonne case of Camels.

During these preliminary exchanges of pleasantries, Prem Narayan studied his host, whom he had never met. Obviously a man of authoritative stance, Wilhelm Vandermeer spoke as one versed in issuing orders. His blue-gray eyes were cold and discerning, giving the impression that their owner rarely displayed his emotions. A trim and pointed goatee, characterized in India as a "Pancham" George or George Fifth beard, camouflaged a receding chin. Longer strands of graying hair were combed over the top of his head, from the left side, covering a balding area. Prem sensed a look of resentment on the part of the Dutchman and interpreted this as being directed against the Indian authorities because of their interference in his activities.

"So you're a part of the Criminal Investigation Department vorking on the so-called cobra murders?" Wilhelm Vandermeer spoke from within a cloud of smoke brought about by the lighting of a fresh cigar.

Hoping to draw his host out in conversation, Prem Narayan chose not to reply verbally and merely nodded his head in assent.

"And vat is it you expect from me?" The Colonel projected a defensive attitude.

"Your United Nations Observer Team makes the rounds of territory not always accessible to us."

The Dutchman laughed mirthlessly as he rolled the tip of his cigar in the ash tray. "You mean our patrolling of the Cease Fire Line might turn up something connected vith the murders?" He tried to sound incredulous.

"That's exactly what I mean," the Captain replied firmly.

"But my team gives attention only to the Kashmir-Pakistan boundary. Ve're not involved in running down criminals." He shook his head and threw up both hands in disavowal.

"Then I'm to take it you've come across nothing unusual ... nothing that might relate in any way to the cobra killings?"

"Nothing." His reply was definite.

A ringing telephone interrupted the conversation. The Colonel reached over to pick up the instrument on an adjacent table. Sensing a possible desire for privacy on the part of his host, the Captain stood and started for the door. The Dutchman waved him back to his seat.

"Vandermeer, here," he addressed the mouthpiece in a low voice, then for a time listened, occasionally grunting and nodding in affirmation.

Prem picked up a newspaper and slowly thumbed through its pages, all the while giving close attention to the Colonel's words and reactions.

"Good God!" the Dutchman suddenly exploded, then muttered a series of incomprehensive words, finally raising his voice to exclaim, "Blithering idiots ... bloody fools!" With these expletives, he gave an angry grunt and slammed the receiver down.

"Problems?" The Captain's voice was solicitous.

Vandermeer chose not to reply but sat glowering at the telephone, his face suffused and perspiring. For a period both men sat in an uncomfortable silence.

"You are acquainted with the American, James Appleton?" Prem broached the subject cautiously, hoping not to trigger another outburst.

"Ya. I know him." The colonel struggled to regain his composure.

"He's not a part of your U.N. force here?" the Captain asked with an assumed naivete.

"No, no connection." He shook his head in a vigorous denial.

"But according to my information you've not only been conferring with the chap, but on occasion he's been riding patrol with you over the Cease Fire Line."

"Ya, ya. Quite true. He's writing a book on the Indo-Pakistan border conflict. Ve only are giving him information for his book."

"So the blighter's writing a book." Prem pretended an ignorance of the fact.

"This Appleton, he is American diplomatic, ya?"

"I'm not certain of his diplomatic status," The Captain shrugged his shoulders with a studied vagueness.

"And you know the other American ... Montague Brown?"

Prem nodded as he stubbed out his cigarette and reached into his case for a fresh Camel. "Of course you must know him. He rooms right next to you here."

Vandermeer grunted acquiescence, pointing his cigar toward the adjacent wall.

"Any idea what the chap's doing in Kashmir?"

The Dutchman's stare coldly probed the Indian's eyes for a moment as he slowly drew on his cigar. "Very close mouthed ... friendly but says very little. Listed here in the registry as a geologist." His words projected incredulity.

"Then you don't think the bloke's studying rocks?"

Vandermeer gave out a sarcastic laugh and shook his head.

"Colonel, have you or your men in patrolling run across the so-called Pakistani dacoits?"

"No, ve have not."

"Do you believe these dacoits exist ... led by a woman?"

The Dutchman carefully flicked his cigar ashes into the tray, then shrugged his shoulders noncommittally. "Bands of people go back and forth across the border, political and economic refugees. Some may become dacoits." He again shrugged his shoulders.

A loud single knock on the door brought Colonel Vandermeer to his feet to admit a man whom Prem recognized immediately as James Appleton. He wore a black eye patch on the left side.

"Am I intruding?" the American asked hesitantly, looking back and forth at the two men.

"Meet Captain Narayan of the C.I.D.," the Dutchman said, without answering his question.

"Pleasure to meet you, Captain," Appleton greeted the Indian officer with an extended hand, and went on to say, "Just had a visit with your Lieutenant McVey. He's got plenty up here." The American tapped his forehead with an index finger.

Seeing the eye patch, Prem Narayan's thoughts flashed back to the Hakim's darkened room and the second of the riddles: Beware of the unseeing eye that hides a festering hatred.

"And vat brings you here?" the Colonel asked, stabbing his cigar in the direction of Appleton. "Thought you were in Delhi."

"Just got in on the morning flight. Rough flying from Amritsar here."

"No patrolling today ... roads are in a bloody mess," Vandermeer grumbled.

"How's the book coming?" Prem interjected with a disarming smile.

The Captain was seated on the left side of Appleton, forcing the American to turn in his chair and face his questioner. "So you've heard I'm writing a book?" He sounded surprised.

Prem nodded. "How's it doing?"

"Pretty well ... have all the facts collected. The manuscript is almost completed."

"You're getting information from both sides of the border, Pakistan as well as India?" Prem persisted in his questioning.

"Absolutely, absolutely," Appleton repeated with emphasis and continued, "This book will be factual, very accurate, a chapter of Indian history."

"Being an historical buff of sorts, I shall look forward to reading it. By the way, what's the title of the book?" Prem threw a questioning look at the American.

Caught off guard, Appleton's face flushed and he mumbled in a barely audible voice, "Several titles in mind but I'm not sure which I'll ultimately choose."

"Tremendous emotional turmoil in those early days of partition. Things were touch and go during the first few hours after Jinnah's raiders invaded the Vale of Kashmir," Prem recalled, endeavoring to assess the American's mastery of the facts.

"Oh ... yes ... yes. August of 1947 when the Pakistani troops fought their way to the very outskirts of Srinagar."

"You must have been thinking of the day of Indian independence which was midnight of the fifteenth of August. The invasion of Kashmir was in October," the Captain countered.

"Of course you're right. Date just slipped my mind," he replied self-consciously.

"And actually the invaders were Pathans. No Pakistani regulars were involved in that initial push on the twenty-seventh of October. Jinnah was using the irregulars to pull his acorns out of the fire."

"Quite right. I should have known better than to trust my memory on such details. But let me assure you all of these facts are accurately recorded in my manuscript." The American was showing signs of embarrassment, his single shifty eye focusing on and off the Captain's face.

"Of course you must have recorded what delayed the Pathans?" Prem casually pushed his attack.

Appleton hesitated before nodding a weak affirmation as he squirmed uneasily in his chair.

"They, the Pathans, made a crucial mistake by pausing to sack and loot the convent of the Franciscan Missionaries of Mary in Baramula, raping and killing the nuns and their patients. This delay on the part of the raiders gave the First Sikh Regiment the critical hours needed to secure the Srinagar airfield during the early dawn of Monday, October twenty-seventh."

Colonel Vandermeer was observing the ruthless cross-examination with a detached air, almost of amusement, as if he actually was enjoying the American's discomfiture.

"Drawing the boundary between Pakistan and India ... my God what a thankless task," Prem continued his grilling, "and what was the poor blighter's name, the Englishman who redrew the map of this vast subcontinent?" Pretending a lapse of memory, the Captain directed a questioning look at Appleton who sat glowering with his lips pursed. "Oh yes," he picked up again as if he had just remembered the name, "Radcliffe, Sir Cyril Radcliffe."

Realizing his exposure, the American made no further effort to reply and sat staring balefully at his inquisitor out of the single eye.

"Oh well, I'm certain you'll have all of this in your book and don't forget I shall be looking forward to reading it." Prem's words dripped with sarcasm. He had exploded the myth of Appleton's authorship.

"Sorry," Colonel Vandermeer announced rising and looking at his wrist watch, "I have an appointment to keep."

"*Accha* ... I thank you for giving me this time. The meeting has been most fortunate for me. I've learned a lot." Prem shook hands with both men, staring back into the American's eye and recognizing in its depth a hint of fear. Then, with his hand on the doorknob, the Captain turned to announce, "Anyone for Pahalgam tonight? I'll be driving up there solo after dinner." He paused briefly for a possible reply and hearing none, stepped out onto the verandah.

Ian was seated in the jeep waiting for Prem and soon the three were on their way back to the Kashmir Princess. A light drizzle had started, just enough to warrant the use of windshield wipers.

"So you met Appleton?" Prem asked, turning to face his associate.

"Fellow's a phony, as the Americans say." Ian grimaced and shook his head disparagingly. "Tried his damndest to impress me with his past positions with the United States Department of State."

"Remember the Hakim's riddle?"

"The unseeing eye that hides a festering hatred."

"That single seeing eye was full of festering hatred when I left just a couple of minutes ago."

"What about Vandermeer?"

"The chap's a bit of an enigma ... quite noncommittal really. Ambivalent about the Pakistani dacoits. I've a notion he knows what Monty's doing. Not much love lost between him and Appleton."

"What about the book Appleton's writing?"

Prem exploded in a loud laugh. "The bloody fool's not writing a book, all the talk is just a facade. Wish I knew exactly what the bloke's doing here."

"Did he admit to this?" Ian asked with raised eyebrows.

"I rather brutally cross-examined him on the border history and the blighter displayed an abysmal ignorance of the subject."

Sardar Khan met the Captain and Lieutenant on the rear deck of the houseboat. The morning had been unusually quiet, not even a telephone call. Bruce and Maureen had not arrived as yet. Doreen had slept most of the morning and still was asleep. Fatima was scurrying about setting the table in preparation for tiffin.

"As soon as the two of you are washed up, join me in my quarters," Prem proposed, "I've an important action to discuss."

Rustum followed the Captain into his cabin with a bucket of fresh charcoal to replenish the brazier. Prem was stretched out on the bed, fully dressed except for his shoes, when the two associates joined him.

"We know at least something about the cobra killers," the Captain began, after Ian and Sardar were seated, "but as yet we have no pakka evidence. Monty and Doreen have seen a couple of the goondas, in fact the American liquidated two. However a shrewd barrister could tear that meager evidence to shreds. And of course we're in no position to pull in the Pakistani dacoits as witnesses. Although we might ferret out local people as supporting evidence, such as the milkwoman Lakshmi or Ameena the maid, they would hardly dare testify for fear of their lives. Don't you agree?"

Both Ian and Sardar nodded soberly. The cabin was quiet while Prem selected a Camel, rolled it gently back and forth between his finger tips and lit it. Blowing a symmetrical smoke ring at the ceiling, he watched it spiral upward.

"How about deliberately precipitating a crisis in order to collect substantial evidence?" Ian suggested, breaking the silence.

"Precisely!" Prem approved, sitting up on the edge of the bed. "You know the old saying, 'If the mountain will not come to Mohammed, Mohammed will go to the mountain'."

"You're talking about purposely falling into the hands of the killers?" Ian sounded dubious.

"We've had the cobra antivenin . . . a fact the bastards don't know . . . " Prem picked a shred of tobacco off his lower lip before continuing . . . "so why not beard the lion in his den?"

"Righto, let's have with it." Ian projected his excitement.

"*Accha.*" The Captain held up his hand for attention. "We have the bait for the trap and I am that bait."

"You can't be serious. I just don't . . . " Ian began.

"Hold it," Prem cut in firmly, "and hear me through."

The Lieutenant frowned but nodded in acquiescence.

"By virtue of the fact that I'm the senior officer in this investigative team, my rating as desirable bait runs quite high. Then there's another factor in our consideration . . . and you'll have to excuse me if this sounds presumptuous . . . I've had more experience in situations such as this than either of you."

"But, sir, why not two baits?" Sardar Khan proposed.

"Can't afford two of us incapacitated. You'll both be needed to work from the outside. So, based on the probability of success in such a mission, I must be the bait . . . and alone.'' Prem brought his fist down into the palm of his hand with a decisive finality.

"And what about our parts in this . . . this trap?'' Ian asked.

"I'll be getting to that, but first let me share a few thoughts. We may have to put out our bait several times before it's taken, sort of a trial and error probing. My first action will be tonight. We may find out what role or roles Vandermeer and Appleton play in the cobra murders. This morning in the hearing of both these men I casually dropped the word that after dinner tonight I'd be driving by myself to Pahalgam. It's my intention to do exactly that. And if this doesn't work we'll look for other potentially inquisitive ears.''

"Such as?'' Ian broke in.

"Parkozian would be a good one.'' Prem grimly scanned the faces of his two associates.

"And?'' Ian persisted.

"Baldev Raj, Deputy Superintendent of the Srinagar Police.''

"Really, sir?'' The Sergeant Major evoked surprise.

Prem nodded. "The man worries me a bit. He's suddenly become antagonistic to Ali Aurangzeb, for no understandable reason, and is showing an inordinate interest in the cobra killings. Sardar, get to your friend on the police force here and see what the hell's going on, eh?''

"Jolly good, sir, I shall do the needful.''

For a moment Ian McVey and Sarder Khan sat in silence absorbing the implications of what Prem Narayan had just announced.

"We'll give you back up tonight . . . follow a safe distance in another vehicle,'' the Lieutenant proposed, breaking the quiet.

The Captain shook his head. "Can't take the chance of scaring them off. I'll have to be on my own. Shan't resist capture too efficiently.''

"The bastards'll hold you for ransom,'' Ian muttered.

"Precisely!'' Prem countered. "While negotiations are going on, we have time to round up the cads. This will be where the two of you'll come in. And let me add, there'll be no ransom . . . it's against government policy.''

"Dash it all, you make me feel like a blithering idiot, sitting on the outside of this action,'' Ian groaned.

"My dear chap, you'll both have plenty of action once the bait's taken.''

"And sir, what about Lieutenant Aurangzeb?'' Sardar asked.

"I'll be putting in a call to him right after tiffin. He'll know about my Pahalgam trip tonight. We must keep him informed. Please take note of this . . . '' Prem stared for a moment out through the louvered window before going on . . . "under no circumstances must any move in my support be made unless I fail to show up here for breakfast in the morning.''

"Why so late ... I mean Pahalgam's not all that far away? If nothing happens, you should be back here easily by midnight," Ian questioned.

"Don't want to set off the trap until the prey is actually snared. And finally, should I fall into their hands, Ian will take over. Don't forget to inform Pritham Singh in Delhi immediately."

"Damn ... I hate to see you walk into that gang of assassins!" Ian burst out angrily.

"We've played with much stickier wickets than these," Prem said with an encouraging chuckle.

Rustum knocked on the cabin door to announce the arrival of the Duncans. The three men walked out into the dining room to welcome the newcomers. Doreen, awakened by the happy greetings, quickly dressed and joined the assemblage. As the emotion-packed conversation quieted, Prem called Bruce Duncan aside.

"Doctor, I need your advice," the Captain solicited.

"Carry on." Bruce nodded.

"If I were to take another dose of antivenin would my immunity to the cobra venom be increased significantly?"

"Rather. Quite some increased. But why the question?" A puzzled frown crossed the Doctor's face. "Are you expecting immediate exposure, I mean exposure to a cobra?"

"Quite possibly."

"The three of you?"

Prem shook his head. "Just me."

"I have the antivenin as you requested," the Doctor reported, stooping down and picking up his medical bag.

"*Accha.* Let's have done with it," the Captain proposed, leading the way to his cabin.

Directly after tiffin, Bruce and Maureen Duncan returned to Gulmarg, happy in the comforting assurance that Doreen would be kept under C.I.D. surveillance aboard the Kashmir Princess. Sardar Khan spent the afternoon checking with friends at the Srinagar police headquarters, delving into the activities of the Deputy Superintendent, Baldev Raj. Ian used the official jeep to run down several possible leads on James Appleton. Prem shut himself up in his cabin, after making certain that Doreen was comfortable, and began his report for Delhi. He covered the abduction and Monty's rescue efforts with the assistance of the Pakistani dacoits, as well as his interviews with Colonel Vandermeer and James Appleton. Having completed his account of activities, he turned his attention to compiling a letter for his wife Bubli, a particularly tender message in the light of his perilous project, the hazards of which he did not divulge.

That night, as the dinner dishes were being cleared, Doreen excused herself, explaining that she planned to turn in early. "Can't seem to get enough sleep,'' she apologized.

The three men pulled their chairs away from the table and rearranged them around a brazier. Ian went through his meticulous routine of pipe lighting while his associates watched with amused tolerance. Very soon a cloud of tobacco smoke gathered about the Lieutenant's head as evidence of the successful completion of his ritual.

Prem heaved a sigh and turned to face Sardar Khan. "Did you find out anything mucking around the local police department?"

The Sergeant Major nodded solemnly. "My friends are saying Baldev Raj is good police officer. He is brave ... respected by policemen ... but now is much worried about cobra murders."

"Any particular reason why?" Ian asked.

"He is thinking some official is working with the cobra killers ... perhaps their leader he is."

"The hell you say!" Ian exploded with a dubious shake of his head. "What makes the bloke think so?"

"Information ... official information ... going to the goondas."

"Does he have any idea as to who the traitor might be?" Ian persisted.

"My police friends are thinking Baldev Raj might be knowing."

"I'll be damned," Ian muttered reflectively, "the chap could've at least shared the information with us."

Prem snorted, "Not on your life if the blighter can disadvantage the C.I.D. with some personal sleuthing accolade."

"Probably so," Ian admitted grudgingly.

"Good work, Sardar," the Captain commended and turned to ask the Lieutenant, "What did you pick up?"

Ian was in the midst of tamping down the tobacco in the bowl of his pipe and drawing short puffs of smoke. After a bout of coughing, he cleared his throat to say, "Phone call to Delhi brought information on Appleton as well as Maya Reznikoff."

"Jolly good." Prem raised his eyebrows expectantly.

"Talked to a contact who attended a series of lectures with me several years ago on police intelligence. We've been good friends ever since. He's now the Indian liaison with Interpol. You probably know him, Ram Singh."

Prem nodded. "Know him well. In fact I just finished a case in which we worked together, espionage aboard a foreign freighter. Good man that Ram Singh. Been with the International Criminal Police Organization or Interpol for quite a few years ... anti-drug section."

"Well, Appleton's on their list."

"On their list for what?"

"Smuggling hard drugs. Bugger's been on and off their list ever since he was booted out of the American Embassy in Moscow. Currently Interpol's hot on his trail."

"I'll be damned," Prem swore softly.

"Interpol's in close touch about this with Europe and North America. Drug shipments seem to end up in Canada and the United States."

"Exactly what's the bloke shipping and from where?"

"Heroin out of Afghanistan. Ram Singh says some of the stuff may be coming from Iran into Afghanistan."

"And who are Appleton's contacts here in Kashmir?"

Ian shook his head. "He wouldn't say."

"Did you bring up the Colonel . . . Vandermeer?"

"Yes, but Ram Singh shut up like a clam. Incidentally, Interpol is aware of Dowry of Death."

"You mentioned Maya Reznikoff," Prem reminded Ian.

"Maya Reznikoff is known to the Interpol staff. She is a White Russian who hates the current Moscow powers, bitterly hates them according to Ram Singh. Her grandparents, relatives of the Czar, were disposed of in an ignominious manner during the early days of the revolution. Her mother somehow escaped the purge and fled to France where Maya was born. The Moscow O.G.P.U. infiltrated the White Russian colony in Paris and murdered her mother before the daughter's eyes. So she now directs this bitter hatred in the discomfiture of the Moscow bear. The invasion of Afghanistan provided a specific opportunity for venting her wrath. Reznikoff is her pseudonym. She's married to a French industrialist . . . Citroen cars . . . and has ample resources."

"And what's she doing to discomfit the Soviet bear?" Prem asked.

"Maya's an important backer of the Dowry of Death."

"*Accha*," the Captain muttered under his breath.

"That means that Monty in some way must be linked to it . . . I mean the Dowry of Death," Ian suggested.

"You're probably right." Prem stared abstractedly at the cigarette in his fingers for a moment. "I only wish we knew exactly what the link was."

"Sir . . . " Sardar Khan broke in quietly . . . "maybe the drug trade is touching the cobra murderers?"

"Precisely what crossed my mind," Prem responded, "but I doubt there's any connection between the Dowry of Death activities and this drug traffic."

"None," Ian interrupted quickly, "Ram Singh intimated as much . . . I mean that there was no connection."

"You know, it's a possibility that the drug ring, under the control of the Russians and their Afghani puppets, has been functioning here for some time and just recently has been assigned the added duty of discouraging the Dowry of Death by cobra assassinations," Prem proposed.

"Sounds reasonable," Ian agreed.

"Sir, you informed Lieutenant Aurangzeb of your trip tonight to Pahalgam?" Sardar Khan asked the Captain.

Prem nodded. "Called the chap just after tiffin. Informed him I had business there. Didn't say anything about the bait and trap business. He wished me a safe trip."

"Can't exactly say I'm enthusiastic about what you're doing tonight, particularly that it's being done solo," Ian admitted, a pull of worry about his face.

"You've Bubli's phone number. For God's sake don't call Bombay unless things definitely go bad for me. Incidentally, I had Bruce give me a second injection of cobra antivenin."

Chapter Nineteen

Dark moisture-laden clouds anxiously jostled each other overhead, at times dipping low enough to brush the treetops. Denied the light of moon or stars, the night was black. The incessant patter of a wind-driven rain drummed a dreary nocturnal tattoo on the fluttering leaves and puddled ground.

Prem Narayan sat crouched forward over the steering wheel, straining to catch glimpses of the road ahead between swipes of the windshield wipers. Bright headlights bored forward into the threatening weather, illuminating showers of meteoric rain droplets. A fine cold mist invaded the inside of the jeep, filtering through the many cracks and apertures where side curtains loosely snapped onto the vehicle's frame. The Captain shivered and explored the neck of his trench coat. Finding the top button, he fingered it into place snugging up the collar. He drove slowly, not only because an obscure and sodden road limited the rate of progress, but also because of the purpose of his trip. A cautious and measured approach to any roadblock would be more likely to prevent a shoot out and permit his kidnapping without undue violence.

Probably turn out a fizzle, Prem thought, as his eyes scanned the lighted route ahead. Anyone would have to be a bit daft to venture out on a night like this. But if I am stopped, the search narrows down to two, Vandermeer and Appleton, one or both of them. They were the only outsiders to know of the Pahalgam trip. He wondered if the Hakim's third riddle might relate to the Dutchman, the one about an arbitrator who barters justice for wealth and prestige. Of course the Colonel or the American could have leaked it.

"There they are," Captain Narayan muttered through clenched teeth, as he swung the car around an abrupt curve to the left. The vehicle came to a quick stop, the headlights focused on a bullock cart standing crosswise and blocking the highway. A lone individual, covered by a tarpaulin, sat huddled and motionless on the tongue of the two-wheeler. Hardly had he come to a standstill when four men with drawn guns and torches converged on the jeep, two from each side. "Damned good orchestration, this holdup," he continued muttering under his breath, "a roadblock hidden just around a corner in the path and four men coming at me separately from front and rear."

Having anticipated his plan of action, Prem moved slowly and deliberately, first shutting off the motor, then opening the door, in each instance making certain the action was understood by the raiders. Stepping out into the rain, he raised both hands and was frisked immediately and relieved of his automatic. During all of the last procedure he felt the muzzle of a gun pressed firmly into his back. Up to this point no words had been spoken.

"You will not try to escape," one of the four warned in English, adding ominously, "for our orders are to capture you dead or alive."

Prem chose not to reply, but deliberately turned down his collar so as to expose the left side of his face, thus insuring his recognition as Captain Narayan of the C.I.D.

The four captors were bearded and mustached with clothes very much alike. Each wore a turban of dark cloth wrapped loosely about his head with the tail of the headdress drawn around the neck as a muffler. From below their heavy knee-length military khaki overcoats, full Afghani pantaloons emerged and dropped to fit snugly about the ankles.

Beckoning with his handgun, the spokesman moved up the road as the three others closed in to escort their captive. A short distance ahead, a side path led off into the woods where five hill ponies were tethered. After fastening Prem's wrists in front of him with a homemade pair of leather thong handcuffs, two of the men assisted him to mount. The saddle was a crude wooden contraption used for carrying bazaar goods, made slightly more comfortable for the human rider by an overlying folded blanket. There were no stirrups, so the Captain's legs dangled awkwardly to be used on demand as a steadying grip around the animal's belly. A rein extended from the pony's bridle to the harness crupper of the mount ahead. The convoy plodded forward in single file over a narrow path which followed a circuitous route deeper and higher into the mountains. As the five steeds and their riders slowly moved ahead, a cold and pelting rain plagued them.

At first thought, Captain Narayan wondered why he had not been blindfolded, then realized that the darkness of the night, surrounding dense forest as well as the constantly changing course had robbed him of all directional senses. After about forty minutes, the caravan came to a halt and all five dismounted to stretch their legs. Prem's thighs were getting raw on the inner sides from a constant chafing against the angled wooden saddle. Moving to the far side of his mount, away from his captors, he worked at rearranging the blanket. With the Afghanis' attention centered on his hands, the Captain scraped a swastika in the mud with the toe of his boot, hoping the weather would not erase the emergency sign.

Another half-hour passed on the trail. The rain had changed, first through a period of sleet and then on into a snowfall. Initially the wet flakes melted on contact with the ground, but as the convoy climbed upward they moved into a countryside covered by a thin blanket of white. The stinging fingers of an icy wind probed the exposed parts of the travelers' faces. Prem's hands and feet were numb with cold but he refused to complain, choosing instead to maintain some level of circulation by a constant exercising of his toes and fingers. Because of a similarity of some words with Hindustani, he understood bits of the Pushtu conversation between the men riding behind him. From what the Captain could gather through his eavesdropping, the party was headed for a solitary dwelling built on the side of a mountain. The quarters were described by the narrating Afghani as rustic but quite *"masbut"* or solid. A wealthy Hindu merchant had decided to enter ascetic seclusion, but on his own terms rather than accepting the austerity of a bleak mountain cave. The recluse had died unexpectedly a couple of years ago and the house recently had been purchased by a Srinagar Muslim as a holiday retreat.

Abruptly, without warning of the immediacy of human habitation, the jungle path led the convoy through a gate into a small enclosed compound circled by a five feet high stone wall. A two-story building rose from the back of the flat yard, appearing to rest against a sheer cliff directly behind. Propped on a window sill of the first floor, a kerosene lamp lighted the scene as the men dismounted and two servants collected the ponies, leading them inside a lean-to for shelter and provender. Relieved of his thong handcuffs, Prem followed the leader up a crude stairway cut out of a single large log reaching from the compound below to the porch of the upper story. Climbing the precipitous and narrow steps necessitated a steadying grasp of the timber on either side, a difficult feat for one whose hands were numb from being fettered and frozen. There were three rooms upstairs and the Captain was directed into one whose only source of warmth was a single kerosene lamp resting on a table.

"Dry clothes and bed covers," the leader announced tersely, waving toward a stack of garments and blankets on a wooden bunk built against the wall.

"Thanks," Prem responded, rubbing his hands together in an effort to warm them.

"The maid servant will serve you some tea," the Afghani added crustily as he turned and marched out of the room, bolting the door shut after him.

Quickly removing his clothes and drying himself, Prem put on a fresh outfit of long cotton underwear and a homespun woolen suit. Then seating himself on a wooden stool, the only chair in the room, he briskly massaged chilled feet until they responded with a tingling and almost unbearable pain. Satisfied with the improved circulation, he encased them in unwieldy rough-woven woolen socks. His further

efforts at dressing were interrupted by a knocking followed by the rattling of the door bolt.

"*Andar aiye*—Please come in," the Captain called out.

The person who entered with the tea was a slender elderly woman dressed in a heavy sweater and salwar pantaloons. A knitted woolen scarf, snugly tied, framed her face and corralled straying wisps of gray hair. She said nothing but set the tray on a round table beside the bunk and started to leave.

"*Dhanyavad*—Thank you," Prem addressed her gently.

She paused with her hand on the door latch and turned to stare inquisitively at the Captain.

"*Ap-ka nam kya hai*—What is your name?" he asked her in Hindustani, smiling good humoredly.

She gave him a long questioning look before responding in a barely audible voice, "*Mera nam Ameena hai*—My name is Ameena." Having divulged this information she slipped out of the room and bolted the door behind.

Prem found it difficult to believe his good fortune as he sat sipping the hot drink. This must be the same Ameena, he thought, who helped free Doreen and Mos from their captors the night before. As Monty had intimated, the whole gang of kidnapping goondas must have evacuated those quarters during the day and moved to this building which now held him captive. "In Ameena I should have an ally," the Captain mused aloud, "a Muslim from India or Pakistan."

Finishing his tea and feeling the warmer for it, Prem rose and surveyed the room. Besides the built-in wooden bed, the table and the stool, there were no other pieces of furniture. On the floor, a large brass pitcher of water nestled in a metal washbowl and adjacent to these sat an enamel commode. A barred window overlooked a narrow porch just outside and a story below lay the compound. The only other opening into his quarters was the single door leading in from a short hallway offering a common access to the three upstairs rooms. Cold and tired, the Captain draped his wet clothes over the stool, made up his bed, blew out the lamp and crawled in between the blankets fully clothed. In spite of the hard boards underneath, within a few minutes he was fast asleep.

At sometime during the night, Prem's rest was disturbed by the sound of voices. Sitting up in bed he first yawned to sensitize his ear drums, then listened with mouth open. Two people were conversing in the adjacent room but the words were baffled by the intervening wall. Cupping both hands about his ear, he used them as a stethoscope against the partition. To his gratification he now could hear most of the words. "They're speaking in English," the Captain mused out loud, "which means the buggers probably are of different nationalities using different vernaculars. One's a bass and the other's a tenor."

" . . . and the chap offered no resistance?" the bass voice completed a question.

"None, not a bit of trouble," a male responded in higher pitch.

"Strange, that. Can't imagine the Captain giving in without a struggle."

"Bounder just might've wanted to be captured, eh?"

"You may be right. Better not let our guard down. Prem Narayan's one helluva bright detective."

A bout of coughing interrupted the dialogue briefly until the tenor picked up the conversation. "When's the American . . . " the voice faded and became unintelligible.

"Talked to him just before I left Srinagar. He'll be here first thing in the morning."

"Oh God! Not Monty," Prem groaned to himself.

"What about the money?" the tenor asked.

"He'll have it with him and in American dollars. Said that his colleague, the Dutchman Vandermeer, would be coming with him."

"Thank God!" Prem sighed with relief, "They're talking about Appleton."

"Remember our agreement, dipping into the sales cash for our own pockets. Better keep absolute secrecy. If those dogs in Kabul ever find out they'll stand me up before a wall for a firing squad."

"Talking about Kabul," the bass broke in, "the officials say the cobra assassinations haven't slowed down arms shipments to the mujahidin rebels and . . . " Prem lost the flow of words then picked them up again . . . "to step up action against the Dowry of Death."

"We've kidnapped the top C.I.D. investigator, haven't we?"

"But damn it, that doesn't slow down the smuggling of arms to Afghanistan," the bass projected his exasperation.

"Did the Russians have any suggestions?"

"More cobra murders. The idiots . . . " again the words became unintelligible.

"Just who?" the tenor countered.

"The Armenian for one . . . that bastard Parkozian."

"If you can ever get the bloke out into the open."

"Almost had him the other night with a forged key to his room but that son of a swine Kafir Jacub fouled things up. We may get the damned Armenian tonight. We're trying a new trap."

"That chump Jacub lost out against the Captain the other night on the Kashmir Princess."

The bass grunted in disdain, then picked up the conversation, "The fool lost out again last night when the Pakistani dacoits took off his remaining right hand. They should have slit his damned throat." There was a cold and heartless cruelty in the words. In spite of Prem's exposure through the years to the criminal world, he experienced an involuntary chill course through his body.

"What about Reznikoff?" the tenor asked.

"A French citizen; she's tied into the French Embassy in Delhi ... don't want to muddy international waters."

"But we got rid of the Chinese Allabaksh and he was ... " the following words were lost.

"Peking doesn't carry the clout with Delhi that Paris does."

The tenor's opening words were unintelligible but cleared up as Prem strained to hear. " ... waiting for the American ... the black."

"Wish we could get rid of that bastard. Don't ever underestimate that damn bloke. He's not only bright but a physical whirlwind. Look what he did to two of our men last night, singlehanded. Bugger knows his manual of arms ... " the remaining words of the sentence could not be heard by Prem, but soon became intelligible again, " ... force him into leaving by kidnapping his lover and that orphan waif that's been tagging after him."

"That jackal Achmed swallowed the bait planted by the Pakistani dacoits," the tenor sneered "and lost his left hand in the process."

"His blooming head's getting too big for his hat. He's been trying to take over this project from me." The bass gave out a mirthless laugh.

"And now what do we do with our captive, the Captain? Perhaps scare him so he'll quit mucking about with the cobra murders and bugger off?"

"Hell no! That bloke will never quit the investigation. He'll never funk and run."

"So?"

"He's got to be done away with. If not I'm in bad with Kabul ... " the words faded out into a mumble.

"How do we liquidate?" the tenor broke in.

"The cobra treatment."

There was the sound of chairs scraping on the wooden floor as the two men separated, one of them leaving for the other quarters, his progress marked by the sound of receding footsteps and the noise of opening and closing doors.

Prem crawled back into bed to enjoy the warmth of the blankets. In the quiet of the darkness he methodically went over the dialogue just terminated in the adjoining room. Of special comfort to him was the realization that Monty was not connected with the cobra killings. The eavesdropping also had pointed up the fact that Doreen's and his kidnappers were one and the same outfit. Furthermore, the conversation just overheard substantiated the veracity of Parkozian's narration of his personal association with the Dowry of Death. Prem was intrigued by the bass voice, for although the words were muffled, the cadence had a familiar flow. In spite of the macabre implications of what he had just heard the Captain was satisfied with the state of affairs ... his capture and incarceration. If this train of events continued, pakka evidence would be forthcoming.

"This is going to be one big gamble of a clinical trial with Bruce Duncan's antivenin," Prem muttered with a chuckle. "I may be a bit daft betting my life that the ruddy experiment works."

Then the Captain, with his accustomed discipline, brushed aside all immediate problems and entered into his autogenic mental exercises, finally reveling in a total relaxation with the resolution of a deep fatigue. Just before falling asleep, his thoughts turned tenderly to his wife Bubli. He sensed an inner relief that she knew nothing of his immediate predicament. In the distance, the hoarse coughing of a Himalayan leopard triggered the high pitched cries of barking deer warning their herd of the prowling predator.

Chapter Twenty

Ian McVey slept fitfully through the night, making several trips to Prem Narayan's cabin and each time finding the bunk empty. In the early hours of the morning the rain had stopped but the wind continued gusting. As the Lieutenant looked out through the window on the ruffled gray waters of Dal Lake, dawn's paintbrush was applying the early tintings of red and orange to the undersides of the clouds. Restless, he slipped out of his quarters to shave and wash, then returned to dress quietly without disturbing the snoring Sergeant Major. In the dining room he found Rustum refurbishing and firing the charcoal in the braziers. The table had been set for breakfast. Fatima entered at the same moment as Ian, carrying a brass pot of coffee, some of which she poured steaming into a cup for him. Between hissing sips of the lip-burning brew, he groaned inwardly, his mind deeply troubled.

"Damned murderers," the Lieutenant muttered in an aside to himself, "must've taken the bait." He paused to fill his pipe, then flared a wooden match by touching it to a glowing coal and lit the bowl of tobacco. "Sure as hell points the finger of suspicion at Appleton and Vandermeer. Thank God Bruce gave Prem that booster shot of antivenin."

"Sir, breakfast?" Rustum asked deferentially, aware of the Lieutenant's sober contemplation.

"What say we hold it up a bit," Ian suggested, and went on to add, "the others should be joining us shortly.

"The Captain is coming back last night," Rustum volunteered.

Ian shook his head. "No, he hasn't come back."

But, sir, the jeep . . . it is there." the driver insisted, pointing toward the lake shore.

The Lieutenant set his cup of coffee down, in his haste spilling some of it across the table, and dashed toward the rear deck. To his surprise, there was the vehicle parked atop the embankment. With his heart pounding, he sprinted across the gangplank, afraid of what he might find inside the car. He grunted with relief to discover it to be unoccupied. The keys were in the ignition and on the driver's seat lay a water-smeared and muddy envelope addressed "Criminal Investigation Department." Taking the communication back on board, he sat at the dining table and pulled the kerosene lamp closer. Within the cover, there was a single sheet of paper, on which in long hand was written the message, "Desist your investigation or feel the cobra's fangs." It was signed, "The cobra assassins." Ian was still staring at the missive as Sardar Khan entered the room. Beckoning the Sergeant Major over, he handed him the note.

"How did it come?" Sardar asked after reading its contents.

"Found it in the jeep parked up there." Ian gestured toward the embankment. "Someone drove the car here and just left it. Which means the bloody goondas have the Captain."

For a moment both men sat staring at each other, the only sounds being the spluttering of the charcoal in the braziers and the gusting winds outside.

"We're going to have our hands full," Ian spoke soberly, breaking the silence, "and let's get on with it."

"Sir . . . you are the commanding officer," the Sergeant Major said with an encouraging smile.

"And I'm going to need your help. First I want you to take the jeep and give a dekko along the Pahalgam road. Have Rustum go with you, the chap knows the territory."

"Very good, sir."

"I've got to get the news to Pritham Singh in Delhi. He's not going to be exactly happy about the ruddy situation. Also must contact Monty. Said he'd be back this morning. Want the American to watch Doreen here while we're mucking about."

"How do I reach you, sir?"

"Telephone. Someone will be aboard the Kashmir Princess all the time. Both of us had better check in here from time to time."

"What about Lieutenant Aurangzeb, sir?"

"I'll be calling Ali shortly. We can certainly use the chap."

Fatima and Rustum brought in the servings for breakfast and the two men set upon the food. Hearing the telephone ring, Ian dropped his knife and fork, heading for Prem's quarters.

"Lieutenant McVey here," he announced incisively.

"Hope I didn't wake you up," Monty apologized and paused briefly before asking, "Something the matter with the Captain?"

"No, I was awake, but why the question, I mean about the Captain?"

"Well, the phone's in his cabin and at this ungodly time of the morning I expected him to answer."

"Monty come right over and make it jaldi, eh?"

"Be there in a jiffy . . . was on my way . . . something to tell you fellows."

The Red Chariot cautiously rolled out through the compound gates at Nedou's and then moved with greater speed down the road toward Dal Lake. The headlight beams became less distinct as dawn continued to erase the night's darkness. An occasional bullock cart or horse tonga braved the morning cold, the draft animals' flaring nostrils intermittently exhaling white mists of congealed breath. As a broken field runner in football, the American daringly maneuvered the Chariot between and around the vehicular obstacles. On the outskirts of Srinagar the road cleared permitting an increased acceleration.

Ian sounded concerned, Monty mused as he drove along. I'll bet something's gone wrong. That message of Aisha's last night presaged no good for the C.I.D. trio. Sardar Khan and Rustum had just pulled out ahead in the jeep as the Red Chariot came to a halt alongside the Kashmir Princess. Loping across the gangplank, Monty stepped aboard and moved on into the dining room without knocking. Jumping up from his chair beside the breakfast table, Ian firmly grasped the American's extended hand.

"Where's Doreen?" Monty asked, his eyes anxiously searching the room.

"She's alright ... in the W.C. washing up."

"Great!" The American heaved a sigh of relief. "What's the trouble?"

"They've kidnapped Prem."

"What do you mean, they've kidnapped Prem?"

Waving Monty to a seat at the table, Ian related the story of the Captain's decision to be captured deliberately, his failure to show up during the night and the threatening message left in the jeep. The Lieutenant had decided to take the American wholly into his confidence and told him so.

Monty listened soberly to the recounting of the past night's happenings before confiding, "Look, Ian, last night I received a message by word of mouth from Aisha. She's learned ... pakka evidence ... that the cobra murderers have definite plans to kill the three of you and Parkozian. According to her these orders came directly from Kabul."

"Well ... the Captain sure as hell obliged them last night."

"You can say that again!"

"Monty I'm going to ask you to act as an unofficial liaison between me and the Pakistani dacoits. We've got to get on top of the situation, and damned quickly. I've decided that any ally against this common enemy is welcome. The C.I.D. may kick me out on my ass for working with dacoits but that's a risk I've decided to take."

"Good, Ian, I was hoping you'd see things that way."

"We need two bits of information: Exactly where the blokes are hiding with Prem and if Aisha still has a contact among the assassins."

"Will do. We may just luck out on the contact. Remember the maid, Ameena?"

"Uh-huh, I remember. And Monty, make it clear with Aisha that we'll handle any engagements such as a raid. There'll be no risks for the

Pakistanis.''

Doreen, dressed in a snugly fitting white ski sweater and dark blue slacks, stepped into the dining room, paused for an instant and then moved quickly toward Monty, who rose and drew her into his arms.

"You two enjoy your breakfast together," Ian broke into their whispering, "while I make some telephone calls."

"That we'll do," the American replied with a self-conscious grin, "and I'll contact Aisha as soon as the phone's available."

"Monty, you might bring Doreen up to date on the night's events."

Lieutenant McVey stepped into the Captain's cabin and closed the door. Moodily he crossed to the window and opened it to look out over Dal Lake, its wind-ruffled waters reflecting the sober gray of clouds overhead. He found himself reacting ambivalently to his assumption of leadership in the cobra murders investigation. The heady challenge of a position of command was counterbalanced by the awesome weight of its responsibility, particularly at this moment with his chief a captive in the hands of a murderous gang.

"Pritham Singh here," the Deputy Inspector General of the C.I.D. responded, a touch of irritation in his voice at being awakened so early.

"Lieutenant McVey, sir. Sorry for this botheration, but Captain Narayan was kidnapped sometime during the night."

"Captain Narayan was what!" The Sikh's words reverberated in Ian's ear.

"Kidnapped . . . captured by the cobra murderers."

For a moment there was only the sound of deep breathing at the Delhi end of the telephone line, then Pritham Singh broke in quietly, "Alright McVey, give me the details."

Ian quickly narrated the events of the past twenty-four hours, emphasizing Prem's deliberate effort to be captured and relating the fact that the Captain had received a second injection of the cobra antivenin.

"Righto Lieutenant, carry on. You take command of the investigation. Pull Ali Aurangzeb in full time on your team. Call for any help my office can give and McVey . . . keep me informed."

"Very good, sir. We have some leads and also the possibility of assistance . . . assistance from unorthodox sources."

"What the devil do you mean by unorthodox sources?"

"Sir, it might be in the Department's best interest that I not answer your question."

"Damn it, McVey, you're already beginning to sound and act like the Captain." There was an intimation of approval in the Sikh's words. "Cheerio and do the needful."

Ian returned to the dining room and joined the other two about the breakfast table. "Why don't you go ahead and make your call," he suggested to Monty, who jumped up and headed for the telephone.

"Slept soundly through the night," Doreen confessed, "must have been dead tired.

"Wish I could say the same," Ian groaned, "That was one helluva night for me."

"Sorry. I feel terrible about Captain Narayan. Are we going to be able to get him free?"

"We're going to give it all we have. I'm breaking regulations that may get me into trouble with the authorities, but under the circumstances I really don't give a damn."

"Will Monty be working with you?" Her voice projected worry.

"You're in love with him, aren't you?"

Doreen broke out into a smile and nodded coyly. "Head over heels. Do you approve?"

Ian studied her face over the rim of his coffee cup for a moment before replying, "That chap's a bit of alright. The match should be a smashing one. You have my blessings."

Monty made several attempts to get his call through to the Pakistani dacoit headquarters before finally hearing the telephone ring at the other end.

"*Kaun hai*—Who is it?" The words were spoken cautiously.

"*American Hakim.*"

"*Bahut accha*—Very well." There was the clattering sound of the receiver being set down on a hard surface, then the slapping steps of sandaled feet fading into the distance. Thank goodness she's in, Monty thought as he waited. She could have been off on one of her trips to Pakistan.

"American . . . it is you, yes?" Aisha's voice came through clearly.

"Yup."

"You received my message last night?"

"I did, and thank you. It's already been relayed to Lieutenant McVey."

"You sound troubled. Have they struck already?"

"Captain Narayan's been kidnapped . . . late last night."

"Swine! Bloody swine!" Her voice was bitter as bile.

Monty went on to explain that Prem had deliberately set himself up to be captured.

"The Captain's a brave man . . . a bit foolhardy perhaps but brave."

"Only outsiders who knew where he would be last night were Vandermeer and Appleton. Sort of puts the finger of suspicion on those two."

"Yes, but don't shut out all other options. They could easily pass the word to others; the wind has many ears."

"Aisha . . . we need your help again."

"A bit cheeky isn't it? The Indian Criminal Investigation Department coming to a band of foreign outlaws for help is after all frightfully extraordinary.'' She broke into a teasing laugh.

"They can't contact you directly, not quite cricket as you British say, so I'm the go-between . . . the broker. After all the cobra murderers are a common enemy.''

"Precisely. I was just ragging you a bit. Let's on with it . . . how can I help?''

"In the first place, can you find where they've moved from their Baramula headquarters, the one we raided?''

"Actually my men at the moment are ferreting that out.''

"Secondly, do you still have a contact in their camp . . . like the maid Ameena?''

"We do, in fact Ameena's still with them.''

"Good! We need to contact Captain Narayan.''

"But, American, do you have time for all this? The cads may already have done the chap in.''

"Aisha, he's had two immunizations . . . anitvenin . . . against cobra venom. Keep this under your hat . . . I mean no one else should know about his protective injections.''

"And this will protect him?'' She sounded skeptical.

"Doreen's brother, Doctor Duncan, is a specialist in snakes . . . herpetologist . . . and he assures us it will prevent a lethal effect.''

"Splendid! I'll keep the secret.'' She breathed a sigh of relief.

"You'll be able to reach me here on the Kashmir Princess. Ask the operator for CID 321.''

"Righto and cheerio American.''

"Cheerio, Aisha, you're quite some gal,'' he said with sincerity.

Monty shared with Ian and Doreen the details of his conversation with the leader of the dacoits. Her promised cooperation was encouraging news.

"We should have information by this evening,'' the American observed hopefully, "and perhaps we'll be able to contact Prem through Ameena.''

"I've got to get in touch with Ali,'' Ian announced, rising from the table and heading for the phone. His attempts to reach the Lieutenant at his home were unsuccessful. He rang Ali's office.

"McVey here. I need to get in touch with Lieutenant Aurangzeb,'' he stated slowly and precisely to the clerk who answered.

After a brief pause, a male voice replied hesitantly, "I am sorry, sir, with apologies, but the Lieutenant this morning has not arrived.''

"Did he leave a message, I mean anything about his being late or not reporting in?''

"No, sir, no message is here.''

"Dash it all, this is a bit of a nuisance. Better send someone over to check his residence. Have the Lieutenant contact me. Tell him it's an emergency.''

"Please not to worry, sir, I shall do the necessary." There was a hint of anxiety in the clerk's voice.

Ian hung up the receiver and sat in thought, disturbed by the telephone conversation. He chewed on his pipestem in sober reflection, his forehead wrinkled in a frown. "Could the bloody murderers have kidnapped Ali as well?" he muttered uneasily.

Chapter Twenty-one

Prem Narayan awoke to the clattering of pots and pans somewhere below. Throwing off his covers he stepped over to the window. The past night's wet clouds had fled the skies and the warm glow of a pink dawn was creeping stealthily over the white-pinnacled Himalayas to the east like a cat stalking its quarry. There was just sufficient light for the Captain to study his surroundings. A thin layer of snow mantled the ground and artistically flecked the pine boughs. In the distance evergreen forests climbed from the valleys below, skirting the mountains upward to the timber line, above which rose massive barren crags separated by glaciers and snowdrifts.

Meticulously scanning the area, Prem could find no evidence of other buildings or human habitation. The two-story house in which he was captive stood on a fairly wide rock ledge and directly in front of a sheer granite cliff rising behind it to roof top level. The three rooms on the upper floor each connected separately with a short hall opening onto a covered porch from which a solid log ladder dropped steeply to the courtyard below. These crudely notched stairs offered the only access to the second story. A stone wall about five feet high, breached at one point by a swinging wooden gate, encircled the compound. Breaking out of the forest on the east or front of the building, a single narrow path headed directly into the compound portal. Captain Narayan was impressed by the solid construction of the walls. Square cut timbers of good size were staggered at the structural corners, one end overlapping another, and the space between them cemented in with gravel. A solid and quite massive door and a window secured by metal bars made any hope of a forced escape untenable.

The prisoner's inspection of his surroundings was interrupted by a knock followed by the grating metallic sound of a sliding bolt. Swinging the door inwards, Ameena entered with a tray of food, including a pot of steaming coffee. Without speaking she unloaded the dishes onto the table and poured the drink, then turned to leave.

"Ameena," the Captain addressed her in a low voice. She stopped and faced him, a friendly look in her eyes. He went on, "*Dhanyavad, aur apse milkar mujhe bahut khusi hui*— Thank you, and I am very glad to have met you." Choosing not to reply, the maid gave him a shy smile and left the room.

Prem moved his breakfast table over in front of the window so he could keep an eye on the activities outside while eating. The sun's rays beamed in through the bars, warming to a stage of comfort for the first time since his capture. Suddenly three riders on horseback broke out of the forest, single file, moving up the path toward the residence. The central figure was obviously a prisoner of the others for his wrists were bound. The Captain's muscles tensed and he felt his temple pulses throb as he strained to identify the captive. Because of the cold, all three horsemen were bundled with scarves wrapped about their heads and necks, making recognition at a distance quite impossible. Reaching the compound, the lead figure dismounted and opened the gate, permitting the cortege to enter. At this closer range, Prem decided with a great sense of relief that the person in custody was neither one of his C.I.D. associates nor Monty.

After freeing his wrists, the two guards assisted their prisoner off the horse, only to have him collapse on the ground. On command, a servant ran out from the building and commenced massaging and exercising the legs of the stricken man. Finally he sat up and then with assistance stood, leaning shakily against his mentor. After a brief period of stationary stepping up and down, the captive's stability appeared to have returned and he was led limping indoors. Just before he moved under the eaves of the porch below, he looked up, his face distorted with pain. It was Parkozian, room seven at Nedou's and the administrator of the Dowry of Death.

"Poor bloke," Prem groaned out loud, "he's bloody well finished, what with his bad heart and all."

Apathetically finishing his breakfast, the Captain began a brisk walk about the room with intervals of knee bends and push-ups thrown in for good measure. On each tour he paused briefly before the window to take stock of the compound. His curiosity was aroused by a servant building something with mud in the center of the yard, shaping and smoothing the surface with his bare hands. As the object began to take shape, Prem recognized it for what it was, a special kind of clay oven peculiar to the northern parts of India and known as a tandur. Shaped like a monstrous jar, it was heated by burning charcoal or wood at the bottom for a couple of hours until the proper temperature for baking was attained. Recipes for famous dishes produced by these ovens have been passed down through the centuries from family to family, delicacies such as tanduri murg and tanduri roti, the uniquely baked chicken and bread. As the morning wore on the clay oven was completed and charcoals lit within to dry the wall into firmness.

Shortly past noon, Ameena brought a luncheon tray and, after gathering up the dirty breakfast dishes, set up the warm brass plates of mutton curry and rice. While the Captain ate, she hovered about as if loathe to leave.

"*Sub thik hai*—Is everything in order?" Prem finally asked.

"*Ha ji*—Yes sir," she responded in a barely audible voice, then moved closer to add in a whisper, "*Mai bazar jaa rahaa huu*—I'm going to the bazaar."

"Srinagar?"

She nodded in affirmation, slipping the Captain a pencil stub and a scrap of paper. He quickly sketched a swastika and wrote under it, "Ameena knows where I'm being held captive. Prem Narayan." Folding the note, he handed it back to the maid who tied the message into the loose end of a scarf about her head and quietly left the room.

Having finished his lunch, Prem sat in thought, elbows resting on the table and chin cupped in the palms of his hands, looking abstractedly out of the window. Aisha will get word by this evening, he reflected, and pass it on to Monty who in turn will notify Ian. I must coordinate any raid on this place with those two. The timing has to be exact or the whole purpose of my kidnapping will be lost, he continued musing, his forehead furrowed with worry wrinkles.

Activity in the compound below attracted his attention and he watched Ameena and a male servant each mount a horse. A third hill pony was led out from the animal lean-to and its reins attached to the harness crupper of the maid's mount directly ahead. Fastened to the wooden baggage saddle on the riderless animal's back were several empty woven baskets and gunny sacks. In single file, the pony train headed out of the gate and down the trail. Hardly had they disappeared into the pine forest than a similar entourage of four riders broke out of the woods and approached the premises. As the men dismounted within the compound, Prem recognized James Appleton and Wilhelm Vandermeer. Turning the four ponies over to a syce, the new arrivals entered quarters on the ground floor.

The afternoon moved on tediously for the Captain without evident activity. He drowsed intermittently, resting his head on arms folded atop the table before him. As the sun advanced westward dropping behind the adjacent cliff, a growing chill pervaded the building. Prem awoke with a start, cold and shivering. He pulled a blanket off the bunk and draped it about his shoulders. While he was in the process of doing this, there was a knocking on the door.

"Come in," the Captain called out in a stentorian voice.

The door opened slowly to admit a rather large man, bearded and mustached, dressed in Afghani full flowing pants, boots, a long khaki military overcoat and an astrakhan caracul cap. His left forearm, heavily bandaged, hung in a sling, and on the back of his right hand was tattooed a falcon. Prem studied his face and quickly came to the conclusion that this was not the man who had lighted his cigarette in the foyer of the Ashoka hotel and been a fellow passenger on the flight from Delhi to Srinagar.

"Ah, Achmed, do come in," the Captain invited, waving him toward the lone stool by the window.

The visitor stopped short and stared maliciously at his prisoner. "How in hell did you know my name? I've never met you before," he growled.

"Quite true, quite true," Prem repeated and went on, "Merely a matter of deductive reasoning, my good chap. Left hand missing, falcon tattooed on the back of the right, so, ipso facto, you must be Achmed."

"But my name, Achmed, how . . . how . . . " his voice trailed off hesitantly, the words indistinct and thick-tongued.

The blighter's on narcotics, Prem thought, noticing pupils constricted to pinpoints as well as his slurring speech. He could be an addict or heavily medicated for pain, or possibly both.

"To answer your question further, my informants supply me with many details which I file away up here . . . " the Captain tapped his forehead knowingly before going on . . . "some relevant and some irrelevant, but all are the building blocks of deductive reasoning."

The Afghani licked his lips nervously but made no comment.

Aware of the drug-induced inebriation of his antagonist and thirsting for information, Prem decided to goad him to a point of irrational behavior.

"And how is our mutual friend, Kafir Jacub, the bloody bastard who tried to knife me in my sleep the other night aboard the Kashmir Princess?"

Achmed again chose to maintain a silence, his eyes smoldering with hatred.

The Captain continued his offensive, "You know, my good chap, you and your fellow Afghani puppet traitors are quite a distance from Kabul. What makes you think that any of you will ever get back there alive?"

The blood commenced to drain out of Achmed's face, whether as a result of what he had just heard or from the pain and systemic effects of the recent hand amputation, Prem could not be certain. For the second time the Captain waved him toward the stool and on this occasion he accepted, swaying slightly as he shuffled toward the window. Once seated, his color began to improve.

"You'll pay for this," the Afghani threatened, taking his bandaged left arm out of the sling and waving it menacingly.

"Don't threaten me, you puppet traitor. Neither I nor the C.I.D. had a damned thing to do with the loss of your hand or for that matter the night raid on your hide-out near Baramula."

"You're lying through your teeth! You joined up with those dogs . . . those Pakistani bandits . . . who cut off my hand and then later killed two of our men." Achmed was becoming hysterical.

"What you think or say won't have the slightest effect on the accuracy of what I've just told you, for I have spoken the truth." Prem's voice was as sharp as honed steel.

The Afghani's mouth moved but no words came out. He swallowed forcefully several times and moistened his lips with the tip of his tongue before he could speak. "You won't leave this place alive ... " Achmed broke into angry grunts before continuing ... "as for those Pakistanis, we'll even the score with the swine. The dogs will wish they'd ... they'd ... " again his speech deteriorated into unintelligible mumblings.

Prem continued his goading, "So you're the brave man who beats a woman to the ground and then kicks her in the head." The words projected contempt.

Achmed started to rise from the stool and then sank back unable to stand, his lips trembling with rage. "The Dowry of Death is doomed as is its director, that bastard Parkozian. We captured the fool last night and in the morning he'll feel the poisoned fangs of cobras just as you will. The snakes will rid us of the C.I.D. and the arms smuggling."

"And who pronounces the death sentence? Who's your top man ... Colonel Vandermeer?"

The Afghani shook his head. "No ... no. He and Appleton are into hard drugs ... heroin. They work with us in getting the stuff out of here."

"What do you mean, out of here?"

"Out of Afghanistan. It brings big money to Kabul."

"You say Vandermeer and Appleton have nothing to do with the cobra murders?"

"Nothing."

"That's a bit of rot, if you ask me," Prem egged him on. "I just saw both of them arrive this afternoon."

"They'll be leaving shortly. Couple of jackals living on offal ... on carrion," he sneered. "That Vandermeer tries to order us about sometimes ... bastard hides in the skirts of the United Nations ... even blackmails us. Appleton is a cunning bastard. Just offered his services to kill you and your two henchmen, Parkozian and the nigger American, as he called Brown. He'd do all of this for a substantial package of heroin."

"And you get nothing out of these jackals?" Prem raised his eyebrows in mock surprise. "I mean for yourself?"

A cunning look crossed Achmed's eyes. "A few dollars, something to help make up for living in this blasted place. Let me ask you, what's the price of a hand, eh?" He looked down into his sling and groaned.

Prem decided to change his role from badgering to sympathizing, still in a continued effort to gain information. "Unfortunate thing." His voice was solicitous.

"Unfortunate thing?" the Afghani was defensive.

"Losing your hand."

"Damned right it's unfortunate. Hurt like hell yesterday morning when the doctor sewed the skin over the end. Left two rubber drains in. He'll be taking them out in a couple of days. Worried about infection. Put me on medication for ... for ... " he lost his train of thought and stared balefully at Prem for a moment before going on ... "can hardly wait to watch those cobras sink their fangs into you." He paused to chuckle malevolently. "You'll scream with pain just as they all do and soon you won't be able to breathe, just die of suffocation."

"Why did you kidnap the Duncan woman from Nedou's at Gulmarg?" Prem asked, changing the subject.

"To blackmail that damned Monty Brown into leaving."

"But why?"

"You don't know?"

"Let's hear your story." Prem chose not to answer the question.

"That bastard's been training cadres of mujahidin to use the arms being smuggled them by the Dowry of Death. Then these Afghani rebels go back up into the Hindu Kush mountains in Afghanistan to teach what the American taught them. But you know all about this, don't you?"

"Yes," Prem lied and went on, "but why haven't you assassinated the chap?"

"He's an American and has official connections with his embassy in Delhi. Kabul doesn't want to muddy the waters too much."

"But what about me, an Indian? You mean to say that my demise wouldn't muddy the waters?" Prem pretended that his feelings had been hurt.

Achmed burst out in a short derisive snort. "The Indian authorities would just write you off as another of the many casualties in the ongoing Hindu-Muslim animosity here in Kashmir."

Activity in the compound momentarily interrupted the dialogue. Prem walked over nearer to the window and Achmed turned on his stool for a better view. While three horses were being led out of the lean-to, Appleton and Vandermeer approached their mounts. One syce made ready to accompany them. The American and the Dutchman each carried three containers about the size of cigar boxes. Soon the three riders had disappeared down the trail into the pine forest.

"Who's your chief?" Prem asked bluntly.

"You're not supposed to know," the Afghani replied haughtily.

"Why not? You yourself just said that I'd not get out of here alive."

"The chief doesn't want you to know until the last minute."

"You mean he'll reveal himself just before the cobras get me?"

Achmed nodded. "Just before they sink their fangs into you."

"You're not only sick physically but even worse off mentally. My dear chap you're a sadistic psycho."

"You're the chump, Captain. At least I'll be around after tomorrow," the Afghani retorted and rose to leave. He shuffled haltingly to the door, where he grasped the latch to steady himself and turned slowly to taunt, "I'll be at the execution in the morning, dear chap. Cheerio."

Prem pulled the stool closer to the window and sat down, a woolen blanket drawn snugly about his shoulders. The sun's rays, cut of by the cliff, no longer warmed the building. In the distance Himalayan peaks cast their lengthening somber shadows across deep intervening valleys. The premises were quiet and without evidence of activity. A wisp of charcoal smoke spiraled upward through the gaping mouth of the clay tandur. Wonder how poor old Parkozian's doing, Prem mused sadly. Wish we had been able to give the chap some antivenin. He felt an involuntary shiver course through his body, whether from the cold or thoughts of the morning, he could not be certain.

Chapter Twenty-two

Sardar Khan and Rustum Sharif returned early in the afternoon from their investigative mission along the Pahalgam road. Discouraged by the paucity of their findings, the two men had little to say. The stormy wet weather of the previous night had erased any evidence of Captain Narayan's kidnapping.

"Beastly luck," the Sergeant Major grumbled, "the rain washed out all possible clues. Very little people out on the road during the night."

"Cheer up, old chap," Ian consoled, "Can't possibly win every game, don't you know."

While Fatima served Sardar a late lunch, he was brought up to date on what had transpired during his absence. He evinced a special interest in the fact that the Pakistani dacoits were trying to unearth Prem Narayan's location. Bruce Duncan had been asked by telephone to take over his sister's protective care, in view of the likelihood that all hands might be needed to effect the Captain's rescue. Monty had insisted on participating in any raid, confiding that he had not entirely settled the score for the brutal murder of Mos and the demeaning treatment of Doreen.

"Sardar," Ian proposed, "drive over and take a dekko in Ali's office. Haven't been able to contact him all day. His blooming clerk doesn't seem to know what the hell's going on."

Shortly after the Sergeant Major and Rustum had pulled away from the lake shore embankment, Bruce and Maureen Duncan arrived. In the dining room, Fatima poured hot drinks and passed out toasted and buttered crumpets. For the most part, the conversation dwelt on Prem Narayan's abduction.

"Where'll you be staying?" Monty asked Bruce as they stood to leave.

"With friends here in Srinagar, where we stayed before going up to Gulmarg."

"Do watch her won't you?" There was an obvious anxiety in the American's voice. He reached over and took Doreen's hand in his. She smiled up into his face.

"Don't worry, my dear fellow," Bruce assured, "I shan't let her out of sight."

Both Ian and Monty walked out with the three Duncans across the gangplank and up to the Land Rover. The two lovers embraced ardently, quite oblivious to those about them. Doreen whispered, "Darling, for our sakes do take care of yourself. Don't forget, I'm hopelessly in love with you." Their lips met in a seal of commitment, her eyes projecting the deep sincerity of her words.

Ian McVey spent a good part of the afternoon seated beside the telephone in Prem Narayan's cabin. Its sudden ringing startled him.

"Lieutenant McVey here," he recited reflexly.

"Lieutenant, this is Aisha. May I have a word with the American?"

"Certainly. I'll fetch him." Setting the receiver down, Ian dashed through the dining room and sprang up the stairs several at a time onto the upper deck where Monty was dozing in the sun. On hearing the word, the American leaped to his feet and reversed the sprint to the lower quarters with Ian close on his heels.

"Hi Aisha ... " Monty took a deep breath before going on ... "you've news?"

"Ameena, our agent within the gang of cobra murderers, contacted Ashok in the Srinagar bazaar. She passed on a message from the Captain; a slip of paper with a swastika drawn above and under it words to the effect that Ameena knew where he was being held captive. It was signed by Prem Narayan."

"Great! Just great!" Monty could hardly contain himself.

"She described to Ashok where the bastards had moved and exactly how to get there. It's about six miles off the Pahalgam road over a narrow and steep footpath."

"Okay, Aisha, can we get with Ashok somewhere or can he come here to the Kashmir Princess?"

"American, let me have a word with the Lieutenant, eh?"

"Sure thing." Monty beckoned Ian over and handed him the phone. "McVey here again."

"Lieutenant, technically I'm an outlaw and the C.I.D. is very much a part of the law. However, at the moment we have a common foe. May I suggest in our joint interest that we brush aside this technical difference and join forces just for this particular project? Let me send over, secretly of course, ex-Captain Ashok of the Pakistan Air Force and two more of my men to work with you on the release of Captain Narayan. These chaps have become very adept at jungle fighting as the American will agree. Of course you would be in command of the raid. When the task is completed there will be no debts to be paid by either of us ... no need to be beholden to each other. You document whatever you bloody well please in your C.I.D. report. How does this strike you?"

There was a momentary silence on the telephone as Ian racked his brains seeking a solution to his dilemma. Perhaps the old maxim of the end justifying the means would be acceptable. How could he in good faith turn down an offer which might not only save Prem's life but at the same time destroy the murderous cobra gang? He remembered hearing the Captain say once that when common sense came into conflict with the law, give thought to common sense. He now was the officer in charge and the decision was his. The C.I.D. might sack him, particularly if the raid failed, but that problem he would face in the future.

"Madam, send Captain Ashok and his men over. We'll be moving out just after dark."

"Splendid! I doubt you'll have cause to regret the decision. They'll be on their way over shortly. Ashok has the details as to the layout of the building ... exactly where the Captain's being kept. Ameena also informed us that another man is being held captive, a person she does not recognize."

"Thank you and wish us well."

"Cheerio, Lieutenant, and may Allah be with you."

Hanging up the receiver, Ian immediately shared the telephone dialogue with Monty.

"That extra captive Ameena reported, wonder if they've picked up Ali?" Ian speculated. "The chap's had no antivenin."

"Sardar Khan may have some lead on that when he returns," Monty suggested.

"I say, would you get Bruce on the phone and have him fetch antivenin for three men right away?" the Lieutenant urged the American. "With all this coffee and excitement I'm going to piss my pants if I don't get to the W.C."

"Okay ... let me at the phone." Monty gave a number to the exchange and listened as the bell at the other end rang several times.

"Doctor Duncan here," a voice finally answered.

"Bruce, this is Monty. Ian wants you here pronto with antivenin for three men. Do you read me?"

"Quite. Be there with the necessary in a few minutes."

Rustum braked the jeep to a gravel-scattering stop on the embankment and Sardar Khan jumped out, heading for the Kashmir Princess.

"Ah ... there you are ... " Ian impatiently waved the Sergeant Major inside ... "and what about Ali?"

"Chap's not been around his home or office the whole day," Sardar replied, staring dourly at the two men.

"Did you find his clerk?" Ian pressed his questioning.

"Yes, but the bloke is not knowing where Lieutenant Aurangzeb is. The mother has been in bed with a sickness and the clerk is saying perhaps he is visiting."

"Any idea where his mother lives?" Monty asked.

"Mother is in small village several furlongs before Baramula."

"Could be a prisoner of the cobra goondas," Ian muttered

unhappily.

Fatima fetched hot tea, toasted crumpets and marmalade for the Sergeant Major. As he munched and sipped, Ian brought him up to date on the plans for the night. To the Lieutenant's pleasant surprise, Sardar evinced no adverse reaction to the news that the C.I.D. and the Pakistani dacoits would be partners in the proposed raid. Their further conversation was interrupted by the telephone.

"Lieutenant McVey here," The words were terse and military.

"Ian, old fellow, this is Ram ... Ram Singh ... Interpol."

"Jolly good to hear from you. Something's up, eh Ram?"

"I've just learned that Captain Narayan's a captive of the cobra gang."

"We know this, Ram, but ... but how in hell did you ... " Ian's voice trailed off.

"We've a plant. An Interpol double agent."

"And what're you up to?"

"Tightening up our net on some international drug smuggling. Incidentally, we both may be up against the same bloody bastards."

"Could be, Ram, could be. Thanks for the call and cheerio, old chap," Ian decided against revealing over the telephone their anticipated raid that night.

A nondescript and weather-beaten car, something akin to a Land Rover, pulled up behind the parked jeep and disgorged three men who made their way across the gangplank onto the houseboat. Monty stepped to the rear deck and warmly welcomed Ashok and his two cohorts, inviting them inside where they were introduced to the Lieutenant and Sergeant Major. The Pakistanis were dressed alike in dark green camouflaged jump suits with heavy woolen pull-over khaki sweaters and knitted stocking caps to match.

"Captain Ashok, could you describe the lay out for us ... the plan of the premises?" Ian asked.

"Right you are. My information is secondhand, what Ameena told me, but it should be accurate. Captain Narayan is being held in an upstairs room, one of three rooms on that level, each of which opens into a short hallway which in turn leads out onto a narrow porch or verandah. The only access to these upper areas is a crude log ladder with notched out steps. A vertical granite cliff embraces the building on its rear or western side, rising to roof level. The space between the tops of the two isn't more than three or four feet." Ashok paused to permit questions.

"The verandah upstairs, is it covered or open?" Ian asked.

"I questioned Ameena about this. She's quite certain that the eaves from the roof only partially cover the verandah."

"Now that's what I call good observation, especially when you consider she's been there only twenty-four hours," Monty interjected.

"No. She's been there before. The assassins have occupied those quarters prior to this time," Ashok corrected.

"Basically you're thinking of an approach from the roof, dropping down onto the upper verandah and then into the Captain's room?" Ian queried.

"Precisely!"

"And reversing the procedure once the Captain is in our hands," Monty concluded.

Ashok nodded in agreement.

"A couple of saplings tied together could bridge the gap between the cliff and the roof, then just modest lengths of knotted ropes for us to drop onto the verandah," Ian enlarged on the plans.

Ashok continued, "Ameena states the door into the Captain's room is solid wood ... no window in it ... and there's no lock, only a bolt. But even if we should find a lock, I'll handle it ... " he grinned self-consciously before continuing ... "Should have been a burglar. I seem to have a way with locks."

The conversation came to a temporary halt as Doctor Duncan joined the group. Again there were introductions.

Ian called for attention and directed his words to the Pakistani trio. "Captain Narayan, Sergeant Major Sardar Khan and I, as well as Monty Brown, all have taken injections of cobra antivenin as an immunization against the snake venom. May I suggest that the three of you also take this protection. In the expectation that you would, I have asked Doctor Duncan, a renowned specialist from Kasauli, to come here prepared to give you the injections. What say?"

"Jolly good idea," Ashok responded enthusiastically.

Bruce Duncan took the Pakistanis into Prem Narayan's quarters and administered the immunizations. Then bidding a hasty farewell, he trotted ashore and headed back to Srinagar in his Land Rover.

The three dacoits were shown the W.C. facilities where they washed up for the evening meal being prepared by Fatima and Rustum. Ian, Sardar and Monty excused themselves to dress for the night's engagement. Dusk was settling over Dal Lake as the six men sat down around the dinner table. Conversation for the most part was related to the coming raid ... potential complications and alternate actions.

"If Ali's a prisoner there, we'll have to get him out," Ian insisted.

Ashok nodded and explained, "Ameena will contact Captain Narayan on her return to the premises and notify him of our planned raid. She's probably informed him of this already. Also she'll try to find out who the other captive is, his location as well, and pass the information on to the Captain."

"Incidentally, Ashok, just who is this Ameena?" Monty asked.

"An aunt of Aisha's who's taken on this dangerous and menial task as a plant with the cobra assassins. Actually, she comes from a high class family. Why she deliberately risks her life in this way is a secret known only to her. I've heard, only hearsay mind you, that her husband was executed by the Afghani puppet government in Kabul. Her present activities may represent a method of evening up old scores. Who knows?" Ashok shrugged his shoulders.

"We all carry side arms," Ian announced, and went on to add, "knives as well. Use the latter if you have a choice. Much quieter."

Ashok nodded as the three Pakistanis uncovered their guns and daggers.

"We all carry side arms," Ian announced, and went on to add, "knives as well. Use the latter if you have a choice. Much quieter."

Ashok nodded as the three Pakistanis uncovered their guns and daggers.

Chapter Twenty-three

The short winter twilight had given way to night, with a partial moon cresting the sky. Two vehicles pulled away from the embankment beside the Kashmir Princess, the decrepit Land Rover in the lead and a military jeep in close pursuit. A day of sunshine and wind had dried the muddy road to a firmness which prevented the tires from skidding, so the cars were able to move along at a good speed, occasionally slowed by bullock carts, horse tongas and trains of hill ponies. By agreement Sardar Khan and Monty rode with Ashok while the two other Pakistanis joined Ian in the jeep.

"Give me a bit of a lift on the landmarks, old chap," Ashok asked the American who was in the front seat beside him. "Ameena said that after this village we're passing, there would be a sharp, right angle, turn to the left and on the inside of the curve three large piles of broken rocks, crushed stones for surfacing of the road."

"Roger," Monty came back quickly.

Ashok chuckled and responded, "Good airman's language, that."

"I've a question," the American broke in after a brief silence.

"Carry on."

"Why are you chaps risking your necks tonight?"

"Why are we with you?"

"Uh-huh, why are you with us? These assassins haven't bothered your group."

"Not easy to put in words, American. In simplest terms it's a matter of freedom. That's why we're here ... people without a country. May sound a bit trite but by the beard of the Prophet, it's the truth. These goondas who've been killing with cobras are puppets of the godless Russians, determined to stamp out freedom-loving Afghanis. We know what you're doing, American, at the risk of your life training the mujahidin in the use of arms to strike back at the bastard invaders and their lackeys. Does that answer your question?"

Monty was about to reply when the headlights suddenly outlined a large pile of crushed rock encircled by a sharp turn of the road to the left.

"Here we are," Ashok leaned forward to announce, "just as Ameena described it."

The three occupants of the Land Rover jumped out, torches in hand, and explored until they discovered the path leading off into a pine forest. There was ample evidence that the trail had been used quite recently . . . human and pony tracks. After scouting out an area of firm ground in the underbrush, both vehicles were parked out of sight. Having meticulously checked out their equipment, the six men headed up the pathway in single file. At Ian's insistence, Ashok was in the lead. Very shortly their eyes accommodated to the moon-filtered night. In the distance two jackals commenced howling back and forth in their peculiar undulating disharmony. As the men penetrated deeper into the woods, they stampeded several barking deer who expressed their annoyance by scolding the world at large with shrill staccato cries.

After almost an hour of following the curving path, winding like a mountain stream in and out of the pines, the six raiders broke through into an open meadow. They paused in the shadows to study the building before them, so much a part of the bluff behind that it gave the appearance of a cliff dwelling. The moonlight softly delineated the two-story structure itself and the compound about its base. As the only evidence of human habitation, a lone kerosene lantern flickered from a window on the ground floor. Ian took over command and drew the men around him for instructions.

"The buggers must have one or more sentries about the place, at least we'll consider that they have, so move damned carefully," the Lieutenant cautioned. "Automatics and knives . . . any metals for that matter . . . must be kept covered. We don't want moonlight to reflect and give us away. We'll break into two groups of three each and flank the premises on either side, circling around to meet atop the cliff behind the building. Captain Ashok here will lead the Sergeant Major and one of his own men about the northern perimeter and I'll take Monty and the remaining Pakistani with me to skirt the southern flank. Remember, if you have the choice, use a knife rather than a gun. We just can't afford to alert the bastards."

"A password?" Sardar Khan asked.

"Quite right . . . a password," Ian agreed and went on, "We'll use 'swastika,' and now let's on with it lads."

The two parties separated and almost immediately lost sight of each other as they were swallowed by the forest shadows. Ian moved ahead as point man of his group, deploying Monty and the Pakistani on either flank several yards to the rear. After a few moments of stealthy progress, the Lieutenant and his party were brought to an abrupt and nerve-racking halt by several grunting wild pigs stampeding through the underbrush just ahead. Standing breathless in their tracks, they waited until the normal quiet of the mountainside again prevailed and Ian waved them forward. Steadily climbing upward, they mounted the ridge running behind the building which was hidden from their view and cautiously crept northward to a point judged to be approximately opposite the gang headquarters. Here they paused to await the arrival

of the other party. Because of the dampness of the ground and
undergrowth from the previous night's snow as well as the increasing
darkness due to the lowering of the moon, Ashok was able to come
within a few yards of Ian and his men before they were alerted.

"Anything unusual?" the Pakistani Captain whispered as the raiders
joined forces.

"Only some wild boar that scared the hell out of us," Ian replied
with a quiet chuckle.

"We heard them," Sardar Khan acknowledged.

"Anything unusual with you guys?" Monty asked.

"Not a blooming thing," Ashok responded. "Their sentries, if the
fools have any, must be inside the compound."

"Better check just where the building lies," Ian suggested, pointing
over the crest. "Monty and I'll sneak over and take a quick dekko. For
the record's sake, if anything happens to incapacitate me, Captain
Ashok's in charge."

The two men crept over the ridge, taking particular care not to
dislodge any rocks or gravel. Their estimate of the building's location
had been surprisingly accurate. Ameena had made a fair calculation of
the distance from the cliff's edge to the border of the roof ... a little
over four feet ... and both men agreed that a bridge of sorts would be
necessary to make the crossing safe and noiseless. The level between the
ledge and the top of the building would pose no problem, there being
only a slight variation in height.

Returning to the waiting men, Ian reported their findings and
dispatched Sardar Khan with one of the Pakistanis into the valley
behind to cut three saplings. The distance into the forest and the incline
of the crest were sufficient to blanket the sound of the woodsmen.
Having bound the timber together, the six men quietly inched their way
to the bluff's edge and, with the help of a rope tied to its far end,
lowered the bridge into place on the roof. Stealthily, three men crossed
the sapling span between promontory and building, Ian in the lead with
Monty and Ashok close behind. Moving across the roof to that portion
overlying Prem Narayan's room, they paused briefly to scrutinize the
premises below, barely outlined by the single kerosene lantern hanging
in a window downstairs. The only evident motion or sound was that of
an occasional tail swishing or snorting of a horse in the animal lean-to
just within the compound wall. Satisfied that they were unobserved,
Monty sat down and tied a rope around his waist, lowering the free end
with multiple knots over the eave onto the porch below. It had been
determined that Ian would drop down the rope to make contact, while
Ashok would be available to follow should the need arise, particularly
if there was a lock to be picked.

"Here we go," Ian muttered through teeth clenched over his dagger.

"You look like an honest-to-God pirate," Monty chuckled softly as

Ashok gave the Lieutenant a hand over the roof's edge.

Stepping onto the wooden verandah, Ian swore quietly as the boards squeaked under his weight. Cautiously, as a man walking on thin ice, he eased toward the window. This has to be the room, he thought, peering through the bars into a blackness within. Ameena was to have forewarned Prem of the intended raid that night, so he must be expecting this contact. Holding his breath with mouth open, Ian listened. First he heard the muffled sounds of blankets being shifted on the bed and then the shuffling of slippered feet on the floor. Slowly, as in a mystic seance, a face took form in the shadows, the face of Prem Narayan.

"Prem," Ian whispered eagerly, "I'll move into the hallway and unbolt the door. We'll be escaping over the roof."

"Just a minute ... " the Captain broke off to reach between the bars and grasp the Lieutenant's hand ... "I'm going through with this cobra ritual in the morning and ... "

"Good God Prem! You must be off your chump, man. You can't mean it, you just can't mean it!" Ian pled. "Dash it all, we can get you out of here so easily."

"Ian." The word was commanding. "I do mean it!"

The Lieutenant drew in a deep breath and exhaled with a resigned sigh.

"How many of you?" the Captain asked.

"Six. Three of the Pakistanis, Sardar Khan, Monty and me."

"*Accha*. Hide out where you can watch the proceedings and make your raid immediately on my encounter with the cobras. The signal for your attack will be my shouting, 'swastika.'"

"It'll be daylight and someone's going to get hurt," Ian remonstrated quietly.

"We must get pakka evidence. Short of this the C.I.D. and the whole bloody project loses, with more cobra murders in the offing. Anyway, I've no doubt the six of you can give a good account of yourselves."

"Prem, that's not the point. You're the bloke who's caught in the middle. Even though you survive the cobra fangs, the bastards will shoot or knife you while we're charging in on the rescue."

"Hell, Ian, we've survived stickier wickets than these. We'll turn the tables on the cowards."

"Brought an extra automatic ... here."

"Better keep it. Just make trouble if they found it on me. Toss it in my direction when you raid."

"Righto." Ian slipped the gun back into his coat pocket.

"The goondas kidnapped Parkozian last night and brought him here this past morning. According to Ameena, the poor fellow died shortly after his arrival ... heart attack. Vandermeer and Appleton paid a visit last afternoon. I learned the two are in the drug smuggling business. By the way, Ali's not with you, eh?''

"No. We've been unable to contact him. His mother is sick and the clerk thinks Ali may be with her. Could the poor chap be a captive here?''

"Ameena thinks there's a male prisoner somewhere on the premises. At least she's not been permitted into one of the rooms below. If not a prisoner, it could be someone they wish to keep incognito.''

Ashok, worried by the passage of time, leaned over the eave and whispered, "Everything alright?''

"Be up shortly,'' Ian reassured him.

"*Accha*. Remember, don't attack until after I've had it with the cobras. In the meantime you'll have a good chance to study the premises and plan the raid.''

The Lieutenant reached through the bars and shook Prem's hand, asking hesitantly, "You're sure?''

"Absolutely!''

"Good luck and cheerio.'' Ian moved across the porch to the rope and quickly overhanded himself to the roof.

"What in God's name's going on?'' Monty whispered anxiously.

"Hold it until we get off of here,'' Ian replied, pressing a finger to his lips.

Retracing their steps onto the bluff, the men retrieved the sapling bridge and then all six retreated over the crest into the shadows of a clump of pines, where they were out of sight and sound of the building. Coming to a rest, Ian reported his conversation with Prem Narayan.

"The Captain has a point, this business of seeing the matter through to the bitter end.'' Ashok commented after hearing the Lieutenant out, adding as an aside, "A brave chap, I must admit.''

"You can say that again,'' Monty interjected.

"Freeze!'' Ian ordered in a barely audible whisper, grabbing the American's arm. Through the silence that followed, footsteps could be heard on the hillside a short distance away. "No contact unless we're forced into it,'' the Lieutenant continued, "and if so knives preferred to firearms.'' Hidden in the underbrush, Ian's party watched seven men approach in single file.

"Too damn close, but they're passing below us,'' Ashok muttered with relief.

"Now just who in hell could they be?'' Ian wondered.

"That's got to be Vandermeer,'' Monty announced incredulously.

"And I'll be, if that's not Ram Singh of Interpol in the lead,'' Ian whispered in surprise.

Sardar Khan broke in to add, "Sir, man in last position . . . he is Baldev Raj . . . Deputy Superintendent Police Srinagar.''

"You're right, that's Baldev Raj,'' Ian agreed, "but what is

Vandermeer doing with them? Maybe they've captured the Dutchman.''

"Hold it," Monty interrupted, raising his hand for attention, "they're stopping."

The party of seven began to gather in a circle. One of the men was flashing a torch onto a paper document which was being passed around for study. They were close enough for an occasional word to be picked up by Ian's men. Ram Singh of Interpol appeared to be the one in charge, for he carried the major portion of the conversation and kept pointing over the ridge toward the building.

Beckoning his men closer, Ian whispered, "These chaps are going to bugger up the whole bloody act. No doubt but what they're out to round up the narcotic smugglers who're the same bastards as the cobra murderers. Interpol ... Ram Singh ... must have caught Vandermeer and are forcing him to come along as guide. Damn it, we've got to check them before they alert the goondas. What say, Captain?"

"Precisely!" Ashok nodded an emphatic agreement.

"Jolly good," Ian announced, "it's up to me to do the needful." Then, hand signaling his men to lie low, he cautiously moved within the shadows, circling closer to the newcomers who continued to be absorbed in their document.

"Ram Singh," Ian whispered, carefully enunciating the name.

The effect of the announcement was electrifying. All seven of the party dropped to the ground in unison as if shot. There followed a few seconds of an eerie hush.

"Who calls?" The words, although barely audible, startled the silence.

"Lieutenant McVey."

"For God's sake, Ian, don't scare the hell out of us like that," Ram Singh gasped with relief.

Stepping out of the shadows, Ian walked over and joined the group.

"Vandermeer guided us here," Ram Singh confided, patting the Dutchman on the back.

"And where's the American, James Appleton?"

"Took him into custody a few hours ago. The chump had the evidence stacked in his quarters, packages of pure heroin. He's the number one person on the Western end of the connection. We've been watching the blighter for several months but never could pin him down with the drugs. He's now crossed off our list. We're here to pick up the blokes who were supplying Appleton. The American went into a funk and gave us names. They're all in that building, we think." He nodded toward the crest of the hill.

Drawing Ram Singh aside, Ian asked, "You know, I'm frightfully confused. Weren't Vandermeer and Appleton somehow tied up together in this drug business?"

"The Dutchman's one of our agents, actually an Interpol double agent. With the help of the United Nations International Narcotics Control Board we got the Colonel on the U.N. Kashmir Cease Fire Line Observer Team. The old chap's not only helped us nail the American drug kingpin but set up tonight's raid for us."

"I'll be!" Ian swore under his breath.

"On our request . . . Interpol's request . . . Lieutenant Baldev Raj joined us with four of his undercover police," Ram Singh explained.

"Did you run across any sentries . . . lookouts . . . on your way up here?"

"None."

"Neither did we. A bit strange, eh?"

"The blokes must feel secure here deep in the wilds."

"A bit daft, I'd say. Works to our advantage."

"Bloody fools," Ram muttered in disgust.

"We've a problem to resolve," Ian confided. "Our commitment . . . the cobra assassinations. Your commitment . . . that of Interpol . . . is to terminate the drug smuggling. What say we join forces and capture the whole bloody lot of them and then let the legal departments of Interpol and the C.I.D. fight over their disposition?"

Ram Singh agreed without hesitation. "Sounds good to me. How many of you are there?"

"Six, and each man excellently trained for this type of mission." Ian decided to hide the identity of the Pakistanis in the interest of their safety.

"Righto. What say we get on with it."

"Ram, we've a bit of a problem on timing." Ian shared Prem Narayan's plans to go through with the cobra ordeal, including the fact that the Captain had received immunization against the venom.

"That's what I call guts!" Ram Singh exclaimed, shaking his head incredulously. "The Captain's running true to form."

"He's a fearless blighter, I should know. I've been working with him for several years."

"But . . . but why does the chap have to go through the whole bloody thing . . . actually being bitten by the cobras?" His words projected an anxiety.

"Each assignment becomes an obsession with him. He's a blooming perfectionist. Realizing that these cobra killings have international implications, Prem wants a pakka case. In order to accomplish this, the capture of the criminals, he'll risk his life. So you see, going through the whole murder process step by step with all of us as witnesses, he'll have irrefutable evidence . . . pakka evidence. That's Captain Prem Narayan for you."

On hearing Ian out, Ram Singh drew in a deep breath and let it out with a long sigh. "I've heard rumors about the bloke, and now I'm believing them to be the truth."

"You'll wait and join us in a daylight raid?" Ian asked expectantly.

"Why not? Dash it all man, we can be more accurate and, although a bit more dangerous, less chance of the bastards escaping."

"And we'll have twice as many raiders," Ian concluded, extending his hand to Ram in confirmation of their agreement.

The Lieutenant rejoined his men and brought them up-to-date on the identity of the seven newcomers and the agreement on a joint attack. He suggested to Ashok that the three Pakistanis remain incognito, at least as to their nationality and dacoit affiliation. After the briefing, Ian invited the other group over and made a round of introductions.

"May I suggest that Lieutenant McVey be given command over this raid," Ram Singh proposed.

"Hear! Hear!" Baldev Raj, the police lieutenant responded with enthusiasm, accentuating the peculiar sibilance of his enunciation.

"Righto," Ian accepted the responsibility with a touch of self-consciousness and waved the men into a close circle. "First, let's get a couple of you out on watch, one at each end of the cliff checking out any action about the building or compound. Then we must have lookouts covering the trail . . . about a furlong before it breaks out into the open at this end. We jolly well have to judge whether to stop anyone or let them go through unaware that they're under observation. The success of this raid depends on the element of surprise. I'll set up our command post here in this clump of pines. We'll call all of you in before zero hour for a final go around on tactics."

"Two of my police can take over the cliff," Baldev Raj volunteered.

"Jolly good, and seeing Monty's already checked out the premises, I'll ask him to position your men," Ian explained.

"Okay," the American agreed, starting up toward the crest with the two plainclothes constables trailing him.

"Ashok, I'd like you to head the guards on the trail and . . . " Ian grasped the two Pakistanis by their arms . . . "how about taking these chaps with you. Sardar Khan will accompany you there and return so we'll know exactly where you'll be hiding."

In single file, the Pakistani Captain, his two cohorts and the Sergeant Major, moved out silently, soon absorbed by the forest shadows.

"Colonel Vandermeer," Ian addressed the portly Dutchman standing beside him, "in your dealings as an agent of Interpol you've been in contact with these blokes . . . in fact just this past day you and Appleton were here on the premises. Let me ask you, are the cobra assassins one and the same group with the narcotics smugglers?"

"Ya . . . same group."

"Are they all Afghanis?"

He shook his head. "Their top man, the vun giving final orders, is not from Afghanistan. The rest are Afghanis."

"No Russians?"

"Not any member of the assassins, but a man from the Russian Embassy in Delhi visits with them from time to time."

"What's his name?"

"Ivan something or other. Ivan is all I've heard," the Dutchman replied, scratching his head thoughtfully.

"Colonel, any idea as to who the top man is?"

"Can't say for sure. I've had no direct dealings. The bloke keeps very much in the background. I'm convinced he's either an Indian or Pakistani."

"Just who do you deal with?"

"Don't even know the man's name but they call him 'The Falcon.'"

"Not Achmed?"

The Dutchman shook his head vigorously. "No, not Achmed."

"But this Falcon chap, he's an Afghani?"

"Ya, ya. The Falcon is an Afghani ... " Vandermeer pointed at the back of his hand before going on ... "has falcons tattooed here on both sides."

"Same as Achmed?"

"Ya."

"Colonel, did you by any chance enter the room where Doreen Duncan and the waif Mos were being held captive at the gang's other place near Baramula?"

"I vas the man. The Falcon vould ask for advice and I vould give it ... had to do this in order to keep my cover. Sometimes I vas asked to check up on things. That evening I vas visiting the headquarters and found out about the young voman's kidnapping. I vas asked by the Falcon to drop in on the captives. I tried to protect her ... threatened the bastard Achmed."

"Jolly good. That clears up things a bit. We've been wondering just who the European was that stepped in and intervened on behalf of Doreen and the waif."

"Vun other thing ... Parkozian was kidnapped and brought here yesterday." Vandermeer pointed over the crest toward the building.

"And the poor bloke died ... heart attack," Ian interjected.

"Too bad." The Dutchman sounded surprised. "He vas a good man. Now the Russian lady, Maya Reznikoff, vill direct the Dowry of Death."

"How'd you know that?" It was Ian's turn to be surprised.

Choosing not to speak, Colonel Vandermeer responded with a noncommittal grunt.

"Then we're really dealing with three men: The top leader who may be either Indian or Pakistani, the Falcon and Achmed?" Ian pursued his questioning.

"Ya ... three men here and the Russian Ivan who drops in from time to time. The rest are underlings ... cutthroats and riffraff. One of their retainers is a ne'er-do-vell Kashmiri by the name of Kafir Jacub.''

"I know all about that fellow. He tried to knife Prem Narayan aboard the Kashmir Princess the other night. He'll have a helluva time knifing anybody now with both hands missing.''

"The raid on the Baramula headquarters of the assassins gave the buggers a bit of a shock,'' Vandermeer confided with a chuckle.

"When they freed Miss Duncan?''

"Ya. That Monty Brown really is something ... ya?''

"He's pretty close mouthed about his activities, but I'm willing to take your word. And how did you learn about it?''

"The Falcon told Appleton and me here yesterday.''

"Well at least now you know that the Pakistani dacoits do exist. You weren't so sure when Captain Narayan interviewed you at Nedou's.''

Vandermeer nodded. "This Captain Ashok, he is one of them, ya?''

"He is ... but Colonel let's not talk about it, what say?''

Again he nodded before adding, "My shooting is good even though I'm not light of foot. You vill permit me to join the raid?'' the Colonel asked hesitantly.

"Absolutely ... you're on the team,'' Ian assured him, reaching out to shake the Dutchman's hand.

"Thanks! I have some scores to settle vith the swine.'' Vandermeer's voice was ice.

Chapter Twenty-four

As Ashok and his two men settled into the deeper shadows of the pine forest to monitor the trail, the darkness was intensifying with the lowering of a partial moon. A benumbing cold permeated the still air seeping through their clothes, first to nip and then to torment the skin. In spite of the blackness of the night, they could see the intermittent puffs of condensed breath before their faces. The men took turns pacing back and forth through the trees in order to maintain a minimum of body warmth. As the night crawled on, the tedium of inactivity bore heavily on the sentries. Then suddenly their monotonous state of affairs changed to acute tension at the muffled sound of hoofbeats approaching on the path. Alerted by the warning signal, the three Pakistanis froze into immobility straining their eyes to penetrate the shadows. Shortly the murky outlines of two mounted hill ponies emerged plodding toward them in single file. The riders, bundled up against the weather, slouched in their saddles like inanimate sacks of produce.

"We'll strike at the same time from behind," Ashok whispered, "pull the bloody fools off their mounts and overpower them before they know what's happened. I'll grab the horses. Can't let them get away to warn the bastards up at the building. Remember, use knives ... firearms only as a last resort."

The three men crept closer to the trail and crouched behind separate bushes tensed for action. The scarves and blankets encircling the heads and necks of the two horsemen made their identification next to impossible, even as they drew adjacent to the ambushers. Ashok gave the hand signal to attack and the three engaged in an action so quickly and silently effected that it gave the appearance of a staged pantomime. Simultaneously dislodged from behind, the riders fell to the ground offering no other responses than grunts of surprise. The Captain quietly grasped the bridles of both ponies and soothed them into submission after their initial snorts of fright. Relieving the captives of arms ... each carried an automatic ... Ashok removed the scarves and studied their faces under the light of his torch. One of them appeared to be a bodyguard, probably an Afghani, slender of build and most apprehensive. The other obviously was European, stockily built and greatly disturbed by the fact that he had lost his glasses in the fall from his horse. The man's inept groping for the article gave evidence of his dependence on the missing visual aid. Noting this handicap, Ashok decided that in the interest of the prisoner's continued incapacitation, the spectacles should not be recovered.

"Outrageous, you hoodlums, absolutely outrageous!" the European shouted in heavily accented English.

"Not so loud or I'll take your clothes off and let you run around naked," Ashok warned impatiently.

"Your government shall hear of this ... you dog ... you swine!" The threat was voiced in even louder shouts.

Quickly with one hand Ashok drew his knife and thrust the point forward pricking the pit of the captive's stomach, while with the other he began unbuttoning the man's overcoat.

"*Nyet* ... no," the European pled in a whining voice, trying with trembling fingers to push away the dagger-holding fist of his captor.

"Now that's a helluva lot better," Ashok muttered, replacing his knife in its sheath. "You're a bloody Russian, right?"

"*Da* ... with our embassy in Delhi." He nodded emphatically.

"And you are what?"

"What you just called me, a hoodlum," Ashok laughed in his face, "What the hell are you doing coming along here at this ungodly time of the night?"

"Business for the Russian Embassy."

"The hell you are? Business with those bastard turncoat puppets of yours up there." He nodded toward the building.

'*Nyet*," the Russian replied, shivering and pulling his coat collar high about his neck.

"You lie in your throat and you know it. You're hand-in-glove with those damned bastards." His voice had the cutting edge of a sharp knife. "You're fighting the Dowry of Death, eh?"

"Please ... you must treat me with respect ... I am a diplomatic. I am comrade first secretary Ivan Dostovitch," he begged in words that trembled.

"Relax you blithering idiot. I hate your guts for invading Afghanistan. You may not know it yet but the Russian bear will never conquer those Afghanis. The British never did and you won't either. Those *mujahidin* will fight you till hell freezes over. I really should do away with you right here, but I shan't."

"Thank you ... I shall make no official report against your action. I shall leave now." The Russian started to move toward his pony.

"The hell you will. You're going to spend a cold and lonely night in the forest, but before I place you out there, come here." Ashok opened the Russian's overcoat and went through his inside pockets, finding a sealed official envelope which he confiscated over Ivan's vehement protests. Then leaving his two cohorts in charge of the other captive and ponies, he prodded the stumbling prisoner into the woods. Some hundred yards from the trail, Ashok called a halt beside a fallen log on which he seated the half-blind European.

"Now listen, you cobra murderer, don't you go buggering off from here in any direction, understand?

"*Da . . . da . . .* I shall stay here," the Russian whimpered, dropping his face into the palms of his hands with a loud groan.

Returning to the trailway, Ashok had his men search the captured guard for any letters and, finding none, went through the same maneuvers as with the European, only on the opposite side of the path. Finally they took the two horses in still another direction and tethered them separately to pine saplings. With the situation under control, the three Pakistanis again set up their watch. A barely perceptible blushing of the eastern sky heralded the birth of another day.

Lieutenant Ian McVey had been bitterly disappointed after his graduation from middle school with honors that he had not been selected as a candidate for Sandhurst, the elite military officers' training academy of Great Britain. In spite of this unfulfillment, he maintained a keen interest in the planning and execution of raids such as this against the cobra gang. His superior, Captain Narayan, noting this talent for tactical theory and its practical application, had recommended to the C.I.D. headquarters that the Lieutenant be supported in continued special courses in this particular field.

Using a torch shaded by the circle of seated figures, Ian drew up plans for the morning attack. Welcoming input from his cohorts, details were revised and clarified until they were understood and accepted by all participants present. Alternate action options were prepared for conceivable variant situations. An estimate of the numerical strength of the opposition was placed at not more than twelve.

"At all costs, Ameena the maid must be protected," Ian warned.

It had been decided, with Monty actually checking out the approach personally, that the attackers could station themselves outside the compound without being seen, even from the upper story, by crawling around close to the wall. Their watch from the top of the cliff would be in direct visual contact and could alert them as to the proper timing for moving into the attack positions. Due to the cramped quarters of the rooms, Ian had concluded that the proposed execution would be carried out in the courtyard. A barrier five feet high would pose no problem in achieving rapid entrance into the compound. The easiest site for breaching the wall was at the animal lean-to, where one could gain access without being seen by anyone in the building or courtyard. As the discussion concluded, dawn had come and gone while the sun, still hidden behind the Himalayas, was transforming the ghostly white-summited peaks into glowing pink sentinels.

"Sardar, slip down and fetch Ashok," Lieutenant McVey instructed the Sergeant Major, going on to add, "I want his two men to remain there and prohibit anyone from approaching or leaving this area.''

Within a few minutes the Pakistani Captain had joined the group and immediately recounted the capture and disposition of the Russian, his guard and the ponies. Ian stuffed the confiscated letter in his pocket to be read later.

"Ashok, here are the plans," Ian confided, taking him aside and spreading out a drawing of the premises to be attacked, "As soon as we determine from our cliff watch that the cobra confrontation is imminent, we move into the attack positions. Sardar Khan and Ram Singh of Interpol will remain up here on the cliff's edge from where they can observe the whole action. Baldev Raj with one of his constables will move in behind the animal lean-to there on the north ... '' Ian pointed out the spot and then continued ... "while his three other policemen will spread out separately behind the wall, remaining there throughout the raid to cut off any attempts at escape. Now you and the Dutchman will be at the courtyard gate, here on the east, with the Colonel holding his position throughout the fracas to prevent getaways through that portal. That leaves Monty and me. We'll be covering the south end of the compound, directly across from the horse stall and Baldev Raj. Now with your two men down the trail, that makes up our total force of thirteen. Any questions so far?"

Ashok shook his head and urged in Hindustani, *"Kahte jao*—Keep on talking.''

Ian drew in a deep breath before going on, "Captain Narayan will shout the signal, 'swastika,' immediately after being exposed to the cobras. The constable, who will be hiding inside the lean-to with the animals, will cut their tethers and stampede them into the compound."

"How many horses?" Ashok broke in.

"Five ... and the constable chap who'll be doing the stampeding already has been in the stall and made his acquaintance with the animals." Ian chuckled and Ashok joined in the laughter.

"So we all attack, but exactly how many of us will be involved in the initial rush?"

"In the confusion of the stampede, four of us ... Monty, Baldev Raj, you and I ... jump the wall and capture the cobra gang."

"With much shouting I hope."

"You're damned right. We'll initiate the charge with our whole blooming force shouting. Psychological warfare, don't you know."

It was the Pakistani Captain's time to chuckle. "Blimey, can you imagine the shock those buggers will experience as they look about and see they're surrounded ... totally surrounded."

"Ashok, sometime I'll have to tell you the story of Gideon's army and how a handful of men destroyed the powerful Midianites. But getting back to the raid, we must reach Prem Narayan immediately or one of the bastards might try to do him in. I'm taking on that particular mission. I've an extra automatic to hand him. Then too, we'll have to protect Ameena from harm."

"What about Ali Aurangzeb?"

Ian shook his head. "Wish I knew where in hell the chap is. We just might find him a prisoner here ... " his voice faded into silence.

The two men rose and moved over to join the group who were busy checking out their automatics, tightening shoelaces and doing all those little things that soldiers do just before going into combat.

Chapter Twenty-five

A scintillating sun cautiously crested the serrated snowy summit of the Himalayas to the east, its searching rays relentlessly sweeping out from the valleys below any lingering remnants of the night's shadows. Awakened by the sunlight flooding his room, Prem Narayan sat up, stretched his arms, jumped out of bed and stepped over to the window, all in one seemingly continuous motion. In spite of a morbid dream that disturbed his sleep . . . a dream of hooded cobras circling his bed in single file . . . the Captain felt rested and faced this crucial day with an unusual optimism stemming in large part from the knowledge that his cohorts were close by ready to lend a hand.

There were signs of activity in the compound below. On the far side a syce was feeding the hill ponies in the lean-to and cleaning out their stalls. In the central open area of the courtyard a servant appeared to be removing the ashes from the clay *tandur* or oven which had been molded and fire-hardened the day before. Somewhat unusual was the fact that, except for the horses, there were no other animals about the premises . . . no dogs or goats or chickens. This lack probably was due to the somewhat precipitous move from the previous quarters. All to our advantage, Prem thought, no dogs around to bark an alarm giving away the proximity of the raiders. Having meticulously surveyed the area outside, Captain Narayan moved away from the window and filled the hand basin with cold water from an adjacent pitcher. Removing his clothes he took a shivering sponge bath. The following brisk rubdown with a dry towel brought a welcome tingling warmth to his goose-pimpled skin. Being fastidious in matters of personal toilet, he grunted with dissatisfaction at the stubble of whiskers covering his face. Hearing a gentle knocking on the door, he hurriedly slipped on his trousers and threw a blanket about his shoulders. Ameena discreetly peeked inside and seeing all was in order, entered with a breakfast tray which she began unloading onto the table.

"*Dhanyavad* - Thank you," Prem said, waving his hand at the hot food.

Continuing to set out the dishes and without turning to face him, she asked in a whisper, "*Ap us admi-se mile*-Did you meet that man?"

The Captain grunted to gain her attention and nodded. She responded with a look of relief.

Putting on his socks, shoes and coat, Prem sat down at the table and began his breakfast, while Ameena moved about quietly tidying the room. Several times he caught her eyeing him sadly. She's been through this before, he thought, and knows what I'm facing. But then she also must be aware of my friends hidden in the surrounding forest. Her duties completed, she moved toward the door to leave. On the threshold she paused to whisper, "*Allahu Akbar*-God is most great." Prem, a Hindu, sensed a glowing warmth within as he accepted this sincere benediction from a Muslim.

From his seat at the breakfast table, the Captain again turned his attention to the compound below. He was intrigued by the clay tandur which by now was receiving the attention of two servants. All of the ashes apparently had been removed through a portal at the bottom of the stove. One of the men disappeared into a room on the ground floor and returned shortly carrying a basket which he carefully placed on the ground beside the oven. Then slowly he began removing eggs from it, one by one, and slipping them through the portal at the base onto the floor inside the tandur.

"That's it! My God that's it!" Prem exclaimed, jumping to his feet and staring through the window. "The crushed egg in the hand of each murdered man ... that's it!" He watched incredulously as the servant emptied the basket. "They'll be putting the cobras into that bloody tandur next. Then the victim's forced to reach in from the top to retrieve an egg just to be sure the poor bloke puts his hand down into the damned snake pit ... " his voice trailed off and then picked up again ... "Those murdering sadistic bastards."

A knocking on the door drew the Captain's attention away from the activities in the compound. The metallic rasping of hinges presaged the entrance of a visitor, who stepped into the room without speaking. The top of his head and ears were covered by a knitted stocking cap and his bearded face was almost hidden by the ample collar of a military coat.

"Please be seated," Prem invited, waving toward the stool beside the table. "Unfortunately there is only one of these articles of furniture but courtesy dictates that you, as my guest, be offered its comforts." His words dripped with sarcasm.

The intruder continued to remain silent and made no move toward the seat.

"I say old chap, must I conclude that you don't understand English?" Prem asked impatiently.

"You don't recognize me?" There was a plaintive note in his voice.

"Ali ... Ali Aurangzeb! So the bloody assassins got you too!"

Choosing not to reply, the Lieutenant merely grunted.

"And you didn't get the shots ... the protection ... " Prem broke off in mid-sentence, clenching his teeth and bulging his jaw muscles. Just in time he had seen the expression on the intruder's face.

Ali came closer, eyes staring vacantly and pupils contracted to pin points. "Shots, what the hell do you mean, shots?" His words were thick-tongued and slurred.

"Oh ... you know ... typhus shots ... just a bit of protection," Prem cut in abruptly.

"Righto, Captain, just typhus shots, eh? Not referring to narcotics?" The slurring speech took on a menacing note.

"Just typhus," Prem shot back, grateful that he had stopped short of revealing his antivenin immunization.

"You and your damned C.I.D.!" There was pent-up anger in his words.

"Ali, what in hell do you mean? What in God's name has come over you?"

"It may be hard for you to believe this, but I head up the cobra gang."

"Oh my God," Prem groaned, shaking his head incredulously.

"And in the pay of the Russians in Kabul," he blurted out, then exploded into gales of mirthless laughter.

"But why, Ali, in God's name why?"

"You damn Hindus and Sikhs don't give us Muslims a chance," he sneered. "We're a bloody minority."

"That's a blatant lie and you know it," Prem replied angrily, and went on, "For one thing there are almost as many Muslims in India as in Pakistan, and talking about minorities, what about the Sikhs or for that matter the Christians. Take Lieutenant McVey, he's been facing a double jeopardy, if you will, being a Christian and an Anglo-Indian. Yet Ian's opted to remain in India ... deliberately chosen to be an Indian citizen."

"Tomorrow I'll be heading for Kabul where I'll be somebody."

"With the Russians and their Afghani puppets," Prem taunted.

"Promotions and better pay," Ali quipped with a smirk.

"You damned traitor! Climbing over the dead bodies of fellow Muslims you've murdered. Ali you're sick, completely off your chump, completely daft. I just feel awful." A cramping nausea discomfited the pit of Prem's abdomen.

"I'm glad to share all this with you face to face before the cobras take over." There was a hint of sadness in Ali's words.

"You had a good career ahead of you ... " the Captain shook his head sadly before continuing ... "but you've damned well funked out."

"Not according to my calculations," the Lieutenant growled.

"What about the calculations of your victims: Allabaksh, Ahmed Feroze and Sayad Khan? Or for that matter the calculations of your friends, Ian McVey, Sardar Khan and me?"

Choosing not to reply, Ali stared abstractedly out the window.

"Well, Lieutenant, you'd better bugger off before I vomit." Prem waved him toward the door. Without looking at the Captain he shuffled out, sliding the lock bolt into position behind him.

Captain Narayan sat down onto the stool with a deep and sad sigh, folding his arms on the table before him and laying his head on them. He was sickened, emotionally and physically, finding it difficult to believe what he had just heard. His eyes moistened with remorse as he thought back upon years of association and friendship with Ali Aurangzeb, the very man who now planned his execution. It was he then who had set up the ambush on the Pahalgam road and not Appleton or Vandermeer. The Hakim had warned of the official who barters justice.

Without knocking, Achmed jerked open the bolt, pushed the door ajar and strode into the room to stand, arms akimbo, before Captain Narayan.

"You don't even have the courtesy to knock, do you?" Prem censured the intruder.

"A bloody old fool, that's what you are, arguing about a little matter of courtesy when you'll be dead in a couple of hours."

"My good fellow, courtesy is no little matter. It happens to be that thin line which distinguishes a gentleman from a knave."

"Damn it, Captain, I don't understand you. Aren't you afraid of death?" The Afghani sounded puzzled.

"Achmed, I've faced death many times and lived to ponder these experiences in retrospect. I believe the matter of life and death lies in the hands of the Gods. The English word is fate. We Hindus speak of karma and you Muslims use the word kismet."

"Well, your karma comes to an end today," he sneered with a disparaging laugh.

"Time will tell," Prem muttered in an aside to himself.

"Let me recite the rules of the game, Captain. I'm certain you've observed the tandur in the middle of the compound. That is your executioner's block, so to speak ... " he chuckled at his macabre quip before going on ... "and within it will be three modest sized cobras, more poisonous at this stage of their growth. Spread over the floor of the tandur will be a dozen chicken eggs. On command you will reach inside through the top, arm bare, and fetch out one egg. This insures your getting into the nest of snakes. Simple, isn't it?" Achmed studied the Captain's eyes while reciting the procedure, disappointed at not catching even a hint of fear.

"And should I refuse to reach into the tandur?" The words carried a ring of defiance.

"You'll be shot on the spot."

"Might that not be a kinder death?" Prem smiled enigmatically into his captor's face.

"Possibly," Achmed replied, still disturbed by the Captain's apparent lack of personal concern.

"And what if I retrieve an unbroken egg from this . . . this snake pit of yours?"

Achmed hesitated, momentarily flustered by the unusual question, but regained his composure to reply, "No one's done that yet, and I don't expect you to."

"I take it you'll all be there to watch this . . . this execution?"

"Yes, the important ones. Even our Russian liaison from their embassy in Delhi. For some reason the chap's been delayed, but we're expecting him any minute. If he's not here soon we'll start the show without him."

"Achmed, you're not coming down with smallpox, are you?"

"What the hell do you mean?"

"Those strange blisters or marks on your cheeks.?"

The Afghani reached to feel his face and then muttered self-consciously, "That bloody little bastard waif of the American threw some coals at me the other night."

Chapter Twenty-six

One of the lookouts scrambled back from the edge of the cliff and alerted Lieutenant McVey that someone was being led down the ladder-like steps from the upper story into the compound below. At Ian's request, Monty quickly returned with the constable and verified that the person in question was Captain Narayan. This was the cue to the deployment of the raiding force. As prearranged, each man stealthily crept to his post to await the attack signal, Prem's shout, "Swastika". Seven people were gathered in a semicircle about the tandur, while five others ... guards and syces ... lolled in the background. Including Achmed, who walked behind the Captain, there were thirteen persons in the courtyard.

Erect and with a defiant smile on his face, Prem Narayan strode toward the group, all the while unobtrusively scanning his environs. Thank God, Ameena isn't here, Prem thought. The only ones in the compound whom he could recognize, besides Achmed, were Ali Aurangzeb and Kafir Jacub. Apparently the Russian still had not arrived. All eyes were focused on the Captain as he walked up to the tandur, stopped and briskly about-faced to eye his executioners.

"Traitors to your countries and cowards, each one of you," his ringing words of denunciation were steeped in disgust. He stood for a moment returning the stares of the men before him, then spat deliberately and contemptuously on the ground at their feet.

"Have done with that!" Achmed shouted, angrily waving his bandaged left arm at the Captain. Still mumbling incoherently, the Afghani stepped forward to pull off the victim's coat, leaving him standing in a short-sleeved undershirt. Then moving back into the ranks of the observers, he commanded, "Now let's on with it. You've been instructed on the procedure."

As Prem turned toward the tandur, one of the guards came over and jerked away a metal cooking pan covering its open top. The head of a cobra cautiously raised up out of the clay oven, its cold and unblinking eyes glinting malignantly in the sunlight. For a moment ... startled by the human spectators ... it paused, nervously sampling the morning air with its flicking sensory tongue, then slid back into the pit. Finally thrust into an awareness of what he must do, for the first time the Captain experienced a nauseating wave of revulsion. The surface of his body prickled as tiny beads of perspiration broke through the pores of his skin. For a brief moment his arms rebelled. Then clenching his jaws tightly ... so tightly that the muscles cramped in pain ... he moved up to the tandur and slowly slid one hand toward the upper opening. There was an intense and eerie silence in the courtyard as all eyes focused on the central character in this ghoulish drama. Giving a final quick glance about him to locate the exact positions of those standing near, Prem continued his cautious reach within the oven. The feel of clammy rippling muscles of the cobras against the back of his hand froze him into a moment of inaction. Then biting his lower lip tightly between his teeth, he forced his reluctant fingers deeper into the snake pit.

An expectation of the strike partially dulled the sharp edge of surprise, but did little to assuage the excruciating pain of the injected venom. Synchronous with the butting of the cobra's snout against the Captain's skin was the searing penetration of its poisonous fangs into the muscles of his forearm. It seemed to him that every sensory nerve in his body responded vicariously to this outrageous physical insult. Time stopped for what seemed an eternity to the victim and then the planned action almost automatically went into effect. With a shout, "Swastika," which echoed back from the granite cliffs, Prem firmly grasped a cobra and jerking it out of the tandur, swirled it above his head before releasing the writhing reptile directly at Achmed. To the horror of the spellbound observers, the serpent struck the Afghani's head and slid down about both shoulders where it hung just long enough to sink its fangs into his neck. With a sickening scream Achmed fell to his knees and, wailing the Koran death verses, began flailing his chest with both fists. The cobra, head raised and hood spread, coiled on the ground near by, hissing angrily at its adversary.

A loud shout drew everyone's attention to the animal lean-to just in time to watch a stampede of hill ponies spread out across the courtyard. As a climactic thrust to the resulting pandemonium, a concerted yelling ringed the outside of the compound and in the midst of this noise four men, each carrying an automatic, vaulted the wall to join the fray. Ian sprinted directly to Prem's side, handing him a gun which the Captain grasped with his left hand, the other still numbed by the snake venom. Then, at a warning shout from his chief, the Lieutenant turned just in time to grapple with a knife-wielding assailant, knocking the uplifted weapon out of his hand and crumpling him to the ground with a fist blow to the pit of his stomach.

"Ali ... what in hell ... " Ian broke off at a loss for words and stared incredulously down on his would-be assailant.

"He's one of them," Prem shouted in warning and added with a mixture of sadness and disgust, "He's their leader."

"Oh my God ... no ... no," the Lieutenant groaned, "how bloody awful!" He quickly stooped down and removed Ali Aurangzeb's automatic from its holster. "You must have gone daft, completely off your chump to do this." Ian watched his prisoner's eyelids flutter and then open revealing constricted pupils staring vacantly.

Monty and Ashok were busy rounding up the guards and syces, disarming each one and having them lie on the ground face down with arms above their heads. The surprise and speed of the attack precluded organized resistance, leading to a rapid capitulation. One of the syces, in his desperate effort to escape, climbed the courtyard wall only to fall into the hands of an unsympathetic constable. Unnoticed in the fast-moving fracas, a member of the gang edged his way toward the compound gate. Observing this attempted flight from his vantage point on the cliff, Ram Singh of Interpol started down around the bluff to head off the man. His efforts were unnecessary, for by the time he arrived at the gate, the escapee lay dead on the path just outside the premises. Colonel Vandermeer stood beside the body, his automatic in hand.

"Vas one of their top men . . . an Afghani stooge of the Russians . . . ya," the Dutchman said with bitterness. "He vas a murderer. He shot down a friend of mine in cold blood. Never vill he do that again. He is called 'The Falcon' by the cobra assassins."

Ram Singh inspected the backs of the man's tattooed hands and agreed, "That's the bloke alright . . . The Falcon . . . one of the top narcotics smugglers. This should slow down the traffic, at least for a bit of time."

"Ya," Vandermeer grunted, nodding soberly.

Meanwhile the turmoil within the compound was subsiding. The horses had been rounded up and the three cobras dispatched by Ashok's automatic.

"Monty, let's get Prem on a pony right away. Take him down to the jeep on Pahalgam road and then on to the Srinagar hospital. I alerted Doctor Sahgal yesterday about the possibility of his having a patient or two so he'll be expecting you. Get Bruce Duncan in on this."

"Okay, I'll get the Captain on his way."

Achmed lay cyanotic and comatose on the ground, his respiratory center slowly being paralyzed. At Ian's request, Ashok had examined him and come to the conclusion that the cobra's fangs had sunk into the jugular area of the neck with a massive dose of venom being absorbed rapidly. The Afghani was beyond help of any kind.

"And how's the bugger doing?" Ian asked.

"Blighter's on his last legs. Done in by the damned cobra. Funny thing, but when I opened up his military overcoat to check his condition, the middle button was missing."

"We have it, the missing button. Monty found the blasted thing on the path where Doreen Duncan was abducted in Gulmarg. She probably pulled it off the coat during her struggle to escape."

"Definitely Pakistani . . . the buttons . . . standard military issue."

"That's what Sardar Khan thought."

"Bloke either got it on the black market or filched it off some poor Pakistani soldier."

Under the direction of their chief, Baldev Raj, the four constables sorted and handcuffed the guards and syces. Kafir Jacub, with both hands missing, had manacles applied to his ankles. Lieutenant Ali Aurangzeb, dazed, sullen and noncommunicative, sat with his back against the compound wall under the watchful eye of the Interpol agent, Ram Singh.

"Ashok," Ian called, beckoning him over to where Prem was preparing to mount a pony, "this is Captain Narayan ... and Prem, this is Captain Ashok."

"What an extraordinary nerve! I mean, going through with this cobra encounter and then grabbing that bloody snake and throwing it the way you did," Ashok exclaimed, grasping Prem's outstretched left hand.

Captain Narayan grinned self-consciously, giving a disparaging shrug of his shoulders. "We're indebted to you old chap, not only for helping us here, but for working on Miss Duncan's release."

Don't mention. We had a common enemy," the Pakistani came back with a chuckle, and added sympathetically, "do have care, eh?"

"Ashok, take someone with you and check out the building," Ian broke in, "I'm worried about Ameena."

Calling one of the constables, the Pakistani Captain headed for the building on a run.

Ian held the reins of the two ponies while Monty and Prem mounted. "How do you feel?" he asked, pointing at the Captain's right arm.

"It's sore as hell but nothing I can't handle." He held up the forearm.

"Just one snake bit you?" Monty asked.

"Just one. But don't ask me why. The way I reached down into that tandur and grabbed the bloody cobra, all three should have sunk their fangs into me. Thank God for the antivenin. Bruce Duncan'll have a frightfully good time writing me up in a medical journal, eh what?" Prem chortled.

"Be seeing you in Srinagar shortly," Ian promised, "first have to clean this place up. Baldev Raj has a police lorry for the prisoners parked on the Pahalgam road. And, I say, tell Ashok's two chaps on the trail to stay there with their prisoners until we come along."

"Say, Lieutenant," Prem called back, turning in his saddle and throwing a salute, "jolly good show you put on here, a damned good show!" The two horsemen headed for the compound gate.

"Captain Narayan," Ram Singh called out, as the ponies gingerly stepped around a body on the path, "after this morning I shan't doubt the stories I've heard about you."

Prem hardly noted the words of the Interpol agent but stared incredulously at Colonel Vandermeer. "I don't understand," he muttered, pointing at the Dutchman.

"I'll explain it all," Monty broke in.

"Sorry, Ram Singh, I didn't quite get what you said," the Captain apologized, still staring at Vandermeer.

"After this morning's demonstration, I'll believe all the wild stories about you."

"Don't do that," Prem laughed, "but thanks for the compliment. And incidentally, your assistance came in damned handy."

"Captain, this is The Falcon, second in command of these bloody murderers," the Interpol agent pointed at the dead man on the path.

Prem leaned over to study the face more closely. "That's the same bloke who lit my cigarette in the Delhi hotel and flew up here to Srinagar with us."

"He's not the same man Doreen and I watched in the dining room at Nedou's the night the cobra was planted in the Red Chariot," Monty countered "The chap we saw there was Achmed."

"Bastard was one of the top priorities ... on the wanted list ... of Interpol," Ram Singh confided, "Heavy into heroin smuggling, and with the support of Kabul."

"Better get you on the way to the hospital," Monty urged as the two men started down the trail and soon disappeared into the pine trees.

Remembering the letter Ashok had taken from the captured Russian, Ian retrieved it from his pocket. The embossed letterhead was quite impressive and official looking from the U.S.S.R. Embassy in New Delhi. Brief and to the point, it was addressed to Ali Aurangzeb instructing him in English to liquidate Captain Prem Narayan and dispose of his body in a manner precluding its ever being discovered in a recognizable form. It was not to be retrieved as were the other cobra victim's bodies. The document was signed over the typewritten name of Boris Stepnyak, First Secretary. The scrawled signature was illegible.

Ashok shouted and beckoned Ian to join him in the building. The urgency of the invitation brought the Lieutenant to his side on the run and the two went directly to the kitchen.

"How horrible ... the bloody swine!" Ian muttered through clenched teeth, looking down on Ameena's body sprawled on the floor, a scarf tightly knotted about her neck.

"Must have suspected she was our agent and ... " Ashok's voice choked into silence. After swallowing several times, he added sadly, "Aisha will take this frightfully hard, don't you know."

"Sorry old chap, very sorry." A deep sincerity flooded Ian's words. The two stood quietly for a moment sobered by the tragedy of Ameena's cruel death.

"Couldn't find a trace of Parkozian's body," Ashok broke the silence, "and we searched through all the rooms on both floors."

"Probably buried the poor bloke somewhere. We'll find out."

Rounding up the party, except for the constables who were placed in charge of the prisoners, Ian discussed areas of responsibility. It was agreed that Baldev Raj and his four men would be in charge of all persons captured in the raid, including the guard for the Russian ambushed on the trail. The police lorry waiting on the Pahalgam road would have ample space to transfer the whole lot, including the bodies of The Falcon and Achmed, to the Srinagar jail and the morgue. The proper disposal of Ameena's remains was to be handled by Ashok.

"Vat about the Russian . . . he will make trouble, ya?" Vandermeer asked.

Ian chuckled and shook his head. "We have that bugger right where we want him." With that he took the letter Ashok had confiscated and read its content out loud. "If I know those Russians, we won't hear a peep out of them when they realize this document's in our hands. I've already asked Ashok to drop . . . what's his name . . . "

"Ivan Dostovitch," the Pakistani Captain broke in.

"To drop Ivan off somewhere in Srinagar and let the bloody fool find his own way beyond that point," Ian continued.

"Splendid!" Ram Singh exclaimed, "Burn the paws of the damned bear for supporting narcotic traffic."

"You chaps will have your reports to make and we'll get ours off to the C.I.D. I must insist that no mention be made of Ashok and his two men in any of your reports. They are our undercover agents and their identities must be kept a secret. Baldev, Ali Aurangzeb most certainly will be a target of the Russians and their Kabul stooges. He just knows too damned much about their clandestine moves into India. Better have your police tighten up their security. Of course the C.I.D. will be involved in his trial. God what a sickening mistake the poor blighter made."

"I've been suspicious for several weeks that the chap was into something crooked," Baldev Raj confided in his whistling voice, "I planned to warn you but really had no proper proof."

"As for Interpol, Ram, you should have plenty to report, what with The Falcon and Appleton. This whole thing's such a bloody mess: assassinations by cobras, international narcotic smuggling and the international movement of small arms by the Dowry of Death. The intrigue will heat up the embassies in Delhi." Ian gave out a noisy sigh and reached for his pipe, filling and lighting it under the close observation of his party of raiders. Then with the pipestem clenched between his teeth he asked, "Any questions before we carry on?"

Baldev Raj raised his hand for attention and announced, "We'll be using three ponies for the three bodies so the living will have to walk to the Pahalgam road." He chuckled at his attempt at humor and was supported by a sprinkling of laughter.

"One last thing," Ian interjected, "be certain to notify Doctor Sahgal at the hospital that Achmed died from cobra venom. He and Doctor Duncan are specialists in snake bites and will want to give particular attention to the victim. Righto, let's get on with it." He dispersed the group with a wave.

Chapter Twenty-seven

After two days of hospitalization, over the objections of his medical mentors, Prem Narayan decided to sign himself out of his sick bed and move back to his cabin on the Kashmir Princess. With Ian McVey tied up in the resolution of the many and intricate problems related to the raid, Monty Brown offered the services of his Red Chariot to transport the Captain from hospital to houseboat.

"Sure you're ready to solo?" the American questioned his passenger as they drove through Srinagar.

"Ready to solo?" Prem raised his eyebrows.

"Ready to be on your own?"

"Aha. Wasn't sure whether your terminology was musical or aeronautical. But seriously, I'm feeling quite chipper really. A bit of swelling perhaps but no reason why I can't take the antibiotics on the Princess. Duncan and Sahgal have turned me into a damned guinea pig . . . an experimental animal . . . drawing blood samples every few hours even during the night. I can't even piss in a toilet because they want it all collected. Then they've been banging my arms and legs with that bloody reflex hammer until . . . " Prem rolled his eyes and gave out with a loud laugh.

"You're a rare bird. It's unusual to have a patient who's had the antivenin before the bite."

"So, you've been training members of the Afghani mujahidin in the use of arms being shipped through the Dowry of Death," the Captain said, more as a statement of fact than a question.

The American took a quick side glance at his passenger and nodded in affirmation.

"Of course I shan't ask under whose auspices you've been doing this but my instinct dictates it is the United States Central Intelligence Agency."

Monty grinned, choosing not to reply directly to Prem's question. "Well . . . " he cleared his throat self-consciously . . . "I learned a lot about jungle or guerrilla combat in Vietnam. The Green Berets were tough characters. I've been passing on my experience to the Afghani freedom fighters."

"Now that's an evasive reply if I ever heard one," the Captain chuckled, "but let me say something that might sound a bit maudlin

... '' he turned and caught the American's eye before going on ...
"I'm damned proud of you, Monty."

"Thanks. Thanks very much, Captain. Coming from you that
means an awful lot to me." He braked the Red Chariot to an abrupt
stop, missing a bicycle rickshaw by inches. After an exasperating
whistle, he continued, "You know something for sure, if you ever visit
me in the States, I'm going to take you for a ride on the Los Angeles
freeways. The difference between driving there and here in the streets of
Srinagar is so vast that I can't even begin a comparison. And talking of
the States, my hitch here is over in a couple of weeks and I'll be
returning to academic life again at U.C.L.A."

"Returning alone?" There was a note of teasing in the question.

"I've persuaded Doreen to marry me. We plan to stop off with my
folks in Washington, D.C. and get married."

"A fetching lass, that Doreen," Prem volunteered, "and I must say
she's found a bit of alright, don't you know."

"You can say that again about Doreen. She's a mighty sweet gal.
But I don't quite follow this bit of alright business."

"You ... dash it all ... you. The two of you make a smashing
couple ... " Prem shifted in the seat to exercise his right arm before
continuing ... "and let me repeat that the C.I.D. is deeply grateful for
your help against the cobra murderers. You bloody well risked your life
on the two raids. Above and beyond the call of duty."

"Thanks again. They were our common enemies," Monty replied
with an embarrassed shrug of his shoulders.

"I say, Ian is planning a dinner aboard the Kashmir Princess for
tomorrow night and you must join us."

"He's already invited me and I've accepted," Monty admitted, "and
you couldn't keep me away with a brace of man-eating tigers."

"*Accha*. Nothing official, don't you know, just a few good friends
to spend a social evening together. Ian's idea really. The guests will
include the three Duncans. Then there'll be Sardar Khan, Ian and you
and ... " Prem coughed hesitatingly and threw a sidewise glance at
Monty ... "and two others, both of whom you know."

"Great! Sounds like great fun. Who're the two others?"

"Ashok and Aisha."

"Ashok and Aisha," Monty repeated in surprise.

"Precisely. I reacted in the same way to Ian's proposal, but he
argued, quite convincingly I might add, that there was no official way
to thank the Pakistanis for their assistance at a most critical time and
the least we could do was to meet with them socially."

"I'm with Ian; it's a mighty fine idea!"

"*Accha*. Then you'll understand why the guest list of the dinner
must not be generally known and the occasion be considered as purely
social and of no official significance."

"You bet your life. Mum's the word."

Rustum and Fatima, all smiles, welcomed Captain Narayan aboard the Kashmir Princess. They led the way to the cabin and opened the door with a flourish to display a profusion of fall bouquets set up about the room. Cattails rose straight and arrow-like out of the clustered autumn and fall leaves of shades ranging from a brick-brown to gold. Prem paused at the threshold and surveyed the display at length before turning to each of his benefactors and expressing his appreciation in Hindustani, "*Bahut dhanyavad* - Thank you very much."

The telephone call to C.I.D. headquarters in Delhi went through in good time and the connection was clear. "Captain Prem Narayan here calling Deputy Inspector General Pritham Singh."

"Prem, my good fellow, been expecting your call. Damn it, man, I'm frightfully glad to hear your voice. Lieutenant McVey's been briefing me on the raid and its aftermath."

"Well ... Pritham ... mission accomplished."

"Dash it all, Prem, I'm torn between calling you a bloody fool or an intrepid hero."

"At this point of time, Pritham, I really don't give a damn what you call me. I accomplished what you sent me up here for ... right?"

Pritham Singh broke out into a boisterous guffaw. "Prem, you'll never change, will you? I just hope to God your luck continues to hold out."

"What do you mean?" the Captain countered, "I don't take any chances."

"The hell you don't! Carefully calculated perhaps but they're still chances."

"Pritham, I'm leaving the bally reports on the raid to Ian and I'll stop by your office on my way back to Bombay. Some of the facts are best left out of the official document."

"The unorthodox assistance McVey mentioned to me?"

"Uh-huh."

"We'll discuss this in my office and see what should be done about the information."

"Frightfully distressing, just awful about Ali Aurangzeb. Poor bloke must have gotten deep into drugs."

Pritham Singh gave out a long groan and added,"Helluva blow to the C.I.D."

"Heard anything from the Russian Embassy?" Prem changed the subject.

"Not a blooming whisper and with that letter in our hands from their First Secretary you can bet there won't be any. By the way, when'll you be coming through here?"

"Day after tomorrow. See you early that afternoon. And, I say Pritham, be a good chap and have your office make a reservation on the evening flight for Bombay out of Palam. Believe it leaves around six.''

"Righto. And Prem ... '' he coughed and dropped his voice to a confidential whisper ... "the Department's damned proud of you. Cheerio and take good care of yourself.''

Both Bruce Duncan and Pran Sahgal dropped by the Kashmir Princess to check on their patient. Doctor Sahgal brought with him the autopsy reports on the two victims. The Falcon had died instantly, a gunshot wound directly through the left ventricle of the heart. Prem asked that the records describe the falcons tatooed on the backs of both victims' hands. The cobra had deposited its venom directly adjacent to the large vessels of the neck, the carotid artery and the jugular vein, according to the findings on Achmed. In the opinion of Doctor Duncan, even immediate injections of massive doses of antivenin probably would not have saved his life.

"I understand there were two other deaths?'' Doctor Sahgal's eyes inquisitively probed Prem's face.

The Captain nodded soberly and responded,"Neither of them done in by our chaps. One of them, Parkozian, was an Armenian of Lebanese nationality who was kidnapped by the cobra assassins and apparently while in their hands died a natural death ... heart attack.''

"The body?'' The Doctor broke in to ask.

"Just found today. The murderers dragged his remains out into the woods. Didn't bury it. The vultures and jackals left not much more than the skeleton, which will be turned over to you as soon as they get it to town. The other victim was an elderly Muslim woman who was strangled by the bastards. Friends have removed her remains for burial.'' Sahgal correctly interpreted the restraining look in Prem's eyes and wisely chose to ignore the matter of the body not being brought to the morgue.

Both Doctors meticulously checked their patient. The swelling of the right forearm was minimal and the motions of the extremity quite free and painless. Removing a bandage from the penetration site of the fangs, they noted the small area of necrotic tissue, destroyed by the venom, directly surrounding the skin puncture marks. Evidence of local infection was minimal and apparently well controlled by the antibiotic. A consensus of the physicians was that their patient's progress was remarkably benign.

"*Accha*. You say I'm doing well ... '' Prem studied the faces of his two medical mentors before continuing ... "then I may fly out of Srinigar tomorrow?''

Pran Sahgal drew in a long breath and exhaled with a whistle. "And why not? I'll have my compounder send you over a supply of medications.'' For the first time to the Captain's knowledge, he saw the makings of a smile touch the Doctor's face, a face hauntingly reminiscent of that of Mahatma Gandhi.

Unencumbered by the noises, smells and schedules of the hospital, Prem Narayan slept soundly through the night. Showering and dressing before his two companions had risen, he selected his metal-tipped mountain cane and, after informing Rustum of his intentions, set out for a brisk walk alongside the lake. A bracing cold wind helped clear his thinking which had been dulled somewhat by his systemic reaction to the cobra venom as well as the variety of medications. Testing the alacrity of his injured arm, he neatly severed a dried-up thistle flower from its brittle stalk with a flip of his cane. He continued to be disturbed somewhat by Ian's plan to invite the two Pakistani dacoits for dinner that night. They had been of substantial assistance not only in the freeing of Doreen but also in his own deliverance. Aisha, their leader, had supported Monty's and Ian's raids against the cobra gang. However, in spite of their being allies against a common enemy, they were outlaws and wanted by the authorities. The Captain's law-and-order mind struggled with the dilemma, finally setting it aside as a problem without a definite solution and accepting the Lieutenant's decision as morally, if not legally, correct.

Monty Brown was the first to arrive for the dinner party. It was a clear night with a gentle but biting cold breeze skipping across Dal Lake. He stood on the embankment beside the Kashmir Princess and scanned the skies hemmed in by the mountains, whose summits glowed wraith-like under the luminescent moonlight. Myriads of stars burned bright holes through the dark vault of heaven. The American stared in solemn reverence at the awesome panorama of beauty spread around him. Then with a happy sigh he broke away from the magic spell and trotted over the gangplank onto the deck of the houseboat.

Rustum admitted Monty and quickly closed the door behind to stem the flow of frigid air. The American was received with that cordial camaraderie so often shared by those who have jointly risked their lives in the pursuit of a common cause. He felt within himself an exhilerating friendship for the three men who greeted him. Removing his trench coat, he handed it to Fatima, revealing a muscular body neatly fitted into a white turtle neck sweater and a stylishly tailored dark suit. Prem and his cohorts, in order to emphasize the unofficial status of the dinner party, had put aside their military uniforms and dressed in mufti.

The second contingent to arrive was the Duncan threesome. After embracing her warmly, Monty held Doreen out at arms length to inspect her sari, a turquoise blue with broad gold borders, which flowed down off her shoulders in queenly fashion. Later she had confided to him that her attire had been specifically selected because she was convinced that Aisha would come in some form of Indian dress and she wanted to join the Pakistani in honoring the regional styles.

Everyone faced the door in silent expectation as Rustum walked across the room to answer the knocking. Aisha stepped inside first with Ashok directly behind her. Doreen had been correct. The Pakistani lady was dressed charmingly in a *salwar*, flowing silk pantaloons snugged in about the ankles, and a *kamiz*, the knee-length sheath of matching material and design. Draped over her head and about the neck was a gossamer scarf. Ashok wore a somewhat frayed winter Air Force suit decorated only with his pilot's wings above the left breast coat pocket. Aisha headed for Doreen and the two greeted each other with an arm-encircling embrace.

"Hello American, we meet again," Aisha said, smiling up into Monty's face.

"Hi there beautiful." He grinned back at her.

"You have an extraordinary cheek to say that right in front of Doreen," she countered, breaking into an infectious laugh.

Shepherding Aisha between them, Monty and Doreen introduced her in turn to the other members of the party, then followed the same procedure with Ashok. As Fatima sounded the dinner bell, Prem waved the guests to their places about the table, seating Aisha directly to his right. The conversation, somewhat austere and formal at first, soon flowed into a comfortable give-and-take, with frequent laughter seasoning the verbal exchange.

"Monty tells me you lost your husband in the fighting when President Zia replaced Bhutto," Prem addressed Aisha with concern.

"Quite right . . . " she turned and studied her host's face intently for a moment before continuing . . . "The Colonel was a supporter of the late President Bhutto and was caught up in the strife of the changeover. After Bhutto's death some of us were forced to flee the country. Ashok . . . that is . . . Captain Ashok, actually is my cousin. A few of us have banded together here near the border where we can keep in touch with what's going on in our country. In brief, that explains the origins of the Pakistani dacoits." She punctuated the statement with a flourish of her hands.

"And the Colonel was in what branch of the military?"

"Tank corps . . . Colonel Abdul Uddin of the tank corps."

Prem drew in a quick breath and asked, "Your husband . . . did he attend the Dehra Dun Military Academy?"

Aisha nodded in affirmation. "I met my late husband in Lahore where he was stationed shortly after partition. I was in college at the time. After our marriage, at social gatherings in our homes and officers' clubs, the men would reminisce and tell tales of their days at the Academy. Abdul graduated just a couple of years before partition."

Stubbing out his cigarette in an ash tray, Prem turned to face Aisha, his face softened in a nostalgic smile. "You'll find it hard to believe but years ago your Abdul and I were close friends. We were in the same

class at the Academy, sharing the same dorms. He was an excellent
athlete, playing on the school soccer, field hockey and cricket teams. In
soccer and hockey I played right halfback and he, being left-sided,
played left half."

"You knew Abdul," Aisha whispered, unconsciously reaching out to
touch Prem's hand.

The Captain nodded, his thoughts still savoring the past. "You
know, I just happened to remember, I dragged him out of a swimming
pool ... he was unconscious. Dove in and struck his head on the
bottom."

"So ... you see ... this is kismet. After all these years the fates have
given me the opportunity to repay Abdul's debt."

"Madam, I am grateful, most grateful believe me."

"Don't mention, please ... " she gave him a warm smile and went
on to add ... "they say you're a frightfully brave man."

Prem waved his hands deprecatingly. "A bit of an overstatement if
you ask me."

"Ashok told me of your deliberate encounter with the cobras and
from another source I learned of your saving a Muslim lad's life back at
the time of partition and the scar you now carry."

The Captain dropped his head self-consciously and reminisced in a
subdued voice, "Wonderful days ... those times before our country
was broken into pieces. What a hellish thing to split this great Indian
subcontinent on a religious basis ... turning Muslim against Hindu and
Sikh against Muslim. A terrible tragedy!"

"It all took place when I was a little girl living in Karachi. So
horrible, so horrible and unreal," Aisha concluded sadly.

Leaning over, Prem whispered, "You must excuse my sentimental
nostalgia ... " he studied her face intently before continuing ... "and
accept condolences. I'm saddened to learn of Abdul's death and your
great loss. I know he must have been a brave man."

Aisha smiled her appreciation of the consoling words, blinking hard
to keep back the tears.

A hush fell on the diners about the table as Ian stood and called for
attention. "I wish to propose a toast and in deference to our Muslim
friends, we shall raise our glasses of water. Will you all please stand."
There followed the shuffling of chairs as nine people rose to their feet.
The Lieutenant lifted his tumbler high and proclaimed, "To our
homelands ... Pakistan, the United States, and India." Glass clinked
against glass, sending merry notes ringing through the dining room to
the accompaniment of the chorus of 'Cheers.'

"And before you resume your seats," Prem broke in as the
participants were concluding their drinks, "may I propose a toast to
two brave and courageous young folk ... a man and a woman ... both
of whom defied death, flouting the threats and actions of heinous

assassins, only to discover in each other the nectar of life also known as love. Ladies and gentlemen, I give you Doreen Duncan and Montague Brown!''

"Hear, hear!" Ashok pounded the table with his free hand as the glasses clinked again.

At a loss for words, Monty grinned crazily as he searched his pockets for a handkerchief to stem the flow of Doreen's happy tears.

"Captain," Aisha addressed Prem as the table settled down to a normal level of conversation again, "you may be hard as steel on the outside but you're warm and eloquent in here." She pointed at her heart.

He cleared his throat several times in embarrassment and changed the subject to confide, "Ameena was an unusually valiant woman to risk her life as she did. I'm frightfully sorry about her."

"She's buried right next to the little orphan, Mos. You know Captain, I was deeply touched by the American's obvious love of that waif, the way he risked his own life to try and save him, and then carrying the dead body through the storm to insure his proper burial. Reminds me of another story about a Hindu officer and a Muslim lad down in Delhi during the terrible early weeks of partition."

Bruce Duncan broke into the conversation to remind Prem Narayan that he was to have his physician in Bombay carry out the prescribed tests and relay the results back to the Kasauli Institute. Prem nodded in acquiescence but at the same time grimaced his lack of enthusiasm in the matter.

"How do you plan to handle this Pakistani dacoit matter in your reports?" Aisha leaned over toward the Captain and asked in a whisper.

"There will be nothing, absolutely nothing in the written report, believe me. To do so would be damaging to the C.I.D. as well as to you. I'll allude to your assistance in my conversations tomorrow in Delhi ... no specifics mind you." He grinned at her knowingly. "Let me add that Lieutenant McVey is in full agreement."

"Well that's a relief," Aisha sighed.

"Monty," Prem called across the table, waving a teaspoon at the American, "be frightfully cheeky on your part not to see Doug Gordon before flying out of India."

"Don't worry. We'll be dropping in on him. Doug is arranging Doreen's U.S. visa and we plan to fly out of Bombay. Anyway, I wouldn't think of leaving without showing him the Indian jewel I found." He drew Doreen close and kissed her cheek.

"That reminds me," Prem remembered, "Bubli and I owe Doug and Sharon a dinner at Fernando's. He wagered I'd be working here in Kashmir. That'll give me a chance to inform that Dutch uncle ... as you called him ... of your activities."

"He knows what I've been doing," Monty admitted with a laugh.

"I thought as much, but I'll be telling him of what went on above and beyond the call of duty."

"American," Aisha spoke quietly,"you shan't be forgetting us, eh?" There was a melancholy note in her voice and a hint of sadness touched her eyes.

"How could I, Aisha ... " he shared a warm smile with her and continued ... "not on your life."

A loud ringing of the telephone brought Prem to his feet and took him dashing to his cabin. Earlier, the Captain had placed a call to his home in Bombay, the first since his encounter with the cobras.

"Bubli ... Bubli this is Prem."

"Oh, darling ... " her further words were inaudible.

"Can't hear you, speak louder my dear."

"You're coming home, Prem?" She raised her voice.

"Right ... coming home ... be there tomorrow night."

"Wonderful!"

"Haven't the flight number but don't come to the airport. I'll take a taxi. It'll be around ten."

"You're calling from Srinagar?"

"From Srinagar."

"Missed you, darling. Didn't take as long as you thought it might, eh?"

"Investigation moved along frightfully well."

"Anything unusual, Prem?"

"Really nothing all that extraordinary, Bubli, but let me tell you the story tomorrow night, eh what?"

"You're alright ... didn't get hurt?"

"Fit as a fiddle!"

—Finis—

DAD

You will benefit from knowing this man. He is a man whose genius is people and places; an ambassador with inside information unrestricted by international borders.

When in the active practice of medicine, his skills were complimented by his compassion for all mankind, and kings and the common man shared in both.

His guidance and wisdom has shaped lives by example.

He is a perceptive intellectual who can abstract facts and develop standards of accountability with fairness.

He is my much-loved father. I am proud to be the son of a man who came into the present from a time when giants strode the earth.

Melvin A. Casberg, Jr., M.D. (Bud)

It's impossible to speak of my dad without including the influence of my mother. The only times they were separated, the world was in crisis. During the last pangs of the Great Depression, Dad was in medical school. My folks couldn't afford a house together, so Mother and us kids lived with two old maids, and Dad slept in the anatomy lab at the St. Louis School of Medicine. Dad's Army Reserve status called him into the Second World War to serve in North Africa, Burma, and China. But other than these times, my parents were always together.

My earliest memories include picnics on old blankets, drives through huge redwood trees, sailing under the Golden Gate Bridge on our way to India as a missionary family, and holding Daddy's hand on board a rocking ship.

It was in India, at the age of six, that I began to sense the kind of a parent my dad is. We had a vegetable garden on the edge of our mission compound which had to be protected from the night-prowling animals. My folks hired someone to sit with a flashlight and frighten away these nocturnal visitors. I wanted that job. Dad said, "Fine, go ahead." He and mother walked me down the garden at dusk, and then they returned to our bungalow. My employment was brief. The next thing I remembered was hysterical running and screaming out of the night and into my dad's lap.

This has been the pattern of my dad's parenting: Giving support and encouragement whenever his children stretched beyond the well-trodden paths into the challenge of the unknown. By modeling this kind of friendly persuasion, we kids grew up able to risk the "night" on our own, and happy to provide "laps" to comfort others.

"Fine, go ahead."

Thank you, Dad and Mother.

The Reverend Sylvia Casberg Guinn